THE
MANY MOTHERS
OF
DOLORES MOORE

THE
MANY MOTHERS
OF
DOLORES MOORE

Anika Fajardo

GALLERY BOOKS

NEW YORK   AMSTERDAM/ANTWERP   LONDON

TORONTO   SYDNEY/MELBOURNE   NEW DELHI

G

Gallery Books
An Imprint of Simon & Schuster, LLC
1230 Avenue of the Americas
New York, NY 10020

This book is a work of fiction. Any references to historical events, real people, or
real places are used fictitiously. Other names, characters, places, and events are
products of the author's imagination, and any resemblance to actual events or places
or persons, living or dead, is entirely coincidental.

First Gallery Books hardcover edition September 2025

GALLERY BOOKS and colophon are registered trademarks of Simon & Schuster, LLC

Simon & Schuster strongly believes in freedom of expression and stands against
censorship in all its forms. For more information, visit BooksBelong.com.

For information about special discounts for bulk purchases, please contact Simon &
Schuster Special Sales at 1-866-506-1949 or business@simonandschuster.com.

The Simon & Schuster Speakers Bureau can bring authors to your live event. For
more information or to book an event, contact the Simon & Schuster Speakers
Bureau at 1-866-248-3049 or visit our website at www.simonspeakers.com.

Interior design by Kathryn A. Kenney-Peterson

Manufactured in the United States of America

10 9 8 7 6 5 4 3 2 1

Library of Congress Cataloging-in-Publication Data is available.

ISBN 978-1-6680-8833-3
ISBN 978-1-6680-8834-0 (ebook)

*In memory of my grandmother Sally
and for all the madres, mothers,
abuelas, and grandmothers*

"It is life, more than death, that has no limits."

—Gabriel García Márquez

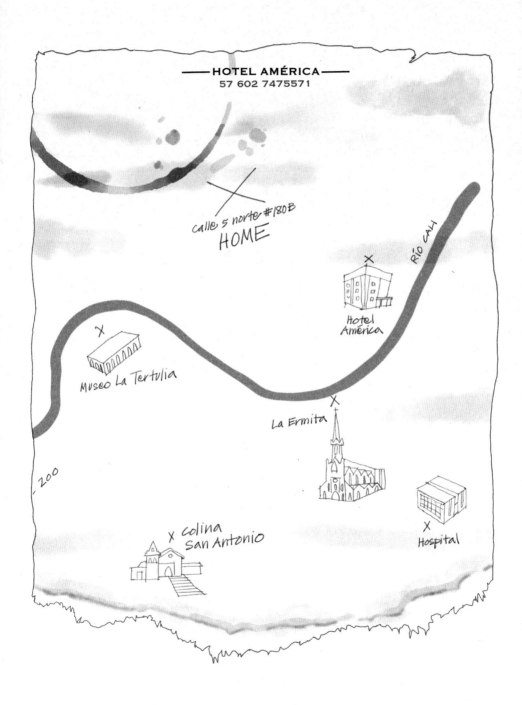

THE
MANY MOTHERS
OF
DOLORES MOORE

PROLOGUE

When I was about fourteen or fifteen, I asked my mothers, "Do you ever hear ghosts?"

"Ghosts?" repeated Jane.

"Hear them?" asked Elizabeth.

My mothers were in the midst of their annual winter holiday decorating blitz, which involved equal measures of Midwestern traditions like the Norway pine and spritz cookies, and also kente cloth and a menorah. Jane had gone to an art fair and bought a Guatemalan nativity scene, which—despite being from the wrong country—was supposed to function as a connection to my roots. They knew their quasi-hippie holiday practice was both culturally appropriative and embarrassingly stereotypical for two middle-aged lesbians, but they had wanted to expose their daughter to as many rituals as possible.

"Right. People who are gone? Do they ever talk to you?"

"I don't think so." Elizabeth lit a candle in the menorah, and the smoke danced into the highest corners of the twelve-foot Victorian ceilings.

"Like who?" Jane was rearranging the nativity scene on the mantel.

"I don't know." I ran my fingers over the wooden ornaments. Mary, Joseph (whose staff was broken), a cow, a manger, and a donkey. "Just . . . just people who aren't around anymore."

"Dorrie, honey, do we need to take you to see Scottie?" Elizabeth had asked. Scottie was a New Age therapist to whom my mothers had taken me several times during my childhood. "Just a tune-up," they would say brightly, and I would sit on his scratchy sofa and insist that I didn't mind having two moms, that I wasn't scarred from my unusual origins, and that I would tell someone if I felt like hurting myself.

"Never mind."

The wooden ass clattered to the floor. Elizabeth extinguished the match in a vintage bubble-glass ashtray and bent to retrieve the figurine.

"I was just wondering."

Even now, I can still smell the tree—a real one, of course—in my mothers' Minneapolis house, see the lights twinkling like a miniature solar system. When I first studied the work of Claudius Ptolemy in college, I had been comforted by the geographer's certainty, by his theory that the arrangement of the stars and planets overhead at the time you were born not only determined everything about you as a human but also situated your place in the world. Destiny set at birth.

But I was born far from here.

PART ONE

MINNEAPOLIS, MINNESOTA

Minneapolis, Minnesota, is in the North Central region of the United States. Located at nearly 45 degrees north latitude, at an elevation of 830 feet (250 meters) above sea level, the urban area spans 58.4 square miles (151.3 square kilometers) of land that is the traditional, ancestral, and contemporary home of the Dakota, as well as Ojibwe and other Indigenous people. Six percent (9.1 square kilometers) of Minneapolis, known as the City of Lakes, is covered in water in the form of lakes, rivers, streams, and wetlands.

PART ONE

CHAPTER 1

I extracted the silk-blend black sweater and charcoal skirt from the staticky plastic of the dry-cleaning bag, where they had been since my last loss. Growing up with an abundance of older and elderly relatives, at thirty-five I had been to every kind of memorial service. The moment I laid my funeral outfit on the back of Mama's green floral sofa, Bojangles leaped up, followed by Django, shedding their long orange hairs all over the V-neck.

(*Cats are for barns, not homes*, came the unseen voices tutting in their typical, unasked for way.)

I ignored them and scratched Bojangles's ears until he purred. Puffs of fur floated in a beam of morning light and settled on Mama's sofa. Mama and Mommy—the names I called them until my first family-tree assignment in elementary school. That's when I decided those weren't quite the right terms and switched to their first names.

(*Dorrie's always liked precision*, commented a voice in the empty house.)

Django kneaded his large paws on the skirt, and more fluffs of hair drifted down onto the sofa. The green had faded over time, turning more mint than kelly, and the pink cabbage roses had yellowed slightly, but no matter how much Mommy and I would tease,

Mama never got around to reupholstering the worn fabric. And now it was mine. All mine. The sofa, the two orange tabbies. Even the Victorian itself, which Jane had bought when the interest rates were high but home prices in Minneapolis were low. It all belonged to me now, and I had no idea what I would do with any of it—the old house, the worn furniture, the cranky cats. My new life.

A hiccup started in my chest, and I pounded it and coughed, willing the choked feeling—whatever it was—to go away. I chewed on a pink tablet of Pepto-Bismol, not sure if it would help, but the chalky taste distracted me enough to pull on the pencil skirt and slip into the black pumps, to get on with it already.

Get on with it already. That's what Jane always said. Or had that been Elizabeth's quip? Did it matter? They were both gone. And now I was the last of the Moores. Alone. Single. And I was an orphan.

Again.

"Please join me in prayer," the chaplain said amid the damp sound of noses being blown. Behind him, red and gold light streamed through the vaguely nondenominational stained glass of the college chapel.

Alone in the front row, I bowed my head but kept my eyes open. Since Jane passed ten days ago, I hadn't cried, as if I were some kind of character in a novel, the proof of my mental state evidenced on the page by my lack of tears. But I didn't want to be a heroine in a book. I *wasn't* a heroine, I had always been a supporting character, the only child in a family of an older generation of academics and Midwestern farmers and do-gooders, the serious analytical one who brought a book to holidays, was used to keeping quiet, listening. Always listening.

Lying open on the pew beside me, the program recounted Jane

Moore's biographical history: undergraduate from UCLA, graduate work in women's studies at the University of Minnesota, two years in London, tenured faculty at the college for twenty-five years, preceded in death by her wife, Elizabeth Pelletier, longtime college library director, survived by her only daughter, Dolores Moore. Mama's whole life summed up in a paragraph of accolades and achievements. Elizabeth had had a similarly impersonal memorial service last year.

(*Dorrie should be paying attention*, the voices scolded.)

I folded the program and tried to listen to the chaplain.

I heard the first voice when I was in kindergarten, after the first loss. My grandma Virginia Pelletier, Elizabeth's mother, who spent her entire life on a farm in Iowa, had passed away from congestive heart failure. I remembered sitting solemnly on a dark, hard pew in the Lutheran church, the hymnal heavy in my lap, wearing my first funeral outfit: a navy blue skirt and cardigan with a calico blouse. My feet, in white tights and patent leather shoes that pinched as much as my heels did today, swung above the burgundy carpet, while Mommy sniffled beside me. I knew I was supposed to be sad, but I was having trouble grasping what Mama had told me: that Gigi was gone.

"Where did she go?" I kept asking, but no one could give me a satisfactory answer.

Gigi's funeral and reception was a large community affair, and while my mothers, aunts, and bereaved grandpa were occupied with cleaning and company and caterers, I was left to wander the Pelletier house alone, the one child among a forest of adults. I stood on a stool in the upstairs bathroom of my grandparents' house, now home to

Baba only, and smoothed my long black hair and straightened my favorite headband—red-checked with cherries.

I'm so glad I chose the cherries and not the sunflower, I heard a voice say. I turned around, but no one was there. *The red goes so much better with Dorrie's complexion.*

I climbed down from the stool and checked behind Gigi's flowered shower curtain. No one was there.

And it was on sale too, added the voice.

Almost ghostly, the voice wasn't coming from inside my head and not outside it, either. Even so, I wasn't frightened; I was pretty sure I knew whose it was.

"Thanks, Gigi?" I whispered timidly.

Instead of responding, the voice tutted, *She sure needs a haircut.*

I asked for a trim when we returned home.

"Amen," recited the crowd, not quite in unison.

"Jane's family has asked that a poem be read in lieu of a eulogy," said the chaplain.

It had been my only request as Jane grew weaker and weaker. At first we blamed the chemo and the third surgery, not quite willing to acknowledge that her frailty was a result of her inevitable mortality. But Jane had insisted we talk about the end. She and Elizabeth had always structured our lives carefully, everything scheduled and organized in their particular way.

"Mama, please don't make me speak at the funeral," I had pleaded.

Jane laughed—or what passed for laughing at that stage—and patted my hand. When speaking at Elizabeth's funeral, I had been so nervous and distraught and—what was it? Something unnamable—that I stopped midsentence and escaped to the chapel's unisex bathroom, where I threw up the donuts I had eaten at the funeral parlor. Jane had agreed to my plea.

" 'For what is it to die,' " recited the chair of the theater department, whom I had asked to read because of her deeply resonant voice, " 'but to stand naked in the wind and to melt into the sun?' "

I tried bringing my focus back to the echoey chapel and the words of Kahlil Gibran chosen by Jane, but I pictured her in the coffin, riddled with the cancer that had taken two tries to kill her.

"And now a reading from Ecclesiastes," said the chaplain.

Jane went into remission after the first bout of breast cancer, when she was in her midfifties, and my mothers had celebrated by getting matching tattoos, sideways figure eights inked on the spot between the breasts, or where Jane's breasts had been. The infinity symbol was supposed to signify "forever."

The new president of the college approached the pulpit and cleared her throat delicately. " 'A time to mourn, and a time to dance,' " she said. Her black two-piece dress gaped at the chest. I was certain *she* didn't have a tattoo on her breast.

"Please rise for 'We Will Walk Together.' "

I stood but didn't sing. I thought about my two mothers' breastbones. Behind them, their hearts. Jane, like those swans that die of heartbreak after losing their mates, rattled around the Victorian after Elizabeth passed away sixteen months ago, until her cancer reappeared in the lymph nodes and I moved home to care for her. Another job I had failed at. Jane had made me talk about the end—the hymns she wanted and the flowers for her gravesite—but not what it would mean for me, the only child left behind. With the exception of the promise I had made her, she hadn't told me what came next for me, the orphan, the last of the Pelletier-Moores. There were some things we never talked about. Across the aisle, a woman's wobbly soprano scratched my ears.

(*A funeral*, said a voice, *is no time to show off one's vibrato*.)

I never told anyone—not even my mothers—about Gigi's auditory appearance after her own funeral. When June Moore, my grandmother on Mama's side, passed away from complications of pneumonia six months later, her voice joined Gigi's. *She's a good kid, my favorite granddaughter*, Grandma June had said, and I giggled, wishing I could remind her (as I had when she was alive), that I was her *only* granddaughter.

"Hi, Grandma June," I had said, although I knew from my experience with Gigi that she wouldn't or couldn't talk with me, only at or about me.

She's got those Moore ballerina hands, she said, an offhand comment that sent me begging for ballet classes like Mama had had when she was young. When Grandma June said, *Dorrie looks nice in that red sweater*, I took to wearing it nearly every day.

Humph, she's awfully small for her age, Gigi commented, a farmer's wife forever. *She should finish her milk*. I doubled down on drinking the glasses of 2 percent Elizabeth poured for me.

What a nice job Dorrie did on that spelling test, Gigi might comment.

All the Moores are good at spelling, Grandma June would agree, the two of them in constant conversation now, unlike they had been in life. *But she should work on her addition and subtraction facts*.

So I worked on math and practiced my ballet moves. As my female relatives—both the Moores and the Pelletiers—left this world, their voices multiplied into what became my own Greek chorus of sorts. Gigi and Grandma June were soon joined by the opinionated

Great-Aunt Maureen, the Moore spinster who had made a fortune on derivatives in the 1980s, after her lifelong pack-a-day habit caught up with her at age seventy-eight. Then Aunt Dot, who wasn't an aunt at all but actually Grandma June's cousin, was suddenly voicing her opinions and often arguing with Great-Aunt Maureen. Judith Pelletier, Elizabeth's bleeding-heart but childless sister, didn't join until I was in college, and by then I wasn't surprised to hear her.

One by one, as my family dwindled, the chorus grew—all of them talking among themselves, observing me as if I were a weekly TV program. Nothing—not even death, it seemed—could stop the Pelletier and Moore women (with one exception) from doling out opinions and commentary from the beyond, and I became accustomed to the cacophony that faded in and out between static as if a radio dial was being turned.

"Please join Jane's daughter in the Community Hall immediately following the service," the chaplain announced after another prayer and a rambling benediction.

The grandly named Community Hall was simply the chapel's basement all-purpose room that smelled perpetually of burned coffee and antiseptic spray. A brick-lined tunnel connected the chapel to Admissions, both of which were erected in the late 1890s, the first buildings on the campus, which had once been a teacher's college. As a child, I used to run back and forth through the tunnel on days my mothers brought me to work with them, a delicious kind of freedom that made me appreciate boundaries and borders.

"Refreshments will be served," added the chaplain as the recessional began.

(*You should have seen the spread at my mother's funeral,* came

Gigi's voice. *Fresh strawberries and meringue. And that liver pâté.* My chorus grumbled that I'd allowed the college-sponsored catering to provide the selection of cheeses and crudités.)

But before I could get to the food, I was intercepted by the condolences and reminiscences from people I couldn't quite place and others I was sure I didn't know. In the impromptu reception line at the back of the chapel, I shook hands and accepted awkward embraces.

"I'm so sorry for your loss," they said.

My mothers' coworkers, who had watched me grow up; Olga and Jenn from my sporadic book club; my mothers' former students; Jane's occupational therapist, who had come to the house a half dozen times over the past six weeks.

"Unseasonably warm for April," they commented.

(*The least Dorrie can do is smile,* said the voices.)

Always obedient, I smiled.

A group of fresh-faced coeds approached wearing what they must have thought passed for funeral wear.

(*In my day,* someone said, *we had to kneel to prove our skirts were long enough.*)

"We're so sorry," said the young women as they glanced at my sensible, low-heeled shoes and neat pencil skirt. What did these girls see in me? Was I a spinster? Did they see an orphan?

"Professor Moore was definitely my favorite teacher ever," one of the young women said.

"We loved your mom *so* much."

Mom, I repeated in my head. *Mom* was a funny word. A palindrome. Backward and forward, it's the same thing. I could feel my lips pursing. Jason had always made fun of me for mumbling my thoughts aloud. Neither of my mothers had planned to become mothers, or even thought they could be. They had chanced upon motherhood and seized the challenge with their typical zealousness, a trait I had neither learned nor inherited. Articulating the *M* made a strange rumble in my chest as if the sound alone was enough to make me weep. I stopped myself from both speaking aloud and crying.

The young women moved on—college students were always drawn to free food—as the longtime sciences dean approached. "We remember when you were running around here in pigtails." Dr. Lundgren's overgrown white beard was yellowing slightly, and his eyes looked rheumy. He reached out as if to pat my head. I ducked.

I shook another hand, murmured another response.

Lundgren moved to my left, apparently having made it his job to stand beside me as if I needed a man—however elderly—to survive this. "Are you still a cartographer?" he asked.

I didn't know how to answer. Despite my education and experience, despite the years of work I had put in, I was unemployed, laid off in what CommSys had said was restructuring, the day after Jane was put on hospice, the week after I moved out of Jason's duplex.

"Sort of," I told Lundgren. But without a job, *was* I cartographer? Without a mother, *was* I still a daughter?

"We'd love to get you over here." He talked about the legacy of my mothers at the college, how important they had been, groundbreakers, how they had been instrumental in the unionization of faculty, the shift to increased renewable energy, the establishment of the first community-wide LGBTQ conference. I only half listened as the endless line of mourners—or gawkers—continued to file out, bombarding me with handshakes and opinions and clouds of eye-watering perfume. I kept my eyes focused on the vibrant map of the college affixed to the wall next to the exit. The library, Ham Hall, the south dorms, the natatorium.

"Might be a vacancy in the Geography Department," Lundgren was saying.

(*Imagine! Dorrie with a job at the college*, exclaimed my chorus. I wished I could roll my eyes in protest, but that's the trouble with people who are gone: you can't argue with them.)

I nodded noncommittally and continued shaking hands and staring at the map on the wall. Something about it wasn't right.

"Be sure to take care of yourself," the funeral-goers advised. I smiled blandly as instructed by the chorus.

"Don't do too much too soon," they said.

But I had stopped paying attention.

I squinted. A key in the lower left-hand corner of the map defined parking rules and walking trails, and the buildings were labeled and color coded, the quad a brilliant green dotted with pink trees as if it were perpetually spring here. But that wasn't the problem.

"What's next for you, Dorrie?" someone asked.

(*That's what we'd like to know*, chorused my voices. *She needs a job. She should sell the house. She should join one of those dating apps.*)

And then I realized that, despite its attention to detail, the map lacked the bright red YOU ARE HERE sticker that the others around campus had. That location marker, combined with an accurate map oriented appropriately, was how a new student found their way to the next building, how the visiting parent located the bursar's office. Even before there was written language, humans used the position of the stars to anchor themselves. In order to move forward and navigate the world, you had to know where you were.

I looked at the map on the chapel wall. How could you find your way if you didn't know where you started?

CHAPTER 2

Back at the Victorian, I slipped off my heels in the foyer to discover blisters on my pinky toes, the skin rubbed raw, an open wound. The house, its own open wound. Home not only for me but for the academics and literati, the misfits and boundary-pushers who had always been welcome for coffee or an afternoon beer, who stopped by unannounced for grievance sessions and were invited to my mothers' monthly symposia. Now there would be no more gatherings—I had finally moved the last of my things out of Jason's duplex a month ago and I wouldn't see my coworkers anymore, not that I would have cared to. I didn't know enough living people to fill the dining table; although, if I could have held a party for the departed, I would have been a great hostess.

The shipman's clock on the mantel ticked and the fridge's motor whirred. Despite some chattering from the ladies in my chorus commenting on the food and the attendance at the reception, the house had that new kind of empty feeling that had settled in its bones since last week, since Jane had taken her last breaths, since she had extracted the promise from me. I felt wobbly and a headache was inching its way up my skull, and I almost didn't answer when my phone rang. But it was Becks, the only person whose voice I wanted to hear.

"How *are* you?" She was pixelated but beautifully familiar: pointy nose that once had a piercing, curls in a haphazard bun, squinting eyes without her glasses, face a little bloated.

(*Is she getting too much salt?* someone wondered. *I couldn't tolerate any salt when I was pregnant with you, Judy,* volunteered Gigi.)

"Oh, Dorrie," Becks said. Although she was now thousands of miles away in California with her lovely husband, I could picture Rebecca Marie Eastman exactly as she had looked at seven, at fifteen, at twenty-two. Birthday parties at the Eastman house, sleepovers in their basement. Flashes of her slide-showed across my memory: tableaus of dinners at the Pelletier-Moore house, swimming lessons with Elizabeth, back-to-school shopping with Jane. "I wish I could have been there."

The first time Becks came to the Victorian, we had just discovered not only that we were "exactly the same" (i.e., we both loved American Girl dolls, the color teal, and our second-grade teacher) but also that we were neighbors. Mommy and I had run into her and her mother at the local playground and invited them over.

"I like your house," Becks had said when we left our moms talking in the kitchen. She had grown up in a postwar split-level with blond furniture and coordinated drapes.

The Victorian hadn't changed much in thirty years. It was more or less exactly as it had been my entire childhood. A solid and permanent token of my existence. Across from Jane's floral sofa was Elizabeth's overstuffed velvet chair in front of the brick fireplace— "Lake Superior sandstone," Jane used to say—which was flanked by two Chinese urns that used to hold firewood but now were empty. The oak floors that I sashayed across in my pale pink leotard still reflected afternoon light.

"Who's that?" Becks had whispered as we crept past the study toward my bedroom upstairs.

"That's my mom," I said. Jane was working at the huge desk, her head bent over student papers as usual.

Becks gave me a funny look. "I thought your mom was at the park with you."

"That's my *other* mom: Mommy. This is Mama. Come look at my American Girl doll—I just got a new dress that my grandma made."

But Becks didn't immediately look at the doll. She pondered a moment. "I only have one mom," she said sadly.

"Do you have a dad?"

"Of course," she said.

"I don't have a dad. I mean, I did, but not now."

"That means," she said in what she would later perfect as her teacherly tone, "there are two things that are different about us." She put one hand on top of her head and the other on mine. "We have different colored hair *and* different moms and dads."

"We're not exactly the same—"

"But almost," we said in unison, and then giggled. Becks was the first person to see me—and accept me—for exactly who and what I was.

"Do you have a sister?" Becks had asked then. I told her I was an only child. "I don't have a sister either—I have a baby brother. So *we* should be sisters."

"Should-be sisters," I had agreed. And that was what we were.

"It's so hard to believe Jane's gone," my should-be sister said now. "I feel like such a terrible friend for not coming to the funeral."

"Don't worry about me."

"I can't help worrying about you."

(*I'm glad Becks's doctor didn't let her travel*, Aunt Dot said. Everyone in my chorus had loved Becks. *She needs to take care of herself*.)

"You keep cooking that baby," I said.

This was her fourth pregnancy and would hopefully be her first baby. I remembered the gurgles of the kettle boiling in the kitchen of Becks's one-bedroom apartment as she took her first pregnancy test. We had both always agreed—since second grade—that we weren't ever going to have babies, and she was terrified. We were twenty-four, still acting like college students, both of us unmarried, although she had been dating the same guy for four years. I clattered cups and spoons to mask the sound of her peeing, and then she burst out, waving the test around, gasping. Two lines. Pregnant. She pointed at the bubbling kettle. "I'm gonna need something stronger," she had said, reaching above the fridge where she kept her amaretto.

I batted her hand away from the alcohol. "You can't—you're pregnant." And then she laughed. Cried and laughed, but mostly laughed. I had to find a paper bag under her sink so she could breathe in and out until she could talk. She called Charlie and I went home.

"Look at how huge I am already." Becks panned the camera down her abdomen and its bump. "I've never been this huge."

Five weeks after that first positive test, I was back in her apartment, bringing her tea as she cramped and bled. "I can't believe I'm saying this, Dorrie," she had said, her voice clogged with snot, "but now I want a baby so badly." And then she cried even harder. Six months after the miscarriage she and Charlie got married and within a month or two she told me, "It's so embarrassing to admit this, but we're trying to conceive for real." She told me I, too, would change my mind someday, but so far all I could see about pregnancy and having children was the uncertainty—something I had, for as long as I could remember, avoided at all costs.

"It's adorable," I assured her now. "You're glowing."

"I am not. Why do they say that about pregnant women? I feel bloated and gross. Look at how cute *you* are."

"I am anything but cute." The V-neck sweater was now dusted in cat hair, the unusually warm April weather had made my black wavy hair limp, and I had dark circles under my eyes. Despite the fact that my chorus had always complimented me on what they called my "olive complexion," my skin looked ashy no matter how much blusher I used.

"You are lovely as always," she said, and I heard the murmurs of my chorus agreeing—mostly—with her.

(*Dorrie could do something about her hair. How about highlights? She could do some amber chunks?*)

"Although you are a little pale," Becks conceded.

"I'm just thirsty." I carried the phone through the dining room where the table still held the detritus of hospice care, and through the swinging door, above which was a large brown stain on the ceiling that my mothers were always meaning to repair, into the kitchen. I took comfort in its shape and smell, the texture of the old cabinets and Formica countertops. Although the house's only full bathroom had never been remodeled—despite Jason insisting it would be a "great return on investment"—the kitchen had been partially updated twenty years ago with newish appliances and tile floors. However, my mothers had never decided on the wall color and the four splotches they had painted years ago were still visible beside the refrigerator. The paint names were labeled in Elizabeth's penciled scrawl: Sea Foam, River Blue, Pewter, and Linen White.

"Why do you need to try out the white?" I had asked my mothers.

"You know what white looks like. Look around. Fridge? White. Stove? White."

I was thirteen at the time, and what I had wanted to add was: *You two? White.* But that was another thing we never talked about. The Pelletier-Moores didn't talk about their Minnesotan—aka Norwegian and German—lineage and Caucasian ancestry. Jane and Elizabeth were Liberals with a capital *L.* They worked at a liberal arts college, for God's sake. And they had me—this brown-skinned, black-haired sprite, this girl, Dolores.

"It's Spanish," Mommy told me when I was in preschool and realized that not everyone called me Dorrie, that I had this other full name.

"Doloreth," I repeated endearingly, a moment captured on a grainy VHS tape that must be around somewhere.

"It's a family name," Mama had explained once.

(*Margaret Dolores,* someone in the chorus had whispered. *Maggie,* said Grandma June softly.)

"It was your biological mother's middle name," she said, a phrase she had used before but that I hadn't understood. Biological mother. As if I needed another mother.

But now. Now I had none.

I propped the phone against the toaster and filled a glass from the tap. Becks asked about the service, and I told her about the crowds, the faces I didn't recognize, and she repeated how she wished she could have been there.

"Did Jason come to the service?"

"Nope." I gulped the water but the pressure on my temples pounded.

Although she was outraged on my behalf that my ex-boyfriend hadn't come to my second mother's funeral, I had been relieved not to see him. Or his mother.

"Well, he could have at least showed up."

"He sent flowers, I think." I hadn't even taken them out of their plastic yet, but their pungency was already filling the kitchen. I unwrapped the bouquet to find a bunch of tall white lilies.

(*Lilies are toxic to cats!* said Elizabeth in a worried tone.)

I set the flowers on top of the fridge, out of the way of the curious tabbies, and threw out the business card for Flynn Lakes Realty he had tucked amid the poisonous blossoms.

"What about food? Did you eat?"

"I had coffee," I said, "and pinwheel cookies. Jane's favorite."

"You can't live on coffee and cookies!"

"Sure I can." I laughed. Or tried to.

There was a silent, choked pause.

"Was it awful?" she asked softly.

"It was just like Elizabeth's. You remember that chaplain? Pretending like he knew her?"

Becks had still been living in Minneapolis when we prepared for Elizabeth's funeral. She had helped us clean the living room and kitchen to get ready for the reception and had made sure Jane and I ate. Both of us missed Becks terribly when she and Charlie moved a few months later, even though we were happy for her. Well, Jane was happy for her.

"I just want whatever is best for the people I love, Dorrie," Jane had said when I complained about my best friend moving away, leaving me. "Just because she's far away, that won't change the bond between you two. You don't need to be physically close to remain emotionally close."

Now Becks yelped. "The baby must have the hiccups." Her face took on that sort of beatific look that you imagine pregnant ladies having as they consider their unborn child. She yelped again. "It's wild, Dorr, this growing-a-baby thing."

I smiled and said something appropriately interested and interesting, but I was thinking about how, soon, it would be not only half a continent separating us but also this experience she and Charlie would have together. She was moving on to someplace I couldn't understand, a future that seemed so unclear to me, the lonely woman in an empty house in Minneapolis.

"Dorrie?"

Looking at her face, I could tell Becks had asked me something, something she wasn't sure she should ask. "What did you say?"

"Oh, never mind. You need some rest."

"What is it?"

She looked at me, bit her lip as if trying to not say anything. Then she asked anyway. "What are you going to do about Jane's request?"

Suddenly the kitchen felt very close. The splotches of paint seemed to be watching me. A meow came from somewhere in the house.

(*Has she fed those cats?* wondered the ladies of my chorus.)

"I'm not . . ." I began. My head swam.

"Are you feeling okay?" Becks was asking, her face close to the screen.

"Just warm."

I opened the window above the sink, letting in the afternoon air that smelled of soil and compost and my mothers. My mothers. They were gone. Elizabeth and Grandma June and Gigi and Aunt Judith. All of them—both here and gone.

"You look kind of gray," Becks was saying.

But I was thinking about how Jane would join the chorus—I knew how this worked. Amid the static and aimless conversation, I would suddenly and without warning hear her voice saying something meaningless and mundane as if she had always been there. For now, before she joined the others, I only had the memory of the last words she said to me.

CHAPTER 3

It was a deathbed wish like in a gothic novel. Jane had asked me as I sat beside her, both too young to lose another parent and too old to be an orphan.

She attempts to speak, then licks her lips. Mama's breath is shallow and slow. I bring a THC lollipop to her mouth, and its cherry flavoring becomes the only color on her pallid face.

"Do you need anything else, Mama?" I ask, smoothing the sheets of the adjustable bed, which the hospice workers have set up in the living room of the Victorian.

My voice sounds distant, more distant than even my chorus, which is murmuring, lamenting the dying of their daughter, niece, sister, wife, but I can also tell they are anxious for her to arrive and join the conversation. I push the sound of them out of my mind, concentrate on the moment, the individual minutes and seconds of this day. It is a Friday, and I can hear the garbage collectors clanking in the alley. I forgot to put out the recycling. This thought intrudes my desire to sanctify this moment.

She shook her head, pushed away the lollipop. "Thank you, Dorrie," she said weakly.

Then she had smiled and reached out. I took her hand—so thin and scarred. "Dorrie."

"Yes, Mama?"

"Dorrie," she repeated. "Dolores, after my sister Margaret Dolores Moore."

"Yes, Mama."

"Why didn't I take you back to Colombia?"

I shushed her, told her not to worry, tried to offer her the lollipop again.

"We always talked about going to Colombia, didn't we?"

We had. My whole life, Colombia—this foreign place that was on my birth certificate—was like a shadow that followed me, like a voice in my chorus. Jane had a pile of woven blankets at the foot of her bed that were made from Colombian wool, and colorful handmade trinkets—ceramics and textiles—decorated her bookshelves. Elizabeth had encouraged me to study Spanish and had learned alongside me "for our trip." They played cumbias and vallenatos on the stereo in the living room and experimented with recipes, scrounging the Midwestern grocery stores for obscure ingredients. "Someday," they would say if I ever asked when we would go. But they had never booked flights or researched hotel rooms, had never contacted travel agents or applied for passports.

And I never pushed them. I would go along with their enthusiasms, saying, "It's pretty," as a child when Jane showed me photos of South America, or, "That sounds cool," as a teenager when Elizabeth talked about guided tours of Cartagena. "We should definitely go," I said vaguely when I was in my twenties and life seemed to stretch out endlessly in front of me. I was curious about my birth country, yes, but also uncertain. And I hated uncertainty.

"Elizabeth wanted to go so badly, she wanted to see where you were born, but there was always—" Jane coughed and then breathed heavily for a moment. "Always some excuse not to go. Don't let the excuses—don't let fear, or anything—keep you from doing what you want, what you need to do, Dorrie."

I nodded, unable to speak.

"You need to do it."

I was sobbing. "How can I, Mama?"

"You can do it. Go back, go see where you were born, to Cali." She pronounced the city's name with a forceful, long *a*, having always hated when people said it wrong, gave it too much twang. *Cali*, I repeated in my head, that long, open sound, the delicate lilt of the *l*.

"Go see where Maggie went, where your—your father lived. Go see your beginnings, maybe you'll see what Maggie saw, what I didn't see, why she chose that place . . ." Mama coughed, held a hand over her heart. "I don't know how you'll ever find that apartment, that lovely little apartment. There was a mango tree." She was breathless with excitement, with urging. "There was something magical about that apartment where they lived. You must go there, find that place.

"You've always been searching, Dorrie, following your maps, charting other people's routes. Maybe it's time to find your own path. I'm sorry that Mommy and I can't go with you. But we know you've always been searching, and maybe going to Colombia will show you the way. Go taste the food and smell the flowers."

She let out a crackly laugh. "Smell the flowers—what a cliché." She had always abhorred clichés and I laughed through my tears. "We should have taken you, shown you where you came from. Elizabeth and me." My mother, my aunt, my mama. She had tears in her eyes but also the hint of something like hope. "Promise me you'll go, and don't let anything stop you."

And then she began to speak faster, her voice insistent but now unintelligible, a garble of thoughts and words and emissions, as if she had so much still to say she didn't know how to slow down enough for me to understand. She squeezed my hand and I pressed my fingers against hers, no longer gentle but urgent.

"I promise," I said, because what else could I say?

Mama let out a long sigh and that was it.

I closed my eyes but still no tears came.

"I don't know what to do," I told Becks. "I promised Jane, but . . ."

"You don't have to decide right now."

I knew, of course, that despite my promise, I was still in charge of my own life, that I could make my own decisions. I frequently tried to remind myself of that, but when the chorus chattered, I usually did as I was told.

"You don't have to go, but you might want to when, you know, when you feel better."

But the prospect of traveling anywhere, much less to Colombia, was overwhelming. I'd never even used my passport, which Jason had insisted I apply for, and I liked home so much I decided to move back to the Victorian. And I hated to fly. Just thinking about it all made me feel woozy. I swayed in the kitchen and gripped the countertop for balance.

"Dorrie," said Becks. "Are you sure you're okay? You don't look good."

"I think it's just the caffeine from the chapel-basement coffee making me feel strange," I said, but the static of my chorus buzzed in my brain. "You know how I hate that."

The summer before Becks and I went away to college, we decided that we needed to experiment a little before heading to school—her to a college out east, me just one state over. We had always been on the same straight and narrow path, serious students, never been invited to big parties, and we were both a little anxious about our next steps. So late one night she bummed a joint off her younger brother, Kyle, and we walked to the big bandshell by the lake. The glassy water reflected the full moon and we spotted a few fireflies in the parking lot but no other humans. We sat cross-legged on a park bench and inhaled.

(*Should they be doing this?* someone in my chorus had worried.)

"I don't feel anything," Becks said.

"Me neither."

"Kyle said this is the good stuff."

We each took another hit, coughing and then laughing. A loon cried from across the lake and a wisp of cloud danced over the moon. The lighted skyline of downtown Minneapolis was reflected in the still water. We smoked more of the joint, watching each other and waiting. And then my head seemed to float off my shoulders, a giggle escaped without my doing anything. Becks's face looked white in the moonlight, lovely and ethereal. She was talking but I couldn't quite understand her. I stood up and swayed as a wave of something pleasant washed over me, and for one moment I felt at ease. I opened my mouth to say . . . I didn't know what. But then the pleasant feeling intensified, it wrapped itself around my chest and my lungs and my head, which was still floating away. It was a wonderful sensation but also terrifying. I tried to sit back on the bench beside my friend, but my body seemed to have other ideas. I twirled and then skipped. I was out of control, couldn't control my movements, my body, my thoughts. I could feel myself smiling, but I didn't know why. I *wanted*—needed—to know why. I walked to the edge of the lake and watched the progress of the moon's reflection.

I kicked a pebble and the water rippled, making the moon shimmer. It was stunning but also unnerving—the scenery, the tableau of this summer night—all perfect and wonderful. And it was too much. Too uncertain. I wanted to feel like *me* again. Not the me that was unpredictable and did things like smoke joints in the middle of the night. The dour, unhappy—or at least middling—me, not this unrestrained, chaotic version.

Later, we agreed that the chill sensation wasn't worth the feeling out of control, and neither of us ever smoked again (to the relief of the disapproving voices).

"Have some more water," Becks told me now. Sweat collected at the back of my neck and I lifted my hair, scooped it into a ponytail.

(*I said she should have worn her hair in a clip*, Grandma June said. *I liked it when it was short*, said Aunt Judith. *She looks better with it out of her face*, said Aunt Dot.)

"You need some rest, Dorrie."

(*Becks is right. I was so exhausted after Vic passed, I could have slept for weeks*, said Grandma June, who was always particularly opinionated around funerals.)

If only they would be quiet for one second. I leaned against the stove, trying to gain some sense of equilibrium. Pressing a finger against my forehead, I willed the chorus to silence or at least switch channels, but then another rush of heat swept over me. My underarms were damp, the V-neck would need dry-cleaning—not that I would ever need it again.

"Dorr—"

"Really, I'm okay. I think." I tried to smile at the phone's camera, but the walls with their splotches of paint pulsed around me. I rubbed the bridge of my nose, tried to clear the sensation of falling. The croupy bark of the neighbor's dog echoed through the open window. The room spun.

"Maybe you should sit down," Becks said. From miles away, she inspected me, her brow wrinkled, with that same concerned expression I used to see on Elizabeth's face when I was sick, parked on Jane's green sofa all day while they brought me chicken soup and Tylenol, played endless games of mancala, the glass stones clinking and clanking.

"You're going to be a great mom," I said.

Becks nodded but stayed focused on me. "Your eyes look glassy." And I thought of those stones.

"Don't worry—" I protested, but my temples throbbed and my heart beat as quickly as hummingbird wings. The sound of the mancala stones clattered in my head. "I don't feel right, Becks."

"Dorrie." Her voice commanding like she was corralling wayward middle schoolers. "You look really sick."

"I don't think I can . . ."

"You need a doctor."

(*It's probably nothing,* the voices said.)

"It's probably nothing," I repeated.

"Come closer."

I leaned toward the camera; the room rotated nauseatingly. Something near my heart fluttered.

"Hmm," Becks said.

"Am I having a heart attack?" I clutched my chest.

"I doubt it, but . . ." She paused, her brow drawn. "But maybe call nine-one-one. Just in case."

"Oh, Becks," I said. A panic was collecting itself deep in my abdomen, working its way up my torso, bumping into things on its way. I looked around the kitchen, watched Bojangles wander in. "What if I die right here and no one finds me for weeks?" I wailed.

"Your mothers' cats will alert the neighbors," Becks assured me—a little too quickly, as if she'd thought about this possibility. I wasn't the only one who hated the sensation of being out of control.

Bojangles sniffed his half-empty food dish and then wandered down the basement stairs.

"They're going to run out of kibbles and then they'll eat my dead body!" I was hysterical now and the spinning wouldn't stop. Django appeared in the kitchen doorway twitching his ears. My feet seemed to fill with blood and my arms were leaden. "I'm—"

"Dorrie." She was firm. "Go out on the porch in case something happens so that those cats don't eat you."

"I . . ."

"Dorrie," she said again. "Hang up and call nine-one-one."

I carried the phone outside. The exterior had been painted many times over the years, each time its gingerbread trim getting a new, vibrant color. Chartreuse, teal, lemon yellow. It was currently dark brown with a bright salmon trim, including the railing enclosing the front porch that ran the length of the house. Despite our early spring, the old wicker furniture hadn't been uncovered yet. The love seat had always been Jane and Elizabeth's spot, and on summer evenings they would sit together reading or just watching the neighborhood kids ride past on bicycles, while I would perch in the little rocker, which was now piled with partially composted leaves. I collapsed on the dirty wooden floorboards, leaning against the love seat for support, as if my mothers were still there.

(*She'll snag the weave,* Great-Aunt Maureen said. *No way to re-pair wool crepe like that,* added Gigi.)

"What's your emergency?"

I told the person who responded to my call that I was having a heart attack. "Or something," I said.

"Massive cardiac event," some physician had said about Elizabeth. As if we should have sold tickets and made seating charts. But there had been no one to witness her final moments. She collapsed at work and her administrative assistant first called Jane and then the hospital. Jane had been teaching a class, and when she arrived at the library, the paramedics had already whisked Elizabeth away. And by the time I arrived at the hospital, her heart had stopped beating for good. Her heart with the infinity symbol inked over it.

I closed and then opened my eyes, the tunnel vision increasing, the edges going black, as black as a funeral outfit. I had no such tattoo, no tangible link left, only ethereal voices, which at this moment seemed to be watching my suffering with silent alarm.

"We're going to need some more information," said the operator. I'd never, I realized, called 911 before, and it turned out that just declaring your emergency wasn't enough to propel them into action. They needed me to tell them where I lived, what my symptoms were. So much talking, I was so tired of the talking. The operator asked questions and I tried to answer them through my gasping breaths.

"We're sending someone now, ma'am," she said at last.

I squinted and everything darkened like a light had gone off. The porch floor seemed to buckle and undulate. Across the street, the neighbor's children shrieked and giggled in the spring dusk, oblivi-ous. The lump pressed against my chest. I tipped one way, then the other.

(*Is she going to faint?*)

I thought about the aneurysm, the pneumonia, the cancers, the accidents, the unforeseen events that had taken my family away. But not really.

My mouth felt lined with cotton and my eyes stung. I thought of Elizabeth with the disconnected machines. I thought of Jane in her adjustable bed, pale against the white sheets, making me promise. I put a hand over my chest. If I died, I would have failed her. Failed Mama and Mommy and Margaret Moore.

1989
Cali, Colombia

From the moment Margaret Moore stepped foot on Colombian soil, she felt an overwhelming sense of certainty. As if the planets had ordained it, she knew that she would stay, that this would become home. After a year of travel from Japan to Thailand to Italy, she hadn't expected to ever be cured of her wanderlust. But as she disembarked at the Alfonso Bonilla Aragón International Airport in Cali with that usual disoriented feeling of the international traveler (the reason she loved travel, really), she felt a prickle of something different.

The smells were airport smells: exhaust and cologne and plastic. The noises were typical of air travel: garbled announcements, weeping in either joy or despair, and the occasional sharp bark of a drug-sniffing dog. Moving from plane to taxi, from train to hostel, she had been to so many intersections, and all of them—no matter the city or country or even continent—were similar in their common foreignness. Until now, until Colombia.

And no, she wanted to say aloud: It wasn't the man beside her. Or, not only that. Although, yes, the fact that Juan Carlos had one hand in hers and the other pressed lightly at the small of her back gave her a frisson of excitement, an otherworldly thrill. The fact that they were in this together now, traveling halfway around the world to his home country, linked by the gold-colored bands they had bought at a kiosk in the Piazza Navona, contributed, she knew, to this sense of familiarity. But there was something more.

As she stood on the sidewalk outside the arrivals gate and watched Juan Carlos flag a taxi, weighed down by suitcases and the ridiculous antiquated Louis Vuitton makeup case her aunt Maureen had insisted she bring on her travels, she realized what felt different.

This place felt like home.

Although, this wasn't her original home. Home had been a big ranch house in Minneapolis, where winters were bitterly cold and summers smotheringly hot. Her childhood had been a place filled with advice from well-meaning relations and aunts and parents. With more than ten years between her and her sister, Jane, Margaret had always been told what to do, what not to do. Jane had indoctrinated her in 1980s counterculture, in individualism and autonomy, in the feminism that she had discovered in college, urging Margaret to choose freedom and independence.

And she had. From the time she was twelve and spent her first week away at Girl Scout camp, Margaret couldn't wait to see the world beyond the Moore household. Even though she had hated the mosquitos and the smoky campfire and the KP duty of camp, she loved being in a new, unfamiliar place. From then on, she sought opportunities for travel—other summer camps, a high school band trip to Canada, a week in Philadelphia with Aunt Dot. Being away from home allowed her to reinvent herself, to claim her identity, whatever it was at that moment.

Now this Colombian version of Margaret was to live with Juan Carlos in the small Cali apartment he had described to her.

"The rest of my family lives in Bogotá," he told Maggie that second night in Rome. "But you'll come to Cali. It's too cold in Bogotá."

"Not as cold as Minnesota," she had said, showing him a snapshot she kept in her diary—Mom, Dad, and Janie on the snowy front steps of their Minneapolis rambler. Looking at it, she could still feel her fingers going numb as she pressed the shutter on the new-to-her Nikon.

"We'll never be cold when we're together," he had said, at least she was pretty sure that was what he said because at that moment he had embraced her and his voice was muffled by his strong arms cradling her.

On the flight from Rome he had told her, "There's a mango tree in the courtyard."

Dizzy with exhaustion and jet lag and new love, she couldn't even imagine what a mango tree looked like. There had been the palms in Thailand and the pines in Italy. She thought of the sugar maple in her parents' backyard, the one that, according to her older sister, had once held a swing. By the time Maggie was born, though, the branch had long since fallen, as if she herself were a failed extension of the family tree.

CHAPTER 4

The most important step in cartography, according to the vigorous lectures of my university professor Dr. Foster (now deceased but, thankfully, not part of my particular Greek chorus) is scale. That representative fraction, in other words, what fraction of the world the map is representing. If the ratio between the distance on a map and the distance in the world isn't accurate, he would say, the map might as well be a child's drawing, a Picasso, a paper towel.

"You might as well blow your nose with it!" Dr. Foster would boom, and the wooden chairs in the old lecture hall, subsequently torn down, would shake.

From the vibrating porch floor of my mothers' Victorian, I had no sense of scale or distance. The beadboard ceiling seemed higher than usual, the shadows harsher. A loud noise whined from somewhere. Footsteps. Voices but not my chorus's—male voices, deep and calm. Something pressed harder on my chest, my heart, my breastbone, that spot where my mothers' tattoos had been. A wave of hot then cold washed over me, adrenaline throttling through my veins. I looked down and suddenly my feet were in white tights and patent leather Mary Janes. A fluttering joined the lump in my chest and I clutched at my sweater. I began to shiver.

"A heart attack," I mumbled, or at least I thought I was saying

39

it. "My mother had a heart attack." A pounding was coming from somewhere, either my chest or inside my head. "There's no air, not enough air."

I felt a gentle hand on my back. "Breathe."

And then everything went gray, no sense of scale.

"How are you feeling?"

I squinted. Someone was passing the bulb of a flashlight back and forth from one eye to the other. I reached out and batted away the hand.

"Your breathing is better."

The person behind me gripped my arm and hoisted me into the wicker rocker after brushing off the seat. Someone else—a large man in a uniform—leaned on the railing, a tablet in his big hands.

"Am I having a heart attack?"

Massive cardiac event.

I heard the rip of Velcro and felt a cuff tighten around my arm. "We don't think so, but let's get you checked out."

(*I* knew *she was fine*, said Aunt Judith. *You were worried, but I never was. She's too young for a heart attack*, Aunt Dot said. *Dorrie—always so dramatic.*)

"I'm not going to die?"

"Not today," said the person taking my blood pressure.

"We couldn't find your mother," said the large man, whose name tag read D. WEST, EMS.

"My mother?"

"You said she had a heart attack. But I've searched the premises and there's no one here."

"My mother is gone," I said.

Paramedic West looked alarmed.

"We had a funeral today."

"Ah," he said, and made a note on his tablet.

"I'm going to monitor your oxygen and heart rate," said the other paramedic, angling his body until we were face-to-face.

My heart pounded again. The eyes, the chin, the black hair. Franklin Liu?

(*Do we know him?*)

"Franklin?"

(*Franklin was always such a handsome boy. Too young—they were too young. No, it was for the best.*)

Franklin Liu connected my index finger to the monitor. "I didn't think you'd remember me."

Franklin Liu. My first real boyfriend. We had met, like some teen cliché, at a party my first week of college. He was a shy sophomore transfer and I had found myself instigating first kisses and then some fumbling on a mildewed plaid hide-a-bed. If there had been actual penetration—and if it were once only—it would have been my first one-night stand.

We met for breakfast the next morning, me on foot and him on an old ten-speed. He walked his bike as we headed to Pat's, a diner that was legendary on campus for being the spot where established couples—including some engaged pairs!—went for morning-after hangover cures. Not a first-date kind of place.

"Are you sure you want to go here?" I asked as we stood in the line that snaked out the door. "We just met."

"Why not?" He shrugged. "I heard they have the best buttermilk pancakes."

I smiled then at the thought of being more concerned with pancakes than what people would think. It was a revolutionary concept at that moment in my life. So even as we jostled among couples who had wandering hands and sparkly rings featuring minuscule diamonds, I ignored them all, and I didn't worry about what our presence there might mean. The tiny diner seemed to shrink until it was just the two of us. All during breakfast he kept his eyes—so black and deep—on me. When the wobble of our table sloshed our coffee out of their cups, he folded a napkin and tucked it under the offending leg, making my world a little steadier.

"You." I stared.

He brushed his hair out of his eyes, and the gesture was so familiar that for one moment I was nineteen again, loved by a sweet-faced boy with baggy jeans and a dimple on his left cheek. After that breakfast at Pat's, I suddenly found that I was a girlfriend—and neither of us remained technical virgins for long.

"I can't believe it's you," I said.

"It's me."

"You're back?"

"I'm back in the Twin Cities."

"And you're here. At my house." It was more of a question. Was he really here?

"What's that line in that Meg Ryan movie? 'In a city of eight million people, you're bound to run into your ex'?"

"There's only three million people in the Twin Cities," I said.

"So even better odds."

"And a mere four hundred thousand in Minneapolis."

He chuckled and then showed me numbers on the monitor to which I was hooked. "Look," he said, "your oxygen is good."

"Textbook panic attack," said Paramedic West.

Panic attack? Not a heart attack? I was both relieved and embarrassed.

"We'll check out your heart just to be sure," said Franklin, "but
you look better now, more color."

Maybe it was the power of suggestion, but I *was* feeling better—
my feet and hands were no longer heavy and my heart felt like just
another organ again.

"When did your mother die?" he asked.

"Ten days ago." My voice snagged.

"I'm so sorry." He exchanged glances with Paramedic West.
"Stress like that can certainly bring on all kinds of symptoms." He
fiddled with his machine. "Based on your vitals and considering your
stress, we both feel confident saying this was a panic attack, but we
can bring you to the hospital for more tests."

I sat up straighter, sending the rocker creaking. "No, I'm fine," I
said hurriedly. Anywhere but a hospital.

"She'll have to sign the release," said Paramedic West, and began
packing their cases of equipment.

Franklin asked, "What about your other mom? What's her name?
Is she home?"

"Elizabeth," I said. "She's the one who had a heart attack. Sixteen months ago. She's gone too." Something caught in my throat.
That lump.

"That's a lot of loss."

I shrugged. He didn't know the half of it.

"I remember them." He touched my hand lightly, and my heart
lurched again. "Your moms were both so nice."

I'm nineteen again. Those awkward meetings during parents'
weekend and trips home, that car ride and that family dinner. This is
months after that first breakfast at Pat's, and my mothers had picked

us up from the bus station, insisted on feeding us. Uncle Harris was coming for dinner, there would be five of us, Jane had said. While we ate her vegetable curry, Uncle Harris and Elizabeth told stories about detasseling corn as kids and argued about who remembered it correctly. Franklin and I had held hands under the table trying to pretend we hadn't spent whole nights together, examining each other's body in the blue glow of campus lighting seeping through thin curtains. The faint scar under his chin, the sharpness of his Adam's apple, the length of his thigh.

"Do you have anyone to help out?" he asked now. "Husband? A relative? A friend?"

"None of those."

(*She has us!* the chorus chimed in, even though I didn't. Not really.)

"I'm the last of the Moores," I said as if it were the punch line of a joke.

"The last?" repeated Franklin. "You're an endling."

"What's that?"

"The last of a species. Like, the last polar bear on Earth will be an endling."

"I guess I am. I'm an endling. *The* endling. But I'll manage," I added because the look on his face was so pitying.

"You're sure?"

I nodded more vigorously than seemed appropriate, but I didn't want him—Franklin Liu!—to worry.

"You should follow up with your doctor, but I think you'll be fine." He stood.

"Be sure to get plenty of fluids and rest." He patted my head as if I were a puppy, or as if he didn't know what else to do with his hands. He gathered his equipment. He was a professional, I saw, and any memory of him as a teenager in love with me faded.

"Liu," called D. West, EMS, as my phone rang. "You ready?"

And just like that, my freshman-year boyfriend exited my life as quickly as he had reappeared.

CHAPTER 5

When the first maps of the world were made, even amateur geographers could see that South America and Africa might have once fit together like pieces of a puzzle. The sixteenth-century cartographer Abraham Ortelius suggested that there was a reason for this jigsaw image: the land must be moving. This seemed impossible to imagine, that the continents—these solid, permanent masses—were once joined and had drifted apart. The ground under our feet moving? Absurd! It wasn't until many centuries later that the idea of continental drift, and eventually plate tectonics, was understood, but Ortelius had been right. Maps and the puzzle pieces of the continents had held the clue long before—as they often do.

I watched the ambulance—and Franklin—drive away, silent, everything surreal. There was a time, I thought, when Franklin and I fit together like two continents. That first winter break in college, I couldn't wait for Becks to meet him and give her stamp of approval. It was the day before New Year's Eve, and she and I took him sledding on the hill behind our old elementary school. It was so cold that morning, the hairs in our nostrils froze as we breathed, but we piled on a red plastic sled and careened down the slope, our shouts visible in the air. The sun was blinding against the white snow, and even when I closed my eyes, I could still see brightness. She grilled him—where was our first date, what does he like best about me, what's his favorite band—until finally whispering to me, "He's nice."

Now, my phone rang. "Are you alive?"

It was Becks—all grown up and six months pregnant—shrieking when I answered.

"I'm alive."

"Oh my god, I was so worried."

"I thought you said I was going to be okay."

"I had to tell you that, didn't I?"

"It wasn't a heart attack; it was a panic attack."

"I'm so relieved."

"Wait until you hear who the EMT was." I told her about the ambulance and my rescuers, the blast from my past.

"Franklin!" she squealed. "Franklin as in freshman-year, love-of-your-life boyfriend Franklin?"

"He was *not* the love of my life," I argued, "so calm down."

But the truth was I could still picture that frigid day and how it felt to be hand in mittened hand with him. On our final run, Becks had stayed at the top and, just before she gave us a running shove, she said, "You two are disgustingly adorable." We laughed and sped down the hill, the fastest we'd gone, clinging to each other until we tipped and crashed in a heap. I lay on my back in the snow, panting, Franklin beside me, and listened to the way the cold distorted sound, making Becks seem miles away—a foreshadowing—and making the crackle of Franklin's jacket sound as if it were inside my head. I opened my eyes to find him looking down at me, his eyelashes coated in snowflakes. His lips were cold on mine, but his mouth was warm. His nose crinkled in a grin and I wished I could save that moment, draw it, map it, keep it in my pocket forever. But eventually, like continents, we drifted apart.

"Well," I said vaguely, "it was a long time ago."

"Did you know he was in the Twin Cities?"

"No idea," I said, although that wasn't quite true. I occasionally searched for him online, but he wasn't on social media and his name never appeared in alumni magazines. We lost touch after graduation and I was embarrassed to even admit that I wondered what had happened to him. You weren't supposed to pine after your first boyfriend, your first love, were you? Especially not when your chorus of relatives seemed convinced it was all for the best.

(*Leave the past in the past*, they would say.)

Jenn Slater from book club said she saw him once a few years ago at the O'Hare Airport when all flights were grounded due to a winter storm. I heard from someone, I'm not sure who, that he had gone to Hong Kong, maybe for work or a family thing? In any case, at some point, it seemed, he had found his way back to the Twin Cities, just in time to answer an emergency call at my mothers' Victorian on an unseasonably warm spring Friday in Minneapolis.

"Is he still cute? I remember he was cute." Becks prodded and teased, and I let her. What did it matter, I thought. I would never see him again. The first yellows of a spring sunset glowed over the bare branches of the linden trees, one pinprick winking in the sky. Looking at the first star, I remembered hunching over my textbook in the college library reading about Ptolemy, the ancient astrologer. He had used the sky to map the earth and imagined a grid of intersecting lines—graticule—based on the stars. These lines eventually became latitude and longitude as geographers now know them.

A memory of Franklin appeared at the thought of graticule. "You and that book are looking pretty intimate," he had said from across the worn library table, its surface a map of its own—the grooves of initials and petroglyphic drawings of penises marking the passing of hundreds of listless students. I ran my fingers over the latticework of the lines, and he had touched my hand with the tip of his finger, an intimate act. "Should we get out of here?" he had whispered with a glint in his eye.

But that was a long time ago.

"Did he carry you in his strong EMT arms? I bet he looked great in a uniform." Becks's teasing was relentless. I gave in and told her that he did, as a matter of fact, look nice in his uniform. "He hasn't aged," I told her.

She groaned. "That's because he's never been pregnant!" Eventually, after she assured me that she would tell me if she got any news at her next doctor appointment and I had assured her that I was okay—and felt no sparks between me and my freshman-year boyfriend—she told me she loved me and then added, "And tell me what you decide about your promise, about going to Colombia."

Long after our call ended, I sat on the rocker in the dusky light of my Minneapolis neighborhood and listened to the first chirps of the crickets. What would I do? Would I go to Colombia like Jane asked? Did I *want* to go to Colombia? *Could* I go to Colombia?

I had never been out of the country, although I did have a valid, if unused, passport. I shivered. Now that the sun had set, my funeral outfit wasn't warm enough for this time of year, and I hugged my bare legs to my chest, sending the rocker creaking back and forth like I was on a boat, tempest tossed.

The very idea of Colombia was as surreal as that of my personal Greek chorus. Its existence both unbelievable and yet irrefutable. It was a fact, yes, that I heard my relatives' voices long after anyone else could, and it was a fact that Colombia was the country in South America in which I had been born, but neither was tangible enough to grasp.

Growing up, I would go for long stretches without even thinking about my origins. I knew nothing and had never seen a single photo of my biological Colombian father or his family, I had no memories of the few weeks I had lived in Santiago de Cali as an infant, and there were no external reminders of half of my heritage other than the Wayuu weavings in the living room and Elizabeth's experimental cooking. And so I would forget—or push it out of my mind. Then, I might come home from visiting Gigi and Baba in Iowa or a sleepover with Becks, and see my brown face reflected in the bathroom mirror, feel that split-second shock that I didn't look like them, that I was different, alone.

"I'm alone," I said aloud, self-pity dripping off the words.

(*Solitude can be healthy*, said Aunt Dot. *She* is *technically alone right now*, Great-Aunt Maureen countered. *She's just missing her friend*, said Grandma June indulgently.)

Then I heard another, new voice.

(*Alone, but not lonely*, I heard Jane say, as she often had.)

Jane. Jane had always insisted that solitude was a luxury and a pleasure, that loneliness was simply a matter of perspective. The quip suddenly struck me as ridiculous, but hearing her voice now made the lump press against my throat and my eyes burn.

I had known, of course, that she would join the chorus; I knew how this worked. But now that it had happened—now that I heard the last new voice there would ever be—I was engulfed in that same out-of-control feeling I had had that night with Becks, that sensation of being rudderless, floating in space, of being unmoored. All my life, the presence of my chorus—all those voices—had reminded me that I wasn't alone and couldn't possibly be lonely.

I glanced down at my phone in my hand—the screen was black. I looked behind me at the dark front window of the Victorian—the house was empty. If I was going to go to Colombia, to fulfill Jane's wish, I would have to do it alone.

An airplane roared. A mosquito buzzed. Above me, Minneapolis light pollution obscured all but the brightest stars: Jupiter, Saturn, and that other one. The vastness of even the light-polluted night sky made me dizzy. When I first learned about Ptolemy's astrological theories, I was comforted by his certainty, but now all those stars just served to remind me that I was lost and alone—no matter what my chorus said. I had promised Jane I would go to Colombia, but that seemed as far away as Saturn and just as impossible to get to. The tears that had been blocked broke free.

1989
Cali, Colombia

Maggie twisted the ring on her finger as the taxi whipped around corners. They weren't married but were pretending to be for the sake of appearances. She didn't believe—yet—in marriage (thanks to her sister), but they would tell his parents—his devout mother, in particular—that they had married in Rome. It was 1989 and she could hardly believe that they had to fake it; after all, she knew her sister and her sister's "roommate" had lived together for years since they graduated from college, and no one ever said anything about it. Sure, the 1980s had Madonna but it was also the era of Reagan's conservatism and the Moral Majority. Juan Carlos had warned her that Colombia, despite being at the cusp of a new decade, was still in the dark ages culturally. And his family was Catholic, so Catholic he wore a gold medallion of Saint Christopher, the patron saint of travelers. So Catholic, in fact, he had been committing Vatican City to memory for his mother when they met.

He had tripped over the huaraches Margaret had left on the cobbles in the square while massaging her sore feet. She saw him stumble and tried to catch him, but of course she was both too slow and too small. He broke his fall by accidentally knocking her to the ground.

Before she looked up, Margaret had been ready to brush herself off, dismiss him. She was a master at ignoring people, one of the many reasons her parents, who were, as they often said, too old to be parents anymore, didn't understand their younger daughter. She had a tendency to be a little too independent, a bit aloof, maybe even detached. Since departing on her world travels after clocking one semester of community college, she had only spoken to her parents once. The last time she had accepted their call was at Christmas at the hotel where she was staying near the beach in Thailand. The line had been scratchy and the call was easy to dismiss.

But instead of ignoring this man who had knocked her over in Saint Peter's Square, she looked up. His eyes were large and dark with hooded lids and long lashes, and as they met her bright, eager blue ones, it could be described as nothing short of love at first sight. They both believed in such a thing, so it was.

He scrambled to his feet and, in his hurry, tripped on his own shoelace. She burst out laughing, and as soon as he had decided neither were injured, he joined her. She extricated the Nikon from around her neck and snapped a picture of him midlaugh, a photo that, when developed, would prove to be blurry and overexposed.

Once upright, he held out his hand and helped her to her feet.

"Grazie," she said, for she knew he must be Italian with that dark curly hair and those black eyes.

He knew she must be American with her short skirt and open face, and so he said, "Thank you," in an accent that didn't quite sound Italian, and in his impeccable English, he explained he was Colombian.

She gasped. "Like *Romancing the Stone?* I loved that movie!"

Now, as she rode in the back of a taxi, her cheeks burned to think she had asked such a thing. She knew better, especially with her travel experience—countries weren't what the movies made them out to be. Colombia, Juan Carlos had explained to her as they wandered the streets of Rome, was many things. Drugs and kidnappings were only a small part. And man-eating crocodiles were not.

"It's like judging Americans by *Footloose.* Or saying everyone in the US eats only McDonald's," he had said.

She giggled. "Well, that's actually true. It's one of the reasons I left." She had had to explain that she was joking. Although everyone in the United States *did* seem to eat McDonald's, her leaving to travel the world at nineteen was so much more complicated than not liking Big Macs. She knew why she needed to travel but not how to explain the feeling.

But now, here in the tropical city of Cali, for the first time since that Girl Scout camp eight years ago, she knew how to explain this new feeling. She was home. And she never wanted to leave.

CHAPTER 6

My childhood home was filled with memories, and the voices of my chorus swirled around me as I wandered the Victorian, wiping my tears with the sleeve of my sweater. What I should do now, I knew, was go to bed and put this whole day—from the funeral to the campus map to Franklin Liu—behind me. Instead, I picked up a book, a mug, a pen, and set them down again, my movements by rote, by heart. I knew every inch of the house from its musty cinder-block basement to its creaky staircase railing.

The cats enjoyed this sort of aimlessness and followed my path from room to room, roaring up the stairs ahead of me. In the study under the eaves, Django jumped on the desk, which was piled with papers. All the medical bills, the insurance forms, the mail. When I first moved back home from Jason's duplex, I had unpacked boxes and tried to maintain a system, but as Jane got sicker, I abandoned all pretense of organization—Elizabeth the librarian was appalled. Now my papers and my mothers' were intertwined and intermixed. The cat pawed at them and flopped half on and half off a messy stack, beginning a careful cleaning of his soft white belly. I pushed him aside, to his great annoyance, looking for my passport, which had to be somewhere in this mess.

A year ago, when Jason had booked an all-inclusive resort with champagne and strawberries in Cabo San Lucas, he helped me apply for one, but when it arrived, I looked at its pristine pages and the prospect of filling them scared me. I suggested we go to Florida instead.

It turned out the location didn't matter much to him. On the last afternoon, strolling the beach in what should have been Cabo but was actually a hotel in the Keys, he had grabbed my hands in both of his and told me he couldn't imagine spending his life with anyone other than me. He fumbled in his shorts pocket and pulled out a box. My chorus was gasping excitedly, but I batted away their voices like a cloud of gnats as he asked me to marry him.

"Think about it. I know you said you weren't ready for marriage and kids and everything, but we're not getting any younger. You know how much I love our life together. I want us to be a family," he said.

I said I wasn't ready, yet I knew, the sand warm under my feet, that it wasn't only that I wasn't ready, but that this—the ring, the life—felt too risky. Our relationship at that point had been faltering, but I was too afraid of change to do anything about it. After growing up in my unconventional household, I had been ready to try something different, so I had moved in with him, spent holidays with the Flynns, tried out a conventional life. He had been so helpful after we lost Elizabeth. But I couldn't imagine what a future with him—with anyone—would look like. I couldn't see where I was going.

"You'll change your mind," he had said. "Did you see that wedding party this morning? White dresses and flowers on a beach? Who doesn't want to do that?"

But I never played bride or dressed up in veils. I preferred pencils and rulers, marking out the boundaries of my world. Besides, I had already had my wedding. Actually, it was my mothers' wedding, but I had worn a white satin dress with a stiff crinoline and held a basket of pink roses as I walked down the aisle. I was four years old, and I stood between Jane, wearing a champagne skirt suit, and Elizabeth, who was in a flowy salmon gown, as their officiant performed the ceremony—symbolic only, because same-sex marriage wouldn't become legal for another two decades. The legal part of the day came when Elizabeth signed the final documentation to formally adopt me.

"Women always want to get married," Jason had insisted. He was certain of the female's vacillation. "You'll see."

But it wasn't indecision. I knew how to make decisions. Six months after his proposal, I put my attempt at the conventional behind me and told Jason that our dead-end relationship was over.

Despite everything, I was grateful to him for the passport that had to be here somewhere. I scanned the topography of the desk, but the light streaming from the hall fixture made everything in the study look useless, like a set from a movie. Two-dimensional, that's how it looked. In third grade, I had made a map of my bedroom for a school project. Bed, desk, dresser, lamp. Squares and circles. Simple shading. Primary colors. I had enjoyed the assignment to chart out the dimensions of my space so much, I moved on to map the house (bathroom, kitchen, living room, porch). Then the neighborhood: the houses, the park, the freeway exit. My mothers bought me a pad of graphing paper and precision straight-edge rulers and mechanical drafting pencils so I could depict my world in neat square boxes, careful lines, and color-coded hues, everything exactly where it was meant to be, no questions, no surprises. Bojangles rubbed against my legs.

(*Has she fed the cats? I hope she fed the cats.*)

Django stopped licking a moment as if he had heard my chorus, but then resumed as Bojangles joined him on the desk. This had been Jane's domain—headquarters for grading and committee work—and I could still picture her in her antique green leather typist chair (an inheritance from my grandpa Vic) at the big wooden desk, me playing on the rug, tracing the Navajo patterns with toy cars and the footsteps of Barbie dolls. The bookcase held my mothers' copy of *Our Bodies, Ourselves*, which I used to sneak under the covers and page through after bedtime. There was the lopsided thumbprint pot I made in an art class, and there was the little tin globe Elizabeth's sister, Judith, had given me one year. The globe was about the size of a softball and mounted on a gold stand. Each country was a different color: the United States was yellow, Australia was pink, Colombia was red.

"This is where you were born," Elizabeth told me, her finger hovering near the plastic tape of the equator. As a serious seven-year-old, I measured the distance between Minnesota and Colombia with the steps of my fingertips.

Without turning on the light, I sat, spinning the chair forty degrees in one direction, forty degrees in the other. I reached down and opened the big bottom drawer not so much because I thought my passport was in there but more to prove to myself that the room existed in 3D. The whole desk wobbled slightly. Jane had always talked about having a woodworker repair the back leg that had come unglued after years of dragging the desk from one room to another, from this corner to that. And now she was gone, and that chore became just another item on her to-do list that she would never tick off.

The wheels of the chair snagged on the rug.

(*She better not rip my rug!* cried Great-Aunt Maureen.)

"I'm always careful," I said, even though I knew they wouldn't or couldn't respond.

The vertical files in the drawer were alphabetized and labeled in Elizabeth's printing. I preferred to organize my files by place, by how much space they took up, by their position in the timeline of my life. This file, for instance, would be in the very back of the drawer, the furthest from the present.

I squinted at the label on the first file folder. *Documents, Dolores.* My name tacked on as if they had been preparing for a second batch of paperwork, another name behind another comma. When I was an adult, they admitted that they *had* considered growing our family, weighed the options, researched the rules of non-kinship adoptions, filled out forms. But ultimately, I had been the only rescued child in the Pelletier-Moore household. "The three of us was all we ever needed," Elizabeth had said as if still placating the feelings of a child.

Since I had last seen it, the cardstock had yellowed with age, frayed a bit on the edges, a little like my fingernails. Every once in a while, I got a manicure—maybe I would get my nails done this week; Grandma June would approve of that.

Inside the folder were loose papers. Mimeographed pages. Signatures. Embossings. These were the documents that declared me to be me, irrefutable proof of my existence in both the world and the Pelletier-Moore family.

I found a United States passport in the file folder, but it wasn't mine. I had opened this one many times, still remembered the corners softened with use. I flipped to the photo and the mysterious and forever young Margaret Dolores Moore stared back at me. Her pale wispy bangs are feathered into a wave above her forehead. Margaret Moore's mouth is partly open as if she had been startled by the flashbulb, giving her a look of bewilderment. Despite Jane's stories of her baby sister's globe-trotting adventures—*All before age twenty,* the chorus would remind me—Margaret had the look of someone who maybe couldn't quite handle the world. Her eyes, blue and set wide, made her seem so innocent.

(*Dorrie has her cheekbones*, said Grandma June, a catch in her voice.)

I might have had her cheekbones, but there was nothing else about her that looked like me. Those questions—who am I? where did I come from?—nagged at me as they sometimes did. I ignored them as I ignored the chorus and flipped through the pages of Margaret Moore's passport, which was filled with stamps smudged by overworked customs agents: Tokyo, Japan. Bangkok, Thailand. Johannesburg, South Africa. Rome, Italy. Cali, Colombia.

It wasn't until after the globe had been pummeled by World War I that the idea of documenting citizens was formalized. Before then, people—men, mostly—could apply for letters of transit to move between kingdoms, chiefly for business. In 1920, the League of Nations came up with the idea of the passport as we know it today, a way of documenting citizens and allowing—or disallowing—them to cross borders, those imaginary lines drawn on maps.

(*Mags was such an adventurer*, said Aunt Dot. *We should have kept her home*, said Grandma June, a sharp edge to her voice. *There was nothing you could have done*.)

I set aside Maggie's passport and opened the folder on my lap. There was my baby picture, my eyes huge and startled looking. Baba and Gigi, descended from Norwegians, used to say, both proud and a bit appalled, "Who would have guessed that we'd have a brown-eyed granddaughter!"

Jane and Elizabeth, also with their coordinated blue eyes, used to gush over the dark brown, almost black, irises and my dark hair. "You were such a little bundle of black hair and chubby legs. From the moment I saw you," Jane used to say, "I wished you were mine."

Elizabeth would kiss me on the top of my head. "If only I had met you when you were that tiny." Then she would add, "But the wait was worth it."

I buried the photo of infant me in a pile of other documents with their blurry typefaces and scratched signatures. Riffling through my mothers' files felt oddly like a violation of privacy. Once, when I was about eight, I had rummaged through the highboy in their bedroom and found a contraption of black leather straps and shiny metal buckles.

"Put that away!" Jane had shouted. My mothers never yelled at me, and I burst into tears.

"What's going on in here?" Elizabeth had cried, arriving out of breath from the kitchen. Jane raised her eyebrows in the direction of the dresser and Elizabeth, I realized later, stifled a laugh. Then they both sat me down on their bed and explained, "Mommies need privacy too, Dorrie. Please don't go into our things without permission."

But there was no one to ask now. Anything I found, any decision I made, was mine alone.

Bojangles stood and stretched with an audible yawn, and I shuffled the file to the side to make room for him. He used to seek out only Jane's lap, but as she grew weaker, he had begun to tolerate mine. As he proceeded to add more cat hairs to my skirt, something fluttered to the floor.

A map.

A hand-drawn map, sketched on a ripped piece of paper. The sketch had been made on half a sheet of stationery from the Hotel América in Cali, Colombia, and each of its locations was identified in the same squat script: a museum, something called La Ermita, and Colina de San Antonio, with the río Cali running between them. Smeared across the upper left corner was a brown half-circle stain of spilled coffee, human evidence on this neatly drawn map. Over time, the brown drips had wrinkled the paper, leaving proof of a life lived, however messily.

(*What did she find?* wondered Elizabeth. Another voice whispered, *Is that . . . ?*)

I thought I had seen every paper in this folder, but this scrap was unfamiliar. I ran my thumb along the torn edge. This piece of paper was proof—of what, I wasn't sure. Staring at this makeshift map in the quiet of my mothers' empty house, I felt a great whoosh of recognition: the map, I was certain, was the key to fulfilling my promise. Tears blurred as I squinted at the X in the middle, where the cartographer had written *calle 5 Norte #180B* in the same careful print.

Home, it was labeled.

I don't know how you'll ever find that apartment, that lovely little apartment, Jane had said.

I reached out, my hand shading the X.

Tell me what you decide about going to Colombia, Becks had said.

I touched the paper, and I knew I had decided. I had found the plan, my next step. Direction. The Hotel América, a museum, a river. I would go there and not let any excuses stop me, just as I had promised. Looking at the map, I felt the opposite of how I had felt that day Becks and I smoked the joint, the opposite of how I felt waking on the porch floor with Franklin leaning over me, the opposite of how it felt to watch Jane take her last breath. I felt grounded and certain. I didn't believe in God or fate or ghosts—despite what could be argued as evidence to the contrary—but I knew a sign when I saw one. Sometimes things align.

Like when Jason wanted me to hire a personal-care assistant for Jane when her cancer came back. That's when I knew it was time to not only move home to care for her but also to break up with him for good. And when I lost my job the week of Jane's terrible scans, I knew it was perfect timing. So even though I was practical and too often literal, I could see that I had uncovered this map for a reason.

(*She's not thinking about going there, is she?* said Aunt Judith. *Is it safe for her to go alone?* asked Grandma June. *She promised,* someone said.)

"Co-LOM-bia," I said aloud, with self-conscious Spanish pronunciation. Elizabeth had insisted they enroll me in a Spanish immersion school. "She needs to connect to her roots," she told Mama, and I pictured the lopsided family tree, the roots of which disappeared off the page. Through the eighth grade, I conjugated verbs and learned matemáticas alongside other neighborhood kids whose almost all white, very liberal parents wanted the global education touted by the charter school. "She probably still remembers from when she was a baby in Colombia," Jane would say when my teachers complimented my accent, which was still, admittedly, filled with flat Midwestern vowels.

Mostly to please my mothers—and because it did come easily to me—I continued to study the language through high school until I unexpectedly had enough credits for a minor in college. Meanwhile, Elizabeth took community ed classes and tried to keep up, insisting we practice at home, and she would fantasize about the trips we would take, the places we would explore with our second language.

We should have taken you, shown you where you came from.

I picked up the map.

And then—a hiss and a flash. The lightbulb in the fixture in the hallway sputtered out, plunging me into darkness.

(*How many tax accountants does it take to screw in a lightbulb?* chuckled Aunt Dot, who had been an accountant's secretary, and I wished she—all of them—would be quiet for once.)

The cat startled and sprang from my lap, sending all the papers scattering to the floor. The sudden darkness disoriented me, made the world spin. Impressions of the X on the map and the squiggly line for the river flashed, and images of Margaret Moore's passport photo and my own baby picture morphed in my head. I half stood, leaning in the direction of the switch near the study's door, but my foot encountered something soft and fluffy.

"MEOW!"

I reached down, feeling in the dark, hoping I hadn't stepped on the cat's tail, when the back edge of my silk-blend sweater caught on a bolt of the typist chair.

(The chorus cried, *Watch out—!*)

I lurched and a tearing sound came from the side seam as another furry body brushed past my leg. I tripped, this time on the fold of the rug that had been displaced by the chair.

(*My rug!*)

The bolt scraped angrily against my flank.

"YEOW!" cried the other cat.

(*Oh, dear,* said the voices.)

I could make out the bulking shape of Jane's desk and, with one hand, grabbed at the smooth corner. And then the world was spinning—or tipping. Me and the world, together we tipped and then tipped some more. I could almost feel Mama's hands gripping mine the way she used to spin me around the backyard. My two mothers would take turns, rotating me until my feet left the ground, the centripetal force sending me airborne, the only thing tethering me to the planet the grip of my mothers' hands.

Would I ever be tethered again?

(*I'm afraid she's going to . . .*)

Then a crash, a crack, and another shriek from a cat and the desk came tumbling down, the pens, the ink blotter, the framed photographs all slid to the floor in a hurricane of papers and paper-clips, history and memories. I yelled into what now felt like the void. "Fucking universe!" I cried as I tried to scramble to my feet, only managing to tip over the typist chair, which landed with a thud on the rug. The desk lamp hung suspended by its electrical cord over the now vertical surface of the desk. I reached up and pulled the switch, illuminating the upset furniture, the rumpled rug, and the memorabilia of my history that littered the room. The scrape on my side burned. And on the floor, faceup in a circle of yellow lamplight, was the map.

X.

1989
Cali, Colombia

Juan Carlos reached up and picked a fruit hanging from the tree in the courtyard of his—*their*—apartment building. The branches reached toward the small balconies of the units above. "See?" he whispered and bit into the flesh, peeling away the skin with his teeth. "Mangos." Just as he had promised.

He offered the fruit to Maggie and she put her mouth on the orange flesh that he had just cleared, a sensual, private act. The mango was sweet and soft like the inside of his mouth, and she wanted to be in this spot—in this courtyard with this mango, with this man—forever, for the rest of her life. She knew, the way she had never known anything before in her almost twenty years.

He must have had the same thought, because he leaned in and kissed her, even as she swallowed. "Te amo, Margarita."

"But why Colombia?" her mother exclaimed after accepting the charges of the collect call.

"It's beautiful here, Mom," Maggie insisted. She was in the foyer of the first-floor apartment, borrowing the landlady's phone. When they first arrived, the dueña and her pale, slight daughter were waiting for them. Juan Carlos kissed them each on the cheek. "Buenas tardes, Doña Rojas. Hola, Cristina."

The young teenager's cheeks reddened and she stood shyly behind the old woman, who was hunched and ancient looking, and seemed too old to be the mother of the girl. Doña Rojas wore all black: a shapeless black dress, a black cardigan, black shoes, and a black scarf around her head, even in the heat. Maggie couldn't wait to photograph her.

"Le presento a Margarita," Juan Carlos said. She loved the way he Spanish-ized her name. She had always hated it, hated that her sister called her "Mags" or "Magpie," like she was a flighty bird. Although perhaps she was.

"Mi novia," he added. *Novia*, meaning bride. Maggie blushed.

"Mucho gusto." The woman's face reminded Margaret of the witches in old Disney movies, but when she spoke her black eyes twinkled and she laid a comforting hand on Maggie's arm. "Bienvenida."

The long-distance line crackled, and her mother asked, "Isn't Colombia where that romance writer got abducted?"

"That was a movie, Mom," Maggie said. "You're thinking of the Michael Douglas film, not real life."

"Thailand was bad enough, dear. Why couldn't you have stayed in Italy? Everyone loves Italy. All that pizza."

"Colombia is beautiful. It's March and instead of gray melting snow, there are flowers everywhere. Just imagine."

"I could imagine better if you sent us a letter."

"Didn't you get the photos I sent?" Maggie had spent a small fortune having the film developed and the pictures of Florence and Rome sent via airmail to Minnesota. But she had hoped the expense would be worth it, that they would see how her photography justified her leaving home.

"You know we don't know much about art," said her mother.

"We gave them to your sister." Maggie could hear rustling. "I'll put your father on the extension. Vic!" shouted her mother. "Pick up, it's Magpie!"

"Can you hear me? Hello?" he shouted. She pictured her father in his workroom, a small wood-paneled room next to the garage.

"I can hear you, Dad."

"You should come home," he said gruffly. "Too dangerous there. Did you see the *Tribune*? Kidnappings, assassinations. You can't stay there, Mags."

"Dad." Margaret took a deep breath. She knew the news about this place; after all, she too had seen the reports and had never imagined herself here. "It's not like what you see on TV. It's a normal city, a nice place." She tried to describe what made Cali different, special. She told her parents about the salsa dancing in the nightclubs that were filled with beautiful young people, all friendly and laughing. She told them about the new construction in the city, the way it bustled and moved, almost in the rhythm of a dance.

She didn't tell them about seeing a man thrown into the back of a car or about the sharp reports of what sounded like gunfire but Juan Carlos assured her were only fireworks. She didn't describe the glimpses of ostentatious wealth or where that money might have come from. She did not describe the bribes or the risks, because Juan Carlos kept her shielded from all that.

She told them about the open-air market, where the chaos reminded her of Thailand—but without British Andrew, the short-lived boyfriend who had brought her to Italy. The smells here were different than in Bangkok, the bulbs of garlic somehow whiter, the fruit larger, the women hawking their wares louder. She snapped pictures of the stacks of potatoes, the piles of bananas, the rows of carrots and yucca. She tried to describe Juan Carlos haggling and joking, clapping the backs of the male vendors and kissing the old ladies on the cheek.

She did not describe how, when a large dark-skinned woman in a colorful turban called to her, selling something orange from a large basket between her knees, Juan Carlos had explained that the fruit was chontaduros. He had pulled her toward the woman and unfolded the bills of pesos from his wallet. He handed her a plastic bag filled with small orange spheres and whispered, "The chontaduro is an aphrodisiac." His breath was hot in her ear. "So we better head straight home."

Maggie didn't tell her parents how she hadn't liked the texture of the hard, pulpy fruit but did enjoy their afternoon in the apartment, in the privacy of his—*their*—home without interruptions from housekeeping in a hotel or other guests in a hostel.

"What will you do there?" Dad asked, always practical. "Isn't Aunt Maureen's money running out?"

"Don't worry, Dad. I'll enroll in school, finish college. You know I've always been good at languages."

None of this was true. She would not enroll in school, had no intention of finishing college right now, and she had never been good at languages (French class with Mme. Lewandowski in high school had been her worst subject). She couldn't quite admit that she was playing house, pretending to be married, that now that she had found this place—this man—she no longer felt restless and let Juan Carlos navigate the city, translate for her, and provide for her. She couldn't tell them all this because if they knew that she had lost her drive to travel, they would know—like she knew—that she was never coming home.

CHAPTER 7

Django meowed, alarmed at the disaster I had made of the study. From the floor, I stared at the X.

A map begins with a set of data. Distance, measurements, relativity. Information that is collected through observation or experience, by camera or satellite. Once the inputs are established, the cartographer begins to formulate the graphical representation through lines and pictures. Depending on the purpose or the intents, the same dataset can create an infinity of maps. With the right information, the right data, anyplace can be mapped. Even a birthplace. So it shouldn't have been a shock to find that thirty-some years ago an amateur cartographer had drawn a map of Cali, Colombia.

Go taste the food and smell the flowers, Jane had said.

"Cali," I said aloud, pronouncing the long *a* like she had taught me. Django meowed again, pawing the papers.

And then there was a bang from downstairs.

My fingers went cold. Bojangles puffed to twice his size. The voices gasped in unison and then chattered nervously. Django stopped his pawing and growled deeply. "Hush," I whispered. I extricated myself from under the chair, head pounding and muscles tensed, my fight-or-flight activated. I looked around the study— I needed to arm myself.

Another bang.

Surely a very large abridged *Oxford English Dictionary* was the right heft for self-defense.

(*A book won't help*, said Judith as I grabbed for it. *Find the letter opener*, someone else said.)

"Hello?" a voice—a real one—called.

Would an intruder say hello? I scrambled to my feet.

"Hi there!" the voice called again. "Dorrie?"

Would an intruder know my name? I crept to the doorway, clutching the dictionary to my chest. "Who is it?" My family was gone, Becks was far away.

"Dorrie, are you okay?"

I peered into the dark hallway.

"It's Franklin."

Another thud and the telltale creak of the railing.

"From before."

Did that mean *before* as in earlier today or as in all those years ago?

"What are you doing here?" I called back. "How did you get—"

And Franklin Liu, who was bounding up the stairs two at a time, and I, coming around the corner, collided.

"Ow," he cried as the dictionary thumped against his chest.

"Sorry. I—"

"Why are you in the dark?"

"The light bulb—" I began.

I fumbled with the wall switch in the study and suddenly the disaster of my accident and the five-foot-ten man still in a paramedic uniform were bathed in bright 75-watt light.

"*What* are you doing here?"

"I know you said you didn't need me to check on you, but your neighborhood is on my way home." He laughed uneasily as I set down my dictionary-slash-weapon. "Or, not *my* way home, but *a* way home. And then I heard a crash, the front door was open, are you all right?" he said in one breath and then he looked at the study. "What happened in here?"

"It could have happened to anyone," I said. But as I described the accident, he kept interrupting with gales of laughter. I told him about tipping, the lights, the cats—the cats sent him into spasms. "I blame the cats!" I concluded as he wiped his tears.

"You were supposed to be resting. But—" He righted Jane's typist chair and collapsed on it, still chuckling. "Thank you. I haven't laughed that hard in years."

"I don't think it was *that* funny."

"It wouldn't be funny if you were injured, but since you weren't . . ." He burst into gales again.

"I *was* injured!" I lifted the torn sweater to reveal a vertical bright red scrape about three inches long on my side. Franklin reached out as if he was going to touch the broken skin. For a moment, something coursed through the acrid air of the study, something fragile and tender. He glanced up. Those eyes I remembered. I backed away, my cheeks unaccountably hot.

"Don't worry," he said, "that won't leave a scar."

"Not like the bike accident?" I asked, desperate to say something about anything. I felt flustered and embarrassed and ridiculous. I pulled down my sweater, smoothed my skirt.

"Now, *that* wasn't my fault," he said, and laughed.

"It was absolutely your fault. You were the one who forced me to do tricks."

"I never forced you—no one can actually force you to do dumb stuff on a bicycle."

"But you were the one riding up and down the curbs, making it look so easy."

We had returned from an afternoon ride to a shady lake near campus, where we lay on the new grass, inhaling the early spring air that we didn't know would be so fleeting. On the way back, we took a meandering route through the neighborhood where all the professors lived, city blocks with big, old-growth trees and sun-dappled sidewalks. He led me up driveways and over sidewalks, around tricycles lying on the street and over dirty piles of persistent snow. These tricks were beyond my skill level, but I wanted to keep up, to show him—and me, I suppose—that I could be something different than myself.

"I shouldn't have jumped that last curb," he admitted, but his eyes were still shining with mischief. "But you didn't have to follow me."

I had jumped the curb but the bike had not, and I ended up splayed on the side of the road, a skinned knee bleeding down my shin. His bike skidded to a stop in a cloud of gravel and he knelt at my side, blotting the bleeding with his T-shirt.

"I still have the scar," I said.

My body, I thought, was a map.

Once he had helped me right the desk and collect the papers scattered across the study, I felt obligated—and I wanted?—to ask Franklin to stay.

"Are you hungry?" I asked. We went down to the kitchen, where I found a bottle of Chardonnay in the back of the fridge. And just like that, Franklin Liu, who I hadn't seen in twelve, maybe fifteen years, was in my mothers' kitchen eating leftover crackers and cheese from Jane's funeral.

"After graduation I went to Hong Kong with my grandfather for six months," Franklin said when I asked what he'd been doing since college.

I remembered when he had first told me about his family. We were in my bed in my dorm room, which we had to ourselves that weekend while my roommate was away, eating Doritos after missing dinner. He had explained, "My dad already had this whole other family before I was born. They came from China in the seventies, and he married my mom after his wife died."

At the time, I ran my hand through his black hair and along the slope of his forehead. He licked the orange off his fingers and then resumed his exploration of my abdomen, breasts, hip. I felt a zing that ricocheted through my limbs and then seemed to settle somewhere in my chest as if deciding to stay.

"So that makes me the American one and the white one—half-white counts as completely white in my family."

"I know all about being a half."

"What are your halves?" he had mumbled as he kissed me.

"Half-Colombian."

"Your mom or your dad?"

"It's . . . it's complicated." I had never liked telling this story, the intricacy of my origins. I preferred straightforward paths, clear directions. "According to my very white mom—who's technically my aunt—my biological mom met my dad in Colombia and they had me. Surprise!"

"It's strange to be half and half, isn't it?" He said this almost more to himself than to me. "I'm never quite white enough for my mom's family but too American for my siblings."

"I try not to think about it," I lied.

The first lie I ever told him.

"Have you been to Colombia?" he asked.

"Not since I was born. My parents both died. Thus the adopted mom." I sat up and reached for another handful of chips.

"Grandpa Bao and I weren't too successful in Hong Kong," he told me now. "Turns out I don't have much business sense either. Maybe I'm not as smart as I thought." He laughed. "How about you? You were always so smart. Are you still mapmaking?"

"I am—well, was. I got laid off a month, two months ago. Restructuring at CommSys." I gave him a wry look and poured him another glass of the cloying white. "It worked out, though, because I was able to move home to help take care of my mom Jane."

"I'm so sorry," he said again.

I told him about the illness, the cardiac events, my mothers' matching tattoos, and laid my hand on my chest describing the infinity symbol imprinted over their hearts. "It was supposed to signify 'forever,' although . . ." My voice trailed off.

"Any tattoos on you?"

I smiled, grateful for the change of subject. "An Irish knot on my hip," I admitted.

"Not the knot! Let's see it."

I pushed down the waistband of my skirt until the edge of the knot was visible on my right hip bone. "Eternal life, you know. I thought I was very deep when I was twenty-two." I had gone with Becks after she studied abroad in Ireland our senior year of college and we thought we were so sophisticated getting inked with the ancient symbol. "Never mind that I'm not Irish, not even by adoption."

Franklin placed two fingers and pressed the intricate design gently. A shiver radiated out from the spot, and I was suddenly nineteen again. Maybe he felt it, too, because he snatched away his hand as if he'd touched a hot stove.

"How about you?" I asked.

"No tattoos."

I laughed. "I mean—how did you end up a paramedic?"

"I started med school in Boston, but that didn't go so well. Then Grandpa Bao was in an accident with a bicycle, and that's what inspired me to do the paramedic thing. I thought I wanted to be a doctor, but first responders are so immediate, you don't get bogged down with hard decisions—you just help people when they need it most. I like how no two days are ever the same. You never know what you're going to be doing."

The opposite of me. I calculated our trajectories, placing our routes to this kitchen table on my mental map. While he was in Hong Kong, I was working at a call center in Minneapolis to save money for grad school. When he came back to the United States, that's when I got my master's in geography and started my PhD in the Twin Cities. He later moved to Chicago around the same time I dropped out of the graduate program and moved in with Jason. While Franklin was zigzagging, I had always been here, always in Minnesota.

"I never would have moved to Chicago, except my girlfriend got a job there," he told me. "Her name is Sasha. I met her in Hong Kong but she's from Duluth."

Sasha. A nice name, I thought. "What's she like?"

He picked at the rolled slices of catering ham and then chose a cube of yellow cheese, which he popped in his mouth. "She's a public defender and she's very driven, very serious. But also really talented, really good at her job." I wanted him to tell me what she looked like, how pretty she was, how different from me—or alike—she was. I wanted to ask how she made him feel, if they circled under streetlights in the snow the way we had in college. But of course, he and

Sasha were grown-ups, most likely they had a grown-up relationship. He went on, "We've been on and off for almost seven years now."

"That's a long time. Are you going to marry her?"

"That's what my mom wants. She even gave me her engagement ring last year. She didn't specify who it was for, but I think she assumes it will be Sasha."

He was a year older than me—thirty-six, textbook age for marriage. "Wow," I breathed, thinking of the beach in the Keys last year and the ring that Jason had offered. The ring I had rejected.

"But . . ." He ate the roll of ham and washed it down with a gulp of wine. "But I don't know if she's the one. Not that I believe in 'the one.' It's just that everything is always very complicated with her. Do you think relationships are supposed to be complicated?"

I shrugged. "Probably."

"Anyway, we were living together, but then I moved in with my grandfather in his house in Saint Paul. Because she stayed with her parents during lockdown, I thought she would understand me moving in with him. But she—she didn't."

"I remember your grandfather."

Franklin ate another cube of cheese and smiled. "He remembers you too."

That first and only spring, Franklin had brought me to his grandfather's one-story Saint Paul house that smelled of garlic and dryer sheets and something woodsy.

(*Was he the one with the lovely garden?* someone in my chorus wondered.)

"Does he still have that garden?" I asked. The backyard was filled with flowers I couldn't identify, neatly trimmed shrubs, and a statue of a bird about to take flight. Then, as now, my chorus had chittered excitedly about the plantings, and I had asked his grandfather for the names of the flowers. That visit was the first time Franklin had introduced me as his girlfriend. I remembered the zing of excitement at that word, the possessiveness of it: I had an identity.

"He does, but I'm not sure how long he can stay in that house," Franklin was saying as he poured the last of the Chardonnay into our glasses. "Who knows what will happen in the future, but Grandpa Bao's already out there this spring, raking leaves and digging in the dirt."

"How long have you lived with him?"

"Last September," he said. "Grandpa fell and we realized he couldn't live alone. It was good timing. Not the falling, but because Sasha and I . . ." His voice trailed off.

"My mom's cancer came back just when I was ending things with my boyfriend. So it worked out, I guess."

"It's funny how that happens. I'm glad I could move in with Grandpa Bao. I can't imagine him in a nursing home or whatever. He's so happy to be in his house, especially the yard."

He stretched and yawned. Was he going already? I looked at the display on the microwave. It was past eleven on a Friday, and he surely had places to be. He wasn't stuck in an old Victorian with ghosts like me. But then he didn't get up and didn't leave, and instead he looked at me and said, "I can't believe it's been fifteen years."

"I think it's sixteen, actually."

Sixteen years that, looking at him now, felt like moments, as if we were still a couple of college kids. We both looked older, but we were essentially the same. He used to wear his hair long, flopped over one high cheekbone, and he would toss it out of his face with a quick jerk of his head. "My dad hates it long," he would say when I ran my fingers through it. Now he had a neat, short cut, a little longer on top, with sideburns that were maybe just a little longer than was in style. A few strands of silver sparkled in the black and I wondered if he was noticing my grays and if he thought they fit me as well as I thought his did. The Victorian felt empty, like a void, like he and I were in a spotlight here at the kitchen table, highlighted and surrounded by darkness, the same way the X on the map had been.

"But who's counting?" I self-consciously pushed a chunk of hair behind my ear and laughed, suddenly feeling awkward.

He smiled, his eyes crinkling. He was very close.

My head swam with the memories of what had been and the possibilities of what could be. My chorus was quiet, only a vague background static audible. I pushed away the cold cuts platter and swigged the rest of my wine. He was so close I could see the stubble on his chin, the two fine lines like faint parentheses on his cheeks.

"Remember . . ." he began.

"I remember." A whisper. The words swirled around the kitchen. My mind flashed—just for a moment—to my freshman year dorm room. Those fumbles in the dark. After that, after Franklin, my later boyfriends and hookups and I were experienced; we knew what went where and how. But before. Before it was just our bodies, exploring what was possible. Uninhibited passion and indulgence. A first love, the naïveté of ignorance. I shook my head as if I could shake away the memories. They were good, but they were part of a long gone moment in my life. But Franklin didn't move. His eyes were even darker than mine.

The spinning stopped. Neither of us moved. I could smell the acrid wine on his breath.

And then I reached for him and placed both hands on the sides of his face. His mouth met mine and I took his hand, pulling him toward me. He slid his fingers under my ripped sweater, making me gasp with cold, with memory, with something raw and pulsating. Bojangles—or maybe it was Django—meowed as we moved toward the stairs. For a moment, I almost stopped to wonder what I was doing. But then I pulled at his shirt collar. This wasn't part of the plan or the direction my life was supposed to take.

In the early days of Western exploration, expeditions to the region that became California determined that the southern portion was an island, separated from the rest of North America by a strait. Of course, this wasn't true; it was a peninsula. After the first miscalculation, though, each following cartographer repeated the inaccuracy, proving that mistakes are often the result of compounded errors from multiple parties. That fact had always comforted me as a mapmaker, knowing I wasn't alone responsible.

And so I couldn't possibly be the only one responsible for my momentary lack of sanity the day of my second mother's funeral. It was grief, I told myself, feeling the weight of a warm body beside me. Grief combined with a bottle of cheap Chardonnay, soft hands, and nostalgia. The memory of that brief time when we orbited around each other, always swaying and reaching, when the days and the nights were a blur, only the nuisance of schoolwork grounding us. I had been floaty and alive, awake, and at first, it was magnificent. We had laughed at everything and nothing and felt sorry for anyone who wasn't us. And for just a moment we had re-created that feeling.

In the dark, I could just make out my rumpled charcoal skirt and black sweater on the floor. I closed my eyes and laid my head on Franklin's bare chest, lulled by his steady breathing. There's a movie in which the character has just lost her dad, and the on-again, off-again boyfriend comes to the funeral and they have sex. She tells him she just wants to feel something. *Something.* Anything.

That wasn't an excuse, I knew, but it was a reason.

Later. The room was dark, the man beside me nothing more than a mound under the blanket. I tiptoed to the study, where I found the scrap of paper. Cali, Colombia, and all the places I'd never been. *Maybe you'll see what Maggie saw,* Jane had said. I held the map on the palm of my hand as if it were a feather, delicate and precious.

(The chorus was silent, but I could feel them wondering what I would do.)

I slipped back into bed and Franklin murmured and reached for me, his eyes closed.

Much later. I'm conscious of rustling paper, a soft scratching sound that could be mistaken for feline antics. I open my eyes to see Franklin sitting up in bed, studying the half sheet of stationery in the glow of blue moonlight.

I watch him smooth out the paper on his lap, squinting at the labeled locations: *San Antonio, Museo la Tertulia, La Ermita.* I want to reach out and cup my hand around his cheek and draw him toward me, but I stop myself.

"Where did this come from? It's like a treasure map."

"I found it in that mess in the study." We were whispering, even though there was no one to disturb. Bojangles and Django were asleep on a blanket that had fallen on the floor, and even my chorus seemed to be sleeping.

"Part of the tornado?"

"It's possible this map was the cause of the tornado. As I said, not my fault."

"Who drew it?"

"I think it belonged to my mother—my biological mother."

He touched the tip of his finger to the X labeled *Home*. "What is it a map of?"

"It's Cali, a city in Colombia. The city where I was born," I clarified. Claimed.

"Have you been there?"

I pictured the red shape on the globe and told him about the Colombian textiles (see: the wool blanket we were under), the Spanish lessons, my mothers' great desire for me to go with them.

"In all these years, they never went back? What stopped them?"

For my mothers, there had always been papers to write, presentations to give, symposia to host. And, of course, the nagging questions about the safety of that country as the politics ebbed and flowed, and there had also been the lulling comfort and security of home. The joy and responsibility of not only jobs they loved but also this house, the Victorian. Unlike Margaret Moore, my adoptive mothers hadn't been adventurers.

"I don't know why, but I suppose it was just easier not to," I said.

"And now? What about you?"

I fiddled with the hem of the sheet, my fingers weaving the cotton into twists and patterns. What I really wanted was to reach out and take his hand, entwine my fingers in his, hold on to something.

"My mom—Jane—asked me to go to Colombia. Right before she—" The words threatened to choke me, but I continued. "She told me that maybe going to my birthplace would help me . . . help me find myself. Or help me find what's missing."

"Something's missing?"

"I don't know, I guess so. I mean, I might be a bit lost."

His eyebrows furrowed, but he didn't say anything.

"I lost my entire family and my best friend moved across the country. There used to be a boyfriend. And then there's the job I don't have . . ." I let my voice trail off as he nodded slowly in the dim light. I didn't think I was crying, but my cheeks were wet. "She didn't just ask me," I revised. "She made me promise."

"Do you want to go?"

"I want to keep my promise."

The word—*promise*—hung in the dark bedroom like a helium balloon that's lost its lift. One of the cats began licking his fur and the smacking of his tongue punctuated the stillness. I could feel Franklin beside me, this familiar body, this unfamiliar man—both things true. Strange and intimate at the same time.

"I don't believe in this kind of thing," I said, closing my eyes as if that would help everything make sense, "but it's like it was meant to be. I was in the study looking for my passport trying to decide if I should do what Jane asked me to do when this map appeared. I mean, I've been through all those papers before and I've never seen this. And now, when I'm thinking about it all, it appears. Does that make any sense?"

Franklin shook his head. "You're asking the wrong question."

"What's the right question?"

"Will you go?" And he pulled me close until our heads were touching, the only thing grounding me in the dark of the room.

Don't let anything stop you, Jane had said.

CHAPTER 8

Sunlight is peeking through the bedroom window, and my mouth is dry. The room is washed new, like last night never happened. Maybe it *didn't* happen, I think as I stretch like Django, first one limb, then the other. But now Franklin is leaning over me, covering me with one of the heavy blankets. His shirt is buttoned and his belt is buckled.

"Dorrie—"

I jerked, fully awake. I struggled to sit up and clutched the lanolin-scented wool to my chest. "I—" I began.

"Do you—"

I tried again. "Franklin—"

And so did he. "Don't you—"

And then our eyes met and the ridiculousness or the embarrassment or the inevitability of what had happened seemed to sink in. We stared, frozen in time and space, the intricate cogs and springs of our brains whirring and turning, trying to make sense of this sunny late April morning in my mothers' Victorian. And then, as if we simultaneously considered and rejected various reactions (cry? hide? vomit?), we began to laugh. Small chuckles bubbled and grew. We sputtered incoherently, apologizing and excusing ourselves and generally blushing furiously. We both became very red cheeked.

"We're a cliché!" I said, finally extracting words that made sense. I buried my head under the blanket.

"The worst kind of rom-com."

"The clichéd kind."

"The kind where you see it coming a mile away." I peeked out to see him brush his hair out of his face with one hand, serious suddenly. He said quickly, "You know I didn't see this coming. I didn't come over here last night with any expectation . . . or even an idea. Not an inkling."

"Me neither." And then something occurred to me and I buried my head once again, groaning. "And you have a girlfriend!" What was her name? Sasha. Poor Sasha.

From under the blanket, I felt his weight as he sat on the edge of the bed. "We're 'on a break,' as the saying goes." I emerged from under the blanket as he made air quotes with his fingers. "I never would have . . . if I wasn't . . . it's fine . . ." he concluded awkwardly. My heart rate slowed to normal. "But it was . . . it was nice."

"It was," I whispered.

It *was* nice. It had effectively made me feel something, something that wasn't sadness or grief, at least for a little while. And anyway—it wasn't as if we hadn't done that before. I inhaled. This was going to be okay, I told myself. No big deal. But then I sat up to find that, of course, I was topless, and a strange concoction of conflicting emotions—embarrassment and bliss and exhaustion— made me feel slightly nauseated. What had I been thinking? I hadn't been thinking, obviously, otherwise I would have thought better of this. I needed to make sure we were both clear on what had happened.

"You know I just lost my mom. I lost everyone." I tried to explain—again—my situation. The more I talked, the more I was able to compartmentalize this strange night, chalk it up to experience, grief, whatnot. Like any cartographer, I was skilled at taking input and making sense of it, interpreting it for others. And for myself. "I'm out of work. I'm in a really bad—"

"You don't have to explain anything," he said.

"And," I continued. I was grasping for reasons, not excuses, but good reasons for why this—whatever it had been—wasn't anything, couldn't be anything. I wanted to say that we should just be friends, but I had used that word all those years ago and it didn't feel right this time. At nineteen, certain of my choices, I had said it. When we returned to campus after spring break, he had a letter waiting, news that he had been moved off the wait list and accepted into a public-health program in Appalachia. I had thought of that sensation on the sledding hill and how similar intense pleasure was to a sense of a loss of control. The trouble with loving someone, I knew well, even then, was that they would leave you. So I told him I wanted to be friends. "Quit while we're ahead," I had added lamely. Then he insisted he couldn't, wouldn't understand, that a distance of a thousand miles shouldn't matter. "We love each other," he had pleaded. But that had been the exact reason, and each time I looked into his eyes, that out-of-control feeling I remembered from the park bench with Becks threatened to suck me down into its clutches. I couldn't see what was coming next, what was around the bend with him; I needed to know my place in the world.

And now, today, just a couple weeks into my new identity as an orphan, I was further than ever from knowing my place. What was next. I rubbed my face, held my chilly hands over my eyes, and I saw the map, the X, on the bedside table, remembered the certainty I had felt last night in the safety of darkness. Maybe I *did* know what my next step was.

"And I guess I'm going to Colombia?" I sounded less certain, so I tried again: "I'm going to Colombia, so . . ."

"That's great, Dorrie. I'm proud of you."

He slid his feet into his shoes and knelt to tie the laces. Already last night felt like a dream, and Aunt Judith always said it was bad luck to say anything about what you dreamed before breakfast. Grandma June had taken that one step further, contending that talking about dreams at any time was simply rude. So I didn't say anything more.

Then he stood and held out his hand—a formal handshake. "Friends, right?"

The word felt as solid as his fingers gripping mine.

"Of course," I said, as if I had no memory of that heartbreaking spring. "Friends."

Over the past month and a half, life had been all about dying. It hadn't mattered whether there was cereal in the cupboard or extra rolls of toilet paper in the hall closet; it only mattered if Jane was comfortable, if the physical therapist had been scheduled, if the medications had been picked up. I didn't think about food because Jane's coworkers brought casseroles and pasta salads, which she couldn't eat and I barely stomached. I didn't vacuum or dust because the Victorian was in a holding pattern, and only the most urgent tasks were completed, like shoveling the walk and taking a quick shower, and even the chorus had let me be, mostly without criticisms of my housekeeping or personal hygiene. It didn't matter if my jeans were clean or the toilet scrubbed while Jane had lain in the bed in the living room. I had been concentrating on my last moments as the daughter of my last mother, holding on as long as possible.

But now, apparently, I had an international trip to plan, as well as getting through the onerous tasks that followed a loss. I had watched the bereaved partners and offspring as my relatives had passed, the ones left behind who had to deal with wills and probate, real estate and banks, certificates and insurance.

Franklin had offered to help with some of the bigger spring chores. "I can bag those leaves and clear out your gutters," he had said that morning we agreed to be friends, standing at the bedroom window that overlooked the garage, where miniature forests grew along the shingles. "And we can glue that desk back together."

"I'll let you know," I had said, not quite ready to start life again. But one week after my second mother's funeral, I peered into the empty coffee canister and realized that it was no longer tenable to ignore the demands of the living. I would need coffee beans and maybe some bread to pair with those never-ending leftover cold cuts. There was no more laundry detergent or conditioner, and the cats were almost out of both food and litter. Jane had passed away seventeen days ago, meaning I had been an orphan—a parentless, childless, single woman living alone—for more than two weeks, but time continued on. So I buttoned my coat against the first spring rain, which turned out to be more of a drizzle, and drove by rote memory to the nearest drive-thru coffee shop and then to the pet store, lugging the container of kitty litter to the car.

But at the grocery store—my mothers' favorite one that had mounds of vibrant produce and a hearty organic section—I forgot what I needed and aimlessly walked up and down the aisles. The chorus chattered about recipes and the price of bananas, and I tossed random items in my cart until, near the meat counter, I caught a whiff of seafood and was suddenly transported to cookouts in the backyard when Elizabeth would grill scallops for her and Mama, and they would allow me the special treat of one hot dog smeared in ketchup. "All those nitrates are unhealthy," Mommy used to say before tickling my belly. She would scoop me up and I would laugh until I cried, and the memory felt—for one moment—as real as if I were in her arms right now. But then the sensation dissipated, quickly and a little painfully, like a Band-Aid being torn off, and I realized all over again that, even if I could hear their voices, I would never be embraced like that again, and then I was crying beside the spiral-cut hams.

Once, when I was in high school, I had stopped at a grocery store late at night to pick up milk—a request made in exchange for borrowing Elizabeth's Volvo station wagon. The store had glowed in persistent fluorescent daylight although it was past midnight. Just as I lugged the gallon to the checkout lane, a wailing smoke alarm startled the half-asleep shoppers. With a screech over the loudspeakers, a voice announced almost immediately that it was a false alarm, but I had had enough. I deposited the gallon jug on a display table of donuts and exited the building. Like that night, I returned to my car grocery-less, and sat with the engine off, trying to slow my breathing, stop the tears.

(*I cried like that after Dad died*, Aunt Judith said. *Tears are cleansing*, said Aunt Dot.)

Of course there had been no fire that night, and I got in trouble the next morning for not bringing home milk. We had laughed about the whole thing later, my mothers retelling the encounter as a funny anecdote. But now my mothers were gone and there wouldn't be an amusing story about a grocery store breakdown.

"Damon, stop that right now!"

I jumped as a woman's large behind backed into my driver's side window. She was corralling two children into her minivan, one of whom was running a frosted cupcake along the side of my car. The woman startled to see a person sitting motionless in her car in the grocery store parking lot.

"Sorry," she said through the closed window with a shrug. "Kids, you know." The woman pulled a wad of tissue or paper towel from her jacket pocket and began dabbing at the frosting, only managing to spread it around the rear door.

I rolled down my window. "Don't worry about it," I said, but she was already packing her kids in her car and shutting the door.

I wiped my eyes with the edge of my sleeve and called Becks. Her line rang until the voicemail picked up and I realized that it was noon on a weekday and she must be in her classroom, teaching her last week before bed rest. She was surrounded by children and other teachers, she had a husband with whom to eat dinner, and even when she was by herself, Becks had a baby growing and soon she would have her own unruly kids. The thought made me feel even lonelier.

(*Alone, not lonely.*)

But I didn't want to be alone. If only my chorus could do more than just comment and bicker. I needed someone to talk to, someone to listen. I scrolled my contacts. Who could I call? There was my doctor and the car mechanic and the Andersons, a family I used to babysit for. There was Judith Pelletier, Jane Moore, Rebecca Eastman: all the people who were gone in one way or another. Here was one: Olga Kumeh from my book club—but she was a lawyer in a firm downtown, and I was sure she'd be busy on a weekday, and anyway, we weren't the kind of friends who called just to chat. Scroll. Another: Franklin Liu, EMS. He had entered his number into my phone, proof, I supposed, that we were friends now. My thumb hovered. And when he said hello, I burst into tears again.

———

"The thing about big emotions," Franklin had said when I told him about my breakdown, "is that you have to face them in small chunks, not all at once. Bite-size pieces."

Later he had said, "What you need is distraction. I can come over next weekend and get to that spring cleanup." I protested, said I didn't really need help—although I did, I needed lots of help—but he told me he just needed to be paid in beers, that we would do it together, that it would be done before I knew it.

And he was right; we were almost done, our hands blistered, the scraggly lawn filled with neat piles of leaves. I had made it through the week, had managed eventually to buy groceries at the smaller market, where I wasn't so overwhelmed with memories. I had fed myself and the cats, taken several showers, and even sorted the papers from the study. Now it was Saturday, the first week of May, with the unseasonably warm spell continuing in the Upper Midwest, and we had thrown our sweatshirts across the porch's railing.

"What happened to you at the store, was that you were taking in too much at once. You have to take it one step at a time."

I sighed. "That's what Jane used to say."

"Small steps."

"Like good ol' Saint Isidore," I said.

"Who?"

As we bagged the rotting leaves, I told him about Saint Isidore of Seville. "Elizabeth used to tell me about old Isidore, like a bedtime story." Saint Isidore, who lived around AD 600, had watched water, drop by drop, fall on a stone. He noticed that the stone had a small depression where the water had dripped—eons of droplets had changed the rock.

"A tiny drop of water. A massive stone," I said, the same way Elizabeth used to. "Great progress, he realized, could be made with small steps."

"Exactly," said Franklin. "You need to take it slow, in small steps." He knelt and held open the lawn bag.

A breeze blew and I chased a few escaped leaves. "Right. So, after watching the water on the stone, Isidore was for some reason inspired to write a complete summary of all the knowledge in the world."

(*Typical male*, Elizabeth said, just like she used to when she told me the story. *A few drops and he thought he knew everything.*)

"Typical male," I repeated for Franklin, "a few drops and he thought he knew everything."

He laughed. "I only met your mom a couple times, but that sounds like something she would say."

(The chorus chuckled.)

And my heart seized for one moment. "It does," I said, and then told him I'd do the front lawn. The children across the street shouted and screeched and I raked methodically, one row of bared grass at a time. Step by step.

"Last one!" Franklin called. I looked up to see him tie off a bag and haul it to the alley. We were almost done with a job that would have taken me the whole weekend—or one I wouldn't have done at all. Last fall, when we should have been raking, preparing for the next season had seemed so pointless. Jane had been in and out of chemo, Jason and I didn't agree on anything, and CommSys was rumored to have financial problems. Back then, I couldn't imagine a time when I would consider the future. Now, though, the new shoots of grass would strain for the sun and grow straight and tall. I stretched my back, rubbing the sore spot, and then opened the garage. We hung the rakes on the pegs Elizabeth had installed long ago, and he brushed off the knees of his jeans.

"Doesn't this get your mind off big emotions?" Franklin asked.

My arms ached, my palms were bruised, and a blister was forming on the soft pad of my thumb. I was tired in a physical way that had nothing to do with grief. "It does," I agreed. "Which means I definitely owe you a beer."

I brought the six-pack out to the porch and he switched on some music, a random playlist, he said. The little rocker creaked as I lowered myself into it, and I held my blister to the cool bottle. That one song by Smash Mouth played—or was it Green Day? Across from me on the love seat, Franklin sighed and then told me how many steps the raking had got him. He fiddled with his watch and rambled about sleep and heart rate and how he wanted to get a smartwatch for Grandpa Bao, who was getting more unsteady on his feet. I listened but didn't really pay attention, just let myself be comforted by the sound of his rumbling voice, by his familiarness, which had nothing to do with the other night—right?—but our little blip of shared history, and maybe something more. After all, Franklin and I were friends.

The setting sun glowed orange and then red, and still we sat, companionably, together. We talked about nothing as a chill settled on the Victorian's porch. I hugged myself, tucking my hands close against my body as I rocked gently back and forth. He drummed the arms of the wicker sofa in time to the music—Weezer?—and each song reminded me vaguely of something from the past, of being a college student, a daughter, a girlfriend, a granddaughter. A rendition of myself when I knew what and who I was. Could I be that again?

"You know," I said, "if a little yard work got my mind off the big emotions, I wonder what a trip to South America would do?"

He grinned. "Only one way to find out."

"To go?"

"To go." And he reached his long arm toward me to clink bottles.

"Here's to trips to Colombia," I said, and the glass on glass reverberated through the springtime dusk.

1989
Cali, Colombia

Despite the lies and half-truths they told their families—or perhaps because of them—la americana and the Colombian lived blissfully in their little cocoon. News of the cartels and the bombs couldn't touch them, worries about what she would do for a job or vocation were ignored, his plan to fix the leaking toilet put off.

Margaret was so happy in her small world of Juan Carlos, she barely gave her own family a single thought, not even her sister, and his parents showed no interest in coming to Cali, because, she had finally gotten him to admit, they didn't approve of his American novia—married or not. Juan Carlos told Maggie that his mother was very traditional and went to Mass every morning, while his father, he said, worked all the time and kept his head down. There was trouble, he hinted, in the capital city, and it was better that they stay away. She didn't know what kind of trouble he might mean but she knew it was true, and she told herself it didn't bother her that she might never visit them in Bogotá or that they had lied to his mother about being married, and anyway she didn't want to be married, she reminded herself. She was like her sister: unconventional, interesting, a free spirit. There were moments when she twisted the fake band around her finger and felt the cheap paint flecking off and staining her skin a dark green, but then she would look over at Juan Carlos asleep on the tangled sheets and know that she didn't care.

"They'll come around," he promised, and then kissed her forehead in the spot where her blond hair met her pale face. She looked so vulnerable and trusting, he didn't want anything to ever wrinkle that brow. "Te prometo," he promised.

Soon they had a rhythm, the two of them. Their world was his bachelor pad: a mattress on the floor, a scratched table in the kitchenette, three mugs and two plates, a couple of spoons. And she thought it was magnificent. They lived in the present, the moment. Every morning he would make her café con leche, carefully pouring hot water over the filter and heating milk in a pan on the hot plate. In the cool of the evenings, they would stroll along the river arm in arm.

The city was a jigsaw of roads and byways intercut by the río Cali, lumpy with hills and a mix of flat and vertical topography. Its reputation as the most dangerous city in the world stayed in the back of her citizens' minds, but they bustled and traversed just like anywhere. For more than a million people, it was home, whether they were descended from Spanish invaders, los indígenas, or carried the blood of enslaved Africans. And Margaret Moore, despite being born in Minneapolis, Minnesota, fit right in.

She didn't understand the Spanish swirling around her, but Maggie slowly became accustomed to her barrio and daily errands, like the market. She learned to say *por favor* and *cuánto* and ask for *pan*. She sliced mango and pineapple for breakfast. When Juan Carlos left in the mornings, she would lazily get dressed, pulling on a light sundress or pedal pushers and a halter top, her hair in a headband. Sometimes she went shopping at the little kiosks and managed a few Spanish words, buying a T-shirt for Juan Carlos, a bottle of perfume for herself. Back home, this kind of routine would have bored her and made her antsy, anxious to leave, but somehow the slow pace of life here fit her changing idea of who she was, now that she was in this country, with this man.

Although the landlady's daughter—what was her name again? Cristina—came to clean the apartment once a week, each day Maggie swept the floors and aired out the bedclothes on the little balcony that overlooked the courtyard. Even when she was screeching at the sight of the roaches that inevitably scurried out from under the bureau and burning the chicken and undercooking the rice, she knew that this was where she belonged.

"When the shop is done, we'll get a bigger apartment," he told her. He was setting up a branch of his parents' travel agency in Cali and promised that they would get a real bed one of these days and that they would travel again, but she never wanted to leave the little studio with its makeshift kitchen, battered furniture, bare white walls. She loved the way the tall ceilings made the space feel almost reverential, how the sticky breeze moving the cotton curtains at the window seemed to whisper secrets, and how she could recognize every creak and groan of the floorboards.

"I might lose you if we have too much space."

The first time Juan Carlos left for Bogotá, he thought Margaret would be lonely, maybe even frightened. After all, there were frequent news reports of random violence in the city related to the cartels and occasional explosions. But she was a traveler, an explorer, an artist. She pointed at the Nikon. "I'll be fine."

He kissed her and told her, "Doña Rojas will be here if you need anything."

Maggie protested that their landlady didn't know any more English than she knew Spanish. "How will we communicate?"

"Cristina is taking English classes in school," he reminded her.

He had on his sport coat and leather shoes, but Maggie looked so appealing, lying there in bed, that he slipped off his jacket and slid in beside her again. He had a few extra minutes. Later, when she had gotten out of bed and he had rebuttoned his shirt, he suggested a few places she might want to visit while he was away.

"These are some of my favorite spots." His pencil hovered over a dog-eared map of Santiago de Cali from his parents' travel agency.

The colors depicting the blue river and red roads had faded, and the stamp that said Agencia de Viajes was smudged so that his family name was obscured. This piece of paper, he told her, had been his lifeline when he first came to Cali to study business. It held the evidence of the life he had before her—greasy stains left by the street vendors whom he had asked for directions, a rip in the corner where a friend had tried to grab it from him, and the well-worn creases where he had folded and refolded it ever smaller—and now, as he marked on the map, it would serve as proof of the two of them together.

"You can walk to La Ermita," he said, circling the location. "You'll need a taxi to get to La Colina de San Antonio, but the views will be worth it, Margarita, mi amor."

And so, Juan Carlos left, took a direct flight to the capital, and she managed alone. She made her own coffee, adding plenty of milk the way she preferred it; used her new, if limited, language skills to buy food at the market; and remembered to close the windows before the zancudos got in at dusk. She took pictures of the leaves and texture of the plants along the river path, and she practiced her Spanish by looking for words she recognized in the inky pages of old issues of *El Tiempo* that Juan Carlos had piled by the bed. True, she had to ask Cristina for help with the water heater to wash her hair and needed directions to the pharmacy, but she found that being alone in the apartment, in the city, wasn't so bad. In fact, as much as she missed Juan Carlos, she loved the feeling of the foreignness of Cali slowly being replaced with familiarity, as if her old self, Margaret, was being reborn as Margarita.

CHAPTER 9

The Babylonians, the Greeks, the Persians, and the Romans were all making maps in ancient times. They carved on stone, shaped clay, and wrote books about the world in which they lived, with the purpose not only of navigating from one place to another but also to explain the afterlife, educate about religion and beliefs, and generally express their worldview. We think of cartography as being complex, something that requires years of schooling to learn (in my case, a master's and half a PhD), but the classical world had figured out how to locate their place through experience and adventure, through mathematics and teamwork. But really, I thought as I studied the hand-drawn map of Cali, Colombia, all it took to make a map was a pen and a sheet of stationery from the Hotel América.

"I'm so proud of you," Becks said when I told her my plan. "This is what you need," she said with certainty.

My chorus was less sure. Elizabeth was cautiously optimistic (*She can't stay at home her whole life*), Grandma June adamantly did *not* want me to go (*I should have stopped Maggie*), and Gigi was worried that Colombia was too dangerous. Great-Aunt Maureen was all for any kind of travel (*About time she uses that passport*). Aunt Judith didn't think I could afford it since I was unemployed, but

Jane reminded her—and me—that I now had access to their bank account. Even if I didn't have a regular paycheck for a while, I had a paid-for home and car, and my mothers' modest life insurance would come through eventually.

(*Isn't that what money's for? This is what she needs to do,* Jane insisted.)

"I wish you didn't have to do this alone," Becks said.

"Me too. But I'll be okay," I reassured both of us.

"I know it's not exactly 'on the way,'" she said, "but maybe you can come here before you go home? So I can see you before the baby's born?"

"Are you sure you don't want me *after* the baby is born? I can help out. I want to help; you're my best friend."

"I'll have plenty of help. Charlie's mom will come out. My mother's coming to stay with us for three weeks." I could hear the eye roll in Becks's tone. "I don't know if it's a promise or a threat."

I laughed. Mrs. Eastman was as different from my mothers—and Becks—as a woman could be. She had all the qualities of a perfect grandmother and I could picture her with a swarm of grandchildren at holidays.

"It'll be better to see you before the chaos begins. Plus, I'll get to hear all about your trip and you can bring me presents."

So I bought my ticket—three legs on the way back—and booked a room at the Hotel América, which miraculously still existed. I had found it online, the website showing it to be an older boutique hotel with reasonable rates.

I would miss my book club's June meeting (something by Hemingway—I didn't mind), but Olga and Jenn and the others had each emailed me encouraging messages ending with "bon voyage." Franklin took his role as friend seriously, promising to pick up mail, put out the trash, and even offered to take in the cats while I was away.

"I'll hire a cat-sitter," I argued. He was on the phone so couldn't see that Bojangles was currently on the kitchen counter investigating the chicken salad I had eaten for lunch or that Django had recently spit up an enormous hair ball on my mothers' bed.

"Grandpa Bao loves animals, so you'll be doing us a favor," he said, so the night before my flight (red-eye MSP to MIA for a six-hour layover, then CLO), I loaded the car with litter, food, and the cats in their carriers and drove to Saint Paul. The yowling started the moment I turned onto the freeway, and each time a semi sped past, Django, in particular, let his displeasure be known. I could hear Bojangles rattling the carrier's latch and emitting an occasional hiss from behind the passenger seat.

"Shh. You're okay," I cooed at them. Bojangles yowled in response, throwing his weight against the door of the carrier.

"They're monsters," Jane had always complained when they returned from a vet visit.

"They're just scared," Elizabeth would say. "Poor babies." She was the only one who was willing to drive them, and the cats hadn't been to the clinic since her death.

"Turn right," said my phone's GPS as we exited the freeway. The side streets seemed to quiet my mothers' cats. "After two hundred feet, turn left."

I obeyed the clipped feminine voice much as I did my chorus, following without question, without really thinking, and before I knew it, I was pulling up to the little mustard-colored house I remembered from all those years ago. I vaguely recognized the yellow vinyl siding, brown asphalt roof shingles, and the just-budding garden.

"Yeow," said Bojangles.

"I'm getting you out right now," I said to the cats as Franklin emerged from the house. We unpacked the carriers first, then the food and litter.

"Grandpa Bao is so excited."

I followed Franklin into his grandfather's house, prepared for a bachelor pad. Growing up not only in a household of women but with women's voices in my head, I couldn't even imagine a home for two men. In my memory, there had been green shag carpeting, but that had been replaced with gleaming hardwood floors, and under the window in the entryway, several plants in water-stained pots crowded each other.

(*A Pathos, a philodendron, and a jade*, commented Aunt Dot. Someone *has a green thumb*, said Gigi.)

Beyond the small foyer, the living room was bright and sunny, and there sat Franklin's grandfather in a recliner. He smiled broadly as Django cautiously sniffed his way toward him.

"Hi, Mr. Lui." He looked older, smaller than I remembered. But his smile was just as bright.

"Call me Grandpa Bao," he insisted. "Who's this?"

"This is Dorrie. Do you remember her?"

"I know who the pretty girl is," said Grandpa Bao, "but I want to know who this handsome ginger is."

We laughed. "That's Django. He's not super friendly," I warned, but the cat was already making an experimental leap into Grandpa Bao's lap.

"He's the cat whisperer," said Franklin. We watched as Django circled Grandpa Bao's knobby knees and finally settled as if this had always been his home. "Are you hungry?"

"No, I should go," I said, but I followed him into the little galley kitchen. It was a postwar house with a simple layout: living room, kitchen, dining room, a hallway that surely led to bedrooms. I told Franklin I had to get home to finish packing (although I had already reorganized the green Travelpro several times), but I would stay long enough to make sure the cats were adjusting. Then my stomach audibly growled.

He grinned. "Should we order in?" He stood in front of his cupboards. "Unless you want rice pudding?"

We're nineteen, coming back to the dorms from a movie (I don't remember the film or the story) that featured rice pudding, which Franklin had never tried.

"How have you never had rice pudding?" I cried as we walked home from the theater in the lamplit dark. "Isn't rice pudding a Chinese dish?"

"I don't know, my dad never cooks and my mom is white."

"Even so. Rice pudding is a dish that defies boundaries—it's in every culture," I claimed without actually knowing. "My Iowan grandmother used to make it. She said it's from the Depression—a way of using leftover rice. But my mom's is the best. She perfected a Colombian recipe. They call it arroz con leche. I'll make it for you someday."

"When?" he had asked, spinning me around and then pulling me in until our bodies were pressed together from chin to knee, blocking the cold November air.

"Right now?" While we made a detour to the convenience store a couple blocks from our dorm, I called home. "Elizabeth! I have a favor to ask." Mommy loved when I called her from college, loved when I needed her. I asked for her recipe.

"I thought you hated arroz con leche."

"Never!" I protested, although it hadn't been my favorite. As part of her exploration of Colombian cuisine, Elizabeth had decided that her daughter would love the sickly sweet dessert and made it over and over, trying to get the consistency just right. Jane would tease her about her obsession, and we would both laugh at her. Elizabeth's cooking—and our teasing her—was part of my family lore, my legacy. In that moment during my freshman year of college, walking in the dark with this boy at my side, his hand in mine, I had felt the need to share something of myself, something real.

After reciting the simple recipe, I snapped my phone closed, and Franklin propelled me out and then pulled me in. I laughed in that self-conscious way of teenagers, that helpless giddiness that comes from somewhere new and deep within yourself when you're young and in love for the first time.

Later we stood at the dorm kitchen's stove and ate the rice pudding out of the pan, scraping the sticky rice off the bottom as if it were our last meal. All the other moments in the Victorian's messy kitchen came flooding back to me, my childhood self somehow connecting to what I saw at the time as my adult self, all the versions of Dolores and Dorrie coming together. For a split second, on that fall night in a college dorm with a tall boy at my side, I became one whole person.

Now, sixteen years later, I found myself cooking rice pudding again, this time in Grandpa Bao's kitchen. Franklin read the instructions he had pulled from an old recipe box that belonged to his grandmother. "Two cups of water. One cup of rice."

Each card was stained and sun-faded, credit given to the recipe's original chef in the upper right-hand corner: *Mrs. Cochran, Mei's*

daughter, Mrs. Connie Henderson, the nice lady from Hua's Bible study.
Sifting through the cards was like a history lesson, an excavation, like hearing voices of women past—a silent chorus.

"Evaporated milk? Do you have that?"

"I think it's expired." He handed me two cans he had unearthed from a back cupboard.

I squinted at the can, looking for a date. "They seem pretty old."

"Not old—aged," he said, running the can opener around the lid. "Like us."

"What are you making in there?" Grandpa Bao called from the other room.

"We're making rice pudding from Grandma Jia's recipe," Franklin explained as I stirred.

"Ah, from Lunar New Year? Jia loved sweets," said Grandpa Bao. I heard Django's happy coo of a meow.

Franklin laughed and whispered to me, "Actually, *he's* the one who likes sweets."

The rice cooked, we stirred in the milk, added the sugar. The starch of the rice is what thickens the pudding, turning it silky and creamy. Nothing fancy and no additives necessary. Just a couple ingredients would do the trick, even if they were old—aged.

"Bean paste?" he asked, reading the recipe.

"We can skip that," I said with more confidence than I felt. I didn't want to discount his grandmother's recipe, but in the Pelletier-Moore household we made rice pudding with cinnamon. "Do you have cinnamon?"

"Here," he said, and we collided as we both reached into the spice drawer, a warmth radiating off his body. We cleared our throats in unison.

"Now the raisins, right?" I said.

"I forgot about raisins. Let's see if we can find any." He pulled out ziplock bags and canisters. "No raisins."

"My mom would be horrified."

(Right on cue, Elizabeth made an audible gasp. *You can't have arroz con leche without raisins!*)

"She believes—believed—in following recipes exactly, especially ones that she developed. She was a pretty certain person."

"My mom is like that too." He stirred in the cinnamon.

"Mothers think they know everything." I offered him a spoonful of the rice pudding. "Taste test?"

He closed his eyes, chewed, considered, as if he were a TV judge on a cooking show. I tried not to remember what happened after the last time we made rice pudding, about the narrow dorm room bed and the awkward creeping down the hallways afterward. He swallowed and then opened his eyes. "It's delicious even without the raisins," he declared. "I guess moms aren't always right."

Was that possible? The room swayed at the thought. Tomorrow I was leaving on my first international flight (since I was a baby) all because I had listened to—obeyed—my mother. I needed my mothers and my chorus to be right. My entire life, my whole existence, was built on the opinions and advice and certainty of my mothers and aunts and grandmothers.

I stared at Franklin, his eyes crinkled in a grin. "What do you think? A little more cinnamon?"

(*Don't overdo it*, warned Elizabeth.)

"A little more couldn't hurt," I said.

PART TWO

CALI, COLOMBIA

Santiago de Cali, Colombia, is located near the equator at 3 degrees north latitude. The city spans 560 square miles (120.9 square kilometers) and is at an elevation of 3,340 feet (1018 meters). The only major city in Colombia with access to the Pacific Ocean, Cali is bordered on the west by the Farallones de Cali mountain range and the Cauca River to the east.

PART TWO

CHAPTER 10

On a map, you get a sense of the layout and full topography of a place. That bird's-eye view is what gives you a sense of direction. But in real life—even with signs to guide you—you only get a glimpse of what's directly ahead and not much beyond. As I followed the crowds through the winding corridors of the Cali airport toward the migration checkpoint and then baggage claim, I tried to picture the GPS version of myself, a miniature dot or a blinking cursor on a map of the airport, the city, the country. If only I could see the whole picture.

"Something always goes missing."

A woman in a purple sundress and cowboy hat might have been talking to me or maybe someone on the phone she held. We were both watching the luggage circling the carousel in the baggage claim area. The low ceiling gave me claustrophobia, and I glugged the last of my American water in my bottle. A pink suitcase went by, then a lemon-yellow duffel. A large roller bag was wrapped tightly in plastic and another one had been personalized with a rainbow strap. A small green suitcase came around, but it wasn't my Travelpro.

The area buzzed with noise and people. With my book-learned Spanish, I caught snippets of the conversations around me (*casa, primos, contento*), and I was consumed with a sudden ache to recognize their voices, their faces. I tried to imagine Margaret Moore, late 1980s, arriving here alone—at least, I assumed she was alone. The family lore was that she had always been a nomad. The ten-year age difference between her and Jane was either an accident or a miracle, depending on whether you asked Grandpa Vic or Grandma June, and was often blamed for her free spirit.

"Your mother had golden hair and blue eyes," Grandma June said once, before she—or anyone else—was part of my chorus. I was four years old, sitting in her lap on a white damask chair. She fingered my brown hair that hung limply in two pigtails. "Your mother's hair was naturally curly—ringlets." I had looked at Mama; Jane's hair was light brown with a few streaks of gray, cut short like a boy's. I couldn't imagine her with curls. It wasn't until years later that I realized Grandma June had been talking about my *biological* mother, her *other* daughter. She had dropped my pigtail then and sighed. "Your father must have been *very* dark," she remarked, touching my forearm with one piano-playing finger.

That's when Mama had scooped me out of Grandma June's arms. "That's enough, Mom," she had said sternly. That night, me, Mama, and Mommy were cuddled together on the floral sofa comparing arms. Mama's was pink, Mommy's was pale with freckles, and mine was coconut brown. "Don't let anyone tell you you're not perfect the way you are," Mama had said firmly.

"Not even your relatives," added Elizabeth, and my mothers exchanged droll glances.

Now I scanned the crowd waiting alongside me for their luggage and wondered if I had relatives among them. Had someone—maybe that elderly couple in the back—known Margaret Moore? Was there a blood relation of mine in line—maybe that little girl gripping her father's hand? But as far as I would ever know, they were all strangers. I knew nothing about Margaret Moore's time in Colombia and even less about my biological father other than his first name, Juan Carlos. And suddenly, surrounded by bustling travelers and cumbersome luggage, I was seized with a tsunami of fear, followed closely by the cold chill of loneliness. What was I doing here?

I pulled out my phone to text Becks, holding it up, searching for bars. Nothing. I tried to connect to the airport's Wi-Fi but got nothing but error messages. I wouldn't panic. No. I forced myself to be present—after all, I was in my birthplace, this was a homecoming. Everything was going to work out perfectly. Soon I would find the apartment on calle 5 Norte as directed by the map and I would fulfill my promise to Jane. And everything would turn out perfectly. I stuffed the useless phone in my carry-on.

The carousel made its lazy circles and time went by very slowly. As I waited, each moment stretched out, begging to be filled with anxiety and worries. Was this trip a terrible idea? Maybe I should have waited a few months? Should I have hired a house sitter instead of accepting a favor from Franklin? Were the cats adjusting to his house? Was *he* adjusting to *them*? What if I can't find my hotel? What if my hotel is a dump? What if the places on the hand-drawn map didn't exist? Maps, while usually accurate, were only as good as their cartographers. And what did I know of my map's maker?

I took a deep yogic breath, trying to push the thoughts from my head. Elizabeth had gone through a yoga phase when I was in high school, and she repeatedly failed to get me to take classes with her. She would make me breathe, tell me to stretch. "Try a downward dog or even mountain pose," she would say. "At least breathe." I had ignored her then but now I inhaled and exhaled.

One by one, the couples and families and solo travelers gathered their belongings and marched through the frosted glass doors, leaving the liminal space of the airport behind. Soon the only other person waiting in the harsh lighting of the low-ceilinged room was the woman in the purple dress and cowboy hat. Three suitcases were piled at her feet, but she continued watching, flipping her blond hair from one shoulder to the other. The carousel creaked and squeaked its way around, the flow of emerging suitcases trickling to nothing, like a shut-off faucet. The woman said something. Now I was pretty sure she was talking to me because there was no one else waiting with us.

I glanced at her and she smiled, saying in American English, "It's not looking good, is it?"

"No, it's not," I agreed, wondering what had made her assume I was American too.

"I thought you might speak English," she said. "The shoes."

I looked down at my feet. I was wearing those brightly colored but hugely comfortable sneakers that slipped on and off without laces. I shifted on their memory foam insoles, noting her heeled espadrilles that laced up the ankles and the way the purple dress showed off her freckled collarbones, and I knew I had worn the wrong clothes—barely twenty minutes here and I already felt out of place.

"My sandals are in my suitcase," I said, as if this stranger would care.

"Here's hoping it shows up!" The woman flashed a white, straight smile.

(*Did Dorrie at least pack a change of underwear in her carry-on?* worried the voices. *Just in case?* I had, as they knew, because they had already given me this advice. *I lost my favorite Louis Vuitton makeup case on a trip to New York in 1963,* said Great-Aunt Maureen, repeating the story she had recited yesterday. *Didn't see it again for a month.*)

"I go back and forth all the time," said the woman, "and I've only had a suitcase go missing twice." Surely, the days of missing luggage were behind us. I remembered Elizabeth having her suitcase—along with her presentation on the metasearch habits of undergrads—go missing years ago en route to a conference in Seattle.

"I'm Trina." The woman smiled and then held out her hand.

"Dorrie."

"Have you been to Cali before?"

"I don't travel much."

"Everything in this country is an adventure." She winked. "You'll get used to it."

A lone beige roller bag appeared.

"Yours?" Trina asked. I shook my head. She and I watched it make its way around the track. "You'll love—" she began.

The carousel shuddered and came to a groaning halt.

"Oh, shit," my companion and I both said.

A man in a red jumpsuit began sweeping the shiny tiled floor of candy wrappers and baggage claim tickets. Trina stopped him and spoke for a moment, then followed him to a room at the back of the baggage claim. I went with them and she interpreted for me, asking for my ticket and phone number. "They'll sort it out," Trina told me at last. "Don't worry."

"I'm not worried."

"Are you sure?" Trina nodded at my hands, the knuckles white as I clutched my backpack. She laughed a loud honk, and I loosened my grip, stretched my fingers, dared to chuckle.

"Okay, I guess I'm a little worried. Will they find my bag?"

"They'll find it. Eventually. Once my kid's Mickey Mouse suitcase went missing on a trip to Disneyland, ironically." With her cowboy hat and sexy sundress and American accent, she didn't look like anyone's mother, especially not one who traveled with a Mickey Mouse suitcase. Not that I was an expert on motherhood. "They only located it after we came back here. But that was unusual," she added, probably seeing my look of horror. "Every time I travel back and forth between here and the US, it works out in the end."

"Where in the US?"

"Los Angeles," Trina said, leading the way through customs (a simple process with no suitcase). "I met my husband when he was going to UCLA," she continued, as we followed the signage toward the airport's exit, "and I was waitressing near campus."

The exit signs blinked. SALIDA. Again, I pictured myself as a marker on a map. Blink, blink. I was the YOU ARE HERE sticker, even though I hardly knew where "here" was, much less what to do next. What would happen when I emerged from the airport? Would I find a taxi? Was it safe?

"Sebastián came back here," Trina was saying, "and I followed."

(*Like Margaret*, someone said.)

"We've been married six years, so at this point I feel more like a caleña—that's someone from Cali—than an LA girl." She paused to reapply lipstick and then fluff her hair. I made a half-hearted attempt to neaten my rumpled T-shirt and smooth back my ponytail. "How about you? Where are you from?"

Where are you from? The question I had been asked over and over again growing up. *Why don't you look like your mom? Where's your dad? Why do you have two moms? Do you speak English? Why don't you have an accent?* The litany of questions, all stemming from the color of my skin and the shape of my face and the blackness of my hair. *They're only asking because they're curious,* members of the chorus would insist.

"I live in Minnesota." The simplest answer, especially here, now.

"Minnesota! I think my grandfather was from Minnesota. Or maybe Michigan? I've never been, but I hear it's really pretty. You don't look like you're from Minnesota. Aren't they all Swedes and Norwegians?"

This—this was what people meant by *Where are you from?* The question was really, *Why do you look different from me?*

But then Trina touched the end of my ponytail as if we were already friends. "You remind me of my husband's cousin. She has the same gorgeous hair as you."

I slipped my hair out of its ponytail. The way Grandma June had looked at my hair, I never thought of it as particularly gorgeous.

"Actually," I said, "I was born here."

"You're Colombian!" Trina exclaimed.

(*Of course she's Colombian,* whispered a voice so soft, I wasn't sure if I heard it or imagined it.)

"I suppose I *am* Colombian," I said.

"Then welcome home."

Home.

Outside the airport, I was greeted by crowds of passengers and teary family members and uniformed soldiers with automatic rifles. People hugged and cried, they grabbed each other's luggage and clutched bouquets of flowers. There was noise and commotion everywhere. Standing on the concrete outside the airport felt like I was in a place no cartographer had yet charted, and I found that I was white-knuckling my backpack again.

Jane had wanted me to see where I came from (how would I ever find that apartment?), but this whole trip had sounded like a much better idea from the safety of the Victorian's living room, in the glow of Franklin's encouragement and Becks's insistence. The hand-drawn map was obviously a ridiculously flimsy reason for being here, and even a deathbed promise seemed ill-thought-out. If only Becks could have been here with me. If only my mothers were here. There was an endless list of "if onlys."

But then, beyond the clouds of diesel fumes and burning motor oil, a grassy and sweet scent wafted over me, reminding me of something the way scents do. A photograph. The only one of me with my birth mother, a blurry picture in an old frame kept on the piano, which I had tucked in my now-missing suitcase. In the photo, Margaret isn't looking at the camera, and sunlight behind her obscures the color of her hair, although Jane had always assured me it was pale, the color of summer corn. My own chubby-cheeked face peeks out from a blue crocheted blanket. I stopped, halting the foot traffic around me, and held on to the memory of that photo, somehow—in the swirl of smells and sounds of the airport's exit—able to feel the scratchy softness of that too-warm wool, catch the aroma of something fresh and sour. Several horns blared and an engine revved. I ignored it all and inhaled, trying to regain a fragment of the memory of the blanket and the mother, even though I knew that that moment in my birth mother's arms couldn't possibly be a memory, not really.

"I remember," I used to tell my mothers when we looked at the photo.

"You were too little to remember," Jane would say.

But the brain has hidden corners and dead ends and skipped

passageways. There isn't a map, there aren't directions. What we perceived as memories were just re-creations in our brain, easily manipulated, perhaps by a yellowing photograph in a silver frame in one's childhood home.

"But I do," I would insist, holding on to the impossibility of my citrusy memory.

CHAPTER 11

When early cartographers began to map their world, they needed to physically traverse the land, to trek from one point to the other, through forests and swamps or along beaches and rivers. No matter how hard the journey, they kept going in the name of discovery. It was the only way. And if I wanted—needed—to find *my* way, I couldn't waste a moment of my time here in my birthplace. So even though I had slept poorly, and even though I was still wearing yesterday's clothes, I stopped by the front desk early that first morning.

Taking a deep breath, I approached reception, where I was dismayed to find the same woman as last night, again in her ill-fitting gray skirt suit and tightly pulled-back gray hair. She looked like the rest of the hotel: elegant but slightly worn with age.

(*This looks familiar!* Jane had gasped. *That old desk, the light. Like it was yesterday.*)

Perhaps this gray woman had been working at this very spot thirty-five years ago; perhaps she had seen a woman with an infant cross the lobby. But if she had, I doubted she would tell me.

Last night she had been unhelpful when she couldn't find my reservation. Thankfully, when we were leaving the airport, I had accepted the help of Trina and her husband, who drove me to my hotel to help me get settled, and as the woman insisted there was no room in my name, Trina joined me at the counter. "Everything okay?"

"I think I'm saying something wrong. She says she can't find my reservation."

Trina leaned her elbows on the desk and swished her blond hair. "Buenas tardes, señora." In fluent, California-accented Spanish, Trina asked about my room. I understood but wouldn't have been able to conjure these words, this vocabulary.

"Do you have a confirmation?" Trina asked me, translating. I nodded mutely as if I were a child and passed the woman my phone with the email.

"No, I'm sorry, I have no reservation with that name." The woman didn't look at all sorry.

"None? Are you sure?" I could feel tears prick my eyes. "I have a confirmation code."

"We'll straighten this out, don't worry," Trina had whispered to me, and several tears escaped at her kindness. "Sebastián!" called Trina. The three of them talked, argued, my new friends explaining that I was already missing my luggage and I needed a room now. The gray woman seemed determined not to apologize, until Seb asked to speak to the hotel's owner and I was suddenly handed a room key.

Now the woman sighed as I approached as if she was already sure she couldn't—and didn't want to—help me.

"Can you tell me how to get to calle cinco Norte?"

With the same grating attitude she had used last night, she repeated, "Calle cinco Norte? Which part of calle cinco Norte?"

I glanced down at the hand-drawn map in my hand. I didn't want to show it to her, as if by sharing it with this woman I would destroy its magic and its connection to me and this country. Instead I asked about the address.

"I am not sure where that would be," she said in a tone that made it clear she didn't want to deal with me anymore. She gave me a few vague directions with a wave of her hand. "Have a lovely walk," she said, peering at me over her eyeglasses as if I might dare not to.

As I turned to leave, the squeaking of my sneakers on the stone floors reminded me I was missing something. "Oh, and—" I said, rushing back. "Any news on my luggage?"

But she was gone.

In the daylight, Cali looked completely different. A low-level humidity hung in the air, casting a blurry haze over everything, playing tricks on my eyes, making shapes and figures appear and then disappear, blink in and out of existence, until the city seemed like nothing more than two-dimensional renderings on a map. For all I knew, it was— my entire known history with this country was nothing more than a birth certificate and documents, a few black-and-white photos, a blue passport. A hand-drawn map. I was a two-dimensional Colombian.

Following the woman's instructions to calle 5 Norte, I turned left at the corner and soon the road started an uphill climb. The back of the hotel was to my right, and on the other side of the street were the redbrick facades of apartment buildings and markets. Shrubs along the center median were a blur of pink and red blooms. In every crack in the pavement, something green grew as if declaring its persistence.

I paused on my uphill climb to let the chattering families pass, wiping the sweat from between my boobs with the inside of my T-shirt. I thought of the airy sundresses and practical shorts packed in my Travelpro and wondered if I would ever find it or the apartment. And then, just as I was considering turning back, I saw the blue sign with white lettering nearly hidden by the branches of a hibiscus: CALLE 5 NORTE. A chill went up my spine; Margaret Moore had walked along this very sidewalk, perhaps hand in hand with Juan Carlos, my father.

There was something magical about that apartment where they lived, Jane had said. *You must go there, find that place.*

"I will, Mama," I whispered, hurrying up the road. As I walked, I studied each building. If the system worked like it did in Minneapolis, I had a few more blocks to go. I pulled the map from my pocket again and fingered the paper as if it were a talisman, a rabbit's foot or a lucky penny. Maps are reassuring in their consistency and honesty. They contain truth, and I was about to find my truth, my past. I wasn't sure what I would discover—I didn't think Jane knew what I would find, either—but it must be something. Please, I thought, please let it show me something.

(*Does anything look familiar?* Elizabeth asked Jane, who said it had changed a lot. I thought I heard someone sigh—or maybe it was only a breeze through the trees.)

And then, halfway down calle 5 Norte, there it was, just where it should be, exactly as it had been depicted on the hand-drawn map. Unbelievably real.

"I first met you," Jane used to tell me, "at Maggie's apartment. A cute studio with a view of the courtyard. I remember the mango tree. I picked one and you loved it, even though you were too young for solid food."

The numbers were affixed crookedly but clearly to the side of the building. It was three stories, attached to the neighboring buildings, which had clearly been built or renovated more recently. Part brick and part concrete, it had two sets of windows on each floor, the lower ones protected by iron bars in intricate designs of fleur-de-lis and vines. And there was a big glass door in the middle, above which was a sign: PELUQUERÍA.

I stood and stared as my chorus chattered.

"Peluquería," I read. I could see the picture in one of my Spanish-language books from high school: *La mujer visita la peluquería.* Elizabeth and I had laughed at the image of a cartoon lady in curlers.

I peered through the glass door. Inside were salon chairs and mirrors, everything a bit dusty and worn looking. A sign taped to the glass said CERRADO. Closed.

(*Oh, poor Dorrie,* sighed the ladies, the voices of my chorus echoing the emptiness I felt in my heart.)

My eyes burned. This wasn't an apartment building. "Home" wasn't a home and it didn't look magical.

1989
Cali, Colombia

Seeing the río Cali as it wound its way through the colonial neighborhood near the apartment Margaret Moore and Juan Carlos shared always made her think of her parents' house in Minneapolis, which was a few blocks away from a creek, where the water was often low, "less of a creek and more of a crick," her dad would say. As a child, she used to stand on a footbridge and imagine the water beneath her feet making its way from her neighborhood in Minnesota, first to the Mississippi and, eventually, to the Gulf of Mexico, where it would mix with seawater and become part of the ocean, free to ride the currents around the globe. She had wanted to be that water.

"The río Cali flows to the Pacific Ocean," Juan Carlos had told her as they stood on their own footbridge and watched the swirling water.

Now she was on her own, following the map he had left for her. Just touching the paper made him feel close. She paused on the sidewalk to double-check that she was headed in the right direction toward the church, La Ermita, and tucked the map back in her new bag.

Before he left again for Bogotá, a package arrived at the Doña's doorstep battered and misshapen. Cristina brought it upstairs, timidly knocking on the apartment door.

"Did you step on this, Cristina?" teased Juan Carlos, and the poor girl blushed crimson.

"Leave her alone," Maggie had scolded as she took a kitchen knife to the tape.

Inside the box was a short satin robe and the colorful woven bag Juan Carlos said was called a *mochila*. He explained, "This is a wedding present for you from Mamá."

It wasn't until later that she realized that when he talked about his family, he never used their names, only identified them as "my father" or "my sister." He talked about his mother as "Mamá," as if she was Maggie's mom too. Maggie, with her older, bossy sister and two grandmothers and even nosy Aunt Maureen, had enough mother figures in her life and continued to refer to her as "*your* mother."

Maggie was sure she would never the wear the silky white robe. She and Juan Carlos had no use for lingerie. But she liked the mochila, which she had seen caleños carrying. So she wrote a thank-you note—the way her mother and grandmothers had taught her—getting help with her grammar and spelling from Cristina, and when Juan Carlos returned, he would address it and carry it off to the post office. And his parents' names would remain unknown and they unmet.

But she didn't worry about that now. She had just caught sight of a cathedral-like spire peeking through the branches of trees all sharp and spiky as if declaring its importance. That must be it. La Ermita. She looked both ways, crossed the busy road, and stood on the plaza in front of the church. The building wasn't as grand as the churches in Italy, but it was somehow still breathtaking in its novelty, this concrete neo-Gothic structure rising from the green, shady banks of the river. With ornate flourishes and whitewash, it reminded her of a wedding cake like the one Aunt Dot had for her first marriage, when Margaret had been a four-year-old flower girl. She snapped off the lens cover of her Nikon and framed the shot, the image that first caught her eye: the spire against the morning's blue sky, a blue that she was certain could only be found in Valle del Cauca.

"You'll love La Ermita," Juan Carlos had promised, and she would love this spot because Juan Carlos had wanted her to see it, to love it, and she loved him.

Inside, the church was cool and smaller than it looked from outside. The domed ceiling was ribbed in gold paint in meticulous, repeating patterns matching the ornaments of the exterior facade. In that space no bigger than her elementary school's gymnasium—and just as echoey—the still air had a hushed feel to it. Her footsteps clattered on the marble floors as she made her way to a hard wooden pew near the back and studied the statue of a beautiful young woman—was it the Virgin Mary?—hands outstretched in prayer or plea, something she hadn't seen until her travels. Maggie had grown up in the confines of a Lutheran upbringing, the unsavory and complicated parts of both religion and humanity hidden from view. She loved messiness and found the documentation of all parts of life was what made it worth living. She refocused her gaze upward, appreciating the way the light filtered through the stained-glass windows of the dome. She fidgeted in the hard pew. Her finger itched to release the shutter, but several elderly women knelt a few rows ahead of her and she knew it would be sacrilegious to snap a photo right now. She would have to commit this place, this moment, to memory.

She closed her eyes and concentrated on the whir of breeze floating through the chapel, the murmur of voices, the musty scent of cold stone. The history of the space, the workmen who had built it, the faithful who had prayed in it, felt palpable. In her mind, even with her eyes closed, she could see this church as clearly as though she had taken the perfect photo; sometimes, she thought, what we feel is more real than what we see.

CHAPTER 12

Triangulation is the process of finding your location from two remote but known points. This simple method has been used for centuries to pinpoint humans' place in the world: one man ventured out, while the other was left behind to light smoke signals, the only way to communicate across the expanse. One early attempt to measure distance in fathoms was thwarted when the area being measured was besieged by wildfires, making the smoke signal impossible to discern. Now, finding myself in a crowded restaurant on my first full day in Cali, Colombia, was like being in the midst of a forest fire, all smoky and confusing. No way to find my location.

After Trina and Seb had helped me with the hotel reservation, they had invited me to dinner tonight. I had tried to resist but they were persistent, and that was how I found myself—disoriented and in well-worn clothes—at a loud Northern Italian cafe surrounded by strangers: friends of Trina and Seb's, who included a couple of Americans and several local Colombians, who all agreed that Trina was very persuasive.

"Trina gets what she wants!" they shouted.

"Eso es la verdad," they laughed.

Someone handed me a drink and someone else passed a plate of bread and butter. The other tables were filled with more groups of boisterously chatting people, and the waiters swiftly moved around the room as if choreographed in a Fred Astaire film. We were on the second floor of the restaurant and the windows were open, letting the smells of the kitchen—tomato sauce, searing meat, salty fish—mix with the city's diesel fumes and floral scents. Besides Trina, there was another blond American whose name I was pretty sure was Hannah, and a gorgeous Colombian woman who had the most delicate features I had ever seen. Two other men about the same height and build as Seb joked and jostled and ordered beers, while the pretty Colombian asked if I spoke Spanish and introduced herself as María Sofía—or maybe it was María Sarita. She worked in a high school (or was it a preschool?) teaching English with Hannah.

"How long since you've come to Santiago de Cali?" Seb was asking me.

"She's never been here," Trina informed him, as if we were friends, as if our relationship spanned more than the time between the baggage claim and the exit doors.

"Never?" asked Hannah.

"I mean, other than being born here." Then the explanation I often offered: "I'm adopted."

"Ah!" the people around the table said.

"Many American families adopt from Colombia," the slimmer of the two Colombian men—Joaquim?—said.

(*Dorrie should explain*, said Elizabeth sternly.)

"Yep," I said, ignoring my chorus.

"Colombians make the best babies." Trina reached out and grabbed Seb's hand from across the table in a youthful gesture I associated with teenage love. Franklin had held my hand, but that was when we were young, and Jason and I had never held hands—he thought it was pointless.

"You mean *you guys* make the best babies," clarified Hannah. "Wait until you see their kid, Dorrie."

"Look at him." Trina let go of her husband's hand and pulled out her phone, holding up a photo of a little boy with black hair, a little overgrown, in a yellow soccer jersey. "He's beautiful, isn't he?"

(*His hair is just like Dorrie's was when she was a baby.*)

"I love Andrés!" cooed María Sofía—that was her name.

"Don't tell anyone, but he's our favorite student," said Hannah.

They must work in a preschool, I thought.

Trina scrolled through more photos and my chorus kept up its commentary as the boy in the photos got younger.

(*He's got nice eyes,* they allowed. *But Dorrie never had that milk rash like this baby has.*)

She scrolled back in time, all the way back until a photo showed a very large, very pregnant Trina with a beaming Seb. "Look at how huge I was!"

"Big as a house," Seb said proudly.

"I didn't know you then," said Hannah.

"She was huge," confirmed Joaquim.

The other man, quiet and smoldering looking, leaned close and asked me, "Do you have children?" I reflexively shrugged my left shoulder and a tingle went up my neck. Trina had introduced him as Oscar, Seb's friend from work. His *single* friend, she had emphasized. Not that it mattered to me. I would not be swept into anything. Not the way Maggie had been.

Spanish and English flew around me in equal measures. I swayed. The group of strangers laughed and tried to include me in their conversations but, despite my learned ability to conjugate verbs and assign articles, I was drowning in a sea of words. I tried to use them as anchors, to triangulate my location between them, but they seemed to circle, to ebb and flow. Individually, each word was familiar, yet, taken together, indecipherable. In order to figure out where you are, you must recognize something, somewhere.

"The winters—" Joaquim, to my right, was saying in English, "—terrible!" Since being introduced to him as a Minnesotan, I had been regaled with his reminisces about his two years at the University of Iowa. "So many layers of clothes, you wouldn't believe it."

"Winter, winter, winter," mimicked Seb, who went to high school with Joaquim. "Is it really that bad, Dolores?"

"Oh, um, yes." I felt like a child again at one of Jane and Elizabeth's symposia invited into the conversation by adults.

"¡Ya te lo dije!" erupted Joaquim, reaching for Seb as if to put him in a headlock. "I told you so! The snow—it gets this high." He reached his long arm high above his head.

I laughed. "Not quite."

"Even the americanas here don't know winter." Joaquim was adamant.

"Guilty of being Californian," said Trina, holding up her hand as if swearing on a Bible.

"And I'm from Arizona," said Hannah. She was tall with dirty-blond shoulder-length hair and had qualified for the Olympic swim team before becoming a teacher.

"I can barely make it across a pool," I said, impressed.

"But then I tore my labrum and spent a whole year rehabbing instead of training for the summer games."

"Exactly," said Joaquim with a satisfied shrug. "You don't know cold." He was clearly unable to let it go.

Hannah laughed and said, "I *have* been skiing."

"I don't ski, at least not in Minnesota," I said. "Too cold."

"So cold you could die, right?" Joaquim said.

"Well," I began. All eyes turned to look at me. "The cold is the worst, I guess." I nodded at Joaquim, who seemed to appreciate my confirmation. "But it can be beautiful too. White everywhere, crisp cold. Todo blanco," I said, trying out some Spanish. "And there's nothing better than coming indoors after spending time sledding or ice-skating. Your hands are frozen, your cheeks are red. And then you curl up in front of a fire with a blanket and maybe some cats and a cup of hot chocolate with your parents."

My audience murmured their awe. I pictured the living room in the Victorian, Jane and Elizabeth under the pilled crocheted blanket, me on the floor in front of the fireplace, Django on my lap and Bojangles basking in the glow of the flames. The image was so vivid, I could feel the heat across my legs, the dripping of my thawing nose. I could even hear the murmurs of my mothers.

María Sofía exclaimed, "You should have brought your parents on this trip!" The others nodded, repeated words about family and togetherness.

(*We should have gone*, murmured Elizabeth. *She's here now; that's all that matters*, said Jane.)

The lump bumped into my heart, its ventricles and arteries momentarily disrupted by the pressure. I stared down at the napkin on my lap. This was a joyous, cheerful group of friends joking and teasing. They didn't need to hear about my losses, my loneliness, my aloneness.

María Sofía pressed on. She was strikingly beautiful with flawless caramel skin, long hair, and equally long legs. "¿Dónde viven tus padres?"

I could be a liar or an orphan.

"My parents are gone," I said at last, swallowing that lump.

A heavy silence fell over the table, exaggerating the sounds of the clattering plates, chattering waiters around us.

"Where did they go?" asked María Sofía earnestly.

Trina and Hannah let out a gasp, as did Seb.

"I'm so sorry," said Trina, reaching for my hand.

"It's okay," I said, a shaky, warm feeling moving from the pit of my core and working its way up. My hands and cheeks tingled. "They're dead," I explained to María Sofía. "Están muertos," I added, hoping I had conjugated the verb correctly. Her face reddened, and her hand flew to her mouth in shock. "All of them."

The later it got, the blurrier and more confusing the dinner became. I ate the pasta and drank rum cocktails ordered by my companions as they popped up and down playing musical chairs. Trina whispered again that Oscar was single. Joaquim confided that he had left behind a boyfriend in the United States, but I shouldn't tell anyone. María Sofía, who seemed to be attempting to compensate for her earlier gaffe, asked about my favorite places to shop in Minnesota.

After dinner, when Hannah and María Sofía went outside to smoke, Oscar whispered in my ear. His breath was hot. "Tell me what you do, Dolores-from-Minnesota."

"I'm a cartographer."

"Maps?"

"But I'm unemployed right now."

"You get to see the world?" His eyes were so dark, they were nearly black, the irises deep.

"I suppose," I said, trying to ignore the warmth in my cheeks (and elsewhere) as Oscar leaned in, his arm brushing mine. "I mean, you can." I'd never really thought of it that way. Cartographers—modern ones, anyway—chart the globe without ever leaving their offices. Pre–World War I and the advent of aerial photography, maps were made by cartographers literally surveying the land, traversing prairies, scaling mountains. Each time a new road was built or a bridge spanned, someone had to see it. They had to witness something to believe it. Now, as the built world changes, we hunch over computers, oblivious to the reality we're delineating. "I haven't traveled much, not like my mother."

My mother. I wasn't sure why I said that. I had been thinking of Maggie.

"Do you remember Colombia?" Seb asked. The whole group was now settled around the table again, still drinking.

"I don't remember anything."

"How old were you when you were adopted?"

"I went to the US when I was three weeks." The truth being more complicated than my explanation suggested, I offered what I could. After all, these strangers had already been so kind and I felt like I owed them something or that I wanted to offer them more than a feeble story. "This is all I have left from . . . from that time." I unfolded the map and passed it around.

Hannah studied it. "Wow, this looks old. The Hotel América," she read from the stationery. "I see now how you found this hotel. Not many tourists know about it."

She passed it to Trina. "Who drew it?"

"I'm not sure," I admitted. "But I want to find these places."

"La Ermita, the Tertulia, la Colina. They're all in the neighborhood near your hotel."

"Yes, I think so," I said, and added, "although the calle cinco Norte spot doesn't exist anymore. I already looked."

Trina turned the sheet of stationery this way and that, running her finger along the torn edge. Then she passed it to her husband.

"It's like a—how do you call it?" he asked. "A—búsqueda del tesoro?"

"A scavenger hunt," Joaquim translated.

Gigi and Baba used to hide Easter eggs in their backyard when I was little. They still lived in their farmhouse, although someone else took care of the land. I remembered cold spring mornings in stiff cotton dresses spying brilliant plastic eggs scattered under piles of leaves and in crooks of trees, and the relatives would watch me, shouting encouragements, sometimes not-too-subtly pointing out the hiding places.

"Or maybe a treasure map?" Trina said.

I pictured pirate maps with buried treasure marked by an X. What treasures would I find here? Although I didn't tell them about the deathbed promise, I found myself explaining the map, the locations, my birth mother in broad strokes, that I was on a quest to find out where I came from. These things I had never really talked about before and yet was now sharing with strangers. The group passed the delicate paper around, commenting on the locations, volunteering which was their favorite, where to start, wondering why the hospital—so incongruous—was on the map.

"You're going to visit all these places?" Oscar asked, his eyes dark and serious.

Was I? What kind of a plan was that? The map suddenly seemed inadequate. A map needed scale and measurement, accuracy and verification, and the hand-drawn sketch had none of these.

"She *needs* to visit all these places," said Trina. She reminded me of Becks in the way she seemed to thrive on taking control. The two of us used to play school in the Eastmans' basement rec room and

I was always the student. "Write 'I am naughty,' twenty times," she would boss, and then hand me a piece of chalk for the real chalkboard that hung on the wall. I always did.

"Alone?" asked María Sofía.

Alone ricocheted off the ceiling and hit me in the stomach. What would Margaret Moore have thought of me—this girl who didn't have the pull to travel, a half-Colombian daughter with black hair and dark eyes, who would rather chart the earth, draw the lines that demarcated one place from another, delineate borders and boundaries from the safety of a desk, than see these things for herself. My throat felt dry despite the humidity. I could only nod.

"Not alone—we're going to help her." Trina handed the map back to me.

1989
Cali, Colombia

Leaving her alone when he traveled back to Bogotá always felt like foolishness, like tempting fate. There were dangers all around them these days; everyone lived with a constant level of surveillance, even if regular citizens had nothing to do with the guerra sucia or the political maneuvering. Juan Carlos mostly went about his days, and he always kept Margarita sheltered from both the news and anything that might end up as news. She wanted to go dancing at the new discoteca that had been advertising incessantly on the radio, but he couldn't protect her there. Instead, he insisted that teaching her the cumbia in the privacy—and safety—of their own apartment was better. Certainly more romantic.

He could feel his body respond to the memory of those nights, and he missed her with an ache that surprised even him. "El amor duele," his grandmother always said, but he had never believed her. Love was beautiful. How could it *ever* be painful?

"¡Juanqui!" His older sister shouted the pet name she had called him since he was in diapers. He tugged on the long braid she always wore and then wrapped her in a hug. "Come eat," she commanded, and ushered him into the little house where they had grown up, always with the background sounds of children playing, mothers telling chismes below their laundry lines, and fathers coming home from work to have a trago or two and asking how was school. Lately, though, the neighborhood in Bogotá was changing. Many families—those with connections or enough plata—had fled to the United

States, some to find jobs, some to escape dangers, either real or perceived, Juan Carlos was never sure. Now the houses, each one connected to the next like a Lego set, were in various states of repair, the front gardens of some forlorn and overgrown while the trumpet flowers of others bloomed in abundance.

"I hope you made something warm for your caleño brother," he told his sister as he greeted his mother, rubbing his hands together for warmth.

"Ay, mijo, your blood is thinning in Cali. It's not cold today," she said, kissing him on the cheek. She was wearing knee socks under her dress and was wrapped in a long sweater of his father's. Juan Carlos smiled and said nothing; his mother was not to be contradicted.

"My ajiaco will warm you in no time," said his sister, laying the table with soup bowls.

"*You're* doing the cooking now? How do I know it'll be safe to eat?" he joked.

"Cállate," scolded his mother. "Your sister is going to make a perfect wife. Ojalá," she added, and made the sign of the cross.

His sister had finished college with a degree in economics, but, ironically, the economy was so bad there were no jobs in economics, and because their father did not believe in women working, instead of taking over the family business, she had been taught to cook and clean for a future husband their mother pictured for her.

"Speaking of wives . . ." his sister said with a wink and a sock in his arm. "How is yours?"

He was certain she and Margarita would love each other.

But before he could answer, his mother shook her head. "Not now, mijo," she muttered.

While mothers want their daughters to find a husband, they don't want their sons to ever leave them. As her youngest and only son, Juan Carlos had been coddled and spoiled, and she had wept when he left for Europe, afraid that he wouldn't come back. But something worse had happened: he had found a woman. And an American one at that.

After lunch, while the women cleaned up, he and his father sat at the table and talked about the business. There was trouble, not enough travelers, but maybe they would make it up during the Christmas holidays. His father blamed the unrest and the fear. "Why are they afraid?" he complained. "Life has always been like this."

Juan Carlos assured him business would be better in Cali, where people were more willing to take some risks in order to live a little. He didn't add that there was also an influx of new money that came from questionable sources. He updated his father about the progress he had made on getting the permit for the office and the contractors he had interviewed. And this felt like the perfect segue into his novia.

"She wants to meet you." He opened his wallet and pulled out a photo of Margaret, which he had borrowed for just this purpose. In the picture, her brilliant eyes had that challenging glint they sometimes had. Although she was flanked by her parents, she was the one who shone as if the sun had selected only her as its mark. "Margarita," he said proudly, handing his father the creased photo.

His father studied the picture, and Juan Carlos could tell that he was fascinated by her exotic look. Still, he said, "Your mother is very unhappy, Juan Carlos. You should have brought her home to your family before you got married. You know she's always imagined the big wedding we would have for your sister, but so far that hasn't happened." His father shook his head sadly. "You should have had a real wedding in the church here in Bogotá."

"We would have come but we have a life in Cali now. You know that, Papá. That was the plan," said Juan Carlos, ignoring the ache of guilt that nagged at his gut for lying about being married. Then he pictured their apartment and her in it and added, "I'm not a little boy anymore."

"Maybe if she wasn't una americana." His father passed the photo back to Juan Carlos. "Your mother is afraid you'll leave Colombia. She's afraid you'll go to the United States, like all the other young people. There's an exodus, and we can't lose you."

"We won't leave, I promise. She loves Colombia as if it were her home."

"Does she even speak Spanish?"

Juan Carlos's cheeks burned. He wanted to lie, but he had already misled his family enough. He admitted that she was still learning their language. "But you would love her. You will all love her. Just like I do."

CHAPTER 13

A shout came from the small blue car pulling up the hotel's curved drive the next day. Trina and her friends had arranged to pick me up later that afternoon for what they were calling the treasure hunt—la búsqueda del tesoro. I had slept poorly without my pajamas or change of socks, which were still damp inside my shoes after washing them in the sink. I tossed and turned under the gentle breeze of the ceiling fan and was bleary-eyed when I greeted them.

"¡Buenas tardes, Dolores!" called Seb from the open driver's window.

I waved back as Trina emerged from the passenger side wearing a short blue dress and delicate thong sandals. I felt frumpy in my sneakers and sagging, overworn jeans, especially when I saw María Sofía in the back of the car. She wore a one-shoulder black top and perfect lipstick.

"Buenas . . ." I began to greet María Sofía, when Oscar jumped out from the other side of an empty booster in the back seat.

"Good afternoon, Dolores," he said, kissing my cheek.

"I didn't know you—all of you—were coming," I said. He smelled like Brent Swenson, best-looking eleventh-grade tenor at Minneapolis East High School. A mix of musky cologne and hard candies.

"You look very beautiful."

I did not, I knew, look beautiful. I had pulled my limp hair into a headache-inducing bun, and my face was blotched with the unfamiliar heat and humidity.

"Hannah and Joaquim apologize they couldn't come," Trina told me. "They want lots of pictures."

"I didn't expect so many of you."

"Good thing they couldn't come," Seb called. "We would have needed another car."

"How will we all fit?" I asked. But what I wanted to know was why all these friends weren't at work on a Monday in June.

Trina offered an explanation, "There's a holiday today, and then we're all going to the coffee region next week. You'll come with us?"

"Oh, um," I stammered.

"Come!" shouted the others with cheers and laughter. They began suggesting other sites I should visit: the natural history museum, the national park, maybe even take a couple days and see the coast.

"You get in there," directed Oscar, holding the rear door open for me.

"I'll fit in Andrés's seat!" said María Sofía.

"No, we move—" protested Trina, but María Sofía was already climbing in. She was right—her narrow hips really did fit in the preschooler's booster. I suddenly felt like I took up a lot of space and that that was a bad thing.

"We got it!" said Oscar, and he climbed in on the other side of María Sofía.

"¡Vámonos!" said Seb, and he yanked the car into gear.

"But where are we going?" asked María Sofía.

"What's your first stop, Dorrie?" Trina asked.

"Maybe we can visit the museum," I said. "What's it called? Tertulia?"

(*Mags loved museums. We never did really understand her photography.*)

"Museo La Tertulia," supplied Seb. "We'll take you. It's not far."

According to the brochure, the Museo La Tertulia was founded in 1956. The modern building was sited perfectly along a bend in the river, exactly as my hand-drawn map showed it would be. A complex of several buildings connected with stone terraces, the grounds were dotted with sculptures as well as young people wandering along the walks and reading on the shaded benches.

Oscar held the door open for me at the main entrance and led me into the foyer, placing his hand on the small of my back for less than a moment, which sent a shiver through me. I pictured Juan Carlos (who was beginning to look something like Oscar now in my imagination) meeting Margaret Moore here in 1989, her in leg warmers (didn't they wear leg warmers then?), him in a black leather jacket. Or maybe it was Jane who had wandered the galleries while waiting for Maggie to go into labor. Maybe she was here, in this very spot, the moment I was born.

"You were the love of her life," Elizabeth used to tell me, repeating Jane's stories. "And now you're ours."

"It was a stroke—it's tragic but happens sometimes. You were two weeks old, honey. Maybe if she had been in the US, closer to a trauma-one center, she would have lived. Although, even then . . ." Jane's voice would trail off, contemplating what could have been.

The unspoken in this tragic story of my birth mother's passing was the contrasting joy.

They say that a sign of true intelligence is the ability to hold opposing thoughts in your mind at once. Maybe a lifetime of doing that had made me a genius? But was it intelligence when all you saw everywhere you looked were the two sides? How could you ever choose that way? How would one ever win out over the other? I was half and half: half Moore, half Colombian; half an orphan, half an only child; half a practical cartographer, half a dreamer wondering what if.

"Do you like this one?" Oscar had led me to a painting in shades of gray. One side was almost black, with nearly invisible shapes obscured by layers of gray. Squares, triangles. A dresser, a desk. The middle of the painting was nearly white and the other side was a paler gray but still with embedded, almost hidden, objects. A computer keyboard, a microchip, a nuclear symbol. *Left and Right*, the painting was titled—two opposites, just like me.

" 'A study on the left brain and right brain,' " read Oscar. "Do you believe in that? The two sides? Left and right? Which are you? Left-brained or right-brained?"

"Right, I suppose. I like cartography because I like logic and reason and precision."

"But don't maps also have artistry?" I looked up at Oscar's dark eyes. Was he teasing me or did he understand maps this way too? I had seen pictures of Chinese maps from 200 BC that were made of woven silk, their details intricately rendered in soft colors, beautiful enough to hang on a wall, to be admired. I began to describe these maps to Oscar when he brushed a strand of hair that had, unaccountably, escaped my ponytail. "And beauty? Like you?"

I felt the gesture in my toes and my stomach flip-flopped at the light touch of Oscar's hand. I needed this location on the map to show me the way, to guide me, to solve the mystery of direction, my

origins, my place in the world. This—*this!*—co
thought I would find here. Could it?

(I heard Elizabeth's voice: *I think he's good
looking?* Great-Aunt Maureen cleared her throat
you like the tall, dark, and handsome type.)

"Where are Trina and Seb?" I asked.

Without a word, Oscar smiled, took my han
side.

"Selfies!" cried Seb from the bottom of the out
when he saw Oscar and me. Seb grabbed his wif
pulled her close, hamming it up for his phone.

"Come here, you two!" shouted Seb. Embarras
hand out of Oscar's.

We all grinned for the camera. All five of us. Ji
just the boys. Multiple permutations: Seb and Mari
Oscar, Oscar and Dorrie.

"Get closer!" shouted Trina, sputtering with lai

I was game. After all, Oscar was pleasant, extr
ing, and smelled heavenly. I moved close, closer. H
over my shoulder, pulled me close. Closer. The sleev
soft against my skin, but for a moment my mind flas
with Franklin: his T-shirt, his hand, the shank of ha
in the back. Friends, we had said—and meant it. I
held up the phone in one hand, but just before the c
and planted his mouth on mine.

1989
Cali, Colombia

r, when Maggie remembered their visit to the museum, she
ld be sure it was on a Sunday, but they went to La Tertulia
ng the week, when a high school class was visiting, teenag-
vho made lewd catcalls whenever Juan Carlos stopped to kiss
iovia. They weren't much younger than she was and her face
ied at the attention, but he had simply laughed and told the high
olers they must be jealous. Juan Carlos and Maggie were certain
yone was envious because they couldn't believe their luck: they
found each other. Hand in hand, they wandered the museum,
protective arm slung loose around her shoulders.

"There's an exhibit of women photographers," Juan Carlos had
her, and when she saw the gallery filled with pictures that took
it she knew about photography and flipped it sideways and back-
d, she couldn't believe that this was what was possible. When she
began taking pictures with her father's Instamatic, her viewers,
consisted mostly of her family, weren't impressed and barely
ied at the resulting snapshots of overexposed teddy bears lined
on her bed or her sister reading a book in the backyard or a dan-
ion in the cracks of the sidewalk. But as she improved—figured
how to frame a shot, what to focus on—she found that she could
nipulate the viewer and introduce them to her world and the way
saw it. That was all anyone wanted, she thought.

She stood inches away from a photo of a woman's ankle sur-
inded by cracked dry earth. The subject's skin was also dry, flaking,

and the intimacy of the close-up sent a shiver down Maggie's spine. That so much could be contained in such a small detail was proof, she thought, that the world was infinite, that the future could hold nothing but promise. The exhibition's prints—some of them ripped and reassembled, some painted on or inked, and some as small as a centavo or as big as the whole gallery wall—gave her the same sensation she had had when she stepped off the plane at the Cali airport. A sort of feeling of arrival, of homecoming. This, she thought, was what mattered.

When they emerged into the still afternoon, the sun danced between the columns of the museum's portico, and she declared breathlessly, "I'm going to take pictures of every single thing in this city."

She lifted the Nikon to her eye and snapped a photo of him just as he moved toward her. She never found out that the last photo ever taken of Juan Carlos turned out blurry, his face nothing but hazy features as fleeting as a ghost's.

After the museum visit, Juan Carlos took her to the restaurant where los arabes served homemade tahini and fresh-squeezed mandarin juice, where they would often sit in the weak sun on the patio surrounded by Middle Eastern expats, counterculture internationals, and local bohemians. That day, Juan Carlos sensed in the changing shadows how fleeting life could be.

"And when the business is set up, I'll take you to Santa Marta and Buenaventura and Antioquia. Wait until you see how beautiful Colombia is. You'll take pictures of the whole country with that thing."

Just like every other time, they ate stacks of flatbread and ensalada turca and drank juice as orange as the sun and talked and planned.

"I could stay here forever," she said, and he promised to bring her a blanket and pillow. "What about my toothbrush?" she asked.

"And your toothbrush."

"Will I have to brush my teeth with mandarin juice?"

"When they water the flowers in these pots, I'll make them stop with their . . . how do you call it? Regadera."

Maggie didn't know the word. He leaped to his feet and pantomimed watering the geraniums.

"Watering can," she translated.

"Watering can," he repeated, but his mouth caught on the loose *w* and staccato consonants, and she pulled him back down and kissed him.

On the walk back to the apartment, they strolled along the river, where the campesinos set up their makeshift stalls selling rugs and tablecloths, plastic coin purses and rubber overshoes, avocados and granadillas, eking out a living beyond and between harvests and luck— good or bad.

"¡Una regadera!" Maggie exclaimed, pointing at a pink watering can on display, trying out her new vocabulary. *Regadera. Paraguas. Equipaje. Paraíso.* She collected words like little treasures, the same way she collected photos with the Nikon, each picture and each word holding in it a moment but also a lifetime.

But Juan Carlos wasn't really listening. Something shiny displayed among the trinkets and beaded bracelets caught his attention. The salesman eyed Juan Carlos and the pretty rubia. "Oro puro," he boasted. He didn't know for sure if the ring really was pure gold, but he did know that it was a very convincing copy of one of the sixteenth-century Spanish rings in the capital's gold museum. It was well-crafted enough that his usual customers rarely touched it, sure that it was too expensive for them. But this tall man dressed in bogotano clothes was boldly holding the ring out to his novia. The salesman named a price high enough that he could comfortably barter.

"Real gold," translated Juan Carlos, and something about this filigreed circle and the sound of Margaret's Spanish chatter and the glow of the streetlight made him tender and romantic and he asked her to marry him. She giggled and held out her hand, on which the ring they had bought at the kiosk in Rome was tarnishing.

"I thought we were already married," she teased.

"For real this time."

Her eyes glistened and Juan Carlos gripped her outstretched hand, solid and sure. Permanent. His strength made her feel like nothing could ever touch her, like she would be protected forever, and no matter what kind of perils they faced, they would do it all together. That life would be an adventure for two. He knelt on the sidewalk, the way he had seen characters do in movies, and asked her to be his wife for as long as they both lived.

"Even longer than that," Maggie promised.

And as they walked home through the darkening neighborhood, Maggie admired the tiny swirls that reminded her of plumeria blossoms. Her mom had always worn a simple gold band and her grandmother had a platinum ring with two chips of diamonds, but this was prettier than any family heirloom. She thought about calling her sister on Doña Rojas's phone when they got home and telling her the news, but when they arrived, Juan Carlos swept her past the landlady's door and into their apartment. He pulled her to the mattress on the floor and she forgot about calling anyone.

Later, they lazed in bed and ate cold chicken and bread for dinner, using the sheets as napkins, until they were too satiated to move. Time and life itself stretched out before them as they talked about the wedding dress she would wear, the family she would meet, the babies they might have someday. Everything seemed a possibility, and Maggie never did make the collect call to Minneapolis. Young couples in love are often too ambitious in their plans, thinking that they have all the time in the world.

CHAPTER 14

Maps can tell you where you are, perhaps where you've been. They can tell you what direction to head in next, but they cannot tell the future. Maps are always only a representation of a moment in time, a location in space. No map—not even the hand-drawn map of Cali—could tell me what would happen next.

I scrolled through the photos from the museum, the one of me and Oscar, his mouth on mine. In the photo, my eyes are popped with shock but also something else, maybe that innate physiology of the first time another person's lips meet yours, the joy of novelty or maybe the pleasure of familiarity. Looking at the picture, at the startled expression on my face, I remembered a cinder-block basement lit only by a few bare bulbs. There's a keg and a guy sitting on the keg as if it were a throne. I remembered a plastic cup and the girl in whose dorm room I had been drinking shots of cheap whiskey. I had been ignoring the voices as I followed her to the party, dismissing their judgmental tones and inane idioms. *Better safe than sorry. Beer before liquor, never been sicker.* The girl—what was her name?—saw someone she knew and abandoned me the moment we came down the stairs at the house party. Franklin, I learned later, saw me before I saw him. He was in a corner, pretending to have a good time. He watched me, he told me later, accept a cup and wince at the first sip. "You had hair in your mouth," he said, "and all I wanted in the whole world at that moment was to reach out and touch your cheek. Also," Franklin would add every time he told this story, "I was very drunk." Dancing began, or what passed as dancing, and I found myself pressed against a tall and angular Asian guy who laughed every time I tried to say something. He had a dimple and his hair flopped over one eye. I remembered standing on my tiptoes to kiss him.

Now, back on the hotel's Wi-Fi, I sent Becks a couple photos. One of me and Trina. One of Trina and Seb walking hand in hand a few yards in front of me, the río Cali visible in the distance and the terrace of the museum crisp against the green grass.

Becks: How's my should-be sister?

I said I wasn't sure what I was doing here. I told her about the shuttered storefront.

Becks: You'll figure it out.

I sent the photo of Oscar.

Becks: He's cute!!! ☺

My phone pinged again and a picture of Franklin appeared. With both his grandfather and the cats. Only half his face was visible, the two orange tabbies squeezed together on Grandpa Bao's narrow lap. The old man was grinning broadly and I felt a moment of nostalgia for the lined faces of my deceased relatives. Hearing them wasn't the same as seeing them. I touched the screen, enlarged first the cats' faces, then zoomed in on Franklin. He still had that dimple, barely visible but there if you knew where to look.

Dorrie: Looks like you're enjoying the cats?

Franklin: So. Much. Cat hair.

Dorrie: Sorry!

I could picture the long, white hairs that would coat everything in Franklin's house, from his jeans to his bedspread. If he had a bedspread. I didn't know what his bed looked like. Or care.

Dorrie: Is Bojangles using the litter box?

(*Is she discussing defecation with that nice boy?* someone in my chorus asked. Several voices murmured in horror; others giggled.)

Franklin responded with a poop emoji and a thumbs-up.

I never was good at casual conversation, whether in person or via texts. Like my mothers, I had a tendency to get to the point too soon, to ignore the inanities of polite chatting. I scrolled through my photos. I needed a second message that was more normal, less like something they would have said. I sent him a photo from the museum.

Dorrie: Here's some pics!

And then another ping.

Becks: I needed that. So bored.

She was on bed rest. I felt like a terrible friend for having forgotten this life-altering event, to have been obsessing about boys and maps like I was still a seventh grader. So I called her. "Are you okay, Becks?"

She laughed her beautiful, familiar laugh. "I'm bored, Dorrie. So bored. It's only been three days of being stuck in bed and I'm already going crazy. I needed those photos. I can't wait until you get here and tell me all about your trip. Or you could start now. Tell me all about your trip."

"Yes, but are you sure you're okay? Is the baby okay?" When she first told me that this pregnancy was going to stick, we had decided that her baby was going to be my niece or nephew. She had told me that it would be a big job and she hoped I was prepared to send lots of gifts and take the kid for a month in the summers. I had told her that no one should trust me with a child for that long and we had laughed both because it wasn't really true and also because we were having the conversation in the first place.

"Is Charlie spoiling you?"

"Are you spoiling me?" she asked, and I heard a mumble in the background. "He wants to talk to you, but don't believe anything he tells you." Becks laughed again and then Charlie said hello.

"How's the patient? Or I guess I should say how's the mother-to-be?"

"She's hanging in there," he said. "Thanks for calling." And then his voice got very low and whispery and he told me that the OB was concerned. He said a lot of things about childbirth and pregnancy that I didn't understand, but I could tell by his tone that it was serious. "Even in the twenty-first century," he said, "things can go wrong. Humans can edit genes and see galaxies thirteen billion light years away, but we still haven't figured out how to keep mothers and babies from dying."

Dying. The word swirled in my head, echoed by the voices of my chorus.

"Dorrie," Becks interrupted. "Don't listen to him. I'm fine. I'll be fine. I just know it."

Ping. Another message from Franklin.

"Oh, Becky," I said. "I'm going to listen to both of you. I know you're going to be fine, but you should have told me. It sounds serious. Keep me posted and I can change my flight at any time."

"No," she said firmly, "you have a duty to stay there, fulfill Jane's wish, keep having fun." And then she insisted she needed stories, she wanted to know more about Oscar. So I told her the things that would cheer her up and keep her entertained. I didn't burden her with thoughts of the apartment that wasn't there, the fact that I didn't know how I would keep my promise to Jane, that I wasn't sure where the magic was. Instead, we chatted and gossiped like we were kids again and I could almost forget that she was a bedridden mother-to-be and I was an orphan in a foreign country.

I lay on my back on the hotel bed for a long time after we hung up, just staring up at the ceiling fan making its lazy circles. Even though I was far away from home, far away from Becks Eastman, I felt a sort of calm here. I knew my new friends weren't far, that Trina was helping me, that I was beginning to get my bearings in this city, or at least in this little pocket of it.

I was exhausted and sweaty from the day's activities. I turned on the water, letting it heat and fill the bathroom with steam, and then remembered the text that had pinged earlier.

Franklin: Who's that? Looks like fun.

Period. Looks like fun, *period*.

"You're crabby, Franklin," I said, my voice echoing in the bathroom. I let the message go unanswered. Instead, the warm water coursed over my body. I was glad I had tucked into my toiletry bag a couple pairs of underwear, which I had washed in the sink, but I would give anything for the tank tops and sundresses I had packed so carefully. Those neat piles of T-shirts and shorts and underwear seemed like they were from another lifetime. Even the Victorian itself seemed almost dreamlike, the way, previously, Colombia had always felt to me. It was funny how hard it was to imagine yourself in any other place than where you were.

The early cartographers were often the court astronomers and mathematicians; they were the smart people in the palaces, because they had to be intelligent enough to look at things in new ways, to chart places they'd never seen.

I scrubbed my hair, my face, washing away the day at the museum, thinking about the places on my body that Oscar had touched, picturing his face and arms. He was good looking—probably the best-looking man who had ever shown interest in me. I tended to attract—and be attracted to—more ordinary men. I had always been cute, maybe pretty, but not beautiful the way Becks was. With her striking features, full lips, gobs of curly hair, Rebecca Eastman was Marilyn Monroe to my Katharine Hepburn. She was always—even after she had a ring on her finger—getting attention from men like Oscar. Her husband was one of those traditionally sexy, masculine men who could have starred in action films, while Franklin, for example, even now, was more boyish and charming than dark and handsome. I switched off the water and my skin grew cool, formed goose bumps.

Wrapping myself in a towel, I scrolled through the messages between Franklin and me. What had irritated him? Then I saw the three pictures I had sent him: me and Trina and Seb, me and María Sofía, me and Oscar. With Oscar's mouth on mine. I hadn't meant to send that to him. Not that it mattered. Franklin had—what was her name?—Sasha.

Dorrie: Just goofing around with some people I met!

No, he wouldn't care about a kiss with a man in Colombia. Franklin and I were friends—despite what had happened, nothing for anyone to be jealous about. That night had been a slipup, a reflection of the for-old-times'-sake mentality.

Franklin: Sure, of course.

He wasn't jealous, was he? Should he be? Did I want him to be? Franklin, Oscar. First kisses, old kisses. There wasn't a map for navigating people. I was feeling muddled.

CHAPTER 15

The next day my new friends were back at work, so I spent the morning in the hotel's cool courtyard garden not looking at my phone, and then headed out in search of lunch. Because I would wait for them before going to the next spot on the map—La Colina, I was thinking—I decided to take a walk, heading up the hill, where I could see businesses, and toward the roar of motorcycle traffic.

From the staccato of horns to the humidity, there was already something familiar about the air in Cali even after only a few days. Was this what Jane had meant when she told me to come here? That I would find something familiar, something nostalgic? A scent that I was beginning to associate with big green leaves and small yellow flowers hung in the air. I even recognized the sensation of my foot-steps on the concrete. Had Maggie, I wondered, planned on staying in Cali after she gave birth? Or was she still infected with the wander-lust that had taken her around the world? I knew she had stayed here during her entire pregnancy, longer than she had stayed in other des-tinations. Was it Juan Carlos that made her stay? And would his ab-sence have made her leave? Or had the pull been the city, the country itself? Would she have raised me here, the green mountains in the distance, the rushing brown water of the river, the cries of parrots in the trees?

Like me, Maggie had grown up in Minneapolis. The Moore family—a mom, dad, and two girls—lived just a mile from the Victorian on a shady street lined with postwar houses. The two sisters had shared the second of two bedrooms and the women of the house, Grandma June told me, shared the main bath while Grandpa Vic was forced to make do with a half-finished bathroom in the basement: just a toilet, unenclosed shower, and utility sink. Was being crowded what made her flee at eighteen? Did she need space as badly as I needed direction?

(*Where is she going?* fretted Gigi as I walked. *Does she know where she is?* asked Elizabeth. *For a mapmaker, she's good at getting lost.*)

I paused, looking around.

Without realizing it, I had arrived once again at calle 5 Norte. My heart squeezed at the thought of that empty hair salon, its CLOSED sign. But my feet kept me headed in that direction until there it was again: #180B. The dark storefront. The disappointment ached in my bones. But I still had plenty of time left—more than ten days until my flight to San Francisco—to find whatever it was that I was looking for.

Above me the shuttered windows made me wonder if the walls that had once defined Maggie and Juan Carlos's apartment were still there, if ghosts wandered the halls of offices or storage units or whatever this building was now. I sniffled away the tears that were threatening to flow and as I did, pungent smoke drifted from a food vendor's cart, and I headed toward the enticing aroma.

The voices cautioned against street food, but I listened instead to my grumbling stomach, watching the man drop something in a vat of hot oil. Bubbles collected and the outside slowly turned a golden brown. Two other customers were ahead of me and each walked away with a greasy paper envelope holding what looked like the most perfect golden-brown empanadas I had ever seen.

"Meat pockets!" Elizabeth had called them. During one of her Colombian cooking sprees, she had experimented with empanadas as part of her mission to expose me to my heritage—without leaving the comfort and safety of the Victorian.

"Yum," I said with my mouth full.

"Much better than your arroz con leche," Jane had remarked. She had never liked anything sticky or cloying.

Buoyed by our praise, Elizabeth had expanded to other types of empanadas. Spanish, Argentinian, Ecuadorian. Pork, ground beef, tuna. Deep fried, baked, skillet sautéed. She also branched out to other meat pockets—pierogies and pasties and then ravioli and dumplings.

"The trick," she would say, "is to get the filling as flavorful and moist as possible." I would watch her stir and taste, break apart the meat with the back of a wooden spoon, adjust the seasonings. The Victorian's kitchen would fill with the aroma of onions and garlic, turmeric or paprika, peppers and ginger. Sometimes the spices made my nose wrinkle and she would laugh and tell me to try it.

"You can't always tell what something will taste like just from the way it smells or how it looks." She would hold out her battered wooden spoon and I would cautiously take a bite. I was always surprised that something that smelled so strange could have a delicate and complex flavor, that the lumps of raisins or hardboiled eggs or peas—which I hated as a child—would transform themselves into part of a bouquet of flavors, all of it a lesson in not judging, not jumping to conclusions. A lesson I perhaps took too seriously, never quite being sure of my own opinions or trusting what I saw. The unknown only made sense when there was a map.

When it was time to fill the dough—rolled out, patted down, store-bought—she would say, "Take your time, Dorrie."

She would give me a piece of dough to experiment with, letting me create lopsided circles and carefully spoon in filling, me in Jane's apron tied twice around my waist, her with flour in her hair.

"Don't rush."

Her expert fingers pinched here or smoothed there. Later, she would pinch and smooth me, too, as if she could protect me and perfect me, her only daughter.

"Una empanada, por favor," I ordered, wondering if this old man had sold empanadas when Margaret Moore was here, if he had served her a steaming-hot meat pocket. I was suddenly starving and an empanada sounded like the only thing that would quell my hunger.

Under King Louis XVI, France funded a cartographer's survey of the country, with the goal of making the most accurate map ever. A surveyor named Jean Picard led the project, painstakingly measuring the contours of his homeland. France, now that it was being accurately surveyed, began to shrink, and Picard was accused of losing Louis XVI more land than he had in any battle. If the king had had his own persnickety Greek chorus, they might have quipped, *Be careful what you wish for.*

Licking crumbs from my fingers, I walked without direction. Soon I could see the river again. All roads seemed to wind up here. I unfolded the map again. The Cali River, exactly like the squiggly blue line showed it to be. I turned the map and oriented myself. I was near La Ermita. If I couldn't see the apartment, maybe the church would show me something, anything. The empanada, instead of quenching my hunger, had made me homesick. Not for home but for Elizabeth and Jane, for all the ladies of my chorus. The grief, which had been held in check, superimposed with new sights and sounds and smells, reared its head. My cheeks were damp. I could taste salt and it wasn't from the food. I dashed across the road as soon as there was a break, however short, in the traffic.

Following the wide sidewalk lined with trees and flowers that meandered along the river, I passed old men reading newspapers on benches or young au pairs minding neat children. If my mother had never gone, would I have been one of those children in blue-and-yellow school uniforms? Would her voice have called out my name—"¡Dolores!"—from across the crowded yard? If my father had lived, would he have hoisted me on his shoulders for the walk home? Perhaps the two of them would have held my hands as we waited to cross the busy road, to return to the apartment.

"She was in love, I promise you that," Jane had told me when I was fourteen or fifteen. "You were born out of love."

Back then, as a dreamy teenager, I desperately wanted my existence to have come about due to love—a love I conflated with Julia Roberts movies and Norah Jones's lyrics. But now I wasn't so sure that mattered. I had loved Franklin Liu purely, deeply, but that hadn't meant it worked out. I had tried a different kind of relationship with Jason, one built on stability and shared respect, but he used to complain that I wasn't a romantic. He would bring me roses and I would complain about the thorns as I stripped them off with a knife. He would light candles and fill the bathtub, while I crawled into flannel pajamas. "Women love this stuff," he had said as my chorus discussed whether he was right for me or not. "Jason, you don't have to," I would say, brushing aside the bracelets and pink greeting cards.

Wasn't it enough that a sperm and an egg somehow found their way together to create me? Did process really matter? Pragmatism had overtaken any tender feelings about my origins. And, anyway, all that was in the past and I would never know what happened between Maggie and Juan Carlos or what could have been. I lifted my chin to keep the tears from dripping and as I did, I caught a glimpse of steeples above the trees.

La Ermita stuck out with odd architecture. Instead of red brick like the other buildings around it, the temple was white and gray with ominous spires like spikes across a security fence. From my quick internet search, I knew La Ermita was a Gothic-style temple built in the 1930s and had some architectural and historical significance, but its true importance was its inclusion on this map. The doors were open and I stepped inside, momentarily blinded by the darkness.

(*I wish I had been able to visit this church when I was there*, said Jane. Her tone was offhand but caught my attention, because I assumed Jane had visited all the locations on the map. If only she had told me more; if only I had asked more.)

Inside, the church was cool and quiet, all noise from motorbikes and backfiring engines fading away. An old woman shuffled ahead of me, dipping her hand in a basin and then making the sign of the cross. I circumvented the holy water and headed toward a pew in the center. Jane and Elizabeth had been spiritual, not religious, and I knew almost nothing about Christianity, much less Catholicism.

"It's hard to believe in a religion that doesn't believe in you," Elizabeth used to say. For a long time she couldn't shake the habits of her Iowan family and would drag me to a Lutheran church on Christmas and Easter, but by the time I was in elementary school, she had abandoned that pretense as well. Instead, my mothers burned incense and listened to Tibetan monks humming. They kept an ofrenda of their deceased relatives, not knowing that each of them chattered to me. They cleansed with sage and palo santo. They lit candles on Hanukkah and Friday nights, and on Kwanzaa, covering all their bases. But what protection had their beliefs—or maybe just practices—afforded them?

Inside the chapel, the ceiling soared. A few people sat scattered in the wooden pews, and I slipped into one, unfolding the map. Who had visited La Ermita? Why had it been drawn so carefully? Had Juan Carlos sketched the places he thought his American girlfriend would like? Had Maggie made this map for Jane when she visited so that she could sightsee on her own?

I leaned back, squinting at the stained-glass panels, their colors swirling. The white plaster of the interior blended with the gold accents like a Bob Ross painting viewed too close. The colors transmuted themselves, red, yellow, blue. I blinked. Why couldn't I see clearly? Then I realized: I was crying. Again. Not sobbing, not making any noise. I didn't usually cry this much. Was it the exhaustion? I hadn't slept well—the bathroom faucet leaked. Was it the culture shock? My morning coffee at the hotel had had a distinctly foreign acridness. The disappointment? Tears filled my eyes, ran in rivulets down my cheeks, and then refilled. This place with its old woman and damp scent and stained glass—my mother Margaret Moore had been here. Perhaps she had sat in this precise location, her ass going numb on the hard pew. I couldn't hear the chorus, but I could feel their presence, silent and contemplative.

At the front of the chapel, a woman in a pale blue habit appeared, shuffling around, removing blackened candles, wiping down the altar table, folding a cloth. She made no indication that she was being watched; or maybe I was the only heathen here people watching instead of praying. The woman disappeared behind a door only to reappear a few moments later to dust. I thought of my mothers' haphazard religious observances—the menorah and the crèche. How had I ended up in a church and not the apartment, the place I had promised to visit? Was there something here to show me who I was or where I came from? I listened—for the chorus or for something else, I wasn't sure. All was silent.

The nun finished her work and again disappeared behind the door. I stood, carefully studying the stained glass and the decorative flourishes on my way out. As I turned to leave, a placard at the back of the chapel caught my eye. I paused to read, slowly deciphering the Spanish. The church had originally been erected in the seventeenth century but had been destroyed in an earthquake. Lack of funding during the Great Depression halted its resurrection, and it was rebuilt during the 1930s and 1940s, little by little, and that time in the popular Gothic style inspired by German architecture.

Someone in the church sneezed. I scanned the last paragraph.

My toes prickled. I read it, reread it. My breath came short and shallow. I stumbled out of the church back into the blinding sunlight. I waved at a yellow taxi, hoping the system worked just like it did in the United States. My heart pounded as if I had just run a 10K, not that I had ever run one kilometer, much less ten. A taxi passed without slowing down. Another. At last, one pulled over, stopped, I collapsed inside.

La Ermita, the placard said, was dedicated to Our Lady of Sorrows: Nuestra Señora de los Dolores.

1989
Cali, Colombia

Each time Juan Carlos went away, Margaret Moore explored her new city, and each sight and sound, each moment and landmark was framed through her camera, the Nikon FG-20 with built-in light meter and self-timer that she bought from the neighbor of a friend of her parents whose husband had died suddenly. The widow had charged her less than it was worth but more than Maggie could have afforded without the windfall from Aunt Maureen, the rest of which went toward buying her independence from the expectations of her parents. The plane tickets, the money for hostels and trains, the army-green duffel she carried around the globe. She would never have used her share of their aunt's gift for a down payment on an old house a mile from their childhood home like her sister had. Jane's idea of fun was scraping paint off the trim and sanding the floors of her dilapidated investment and faithfully watching episodes of *This Old House* on her black-and-white television. Here, Maggie didn't even have a TV. But she had something better: freedom. And Juan Carlos. And the whole city of Cali at her feet.

And now they had a baby on the way.

She had known, of course, that it could happen. Janie had been the one to give her a talk that touched on the mechanics of sex and the risks of pregnancy. "And AIDS, Mags," she had said. "You have to be careful." But Maggie and Juan Carlos, while intending to be careful, rarely were, and now there would be a baby, proof of their love. They couldn't wait.

She slung the Nikon around her neck and dropped an extra canister of film into her mochila and skipped down the stairs and onto the street below. The baby was, so far, their secret. Maggie was as slim as ever in her denim miniskirt, the only change he could tell was a rosiness to her cheeks that wasn't there before. And her newly found taste for chontaduros.

The camera bounced against her as she walked down the hill toward the river. A passerby watching might have assumed she was a tourist with her blond hair and ready lens, but she was an artist, she told herself. A documentarian. A seeker of truth.

Crossing the river, she stopped to capture the way the light filtered through the bamboo and bounced off the churning water. At the base of a mammoth ceiba, she shot straight up into its branches, capturing the jigsaw of its leaves. At the market, she focused on the piles of guavas and plantains, catching the vendor midsale in the background. Each day that Juan Carlos was either working or in Bogotá, she used her camera as a witness.

At last, she had several rolls of film and she went in search of the laboratorio fotográfico that Juan Carlos had said was in the next barrio. She and the salesman laughed through their awkward language barrier and eventually the film was developed and she clutched the three envelopes as she hurried home. She couldn't wait to show Juan Carlos. She would display the best ones like a gallery, show him how she loved this place and their life.

And when he returned from his latest trip, he was greeted by a map of Cali on the walls of the apartment. Where he had taped a single postcard of Rome was now a panorama of Maggie's world as seen through her eyes. Each photo showed the way she saw light and dark, what she thought was foreign or interesting about his country, where she went when he was away. She followed him as he progressed around the room with her fingers laced through his, slightly behind, averting her eyes as he peered at the work she had created.

"This makes me feel like I was with you," he said. The still photos, affixed somewhat crookedly to the plaster walls, gave the sense of a moving picture, each one seeming to come alive the moment you looked away. His eyes were filling with tears because he had missed her and would again when he had to leave once more.

"You *were* with me."

"Eres una artista, Margarita," he said, and she blushed. "I never knew this place was so beautiful. You show us the way the world could be."

"No," she protested. "I'm simply showing the world as it is."

"¿No extrañas tu familia?" Juan Carlos asked whenever Maggie mentioned her sister or something her father used to say, and she assured him that she didn't miss home. She certainly didn't miss the stifling college courses she had started and abandoned, the barren flatness of the prairies, or the winter with its icy sidewalks and dirty snowbanks.

But at the beginning of her fifth month, when her clothes didn't fit and she began to wear his shirts, her cravings for salty chontaduros and crispy plantains suddenly switched to a longing, inexplicably, for banana bread, the sweet, chewy treat—studded with walnuts—of her childhood. Her mother used to save overripe bananas in the freezer like any good Midwestern housewife, and when there were two or three, she would take out her Tupperware mixing bowls and Pyrex bread pans. Maggie, seven or eight, and then ten or twelve, would stand on the folding step stool to stir and measure.

"You have to be exact, Mags," her mom would instruct whenever Maggie was sloppy with the flour. "Baking shouldn't be an adventure. If it is, you're doing it wrong."

"That's why I like it," Jane might say if she were helping in the kitchen. "Nice and predictable."

As the little sister, it was Maggie's duty to scorn her sister's and mother's lesson. "Predictable is boring."

Her mother, always ready with advice and opinions, would tsk. "Someday you'll appreciate predictability."

Maggie smiled both at the memory and the fact she was no longer beholden to those voices as she smashed ripe brown bananas and mixed the batter. She didn't have measuring spoons, so she used a mug to approximate the cup and a half of flour, and a soup spoon to fold the batter. When the pan was ready, she wiped her hands on Juan Carlos's old blue button-down she had begun to wear over her bump and went down to Doña Rojas's apartment to borrow her oven.

From the moment Maggie's belly began to swell, the landlady had taken her in, offering advice and food and telling her to please ask for whatever she needed. Doña Rojas and her daughter were the only people whom Juan Carlos and Margaret had told their secret to. Although any vecino walking down the street could see that this young woman would soon have a baby, Juan Carlos hadn't yet mentioned the coming arrival to his parents and she still hadn't called home. She sent a few postcards, a few photos, letting the images stand in for what she couldn't seem to say.

"¿El horno?" Maggie asked when the old woman answered the door. She was almost positive that was the word for oven.

"Lo que necesites."

In the kitchen, a small room at the back of the main-floor apartment, Doña Rojas thrust a box of matches into Maggie's hands. Back home, her mother baked in a clean white Kenmore that had four black, spiral heating elements and a glass door that showcased whatever was rising and browning inside, all of it illuminated with the yellow glow of a single lightbulb. But here the burners had to be lit with matches and the gas for the oven had to be turned on. Together, the two women—one elderly and one pregnant—awkwardly knelt with equal effort and peered at the innards of the oven. It took three tries to light the pilot and each time Maggie struck the match, she marveled at the old woman's face illuminated by the flame.

"Eres muy linda." Maggie used a phrase in Spanish that she had learned from Juan Carlos. Doña Rojas threw a dish towel over her face and insisted she wasn't beautiful.

Maggie held up the camera, which was forever slung around her neck. "¿Por favor?" She snapped a picture, advanced the film. She clicked again. Advanced the film again. And again. "Muy bella," she said.

At first Doña Rojas, two spots of pink glowing on her weathered cheeks, held up her hand to block the lens, but as Maggie refocused and clicked the shutter over and over, the old woman seemed to fall under a spell, a trance of smiling and blinking. Several strands of silvered black hair escaped her headscarf, and she pushed them out of her face with the absent gesture of a young woman. Juan Carlos had once said that their landlady must be a bruja, but her nose was straight and her chin elegant. She was old, yes, and stooped, yes, but Doña Rojas was lovely in a way that defied what Margaret Moore had been taught about beauty in *Seventeen* magazine and the halls of her Midwestern high school. She had grown up thinking that there were right ways to do things: that beauty was the smooth skin and full lips of Cindy Crawford, that you weren't successful until you had a career like Clair Huxtable, that a family meant two parents and several children like the Keatons. There had been nothing to suggest that this slight, fair-haired youngest daughter would end up in this kitchen in South America and find beauty in an old woman.

Maggie looked through the viewfinder and marveled at the deep creases of the woman's face. Her mother, her high school friends, even her open-minded sister Jane wouldn't have given Doña Rojas a second glance, and if they had, they might have looked away. Her friends and family didn't always speak out loud, but they always had an opinion. Grandma Moore on her dad's side might have suggested Doña Rojas dye her hair or moisturize her skin. Aunt Maureen would have told her to buy a pantsuit—something cinched at the waist, she might have said. But Doña Rojas moved with grace in her shapeless dress and her wrinkles were wondrous lines that mapped a life lived.

When Cristina arrived home from school, Maggie snapped a photo of the teen, pigeon-toed in a plaid school skirt. As the bread baked and Maggie photographed, the Rojas women peeled potatoes for dinner, haphazardly adding onions and masa without a measuring cup in sight, and chatted about their day. Maggie listened but couldn't decipher their casual, rapid Spanish any more than she could the conversations Jane used to have with their mom about mortgages and taxes, or with their grandmother about pies and garden shears. The Moore women had always been comparing recently read books or discussing optimal routes to avoid traffic, and Maggie had bristled at the inane talk. Listening to Doña Rojas and her daughter in the cramped kitchen, though, made Maggie feel like maybe the conversations—even when they were about nothing— might be important after all.

"Huele rico," Doña Rojas said as the kitchen filled with the damp, sweet smell of Maggie's childhood. She offered the Rojas women a taste, but they declined and instead packed up one of their leaf-wrapped tamales, which she and Juan Carlos would share for dinner. Before she started up the stairs, Cristina laid a hand on her arm, delicate as a butterfly.

"Can I try a photo?" she whispered.

Maggie set down the tamal and the steaming pan of bread and showed the girl how to focus the lens and adjust the f-stop, then she posed on the bottom step and smiled as Cristina's small face disappeared behind the Nikon. The only photo ever of a pregnant Margaret Moore.

"It's delicious," Juan Carlos told her later, even after they discovered Maggie had bought salt instead of sugar. "Muy rico."

CHAPTER 16

I returned to my room, not even bothering to ask at the front desk about my luggage. Nuestra Señora de los Dolores. I had been named after her. I knew it. I hadn't seen the apartment, but I had seen that sign. It was a sign.

I tried to imagine Margaret Moore entering the church, gazing around as I had, a tourist in this foreign city. In my mind, she has the same soft feathered hair as in the photo I had packed in my suitcase and she looks delicate and vulnerable. She passes the placard, sees the dedication. Was she pregnant then? Did she know when she visited La Ermita that she would need to name a child, a daughter?

I peeled off my dirty clothes, hoping to air out the sweat and tears before I needed to put them on again. I was bone-tired, wrung out like a dish towel. First the disappointment of the apartment, then the church. Stretching out on the bed in my underwear, I let the ceiling fan cool my skin until it became goose-pimply.

(*She should at least buy a fresh pair of socks*, said Gigi, launching a debate into whether I should wait for my luggage or consider it a lost cause.)

While the chorus chattered in the background, I sent Becks a photo of La Ermita, explaining it was dedicated to Nuestra Señora de los Dolores. She didn't reply. Then I sent Franklin the same picture and message.

Franklin: Like you?

Hopefully this meant I was forgiven for the other photo. Not that it mattered to me if he was grumpy about a random kiss.

Franklin: How cool!

Yes, I thought. It appeared I was forgiven.

Franklin: What does it mean?

Dorrie: Pain.

"Oh, the pain," I used to say dramatically when I was a child, every time someone called me Dolores. Jane and Elizabeth would laugh and roll their eyes, half-embarrassed and half-proud.

Franklin: That fits.

I smiled and my finger hovered. I wanted to say more, to ask more, to keep him replying, responding, making his existence verify my own.

Dorrie: Thanks

It was all I could think to say.

It meant pain. Pain and agony. Sorrow. Nuestra Señora de los Dolores.

The ceiling fan whirred.

Jane had said, *We should have shown you where you came from.* Was this it? Was this the treasure, I wondered, or was there more?

"There she is!" greeted Trina.

When I went downstairs to meet her and the girls, I left the hand-drawn map on the dresser, a smear of grease added to the original coffee stain. I had been here almost a week and, still, the only locations on the map that I had visited were the church and museum.

Over the past couple of days, I had eaten plenty of ice cream and more empanadas, and I had perfected the art of asking after my luggage. But now, instead of searching for the next site, I was off on a girls' day organized, of course, by Trina.

María Sofía kissed my cheek. She was wearing a strapless pink jumpsuit and carried a straw tote. Her pink sunglasses and lipstick matched the ensemble. Hannah said a gruff hello. She had agreed to come along swimsuit shopping only because she wanted to swim.

It had started with María Sofía's hint when we had coffee yesterday afternoon: "I've heard that the Hotel América has a beautiful pool."

I responded with questionable grammar but enthusiasm that they should come use it. "It's not Olympic-size," I added, glancing at Hannah, who smiled wryly.

"Thank god," she said.

"But you're welcome. I won't swim—no suit," I said. "No equipaje. No traje de baño."

"Then we'll go shopping first to buy you a swimsuit," María Sofía had suggested, and Trina said she knew of a cute boutique near my hotel.

"I hate shopping," Hannah complained now as we walked toward the shop.

María Sofía smiled and said, "It's not so bad, Hannah." I liked the way she pronounced Hannah's name with a quick, hard *h*, making sure she got the American name right.

"There it is," said Trina, and led the way across the street to a little storefront tucked between a motorcycle repair shop and a café. It was called La Moda Natural, the shop's name in big pink letters that matched María Sofía's jumpsuit. I was already regretting this outing.

The mannequins in the front window wore sparkly gold and silver Brazilian-cut one-pieces and five-inch stilettos.

"A la orden," said a salesgirl as we entered. There were racks of swimsuits in every color, most of which would not be found in nature, all of them nothing more than bits of cloth and spangles. María Sofía beelined for a display of minuscule bikinis while Trina and Hannah headed to the hats displayed in the back. "Buenos días," the girl said to me.

"Buenos días," I said, trying hard to imitate María Sofía's accent. Trina didn't seem to mind that she spoke Spanish like a gringa, but I wanted so badly to blend in. I wanted to be seen in that way that I had never experienced growing up in Minnesota. I needed this total stranger to believe that I was a caleña like the beautiful María Sofía examining a sheer cover-up, and that I, with my dark hair and eyes—unlike like the blond Trina and Hannah—was not American, not a transplanted, half-Colombian adoptee from the American Midwest with flat vowels and swallowed consonants. I wanted to belong.

The salesgirl smiled and then asked in English, "How can I help you? A bikini?" I had not fooled her. She could see me for what I was, despite my black hair and those brown eyes that the grandparents had found so exotic. I was exotic everywhere I went, never quite fitting in, always just a little on the outside.

Maybe that was what had drawn me to mapping, everything so clear, the cartographer in charge, almost like playing God. In my undergrad program, I had taken a summer course during which our class got to design a map for a new park and nature preserve. There had been a partnership between the university and the county and my professor knew someone and suddenly these undergrads were plotting the land that had been gifted by a wealthy benefactor. At the end of the summer, we were all proud of our work but also ready to move on to the next class, the next semester, finish college. It wasn't until the next summer that I went to the reserve and was handed a glossy map that I realized the impact we had made, that our work and our choices were now fact and truth for the public. We had played God for that community.

Now, though, I was as far from being a deity as I could be, at the mercy of fashion.

"A one-piece?" I asked. One adventure at a time.

María Sofía told the girl that I needed a suit to show off my chest, that she should find something for my rear end, and that I was cute but stocky. The salesgirl nodded and smiled. She inspected me, her eyes surveying my body from head to toe. I felt like that land waiting to be mapped. She gathered several options and shoved me in a curtained fitting room. There was no mirror, so with each suit I was forced to display myself in the center of the shop and receive her pronouncements.

"Too big in the bosom," María Sofía declared when I tried on the only one-piece the salesgirl had selected.

(*Dorrie's always been small-chested*, said Jane, who had been a double D.)

"Too tight in the back," the salesgirl said when I showed her the two-piece that had more coverage than the others.

(*The two-piece is better, but not flattering on Dorrie's figure*, commented Grandma June, who had kept her slim waist her whole life.)

The salesgirl tugged at the floppy fabric barely covering my ass. "Too loose," she pronounced when I showed the next option.

Hannah groaned from the other fitting room. "Give me a basic tank Speedo any day. I hate this!"

"Me too," I called back in solidarity.

"Check out this gingham!" cried Trina. I peeked from behind my curtain to see her in a blue-checkered high-waisted suit.

(*She looks like Mary Ann from* Gilligan's Island, said Great-Aunt Maureen.)

She was sexier than that. "You're giving *Emily in Paris* vibes," I said.

"I love it!" Trina flounced in front of the mirror. I admired her certainty and the way she had figured out how to be both herself and a caleña, the way I imagined Margaret Moore might have. I was still trying so hard to decide who I was.

María Sofía handed me several more to try on. She had already found three that she loved. "Muy chévere este sitio, Trina," she said approvingly. She loved this shop.

"Well?" I came out of the fitting room for inspection.

"Pretty good," the salesgirl said, and tugged on the ties of the string bikini. It was red and gold with swirls of black, a pattern that complemented my skin tone and did a bit of camouflaging. I wouldn't be caught dead in this at home, but it did fit "pretty good," as she said. My chorus weren't complaining, which was probably a sign of their approval. Although the bottom was skimpy, it was still oddly flattering, and after she exchanged a smaller size for the top, my chest was magically supported. I even had a nice bit of cleavage.

"Yes, good fit," agreed María Sofía.

"It's kind of cute, but . . ." I pulled at the straps and shifted from one foot to the other in front of the mirror and tried to explain that this wasn't my style. This wasn't me. I held both hands over my stomach, which bulged a bit. "But I'm embarrassed."

"¿Embarazada?" the saleslady repeated.

"¿Embarazada?" repeated María Sofía with a clap of her hands. "You're pregnant?"

Hannah and Trina both lunged out of their fitting rooms, half-dressed. "Dorrie's pregnant?"

"Embarazada," repeated María Sofía.

"Pregnant!"

My whole face burned and I laughed.

"Embarrassed!" I enunciated, and Hannah and Trina both burst into giggles.

I had made this mistake once in an oral exam. The word *embarazada* is a false cognate and doesn't mean "embarrassed" but "pregnant"—a terrible accident of similar sounds. I explained the error to the Spanish speakers, and they giggled as the salesgirl wrapped up the bikini in pretty tissue paper and tied the bag with a satin ribbon. I looked at the package and it shone with newness and possibility—the possibility that I could be someone who wore red string bikinis, that I was the type of woman who went to foreign countries. A brave, bold, daring person, perhaps as adventurous as Margaret Moore. I handed over my credit card.

Back in my room, Trina immediately stripped and changed into her new suit, while Hannah shuffled to the bathroom for some privacy, which I would need too. I untied the ribbon on the bag and pulled the bikini out of its tissue paper. I held it up in front of the mirror, thinking of my own suit, currently packed in my Travelpro—wherever that was. Would I really wear this?

"It's perfect," said María Sofía, as if reading my thoughts. "You are really pretty, Dolores."

"Thanks for helping me," I said.

"It will look beautiful on you," she said.

I shrugged.

"You don't wear bikinis?" asked Trina. She tugged on the waist of the gingham bottom and patted her belly. "You have no excuse— you haven't had a kid like me."

"Nope, never been embarazada!" I said, laughing.

When it was my turn for the bathroom, I peeled off my well-worn clothes and yanked up the bottom, tied on the top. Standing on tiptoes to see in the mirror above the sink, I inspected what I could. It would do. I pulled my hair into a high bun as my phone pinged, displaying Franklin's name.

Franklin: Have time for a question?

My stomach dropped. Questions weren't good, I knew. There were questions after Jane's doctor appointment a decade ago, questions when Aunt Dot's face began to sag, questions about Becks's repeated miscarriages. Was Franklin in trouble? Were Django and Bojangles okay?

"How's it going in there?" called Hannah from the other side of the door.

"You guys can go ahead without me," I called back. "I'll be right down."

I heard more laughter and the slam of a door. Franklin answered almost before the first ring, his face popping on the screen.

"Is everything all right?" I asked.

"You look—" he began. He was staring at the camera lens, his eyes darting.

"I'm—" And I realized my chest in its new string bikini was on prominent display on the screen. "Just, um—" I grabbed a towel and wrapped it around my shoulders, asking again, "Are you okay? Is your grandfather okay? Are the cats okay?"

He cleared his throat and looked away from the camera as if he was either embarrassed for me or intrigued—I couldn't tell. "I'm fine.

The cats are fine. I mean, they *seem* fine. But one of them vomited. Is that bad? I don't know which one. Should I take them to the vet?"

I let out a relieved guffaw and the towel slipped.

"Does the laughing mean this isn't a trip to the vet?" His face crinkled in a grin of relief.

"Cats throw up." I pulled at the towel again. "It's gross—sorry!— but it's fine. I should have warned you. My whole childhood was nothing but a lot of cat-puke cleanup," I joked. Before Django and Bojangles, my mothers had taken in a beat-up old alley cat named Princess, who had a chunk of her ear missing, halitosis, and a sensitive digestive tract. As I explained this to Franklin, I tried not to notice his eyes straying to my chest, tried to pretend I didn't care. We were friends who discussed the bodily functions of cats—nothing more.

"I was going to say that Grandpa Bao and I might adopt a cat, but maybe not?" Franklin's face disappeared from the screen and then I felt dizzy as he panned across the room. Then the image refocused and I saw Grandpa Bao in a recliner nearly buried under the bulk of Bojangles. Franklin whispered, "They're best friends."

The man in the recliner said something to Franklin. "Grandpa, say hello to Dorrie." Grandpa Bao waved and his face crinkled in the same way Franklin's did when he smiled. "Remember, she's the owner of these guys."

"Hi, Dorrie!" he said obediently. "We like your cats." I watched him stroke Bojangles's silky back. The cat nuzzled deeper into his lap.

(*What a lovely man,* said Gigi.)

"Hi, Grandpa Bao," I said. "I'm glad you're enjoying my mothers' cats."

Grandpa Bao said something to Franklin that I didn't catch. Franklin faced the camera again. "He says he's sorry about your mom. I told him—"

My throat caught. "Thank you," I cut him off. I wanted to think about bikinis and cats, not loss. "I mean, thank him for me."

"What are you doing? How's it going there?"

"Well, I found my mother's apartment, but it's gone. So that was a disappointment."

"I'm so sorry," Franklin said in such a pitying way that I shrugged, wanting that look on his face to go away.

"But otherwise it's good, I'm good." I smiled as broadly as I could. "I'm about to go swimming with a few friends."

"That sounds nice. It's cold here, especially after that warm April. I found the kitchen window open at your house, so I closed it. They're saying it might freeze overnight and Grandpa is worried about his plants."

"Plenty warm here."

We stared at each other, and I experimented with smiles—broad, casual, breezy. "I guess I should get going," I said.

"You look nice."

I glanced in the mirror again and I could see that María Sofía and the salesgirl had been right, that this bikini did look good on me; it was flattering and attractive.

"Different, but nice," he added. "It looks like Colombia was the right choice, just what you needed."

I held the phone higher, so just the top half of my face was visible in the camera. "Ha," I said. "Well, yes, I'm, yes. You and Grandpa Bao should adopt a cat," I said. "Get a kitten. They're so fun."

"Do they puke as much as these guys?"

"As long as you don't get long-haired cats."

"Why not?"

"Hair balls."

"Oh, *that's* what it was."

The three women were the only people on the pool deck when I got there. I settled into a lounge chair and imitated my new friends: put on sunglasses, lie back, close eyes.

"Was that a boyfriend?" I heard Trina ask.

I opened my eyes. "Who?"

"The phone call."

I chuckled and said no. "He's cat-sitting my mothers' cats and needed some advice." I told them about Franklin and Grandpa Bao.

"Does that mean," she asked, "you're not seeing anyone?"

Of course I wasn't seeing Franklin—we were just friends.

"No boyfriend?" asked María Sofía.

I thought of Jason, Jason with whom I had spent five years and now barely thought of. "Not anymore." I told them about Jason Flynn in broad strokes, the years we were together, how breaking up had been the best decision, how my mother had approved.

"Well," Trina said, "I think our friend Oscar likes you."

My mind flashed to the kiss at the museum, the way my stomach had flip-flopped. "Don't be ridiculous."

"Of course he likes Dorrie," said Hannah. "He likes anything that moves."

"Es un bacán," objected María Sofía. "He's cool." She told me that they had been high school sweethearts, and they had stayed friends. "But we don't date anymore," she said. "He'll make a wonderful husband someday. But we're better as friends."

There was that word: friends. So innocent and yet so complicated. I told them about Franklin, that I knew what it was like to be friends with someone you used to love.

"Sometimes you can love somebody but you're not meant to be together like that," she said. "Now Oscar is one of my best friends."

I could imagine Franklin becoming that—not just a friend but one of my best friends. The thought was surprising, odd. We hadn't seen each other in almost two decades but after only a couple weeks, it already felt as easy and comfortable as it had all those years ago.

"How do you know the difference?" Trina asked. "Seb and I are best friends but I would never want to *only* be friends with him."

María Sofía and I looked at each other, waiting for the other to answer. How *did* you know? I thought about raking leaves with Franklin and how we had just discussed cat vomit. Then I thought about the way he had looked at me in my bikini just now and the way he had kissed me that night, and about his mother's ring meant for Sasha, and the whole thing seemed confusing.

"You just know," María Sofía said.

You just know. Her words echoed and bounced, feeling like a pronouncement from my chorus. I lay on the lounge chair in the sun and heat, letting my newly exposed skin get its first blast of vitamin D and ultraviolet light. I would put on sunscreen in a little bit, but for a moment, I just wanted to soak in the tropical heat, feel the way the sun hit my face, my thigh. I let my eyes close, listening to the distant traffic, the squawks of birds, the clanging of pots somewhere.

From two loungers over, María Sofía said, "I'm glad you're not dating this Franklin person." She lowered her sunglasses and winked at me. "Because I *do* think Oscar likes you."

Trina and Hannah whooped and made kissy sounds.

"Stop! You're embarrassing me." I puffed out my stomach. "¡Embarazada!"

We laughed until we had tears in our eyes and then plunged into the pool. It was shockingly cold but made me feel acutely alive. The others shrieked and shouted and scrambled out, but I treaded water, lay back, and squinted up at the Colombian sky, which was mottled blue and ice gray. Palm trees and the local evergreens leaned down, watching me, watching over me. Every inch of my body was suddenly awake and alert, from the tips of my toes to the ends of my hair. The humiliation of bikini shopping and the burn that would surely follow my afternoon in the sun were worth this feeling of being exactly where I was supposed to be. At least in this one moment.

Later, in the cool of my air-conditioned room, as we dried ourselves and slathered lotion on our sunburns, Trina saw my map on the dresser and asked me about my treasure hunt.

"I went to La Ermita," I explained. "Did you know that the church of La Ermita is dedicated to Nuestra Señora de los Dolores?"

"That's why it's on your map," exclaimed Trina.

"Do you know her?" María Sofía asked, shimmying back into her jumpsuit. "Our Lady of Sorrows? La Virgen," she explained, "reminds us of sus dolores. You know the Seven Sorrows?"

I didn't know that either.

"You're not Catholic?" she asked me.

(Of *course not, she's Lutheran,* Gigi harrumphed. *She is not, Mom,* contradicted Elizabeth, as she often had.)

"No and I know nothing about saints."

"You don't either?" she asked Trina, who shrugged.

"I grew up without religion. Hippie parents."

"Me too." I pictured my mothers' multifaith Christmas ornaments with a pang.

"Don't look at me," said Hannah over the roar of the hair dryer.

"But you must know the Sorrows? Or at least the last ones? Jesus on the cross? Jesus taken down from the cross?"

I shrugged.

"We celebrate Nuestra Señora to remind us of her faithfulness,"

María Sofía said. "She understands pain because she lost both her own son *and* the son of God," said María Sofía.

"Did she lose her luggage too?" I asked as I pulled on my sink-washed socks.

Trina laughed, but María Sofía was not amused and she ignored us.

"Nuestra Señora de los Dolores is about suffering but also compassion."

"What's the difference?" I asked.

"Compassion is about suffering *with*," she explained.

Compassion. That's what my mothers had. They had wanted to make the world a better place through feminism and sticking it to the man and books and information. Their teaching, the symposia they hosted, the holiday gatherings of wayward strays. They had wrapped me in it, cocooned me in their caring, their attention. They hadn't quite understood what I was missing, but they knew I had a hole and had tried to fill it. Even if they never could.

1989
Cali, Colombia

Juan Carlos didn't want to be in Bogotá that day. He wished he was home with Margarita, whose belly was gorgeous and sexy and whose face was radiant. She was improving her Spanish and had started reading the children's books he had bought at the librería. Just the thought of her sent a lightning bolt of warmth through his body as he walked past his high school, where the fumbles with girls behind the soccer field seemed like they had happened to a different boy. Because now that he had his americana, his vida, he couldn't even remember being with any other woman. He had, of course, but they became faceless memories once he met Margaret Moore.

"I'll meet you at the shop," he had told his father when he caught Juan Carlos still in his pajamas dipping arepas con queso in the café con leche his mother had made him. His father had studied him with that same disappointed look that he had used when Juan Carlos was in college and needed his sister's help to pass his statistics course.

As he ran to catch the bus that was just pulling away from the curb, someone on board waved at the driver, and Juan Carlos collapsed in a front seat and watched his hometown go by in a blur of buildings and roads, all of it hazy in the low clouds and a drizzle. He zipped his jacket against the bone-chilling damp of the capital city. He would never, he thought, bring Margarita here. It was too cold and there was too much family. She had told him that her home was also cold and insisted that it was colder than Bogotá, but he couldn't imagine such a thing. What could be colder than this high-altitude climate or these parental expectations?

"¡Oye!" he shouted at the driver when he realized he'd missed his stop. He jumped up. The driver ignored him, even while he hovered behind the man's shoulder. When the bus finally stopped, he was four blocks out of his way. At least the rain had stopped. And then, just as he was shoving his cold hands in his pockets and calculating how many hours until his flight back to Cali, the ground under his feet jolted and a roaring exploded in his ears.

An earthquake?

He fell to the ground and was engulfed in a cloud of debris. He could hear people shouting and the scrape of metal on metal. Cars honked and fire alarms blared. He got to his knees and there, up ahead about a block away, was the epicenter of the disturbance.

"¡Una bomba!" someone cried, and Juan Carlos ran as fast as he had in school when he couldn't wait to get home. The dust swirled in a stormy wind and he coughed. The ground was littered with bricks, bits of paper, a shoe. He wasn't the only one running; anyone who could was running toward the disaster. The wail of police sirens filled the air and the voices of people trapped in cars and under rubble crescendoed. A bomb, they cried. An attack, they said. Help us, they wailed. Who's in charge? they asked.

"¡Señor!" came a man's voice from a battered taxi. "Can you help me? I can't get out."

Juan Carlos approached the car and pulled at the mangled driver's side door. The front glass was shattered in a kaleidoscope of cracks and the back windows were even worse. "Is there anyone else in there with you?"

"No one else, gracias a Dios," said the driver, blood careening down his left cheek.

"I'll pull you out."

By the time Juan Carlos got home that evening, he didn't know how many people he had pulled or dragged. The taxi driver hadn't been injured but the girl trapped under a shop's heavy door couldn't move her legs, and the old woman whom he had scooped up from the road wasn't breathing. His mother, plucking debris from his hair and wiping his face with a warm cloth, told him that the radio news reports coming in fingered the cartels and the neighborhood gossip blamed the militia. It had been planted on a parked bus, its intended target an official in a building high above the street. Nobody said if the official had survived, but that didn't mean there weren't hundreds of families with missing fathers and daughters, uncles and friends. This wasn't the first time Juan Carlos had experienced the destruction his country's war could wreak, and it wouldn't be the last. He brushed aside his mother's ministrations and stood so suddenly the chair tipped to the floor, making his mother jump. He knew it was selfish, but he needed to get back to Cali, back to Margarita. He needed to go home.

Juan Carlos swung Maggie into an embrace, lifting her off the floor and squeezing her as tightly as a boa constrictor. He buried his face in her hair and let the scent of her shampoo erase the memory of smoke and dust. He was home. "Did you miss me, mi amor?"

"Don't ever leave again," she said into the crook of his neck. He had been gone for seventy-two hours this time, and although she had filled the days with wandering the city following his maps just as she had before, it had felt like she had been wandering without her soul.

"I will have to go back," he said, setting her down and switching on the electric kettle. Even though it was nearly ten at night, he wanted a cup of coffee—un tinto, as he called it—after the flight.

She reached into his pockets and removed his wallet and house keys, a candy wrapper and matchbook. Then she began to unbutton his shirt. "If I remove this," she said coyly, "you'll never be able to leave me."

His mouth was on hers, and the glow of the overhead light and the sound of the water gurgling in the kettle faded as they pressed against each another until not one micron of space was between them. She could feel her soul returning to her body.

And then, in an eye blink, they were plunged into darkness. It was Maggie's second blackout, and although Cristina had explained away the unannounced cut in electricity as something that just happened, it made Maggie uneasy. "Así es," the girl had said, and shrugged. Now, Maggie gripped Juan Carlos's hand.

"You're not scared of the dark, are you?"

"Of course not." She tried to make her tone light. "I'm just sorry you won't be able to have your tinto now."

He let go and fumbled his way across the room, cursing when he ran into the rickety table, and she heard him scrape the kettle across the counter. "The water is still warm."

Then a match ignited, and when he lit a candle, the shadows receded. Her shoulders eased. He tossed her the book of matches and told her to light more candles, which she found in the drawer among his socks. Once they were lit, he poured the water over the grounds, filled two cups. In the flickering candlelight, he handed her the coffee and sank into their sole armchair.

"It's magical, isn't it?" he said as he pulled her onto his lap. "The dark? The candles?"

Now, pressed against him with the warm mug in her hands, she could see the romance in the blackout.

"At Christmas," he said, "there's a day when everyone lights candles, and the whole neighborhood is lined with velitas. This year, you will help me make luminarias and line the courtyard and hang paper lanterns from the branches of the mango tree. Ay, mi amor, I can't wait for you to see it. It's a special day because it's for families—my grandmother always made buñuelos and hot chocolate for my family." He told her about his childhood visits to his grandmother's finca, the chickens he would chase, and the tricks he and his sister would play on distant cousins and neighbors. The drive to the farmhouse was bumpy and winding, the little family car would get coated in a film of dust in which he and his sister would draw stick figure battles. In the evenings, while the teenagers swiped bottles of rum and kisses in the dark, the adults would gather on the veranda, backlit by the single bulb in the comedor, and talk, telling stories that sounded true, stories that felt true, and stories that were true.

"On la Noche de Velitas, my grandmother used to tell us to make a wish on a candle. She said that if it burns all night, your wish will come true." As he spoke, his voice, smooth and gentle, rumbled through his body directly into hers while the flames danced. "What would you wish for, mi amor?"

Her only wish was to be with him always, in this city, in this apartment, in this chair. And, of course, he agreed because they were meant to be. Curled together in the armchair, waiting out the black night, they fell asleep before morning and never knew if the candles they had wished on had burned all night.

CHAPTER 17

"Welcome to Monday night's boring dinner," Seb said as he poured me a glass of wine. We were standing in the kitchen of Seb and Trina's apartment, where an open window let in the evening air. A covered pot steamed on the stove, and a large bowl held a pineapple, several limes, and a bunch of green plantains. The refrigerator was plastered with crayon drawings, crooked snapshots, a black-and-white sonogram printout of what must have been Andrés. "I told Trina we should take you out again, but she insisted you wanted to experience a home meal."

"This is just what I wanted," I assured him.

Since arriving in Cali, I had felt pulled in different directions—to search out the locations on the map, go to the pool with new friends, or soak in as much of Colombia as I could. All the moving and switching direction, all the changes and novelties were beginning to take a toll on my body. I had never been so exhausted in my life and was so glad when Trina had invited me for dinner.

"¡Tía Dolores!" said Andrés. I smiled at the term *tía*. I was an aunt already! "Do you want to see my Formers?" he asked, clutching an armful of plastic figures.

"After dinner, mi amor," said Trina.

Before I could ask what a Former was, the front door buzzed. I turned to Trina. "Who else is coming?"

She and Seb exchanged gleeful glances as he opened the door. Trina leaned over and whispered, "You look like one of those innocent girls but then attract the best ones. I'll have you know he asked to be invited. I told you he likes you."

Oscar was wearing crisp dark jeans and a structured black shirt with the sleeves rolled to the elbows, his hair freshly oiled back into neat black waves. My nose tickled pleasantly at the scent of pomade and cologne and that attractive-man smell I associated with the cutest boys in high school. He leaned in and kissed my cheek, briefly placing a hand on the small of my back again, and my stomach flipped. "You look nice, Dolores."

"Thanks to Trina." Last night, the gray concierge had called my room and told me she had a package for me. When I came down, she held out a plastic bag with two fingers as if it were contaminated. I opened it to find a bundle of clothing and a note from Trina: *A few things for you to borrow.* I had to read the note twice because my eyes were clouded. It felt so nice to have someone take care of me, go out of their way, and I couldn't help tearing up.

"My dress looks fabulous on you."

Trina's blue flowered dress hung a little long on me and the halter neck would have been cuter if I hadn't gotten sunburned by the pool. "Wish I had my own clothes, but thank you."

"They still haven't found your suitcase?" she asked. Her missing luggage had arrived three days ago.

"You won't believe this!" I said. "This morning I asked again if there was any news on my luggage."

The front desk had been staffed by a new employee, a man with a receding hairline, and I explained, "We've been trying to track down my missing suitcase since two Saturdays ago. The señora said she called the airline for me."

He shook his head sadly. "Today is her day off. I'll look at her notes." He opened a large ledger and scanned its pages. "I have no record of her correspondence," he said formally. "Would you like me to check?"

"Please." I gave him the flight and baggage claim information.

"I'll try my best." He dialed and I studied the hotel's menu while I waited, even though I'd practically memorized it by now. I listened as he contacted someone at the airline. There were many formalities before he got into my problem. He spelled my last name, pronouncing it with more flair than my Midwestern family probably deserved. He nodded into the receiver and repeated several things. I was losing track of his side of the conversation, my Spanish not quite up to filling in the blanks.

At last he hung up. "Señora Moore," he said. "They say that your luggage has been waiting at the unclaimed baggage department since Wednesday."

Since Wednesday?

"¿Miércoles?" I repeated in Spanish just to make sure we understood one another.

"You must submit a claim," the concierge explained, "which they say you never completed."

Was it possible that the missing suitcase wasn't actually missing?

I said this out loud to Trina and Seb and Oscar: "Is something lost if you're the only one who doesn't know where it is?"

"If a tree falls in a forest . . ." said Trina.

Oscar looked confused. "I thought we were talking about suitcases, not trees."

I laughed. "There's a riddle, do you know it? If a tree falls in a forest and there's no one to hear it, did it make a sound?"

He repeated this under his breath, thinking. His brow furrowed and a little shiver went through me at the way his eyelashes fluttered against his cheekbones.

"The question being, is the sound only a sound because someone hears it?" he mused.

"Ridiculous," said Seb. "Sound isn't dependent on people. This riddle is so American."

Oscar nodded. "Things happen even if we humans don't know about them."

"Oh, you two are taking this too seriously. It's funny," said Trina, returning from the kitchen with a steaming platter of food.

But, as Oscar and Seb continued debating this, I thought that perhaps they were right. It was very self-centered to think that a thing could only happen if we were there to witness it. My suitcase was lost only to me—the airline knew exactly where it was. What happened to my mother—my biological mother—only seemed mysterious because I wasn't there.

My chorus, too, I thought. I had never told anyone about hearing their voices because I knew no one would understand. Because they hadn't experienced it. If you were the only one who heard something, did it really happen?

"¡Pollo a la criolla!" Andrés clapped as Trina set down the platter of food, effectively ending the existential conversation between Seb and Oscar.

(*Goodness, that child is loud,* said Grandma June, and I smiled because I knew the voices were there and real and true.)

"Sí, papi, we're having your favorite. This is one of the few dishes Seb's mother taught me that I can actually make," she explained.

"It looks delicious," I said.

"Is it *your* favorite too?" Andrés asked me.

"Well, no," I admitted, "actually, I've never tried it."

His eyes grew wide at the idea of this woman in his house having never had his most favorite dish. Children grow up thinking their experiences are the way everyone lives. Becks was the first person to show surprise at the fact that I had two mothers, but she wasn't the last. Each time I introduced a new friend to my family, there was always a moment of confusion, often more from my friends' parents than the children themselves. As I got older, I became less likely to invite new people to the Victorian and soon I was reluctant to make new friends altogether. Besides, I always had a steady commentary, was never completely solo. Alone, not lonely.

"You will like the pollo a la criolla." Andrés took a big bite and then said, with his mouth full, "Te lo prometo." He then launched into a story, mostly directed at his parents, in a rapid-fire, child version of Spanish while I tried to keep up. Every once in a while, he would turn to his mother and say, "¿Cierto, mamá?"

"Home is for English, mi amor," said Trina. She turned to me. "We're trying to speak English at home so that he grows up totally bilingual, but it's a challenge."

If I had grown up with both my parents—my biological parents—would I have spoken Spanish and English? Would Juan Carlos have spoken to me, teaching me the sayings and slang? Would Margaret have tried to help me with English, coaching me with a Minnesotan's accent? I looked around Trina's apartment and wondered how it compared to the magical apartment on calle 5 Norte, and my heart faltered for a moment. There must be a way, I thought, to find out more about the apartment, to fulfill my promise to Jane.

"Sí, mamá." I watched Andrés shovel food into his mouth and wondered if I would have been like this child, happy and loved and secure. He turned to say something to Oscar, very sure of himself, and I was certain this child would never feel the need to depend on maps to figure out where he is in the world. He knew his place.

"This one keeps letting him slip back to Spanish." Trina elbowed Seb.

"¡Mentiras!" cried Seb with a big laugh. Lies.

Andrés imitated his father. "¡Mentiras!"

I laughed and did it too. "¡Mentiras!"

Despite the intention to speak English, the conversation swung between languages, making me feel slightly dizzy as if I were on a merry-go-round, spinning and spinning. As far as I could tell, there were lots of comments about "tractomulas" being "grandes y ruidosas" and how the Formers (which turned out to be several vintage Transformers toys) were "muy chévere." We discussed our own childhood toys, pouring more wine, clinking glasses, erupting in laughter.

Dinners with Jane and Elizabeth had always been quiet. We used the dining room because there were only seats for two in the kitchen. They sat across from each other and I was between them at the head of a table large enough for eight. When I was young, there was symmetry between us, each of us points on a triangle. Later, though, I realized it wasn't an equilateral triangle; Jane and Elizabeth were farther from me, we formed an isosceles. I had always longed to be equidistant from someone.

Oscar entertained Andrés with several magic tricks, making spoons and even a bowl of rice disappear, a feat that Andrés begged for over and over. "¡Otra vez, tío Oscar, porfa!"

"Does this mean you're done, mi amor?" Trina asked, clearing away his dishes and sending him off to go play.

After dinner, while Seb put their son to bed, Trina told me and

Oscar to relax in the living room, where big windows overlooked a small park, several taller apartment buildings, and the river beyond. She had gestured at the sofa, but he and I stood at the window, looking out or perhaps in. His black eyes were very close and he smelled like testosterone and possibilities. In the dark, our own reflections blended with the twinkling lights of the city below, making both scenes seem surreal.

"Andrés is requesting a kiss from Tía Dolores and Tío Oscar," announced Seb, with a sneaky glance at his wife.

"Of course!"

I peeked through the cracked-open door to see a yellow glow from a bedside lamp illuminating the twin-size bed, a dresser, a blue-painted box overflowing with stuffed animals and trucks. Like any child's room. Like mine had been, actually. I could still remember the exact way the light shone across the floor from a streetlight outside, the shadow my clock made against the wall, the creak of the bed when I rolled over. Walking into Andrés's room made it all come rushing back—the dotted swiss bedspread and the antique bed and dresser set that had belonged to Margaret Moore when she was a little girl and to Grandma June before that, the comforting glimpse of my mothers' room across the hall. I sat on the edge of his bed like my moms had sat on mine, and a tear rolled its way down my face.

"¿Lloras?" asked Andrés, reaching out with a small hand and touching my wet cheek.

Everything felt so recognizable and yet strange, as every moment in this city had felt so far, that strange combination of the familiar and the foreign. I wished Jane were here to put a hand on my shoulder, to assure me I was in the right place. I wished Elizabeth could have tried Trina's pollo la criolla, discussed the exact proportions of garlic and cilantro. It didn't seem fair or right that I had to be here alone, without them. Hearing their voices wasn't the same as having them beside me.

"Are you okay, Dolores?"

"I'm okay," I whispered. "I miss my mom but I'm happy to be at your home, Andrés. Thank you."

"You're funny," Andrés said.

I smiled, wiping away a second tear. "I think you're funny too."

He sat up then and wrapped his skinny arms around my neck. "Good night," he said into my hair. He smelled like toothpaste and sweaty boy and the guava juice we had at dinner.

"Buenas noches." I gave him a gentle squeeze.

"Buenas noches, Tío Oscar." Oscar got a little-boy hug, too, and then we gently shut his door, leaving the child in his cocoon of Transformers and night-lights.

"You're very good with him," Oscar whispered as we tiptoed down the hall. He laid a hand on my shoulder, just as I had wished Jane could have done for me. The tenderness in his voice—his present, very real voice—made my insides turn gooey.

"He's very sweet. And he really likes you, doesn't he?"

"He likes me; he likes you." Oscar paused and brushed his hand along my arm, turning my flesh to goose bumps. "I like you too." His hand was on my waist now, and he gently pulled me toward him in the dim hallway of Trina and Seb's apartment. I leaned the rest of the way until there was no distance between us, and when our lips met, it wasn't a surprise this time. I closed my eyes and sank into the close feeling of solid arms around me, the tingling sensation that shot down my body, the delicious novelty of an unknown mouth and tongue and scratchy chin.

"Chicos." Oscar and I jolted apart at the sound of Seb's voice. The hallway light snapped on. "My wife says we need to go get rum, the good stuff. Vámonos," Seb said to his friend, either ignorant of or ignoring what was happening between us.

Trina was not ignorant. "You look flushed. A little glowy," she said after they left. I laughed and she gasped. "*Oscar and Dorrie sitting in a tree,*" she singsonged.

"Not like—" I protested.

"If I weren't married to the second-most handsome man in Colombia . . ." She raised her eyebrows at me. "So?"

"I'll need another drink before I tell you anything."

"I have just the thing while we wait for the guys." She went to a cabinet and poured clear liquid into two short glasses. "We can get started with the aguardiente."

"Aguardiente?" I repeated. "Firewater?"

She chuckled. "A spirit made from local sugarcane." She clinked my glass. "Salud."

I coughed as the licorice-flavored liquid burned down my throat, and we both laughed.

"You're a real caleña now!" And we both cheered and laughed and downed our drinks.

"¿Mamá?" Andrés appeared in the room, blinking in the light.

"Mi amor." She sighed and then giggled. "Too loud? Did Tía Dorrie wake you up? Let's get you back to bed."

When she returned, I was comfortably curled on the couch in a pleasant fog of aguardiente. "Your son is really great."

"When he stays in bed he is." She poured us each another shot. "I complain, but he is mi vida, as the mothers say. Although, even if he is the best kid ever, I only want one—to the horror of my mother-in-law and Seb's sister. But I don't want another, and to have another kid you have to make the decision, you have to feel it deep in your bones. No one can tell you or convince you. And it's a lot of work, as you can see."

"I told you about my friend, who's pregnant now after four mis-carriages."

"Yes, have you heard from her?"

"She's bored out of her mind on bed rest," I told Trina. I had had several messages from Becks begging me for photos and news and I had sent her as many pictures as I could, whatever would give her something to do and think about. "She'll do anything to avoid another miscarriage."

"I had one before Andrés was born. It's a special kind of heart-break. Another reason I only want one." She sighed, her usually smiling face serious. "We're lucky to have him."

There was something about the coziness of the apartment, the tender expression of this woman who was a stranger and yet so kind. I thought of the people I had lost, the people I never knew. Why was I always holding others apart, always keeping new friends, new peo-ple distant? I told her what I had not been able to say before, about my birth mother's stroke, the true story of my adoption.

"Oh, Dorrie," she said, laying a hand on mine. My insides squeezed.

We clinked glasses and the sound reminded me of the delicate balance of life.

CHAPTER 18

Oscar, as orchestrated by Trina at the end of the evening, would walk me back to the hotel. "Seb is in no shape to drive," she said, kissing her husband on the cheek. We had been discussing where we should go the next day—"We'll take you dancing!"—but then somehow we began arguing about the differences between men and women, and then, for some reason, Seb and Oscar began singing songs from their primary school days. Trina lit a cigarette to the horror of her husband—"Where did you get that?"—and then Seb pulled a joint from his pocket, and the smoke from each twisted and turned in the breeze of the open window, shrouding everything and all four of us in a haze. As my chorus muttered about us all being too old for this behavior, Trina poured one more trago of rum—when we had all had far too many—and informed us that my hotel was close enough to walk.

"¡Buen idea!" cried Oscar, leaping from the couch and grabbing my hand. We laughed and everyone kissed everyone good night and then Oscar and I headed into the night. A good idea, I agreed, my head fuzzy from aguardiente and rum and smoke and the sudden dark.

(*Romantic*, commented Aunt Judith, and I shook my head, trying to will the voices away, wanting a little privacy from them.)

The moment we were out of sight of our hosts, Oscar caught

me and kissed me and twined his fingers in mine and we kissed as if we had been waiting all night for this moment. We crossed Trina's street and then followed the road until we were at the river, where several other couples—mostly teenagers—were strolling under the streetlights along the wide avenue and the night air was filled with something sweet and heavy. My mind flashed with a collage of other moments, other kisses, and threatened to distract me with questions and logic, but then I tripped on a crack in the sidewalk and Oscar's arm was around my waist and then his face was close to mine. My hips vibrated as if I were dancing. Now we were standing at a vendor's cart and Oscar pulled a few bills from his pocket to buy ice creams. My hip seemed to wiggle again. It wasn't phantom dance moves—my phone, in the pocket of my loaned dress, was vibrating. Franklin's name flashed on the screen.

"Franklin! Everything okay?" I tried a joke: "Or are the cats puking again?"

"She gave me an ultimatum."

"What? They're both *he*," I said. Franklin seemed intent on misgendering my mothers' cats.

"No," Franklin said in my ear, "*she* gave me an ultimatum."

"Who? I can't hear you." A car sputtered, followed by a loud honk, and Oscar called to me, perhaps asking which flavor. I hoped he was ordering maracuyá, which had become my favorite, the perfect combination of sweet and sour, creamy and light. "What did you say?"

"I'm sorry to bother you. Were you sleeping? I thought we're on the same time zone."

"We are," I assured him. "I'm awake. I'm out with some friends—with a friend."

"She found out about the ring."

208

The pieces realigned. This wasn't about my mothers' cats. "Sasha?"

"She just accepted a job in Chicago and stopped by and my mom was there cooking for Grandpa, and she said something about the ring to Sasha." He let out a small groan. "And then she called me, gave me an ultimatum."

"Your mom?"

"Sasha."

I didn't say anything. A nighttime caleño breeze cooled my skin. I thought about the word *ultimatum* with all those *u*'s, so final sounding. My mouth pursed into the shape of the word.

"I don't know why I'm telling you," he said into my silence. "I shouldn't have bothered you. Are you having a great time?"

"Franklin, it's fine. I'm here. I'm listening." I paused.

(*That's what friends are for*, said my chorus.)

"That's what friends are for," I repeated.

"Sasha said she wants to be with me now that she has this new job, she says I can work anywhere, says she knows what she wants now, and she wants to get back together."

"Oh. Well, that's nice. Right?"

"But . . ." Franklin's voice trailed off.

Elizabeth used to say that getting back with an ex is like putting on dirty underwear after taking a shower. I'm not sure where she got that imagery, but it was gross enough to stick in my head. The summer after my sophomore year, Franklin and I happened to take the same Greyhound home. Two of only a few college students heading to Minneapolis, we sat together in the scratchy, rank seats, careful— at first—not to let our elbows touch.

"Hey," he had said.

"Hey."

"Haven't seen you for a while."

"How was your semester?"

"Hard. Glad it's over." We were both silent, then he asked, "How are your parents—I mean, moms?"

"They're good. How are yours? Your grandpa?"

"They're good."

The bus had taken a turn onto the freeway exit and we were jostled together, our bodies touching. Somewhere in the middle of a Midwestern cornfield his hand inched to my lap and I held it. By the time we were in the suburbs of the Twin Cities, we were face-to-face, experimenting with the feeling of our lips touching, so familiar yet exciting.

At the bus depot, Franklin stood with his luggage, staring at his Converse as if they were the most interesting sight. "Do you want to maybe get a coffee this summer? Or dinner? Or just hang out?" His words came tumbling, fast and jumbled. I knew what he meant.

But I had thought of Elizabeth's adage and shook my head. "I don't think that's a good idea," I said, and walked away.

But perhaps life decisions shouldn't be made based on quips.

"I don't know," he was saying now. "This time Sasha wants the ring, a wedding. She and my mom got to talking and they think Grandpa Bao needs to be in assisted living—they don't think I can take care of him. I don't know, maybe they're right—we should sell his house. Sasha doesn't want to live here." Franklin tried to laugh. "I don't blame her. It's ugly and small, hard to get to from the freeway."

I was fully alert now, the rum evaporating from my sweaty pores. "Oh, Franklin, I'm sorry." Perhaps I needed to tell him Elizabeth's vivid advice.

"I care about her, I do. And it's been so long, the two of us."

I thought of my five years with Jason and how, after three or four, he used that time together—he thought of it as an investment—as a reason why we should move to the next step, to that wedding, the family he wanted and thought I should want too. I didn't say any of this to Franklin.

"I don't like the way she's backed me into a corner. And it doesn't feel like the right—the right path, you know?"

I looked up to find Oscar in front of me holding an ice cream cone. I thought of María Sofía saying that *you just know*. Franklin didn't know. Oscar held out the cone but before I took it, I pointed to the phone. "Un momento," I mouthed.

"I keep thinking about the first time I went rock climbing with this friend of mine," Franklin said as Oscar walked to a bench and plopped down with a sulky attitude. Franklin was saying, "He was a super jock, Keng. I started the climb and he's telling me which hold to use, where to put my feet. But then I got higher and he couldn't really see anymore. He said, 'Look for the chalk marks, then you'll know where to go next.' Pretty soon I was doing it, though—the best feeling. Seeing the chalk and following the route. But then I ran out of chalk marks. It was just rock and I had no idea where to go next. I kept calling down for help. I wasn't scared of falling—I was in that harness—but I was freaked out about not knowing what to do next. And then Keng called up, 'You gotta make your own route, dude.'" Franklin chuckled. "That guy."

Keng, Sasha. I was trying to concentrate, make sense of Franklin's story even as I swayed and watched Oscar fold his arms over his chest. "So what happened? Obviously, you never plunged to your death."

"No, right. I made it by following my own route. And now that's what I love about climbing—you make your own route, like you really trust it. And with Sasha . . . I don't know. I mean, I'll always love her, of course. We've been together for . . ." He faltered. "It's been good, it has. But it just doesn't feel like my route, you know?"

I wouldn't advise him, I realized. It wasn't my place. And after several days of putting on dirty clothes after showers, I knew it was something that sometimes made sense.

"It's a tough choice, but only you can make it, Franklin," I said as I finished the ice cream cone, finding it suddenly too cloying.

The phone was back in my pocket, my fingers sticky. I returned to Oscar, who pulled me onto his bench under a broad banyan tree. He reached for me and kissed me again, his mouth on mine, then on my neck, my chest, his hands sneaking up my thigh. I backed away from the embrace so I could look at him. His face was so symmetrical, his skin so smooth, his hair so soft. When we came up for air, our bodies connected like two magnets that won't let go.

He stood, held out his hand, and pulled me up. We walked along the river, which I couldn't see but could hear. Then, a flash of purple then blue flitted through the night like a beacon. Like a sign. It was a little bird in brilliant colors that I didn't think existed in nature. Iridescent green and blue and violet glitters. The bird buzzed around our heads.

"¡Mira! It's a colibrí," Oscar said. The glimpse of blue and a shocking turquoise dove around us again. "I don't know how you call this bird in English."

"A hummingbird," I said.

The colibrí sparkled around a yellow blossom, then it swooped and chattered. We leaned on the low wall that bordered the river and I held out my hand. The bird buzzed again and then landed on me, its head cocking from one side to the other as if listening. I gasped in shock and joy, feeling the ghostlike weight of the tiny feet on my wrist. Then it flew away.

"We have hummingbirds, but they don't look anything like this."

"I think it's a colibrí chillón," he specified. "It's good luck to have a hummingbird land on you."

I wondered if luck had anything to do with anything.

"You're a good luck charm," he said, and brought his mouth close to mine. I wasn't watching the bird anymore. The smell of the water, the flowering trees, and the presence of this man swirled with the night and the alcohol and made me lightheaded. Oscar's face had moved toward mine, and then his mouth was on mine again and mine was on his, and his hands were on my hips, my thigh, under my dress. The hummingbird thrummed or maybe that was me. My knees went to jelly as he held me against the wall so I wouldn't fall. A feeling of letting go washed over me. What was I doing? I didn't care what I was doing.

"When Trina introduced you to us, I thought you were the most beautiful girl when I saw you." He squeezed my hand.

I shook my head and laughed, thinking of María Sofía, who would undoubtedly win a beauty contest against me.

"No, really. You laugh but it's true. There's something very honest about you. Solid."

"I . . ." I started to protest (solid!) but he cut me off.

"You are very real, Dolores."

I let go of his hand and ran my fingers along the leaves of a bamboo that leaned over the wall. The green was vibrant, almost fake looking, and reminded me of the box of Crayola crayons I had as a child. Thirty-six colors, each one pure and distinct. I had used them to make maps, color-coding my world. The real world was less ordered, more confusing.

"Is real a good thing?" I asked.

"Of course. You look more . . ." Oscar turned and studied me. "More comfortable than when I first met you."

I pictured myself following Trina that first night, cautious and timid, unsure of why I was in Colombia and completely baffled as to how I had found myself not only in Cali but among strangers who acted like friends.

"I cannot believe you never came to Colombia before," he said. "You belong here."

Something deep inside me pulsed. I had always wanted to belong, to feel like I could blend in, to be just like the people around me, to not be an outsider or an oddity. Was this why Jane had wanted me to come to Colombia so insistently? Had she had an inkling of what my life had been like growing up without biological parents, without the close genetic link that explained my hair color, my face shape? I looked out over the río Cali and tried to imagine it flowing to the Pacific. Was it true? Did I belong here? I waited for my chorus to comment, but they were silent.

I don't know how long we stayed like that, but my whole body quivered with the city, the dark, the rum coursing through me. And maybe it was also Colombia, this city, my past and my present. The bird flitted away and then back again, it hummed and swooped, and Oscar's hands felt like delicate feathers across my skin.

And then another colibrí flew by, and then another and another. Soon we were surrounded by a cloud of iridescent blue and purple, a tornado of thrumming wings, each colibrí dipping so near that I could feel the air move. They swirled and tittered, circled and flitted, their chirping sounds as insistent as my chorus. I yelped and closed my eyes, and when I opened them, a downy soft blue-purple feather drifted down between us. Maybe this was the magic Jane talked about. I caught the delicate, brilliant feather and spun it between my fingers, rotating it on its axis like a compass.

1989
Cali, Colombia

For a time, in the last few months of the year, of the decade, Margaret Moore was the happiest she had ever been. Even when maneuvering through life got more and more cumbersome, even when her feet disappeared and she could no longer fit into her ballet flats, she glowed with the exhilaration of being alive. Here, not only in Colombia but in Juan Carlos's life. Soon he would return from his latest visit to Bogotá, and she would finally meet his family.

"This time everyone is coming with me!" Juan Carlos had told her when he called on the landlady's phone. Now that they had told his mother and father that they would soon be grandparents, they had softened toward the American novia. Even the sister, whom Juan Carlos said could be jealous of her younger brother's girlfriends, was excited, he promised. Maggie stood in the foyer of Doña Rojas's apartment, the telephone cord twisted around her wrist. She could see the dueña at the stove in the kitchen, adding choclo and cilantro to the sancocho steaming in a large pot. Maggie was amazed that, even in her all black, Doña Rojas didn't have a single bead of sweat on her. Meanwhile, Maggie herself was drenched and her pregnant belly, which seemed to have taken on a life of its own, wriggled as the creature inside did flips.

When Juan Carlos was home, he would talk to it as if it were already its own, independent self. "Mi muñeco," he said to her belly.

"Are you sure the baby can hear you?" Maggie would ask, laughing.

"Whether he listens or not—"

"He?" interrupted Maggie as she always did every time Juan Carlos referred to the baby as a "he."

"I am certain he *or* she can hear us—after all, we love him or her." He leaned down and whispered, just above Maggie's belly button: "Tú eres mi vida."

"I should know what you're saying to my child," Maggie teased him.

"You, mi reina, need to learn more Spanish," he teased back.

"Why do I need to learn when I have you to translate?"

"Because our baby will speak both and you will want to understand our hijo."

"Or hija," she added. She knew enough to recognize the word *son* and added *daughter*. She felt sure the baby would be a girl, even though the old women at the market predicted a boy by the way she was carrying.

"We'll be on the flight home tomorrow," Juan Carlos had promised over the scratchy long-distance line. After he had broken the news, another battered package had arrived at the apartment. This time, instead of a silky robe, there was a stack of mamelucos and a tiny yellow sweater. "Papá, Mamá, and even my sister. They can't wait to meet you."

She knew that his family only wanted to meet "la americana" now that she was having their first grandchild, but she didn't mind. Juan Carlos was hers and the baby would be hers. Theirs—hers and Juan Carlos's alone.

"We'll take a taxi from the airport, so don't worry about us. You just put your feet up and relax."

She couldn't do much more than put her feet up at this point. After ending the call, she lumbered upstairs to the apartment. Cristina had been to clean the day before, so all she had to do was pick up the pajamas she had left on the bed, wash the dirty coffee cup and plate from her breakfast, and water the flowering geraniums in the window. *Regadera*, she thought, and smiled. Then she decided that, in their honor, she would wash her hair.

She skipped lighting the water heater because the day was warm—even in November, something she loved about Cali—and let the cool water run through her hair, which had lost its shape during her pregnancy. She had left Rome with a feathered cut that accented her cheekbones (people said she looked a bit like Princess Di), but now she often clipped back the outgrown layers. After the baby came, she would ask Juan Carlos to find a peluquería that could handle her thin, wispy hair. For now, she toweled it dry and pulled it back with tortoiseshell combs, and then lounged on the bed. Her sister had just sent her a care package with a bag of marshmallows, a jar of Jif, and a new book called *The Joy Luck Club*, which she'd been devouring since it arrived. She propped her feet on several pillows and leaned back with the book, ready to wait for Juan Carlos and his family.

Her family.

CHAPTER 19

The next night, as promised, Trina and her friends took me dancing at a discoteca where music pounded and everyone swapped part-ners, each of them trying to teach me to dance. "Cali is the salsa capital of the world!" they shouted. Hannah danced with Joaquim, both of them tall and strong, while Trina swayed close to Seb. María Sofía rotated on the dance floor between partners, each one twirling her until her hair became a swirl of black and her skirt flared.

I was wearing another too-short dress that Trina claimed to be loaning me but fit me perfectly and smelled new. It was nothing I would have bought—or worn—if given a choice. I tugged at the hem of the dark red fabric, trying to make the dress a bit longer, a little less tight. Oscar had not said anything about the dress but ran the back of his fingers along my bare thigh, clearly forgiving me for my quick departure last night.

As the music thrummed, we danced and took breaks to lean on the bar and drink shots of rum alternated with ice-cold bottles of water. Older couples spun in dizzy circles to cumbias, and younger ones crowded together when the DJ played thumping reggaeton. Other dancers bumped into us as they swayed and moved, but we had formed our own circle, sometimes in partners, sometimes keeping the beat with our feet and shoulders together. Was this, I wondered, what I had missed out on by avoiding groups, by keeping one or two close friends, depending on Becks, on Jason, on my chorus. Maybe I could open my life a bit more to living people.

Now Oscar swung me around and, with his other hand, gripped my waist and pulled me toward him just as he had last night but now in rhythm and with a purpose. The music was loud and insistent, both lazy and unwavering, a constant thrum like hummingbirds, like the nonstop drone of cars and trucks punctuated by shouts and honks, the rhythm of the caleños hurrying but slowly. The cumbia coursed through me and I could feel my Colombian blood pulsing through my veins. My thoughts—my questions and doubts and uncertainties, as well as those of my chorus—were drowned out as his lips landed on my neck. "Last night," he murmured, and I laughed, more because of the surprise than the pleasure of it.

Last night was nothing, but my face burned as his breath tickled my ear.

"How do you like your hotel?" he had whispered as we stood outside the front drive of the Hotel América. "Is it a comfortable bed?"

The guard had opened the gate, wished us buenas noches, averted his eyes. But I caught something between him and Oscar, some congratulatory expression. And it was as if someone had turned a searchlight on me. I pulled back from Oscar and studied his perfect face, felt his warm grip on my waist.

"It *is* a comfortable bed," I had told him. And then I kissed him on the cheek. "See you tomorrow." And I went through the gate—alone.

Now I closed my eyes, dizzy as he spun me around the dance floor, our pelvises locked, and wondered if I had chosen wrong.

"¡Wepa!" shouted Trina as she and Seb danced close to us. She winked at me before being whisked away.

Later. Sultry, dark heat. Tequilas and rum. Amber streetlights, the rushing of the río Cali, a man's hand around my waist, down my thigh. Trina and Hannah marched ahead of us, singing "Who Let the Dogs Out" at the top of their voices, Seb shushing them while María Sofía and Joaquim walked crookedly arm in arm.

"Dolores," whispered Oscar, and then a torrent of Spanish.

There was something familiar now but somehow also sad about the air in Cali. The humidity, the gentle roar of traffic, the echo of cumbia in my head, and the staccato of motorcycle horns. A scent that I was beginning to associate with big green leaves and small yellow flowers hung in the air. A wave of nausea crashed over me.

"Dolores," Oscar repeated in my ear, his hands along my waist, running up and down, eager. We were almost at the hotel now; I could see its gate up ahead. The hotel, within it my room, within that the bed. Would I make the same decision as last night? Which way? Did Maggie, I wondered, need space as badly as I needed direction? I thought of Sasha's ultimatum, of the pang in Franklin's voice. I thought of Jason and his mother. I thought about how Becks was bored and wanted me to live, to experience life. I thought about Jane wanting me to come to Colombia. I needed to choose. I looked at Oscar's symmetrical face and strong hands and reached for him.

But then an engine backfired, followed by an angry shout. An insect as big as my palm scurried across the sidewalk in the spotlight of a streetlamp. I shivered and leaned against a stone wall to keep myself upright as I was drawn farther and farther away from this moment with Oscar's searching eyes and hands, this moment tinged with regret, this moment in which I wasn't sure what I was doing here—here in this man's arms, here in the dark of Cali's night, here in Colombia.

We think of maps as infallible, as nonfiction. But they can be as fantastical as dreams. Atlantis, the Garden of Eden, El Dorado, Brigadoon. Each of these places had been rendered many times by cartographers in great detail. And yet none exist.

Oscar's mouth was near my ear, speaking words I couldn't quite hear or understand. Something didn't feel right. I squeezed my eyes shut.

I felt sick.

Vomiting is the body's response to rid itself of invaders, of pathogens, of infection. The violence of the spasms has no correlation with how much danger the body is in, how urgently it wants to purge the unknown. It has one goal: survival.

I managed to avoid Oscar's soft leather shoes, but I did get vomit on my own.

"¡Puta madre!" Oscar cried, almost levitating in his hurry to escape me.

When the concierge called to me as I crossed the hotel's foyer, I wanted nothing more than to ignore her. I wasn't sure where Oscar had gone, but I needed to get to my room and a cold shower, wash off the stink and mess.

"¡Señorita!"

I was weak and smelled noxious.

"¡Dolores!" the gray woman called again, her voice grating and angular. My stomach hurt, my head ached, the lobby tilted. But she wouldn't let me pass. "Permiso," she said. "Ha llegado su maleta."

My brain whirred, calculating and navigating, reaching for the translation. Maleta . . . There, on the floor beside the desk, was my Travelpro. Green and scuffed with its cardboard ID tag rumpled. I hefted it, rolled it on its clever little wheels. My suitcase.

Back in my room, sticky with sweat and vomit, I opened the suitcase. Margaret Moore's forever-young face smiled up at me from the silver frame, and I pulled it out, set it on the dresser. She looked at home here in this hotel in Cali. I pawed through the other items as stray cat hairs drifted on the air-conditioning's currents. My clean socks and underwear looked so fresh and new; the halter dress was so wrinkled, each fold was like a knife pleat. The leather straps of my sandals were dusty from last summer's walks. It was like digging through a time capsule.

CHAPTER 20

The Egyptians and the Babylonians, the Plains Indians and the Aztecs, the Chinese and the Greeks all created maps with themselves—the cartographers—at the very center. Not only do all early maps depict the mapmaker at the center, Earth is also always the focal point of the universe, the insignificant sun, moons, planets swirling around our impressive blue ball. A visual representation of the world literally revolving around you. Modern mapmakers try to adjust for this human need to put oneself in the center of the action, yet we still end up with Western projections that center North America or Europe. But the human desire to center ourselves doesn't reflect the world. That isn't how it works. In reality, Earth is a tiny speck in the universe, and even our universe is one of many.

A great feeling of insignificance washed over me as I vomited for the third—or fourth?—time that night. This wasn't the alcohol—although that couldn't have helped—because I hadn't actually had that many drinks; mostly the dancing had made me so thirsty, I downed bottles of water. It had to have been the street food—ice cream or maybe the repeated empanadas vallunas. I hadn't felt quite right ever since then and the thought of meat churned my stomach again.

(*Poor Dorrie*, murmured my chorus.)

Poor me, I thought. I laid my head on the cool floor of the hotel bathroom. The black-and-white tiles reminded me of something. Oh, yes. Ancient T-O maps, human's first graphical representation of place. Just a symbol really, a circle intersected by what looks like the letter *t*.

I woke later to the sun streaming through the window and the sound of housekeeping in the corridor. My fresh clothing was strewn about the room. I dragged myself to my feet and stuck the NO MOLESTAR sign on the knob. My mouth felt like wool, my stomach like a corset. My head pulsed. I climbed into bed.

Ping. A text from Becks woke me from a strange, fitful sleep that afternoon. A photo of an ultrasound.

Becks: Made it to 36 weeks!

I didn't know what I was looking at, the image all black and white and gray blobs, but I sent back a heart. I struggled to sit up in bed. The room still wouldn't stop spinning.

I'm sick, I typed. But I didn't click the send button. Did Becks need to know this? She would worry about me but be unable to help. I deleted the words.

I lay back. I could call Trina. There was a stack of unread messages from her, trying to get me to agree to go to another nightclub, another dinner, asking what locations I hadn't been to yet. But did it matter?

My mother's (which one?) hand-drawn map wasn't a representation of Cali; the only locations are those that were important to its cartographer. The rest of the city of Santiago de Cali had existed and would exist before and after me or my parents, even without its appearance on a thirty-five-year-old sketch. We are each of us simply specks, dots. From far away, we are indistinguishable.

Housekeeping had left me clean towels and extra bottles of water outside my door, and I took an experimental sip. It immediately sent me back to the bathroom.

I startled awake at a sound. A crash or a knock. It was my phone. Oscar? There had been no messages from him. I involuntarily shook my head, which my stomach didn't appreciate. I didn't need him; he couldn't help even if he wanted to.

Trina: Hope you're feeling better. Let us know when you're ready to go out dancing again!

I would never dance again, I thought.

(*Does she need a doctor?* worried the chorus.)

I was sure I didn't need a doctor. Not yet, anyway.

(*Or a nurse,* they said.)

I didn't need a nurse, but I could ask an EMT.

Dorrie: I'm sick.

This time I hit send.

Franklin's response was immediate.

Franklin: Symptoms?

I sent a puking emoji.

Dorrie: I think it's food poisoning?

My phone rang and the first thing he said when I answered it was, "How much vomiting?" His face was lined in concern.

I laughed weakly and my insides protested. "Hello to you too."

"Sorry, I get into medical mode." He chuckled. "You don't look so good, Dorrie."

"Hold on." I made it to the bathroom just in time. "Sorry. Did you hear all that?"

"It's fine," he said. "Nothing I haven't heard before." He asked about my symptoms; I told him about the empanadas and the ice cream and rum. Too much of everything. I didn't tell him about Oscar.

"And you've been sick since yesterday? And still vomiting? That seems like a long time to have food poisoning. Maybe it's a virus?" I told him I didn't feel feverish, just nauseous. "You look pale, so you definitely need fluids. As much as you can tolerate."

"That was my two sips of water."

"Bottled?"

"Of course."

"If this keeps going, you need to find a doctor."

(*That's what I said!*)

"Dehydration is the risk. But I'm sure you'll be fine."

My body relaxed at the sound of his certainty—even my stomach seemed to calm. There was a moment of silence, a comforting sense of someone listening, witnessing my existence.

(*She'll be fine*, said Elizabeth with equal certainty. *She has a sensitive stomach*, agreed Jane.)

Even though Franklin's face was still looking at me through the magic of signals and technology all the way from Minnesota, he suddenly seemed far away, and I felt—for just a moment—that it was only me with my mothers in this hotel room in Cali.

"They say I'll be fine," I murmured.

"Who?"

I never told anyone about my voices. Not my mothers, not my best friend. I always told Becks everything, but not that. I never tried to ask my moms again if they heard voices—I didn't want to go see Scottie. Voices in your head just wasn't something you wanted other people to know about.

But now the room rotated to the east, then the west. The purple feather of the colibrí was on the dresser, winking at me. "I hear my mom talking to me," I said quietly.

Franklin, thousands of miles away, waited.

"My moms, my grandmothers. They all speak to me. Well, *at* me."

I told him about the voices and the family members who have left me. Aunt Judith after her canoe capsized in freezing water; Grandma June after her broken hip and a long stay in a nursing home with pneumonia; Great-Aunt Maureen, the lifelong smoker, succumbed to lung cancer. I told him about Gigi in the Iowa house and about Grandma June. I told him about Aunt Dot—who was really Grandma June's cousin—and the stroke she had when I was in seventh grade. I told him about Elizabeth and I told him about Jane. And I told him that they each seemed to have something to say, nothing important maybe, but something.

"Grandpa Bao sometimes talks to my grandmother Jia," he said. "He talks as if she were in the room, and sometimes I almost believe it."

"I don't think anyone else hears them. Just me."

"That makes you special. They must have something special to say to you."

If they were trying to tell me something, I hadn't been listening. I had heard them all my life, but maybe I never really listened. I told him I felt crazy, but maybe it was just the Colombian air. I laughed uncomfortably. "You must think I'm certifiable."

"Hearing voices doesn't make you crazy." His voice was calm, soothing. "Who knows how it all works?" he added. "Have you heard of liminal spaces?"

I hadn't.

"They're places where life and death are close. Spaces where the veil between this life and the other lift and it all gets mixed up together. I see it at work on the worst calls. Have you ever watched someone at the moment they passed?"

I'm in the living room of the Victorian, swearing I'll come to Colombia, promising anything as Jane slips between one world and another, ready to agree to whatever she wants if she'll just stay on my side a bit longer. I'm watching Jane take her last breaths; I'm in the hospital room with Elizabeth; I'm at a funeral in my patent leather shoes and calico blouse, in my charcoal skirt and sensible heels. I keep on living.

"Then you know how mysterious the end of life is," Franklin said.

A breeze fluttered through my room from the open window in the bathroom and the feather drifted to the floor. "A hummingbird landed on me the other night," I said. I told him about the colibrí, but I still didn't mention Oscar. "There was a swarm of them, like a cloud of birds. All of them surrounding me."

"Do you know what a bunch of hummingbirds is called?"

"A flock?"

"That's geese."

"A herd?"

He laughed. "That's elephants. It's called a charm."

"A charm of hummingbirds?" I said, and the memory of the cloud of beating wings was so real I could almost feel the air currents. And I realized that that moment had nothing to do with Oscar; it was about magic and Colombia, about life and possibilities. It was about me.

"Sounds magical."

"It was almost as if they were speaking to me," I admitted. Then I laughed, a motion I felt in my queasy stomach. "Now I sound even more unhinged."

"It's not the existence of the voices, Dorrie," he said. "It's when you start acting on them—then you have to worry." He smiled, his eyes crinkling.

After I hung up, I lay back on the hotel bed, watching the ceiling fan rotate, thoughts of loss and family, birds and promises swirling.

1989
Cali, Colombia

Maggie had fallen asleep with her book in her lap, which she had begun to do frequently since entering the last half of her eighth month. The apartment was dark when she heard a pounding on her door.

"Juan Carlos?" she called, struggling to sit up. He and his family were due to arrive any moment, they were taking a taxi, he had said. She listened for the sputtering sound of a car's retreat. "Is that you, mi amor?"

"¿Señora?" It was the voice of Cristina. Then a tentative knock. "Disculpa, señora Margarita."

"Coming!" Maggie shouted. "Ya voy," she said, proud of her Spanish phrase. She hoisted herself out of bed and opened the door. "Where is Juan Carlos?" She peered beyond the slim form of the daughter into the dark stairwell.

"Come," was all Cristina said, and led her into the Rojas apartment downstairs, where the two women seated her in a stiff-backed dining chair.

It was already all over the news. An organized crime group had quickly claimed credit for the bombing. A flight bound for Cali, more than one hundred on board, although not the intended targets of the cartel. But Juan Carlos and his parents and his sister had been on it, the four of them.

There were no survivors.

"No, no," Maggie said over and over. "It's not true."

"It's on the radio," said Cristina. She was young but she had seen bad news delivered before, most people had. Kidnappings, bombings, accidents. These things happened.

"Así es la vida," said Doña Rojas, which sounded harsh to Maggie's ears. That's life. But that's not how the landlady meant it. She was thinking of the way Juan Carlos looked after this fair-haired American girl, the way he protected her and loved her. She was thinking of the adoration in Margarita's blue eyes as she watched every move of the young man. She knew love when she saw it. So life is tragedy, yes, but it is also love. "Así es la vida, querida."

Her belly felt heavy, her legs and feet were swollen, and her heart was broken. Doña Rojas bustled around Margaret, who would not—or could not—get out of bed. The dueña tried to get la niña to eat, to talk. "La bebé," the old woman would repeat. *La.* She too was certain the child would be a girl.

"Call your parents," said Cristina. She was only thirteen but kept watch over Margarita as if she were the aunt or the nurse. "My mamá says to call your family. Tell them to come."

But Maggie couldn't. There was too much story to tell, too many routes she had taken that they knew nothing of. She had asked about Juan Carlos's remaining family, but the only contact the landlady had was the parents, who were gone, too, and Maggie didn't even know where they lived in Bogotá or their second family name. She had wanted an adventure, Maggie thought bitterly, and now she had one. Alone with a baby on the way.

"Que Dios te bendiga," said Doña Rojas, making the sign of the cross and then laying a gentle hand on Maggie's belly.

—————

"There must be someone," Cristina said. She had brought pandebono, which Maggie couldn't choke down. "Isn't there anyone you can call?" the teenager, thin and petite, pleaded.

Even in the state she was in, Maggie felt sorry for this frightened girl who had somehow become her caretaker. So, through the fog of her grief, she decided. Janie. She would call her big sister Jane and ask her to come. She followed Cristina downstairs, and when she phoned from Doña Rojas's foyer, she told Jane she would explain everything when she arrived. "Please come. I need you. But don't tell Mom and Dad." She didn't know how she would ever be able to make her parents understand. "Not yet."

When Jane arrived via taxi from the airport—the way Juan Carlos should have—she found that her baby sister was huge, her belly as big as a July watermelon.

"Why didn't you tell us?" asked Jane. She wanted to scold her. But when Margaret began shaking, her face turning red, Jane could do nothing more than lie down beside her sister in the little one-room apartment and hold her.

Little by little, Maggie told her sister what had happened, at least in broad strokes. They met in Rome, they moved to Cali, he had died in a plane crash, she would have his baby.

"But why didn't you tell us? Or at least me? You could have told me," said Jane. They were pacing the tiny apartment. Maggie had a sore back and movement helped.

"Dad would have wanted me to come home. Mom would have convinced me. I know what she would say: You can't have a baby in a third-world country. But I love it here, it's home. And Juan Carlos—" Her voice caught. "This is his home. This is *my* home."

Jane looked around the tiny apartment with its bare mattress and two coffee cups and wished she could see whatever her sister saw in this place, whatever magic she felt.

"I could have come earlier, Mags," she insisted. "I could have come over Thanksgiving break, you know I'm on break from teaching, I could have helped you get ready for the baby. Me and Elizabeth both. We could have come sooner."

"It wouldn't have changed anything," said Maggie.

CHAPTER 21

Colombia had always meant the colorful weavings that Elizabeth had made into throw pillows and the heavy wool blankets at the foot of the bed. Colombia had been the blurry photo of me as a baby held by a woman even blurrier. Colombia had been the coffee-table book that my mothers kept in the living room whose pages were filled with glossy photos of green jungles and auburn dirt roads. But here, now, was the real Cali—or as real as it could be for an American tourist. It wasn't imaginary, it wasn't trite. This place was pulsing with people: two taxis going opposite directions, a woman pushing a stroller, a group of teenagers lighting cigarettes. And me.

I hadn't had any breakfast, but after spending almost two days in bed, I was beginning to feel better. I had been able to drink more and more water, and last night I ordered an herbal tea and a few slices of bread from the restaurant.

(*Tea and toast,* the chorus had advised, much as they had done when I was a child.)

And now I was determined to go back to calle 5 Norte. Something about my illness and the charm of hummingbirds and life's transience. *I don't know how you'll ever find that apartment, that lovely little apartment. There was a mango tree,* Jane had said. From the hotel bed, every time I closed my eyes I had seen the brick facade of the building, and I dreamed about the empty peluquería. In the middle of the night, I thought I heard a voice calling for Margarita, but when I looked out the window, all was dark and I knew I had been dreaming. I needed to give that spot on the map one more shot, one more chance to prove to me why it was so important to Jane for me to visit. As I passed the young people, the smoke circled me, made my stomach rise. I coughed and hurried away.

"Buenos días," a woman said, nodding at me. She was maybe in her late forties or early fifties. Streaks of silver veined her dark hair and she wore a striped peplum blouse with jeans.

"Buenos días."

The woman smiled. "American?" she asked.

I nodded. Again, it was clear that I wasn't a Colombian, that I was a foreigner. Despite what Oscar had said, this woman knew I didn't belong.

"I like your dress," she said in accented English.

The dress, still wrinkled from my suitcase, was simple white linen, buttons up the front, cool and comfortable.

(*She looks lovely in white,* said Gigi. *About time she changed clothes,* said Great-Aunt Maureen.)

"Gracias," I said, trying out my Spanish again, hoping to get it right, hoping to get *something* right. "That's a beautiful building," I said, pointing across the street. "Do you know anything about it?"

"Yes, I own that building." She stopped her sweeping and leaned the broom against the doorjamb.

"You own it?" My hands began to tremble.

"Yes, I inherited it, the old thing."

"My m-m-mother lived there." That word, those *m*'s. Mother. Jane. Elizabeth. Margaret Moore. Who got the title when it was in the singular?

"¡Chévere!" she exclaimed. "My mother Doña Rojas owned it before me. She surely knew your mother. My name is Cristina. Cristina Rojas Vargas."

"Nice to meet you." I looked across the street. "Do you live there? Are there apartments?"

"Oh no," said Cristina. "Not for many years. I live here now. But I can show you the building. Would you like to come?"

I followed her across the street, and we entered through the peluquería, which she unlocked with a key from a large ring. The smell of perm solution and antiseptic spray bombarded us as we passed through the back of the abandoned shop through a door that opened, like magic, into a courtyard, overlooked by tiny balconies above. Which one was apartment B? The words on the map swirled in my mind and I felt weak. The apartment. Margaret Moore's apartment. My parents' apartment. My empty stomach churned and I wished I had been able to eat this morning.

"It needs work," said Cristina. The bricks were broken in places, some splattered in moss. A shutter was halfway off its hinges and a coating of bird droppings carpeted the stone floor. A gnarled tree stood sentry in the space, small green fruit dangling from the highest branches. "This hasn't been a home for anyone for many years," she said. "When did your mother live here?"

"Thirty-five years ago."

Cristina invited me to her home and I followed her and her rattling keys back across the street. In a small living room, the shelves were crowded with knickknacks and photos. She insisted I sit on the low red sofa and brought me coffee in a cup and saucer with a delicate blue floral pattern.

(*Lovely china*, murmured Grandma June.)

She held out a bowl of sugar, matching, which I declined, and then she seated herself opposite me and scooped three spoonfuls of sugar into her own cup, stirring as I explained my connection to the building.

"She was young," I said. Cristina nodded when I paused, the only sounds the clinking of her spoon against the porcelain and the breeze through an open window.

"What did she look like, your mother?"

"Not like me. She was blond, had feathered, wispy hair, small eyes, pale skin." I pulled the framed photo of Margaret Moore from my bag. "She was American. And she had a boyfriend from here? Juan Carlos, that's all I know."

Even before Cristina looked at the photo, she let out a yelp, her coffee cup clattering in its saucer. "You! You're the baby."

I was the baby.

(*Such a chubby baby*, Jane said.)

"You're Dolores."

My coffee grew cold as Cristina Rojas Vargas described for me my unknown past, my beginning, or at least some version of it.

"What a tragedy," she kept repeating.

When Margaret Moore first moved into the second-floor one-room apartment, she hadn't been noticeably pregnant, Cristina said. But soon even a thirteen-year-old could recognize the meaning of the bulging stomach. "And of course I was fascinated by them, this pregnant American and her handsome husband, Juan Carlos de la Peña from Bogotá."

Juan Carlos de la Peña. I churned the words in my head like rocks in a tumbler, as if I could make them smooth, shiny, recognizable. A surname. A full name. A name not mine, not my mothers'. Someone else, someone new. A stranger. A father.

"I was thirteen and I thought they were the most beautiful couple. She was so fair and he was so dark. He always held her around the waist like he was afraid something would happen to her or the baby." Cristina picked up the frame and studied my mother's face. "I had a crush on him," she said with a slight blush.

The man had to travel often, she wasn't sure why. Perhaps he had family somewhere else or a job. Doña Rojas tried to keep an eye on the young woman, especially as she got later into her pregnancy and developed horribly swollen feet, so tender she could barely walk.

"My mother would sometimes send me to the market to buy milk and bread for La Niña, as she called your mother. Look, I have one of her photos." Cristina leaped up and handed me one of the picture frames from her crowded shelves. It was a black-and-white image of an old woman with interesting features. "My mother, but the American took it."

I stared at the photo and tried to imagine Margaret Moore snapping the shutter.

"Poor woman. I would use the master key to let myself in and leave the food in her kitchen, because she was often resting. She was still so lovely, even swollen and pregnant. I didn't look anything like that when *I* was pregnant with my two boys." Cristina smiled and I could picture her as a younger woman, maybe even see her as a thirteen-year-old, the girl my birth mother, Margaret Moore, had known.

Then, in November—no one forgets the date, Cristina said—there was the plane crash.

"You know, 1989 was the worst year in Colombian history, everybody still says so."

Juan Carlos had been on the flight, she told me, coming back from Bogotá, when it went down. The most infamous plane crash in history up until then. "A bomb on board," Cristina said.

I had known that my father had died, but a bomb? I couldn't hold the idea of that kind of violence in my head at the same time as the Colombia I had seen. Laughing friends and art museums and mango trees.

A fire near the fuselage of the 727, Cristina explained, and the plane went down, killing everyone on board and several more on the ground. "The cartel," she whispered.

The information exploded, revealing in its wake the times I had defended my birth country, insisting it was safe and not to listen to the biased news reports, the stereotypes. But even a stereotype can be born out of reality.

"That young wife—" Cristina's voice cracked. "I think my mother felt responsible for La Niña after the plane crash. It was everybody's tragedy."

When people think of a place without trouble—no violence or poverty or inequality—they often conjure the idea of a utopia. I had thought, I supposed, that Colombia would be that for me. The location where everything—the pieces of me—would finally fall into place. My past, my life, my future. All questions answered, all doubts quelled. But the word *utopia* literally means "no place." There is no place like that, no place without suffering, without pain. You cannot find it on a map, you cannot navigate your way there. Utopia does not, by definition, exist. It is no place.

"I have to go to work now," Cristina said suddenly, clearing away my coffee cup and tucking her mother's portrait back on the shelf.

Now? She couldn't leave now. Cristina's living room came back into focus, the events of 1989 fading away. I felt disoriented, like I didn't quite know where I was. Panicked bile rose in my throat. "You have to go?"

"I teach English at a night school. I have thirty businessmen waiting for me."

"Your English is amazing," I said politely, but my head spun.

"But come back, Dolores," she said, perhaps sensing my panic. "Can you come back? I'll be home tomorrow morning and we can talk more."

She was being so kind to me, a stranger, so I nodded and said of course and told her I would return tomorrow at ten. But that felt like years, eons away. I needed to know what happened.

As I walked back to the hotel from calle 5 Norte, the city seemed to pulse and vibrate around me. I felt queasy thinking about my father— Juan Carlos de la Peña—dying a horrible death in a plane crash, a senseless crash. I paused, caught my breath, as tears began to stream down my cheeks. My mother—two of my mothers—had walked these streets and witnessed these buildings, these trees, looked up at this sky. I pictured the blond Margaret Moore as she looked in her photo. I pictured Mama as she looked when I was a child, with her pixie cut and a flowing blouse and sneakers with wide toes. Even though Elizabeth hadn't been here, I saw her, too, in overalls and Birkenstocks, her hands dirty from painting the hallway or gardening or cooking. I let the three of them walk beside me as I wandered toward the river, that landmark.

By the time I made it to the water, my feet were blistered from the sandals I had unpacked, and my eyes felt gritty. A few mothers pushed strollers with small children and an elderly couple walked arm in arm along a sidewalk. I turned to the right to follow them, a peaceful promenade of city dwellers. There was no hint today of any past violence or unrest. A bomb. It didn't seem possible that a place as beautiful as this—with its lush trees and shocks of color—could harbor heartbreak and evil.

To the right, I came upon a statue of a cat. Large and proud, the cat stood twenty feet tall, the terra-cotta orange of iron with twirly whiskers and a self-satisfied expression I recognized from Bojangles after he has licked out a cereal bowl. I listened for commentary from the chorus, but all I heard was a bit of faint static. The sculpture was warm to the touch, the metal heated by the tropical sun. I stroked the cat's paw as if it were real—what did I know of real? Beyond the large sculpture I saw more colorful but smaller statues, one with yellow legs, a striped body, and jewels for eyes. A few paces ahead, there was another statue, this cat glittery and purple with black spots and red lips, and it made me think of Bojangles and Django in Franklin's house. No, in Grandpa Bao's house. I was glad they weren't alone in the Victorian. I knew how lonely the house could feel, despite the quips about "alone, not lonely." My mothers would have loved this museum of cats, I could see them each selecting their favorites, perhaps arguing over which design was the best, which I would prefer. As the path turned, I found a placard that said the main sculpture was titled *El Gato del Río*, donated to the city by the artist Hernando Tejada in 1996, and the park around it was now called parque El Gato de Tejada, after the sculptor. I would have been a little girl then, and I imagined us here walking the way we used to—three abreast, me in the center, the anchor. What had kept us away? I would never know, just like I would never know many things about the people who were gone. They might chatter, but they never answered any questions.

I inhaled and the humid air caught in my throat. A bomb, Cristina had said. Maybe I didn't want too many answers. The cartel. I couldn't even imagine what those words meant. Even though she spoke clear English, they felt foreign, incomprehensible, and made me feel my American half grow. Was I really Colombian if I didn't understand these words? I wiped my eyes on my dress and walked among the cat sculptures, and when I came to the end, I walked back again, studying each one. Different artists had designed each of the smaller statues, some with deeper meanings, others more flippant. The same basic shape—a cat shape—but each one distinct, a surprise of color and texture. The sculptures made me think of us humans. We have the same basic human shape—arms and legs, brains and hearts—but we're completely unique with our own personalities and stories and pasts.

Maggie's sister hovered, asked how she was, made quiet but annoying noises in the makeshift kitchen of the apartment. She stayed at a hotel during the night but showed up every morning at dawn, ready to give Maggie pitying looks.

"Are you sure you don't know his family's address? The name of his shop? Anything?"

Maggie knew her sister was just trying to help, but the questions—so many questions—were why she hadn't told her family anything. She tried to be nice, to appreciate her sister's care, but she just wanted Juan Carlos back. And she wanted to cry, to weep great tears, but had been unable to from the moment she found out Juan Carlos wasn't coming back. Maybe it was the shock or the pregnancy or the smell of mangos, but she couldn't. Now she tried to conjure tears but was suddenly gripped by a pain she'd never felt before. It shook her body like an angry spirit. She let out a howl and collapsed to her knees.

"Are you having the baby now?" Jane didn't know what to do. Despite being an overeducated feminist, she knew nothing about childbirth. She also spoke no Spanish and was terrified of admitting how terrified she was. She was useless. She would have done anything to help her little sister.

Maggie stood up, breathed heavily, and then howled again. Now, as contractions gripped her body, she leaned into the pain hoping it would elicit tears. Instead she went silent. Like a tragic heroine in a book, she was unable to weep. She moaned.

"¿Señora?" The apartment door opened and Cristina was there. "We heard Margarita. My mamá says she's on her way."

After hours or days or months of pacing the apartment with the help and guidance of Doña Rojas, Jane insisted it was time to go to the hospital. She didn't know much about childbirth, but she knew she didn't want her baby sister having this child on the floor of this tiny apartment. She should be in a hospital; this she knew.

The infant—a healthy girl as Margaret had guessed and Doña Rojas had known—was born in the hospital after ten hours of labor.

She came out silent and alert. And then the baby took her first deep breath and let out a cry that struck both sisters deep in their marrow. The baby cried for the shock of being born, and the mother cried—at last—for the shock of being alive. And as soon as the baby's tears came, so did Maggie's. She and the baby wept.

"She looks just like Juan Carlos," Maggie said when the baby had fallen asleep at her breast, and her own tears had calmed, and she could breathe again.

Jane marveled at the tiny face, the clawlike hands, the black hair. "She's prettier than you were when you were born," said Jane fondly. She remembered Margaret's birth as the most exciting thing that had happened in her first eleven years—maybe her whole life up until now. She had adored her baby sister from the first time she saw her.

"How did you learn to change a diaper like that?" Maggie asked as her sister changed the little thing in preparation for leaving the hospital. On each attempt, she had so far fumbled the plastic diapers and usually ended up with baby goop on her hands.

"I had practice—with you. I don't think Dad changed a single one of your diapers, thanks to me."

"You should have a baby someday," Margaret said. "You'd be a great mom, probably better than I'll ever be."

When the doctor filled out the birth certificate, Margaret declined to include Juan Carlos's name and left "padre" blank. She entered Moore for the baby's last name. "I don't even know his full name. They have two last names here, you know," she said. "And his family is gone—I'm her family, all she's got."

"I'm here too," said Jane. A promise.

Dolores, she named the baby, after her own middle name, the most obvious choice. "Did you know that Dolores is a Spanish name?" she asked Jane.

"Really? I think you got your middle name from some great-grandmother on Dad's side. But that's neat. What does it mean?"

They didn't have a dictionary handy, didn't know. And if they had, maybe they would have chosen something else.

The first week home with the baby was hard. After being unable to cry, Maggie suddenly found herself weeping every time the baby cried, like a switch had been flipped. She cried for her fatherless daughter and she cried for Juan Carlos and everything that could have been. As many times a day as an infant cries, that's how much Maggie cried.

Jane, who since the baby had arrived had only been back to her hotel to shower and catch a quick nap, kept trying to convince Maggie that she should come home, back to Minnesota, where she would have support raising a child on her own.

"*This* is my home," she insisted. Dolores was on her back on the unmade bed, arms flailing. When the baby was content, Maggie's tears magically dried and she knew she had to get on with it. "Cali is home."

"But you know no one here."

"I know the landlady and her daughter. And the woman who sells bread in the market. That's three people."

Jane shook her head as she picked up the baby and changed Dolores out of her wet onesie. "That's not family. A child needs to be surrounded by family. People who love her. As many as possible." Jane didn't realize she believed this until she said it aloud. But she had been surrounded by people who loved her—even if she was in the closet, she knew they were right outside the door. And now she wanted her baby niece to have the same thing. She already loved this infant more than she thought it was possible to love anyone.

"If I leave Colombia, what will my daughter know of her origins? An entire half of her is Colombian."

"You can't be a whole half, Mags," Jane pointed out.

"You know what I mean."

"She's American too. Half you. Half Moore. Don't forget."

"This baby is Colombian."

CHAPTER 22

I woke up several times that night to check the time, afraid I would oversleep and miss my appointment with Cristina. I knew how generous it was that she was inviting me to her home again, taking time out of her day to talk to me. I didn't know if *I* would do it if I were her, if I had that kind of generosity in me. I had always been so reserved, so used to the sidelines, to watching and listening. I rarely offered help or gave of myself, perhaps too worried about whether I would do it right or not.

There was no way for Cristina to do this wrong. I wanted to hear the rest of her story so badly, and I had also found something soothing about her presence. Maybe it was that courtyard that Jane had remembered so well. As I walked toward calle 5 Norte, I could already smell the mango—although that might have been the scent of this city, always growing and producing, giving.

I had taken extra time with my appearance, so relieved that I had the luxury of a whole suitcase to choose from. I pulled out another sundress and hung it in the bathroom while I showered to try to erase the wrinkles the way Aunt Judith had taught me.

"If you don't have an iron *for some reason*," she had said in a way that made it sound like not having an iron was a true emergency, "you just pop the blouse on a hanger and hang it from the shower rod in a steamy bathroom." I had been about twelve at the time and the word "steamy" made me giggle. As the creases fell out of the dress, I was surprised I didn't hear her voice saying some version of "I told you so." I listened but heard nothing and pulled on my sneakers (too many blisters) to set out for the apartment again. *Home*, as it was labeled on the map.

"Your mother was—how do you say? She was devastated."

Cristina had picked up the story exactly where she had left off. We were in her living room again, with cups of strong coffee stirred with sugar like the previous day. She had a basket lined with a paper napkin containing a pile of pastries, little breads. "Pandebono," she explained as I bit into one. "Your mother loved them when she was pregnant with you."

I stopped chewing. This tidbit, this little piece of knowledge, was like magic, an unexpected gift. To know something about my birth mother, the person to whom I was most closely, most genetically related. I felt a chill even though the heavy Cali humidity hung in the air.

A few days after the crash, Cristina told me, Margaret began acting strange, even for a woman in mourning. "I had brought her a bag of chontaduros—she was craving the salt—and when I let myself into the apartment, la rubia was wailing. Por Dios, she was inconsolable. Crying with no tears. I'd never seen anything like it in my life."

I thought of my own dry eyes at Jane's funeral. What kept the tears inside? What let them out?

"My mother worried about the baby coming, and she made

Margarita call home, get help. She eventually called her sister—is that your aunt, right?"

I nodded. Aunt; mother.

I pictured the phone ringing in the Victorian, maybe Jane answered it from the kitchen, pulling on the yellow cord, winding it around her wrist. The line would have been crackly, the sound muted and warbled. During the era of geosynchronous communication satellites, they each would have heard delays as their voices were translated into signals sent into space and back again. When she finally understood what her baby sister was saying, Jane would have wanted to tell their parents, but she had told me that Maggie asked her not to, and Mama always kept her promises. So she and Elizabeth would have discussed the trip, making decisions about flights and how much money it would cost and if this was the right thing to do.

"She arrived just in time for the birth. We sent them in a taxi to the hospital."

Cristina didn't see much of the women the first week after they came home with the baby. She heard tiny infant cries, and in the middle of the night, the floorboards above her bedroom would creak with the pacing of a new mother soothing a baby.

"I saw the sister—your aunt—leave with the baby in a sling on her back, the kind los indígenas use to carry their babies. My mother wanted to give her the stroller she had used for me and my brothers, but she insisted she liked the sling. My mother thought that was very strange." Cristina laughed. "But now you see many women carry their infants that way."

I pictured Jane walking along the streets toward the river with me strapped to her back. I imagined that Margaret Moore might have drawn the map during those days, leaving breadcrumbs for her sister, showing her the way. Jane would have walked to the Museo, to La Ermita, or maybe just along the river, where the sounds and smells lodged in my infant's memory.

"We wept again when the news came that they had recovered the bodies. Well, my mother and I cried, even the sister, but not Margarita. She still could not weep. I will never forget her vacant face."

Cristina's eyes shone with tears. It must have been traumatic for a young girl of thirteen to witness such events, to see a young woman suffer the way Margaret Moore must have suffered. Even though Cristina was older than me, I felt suddenly protective of her, as if she were still that teenager.

"After the baby was born and her sister arrived, I never saw Margarita leave the apartment again. But one day," Cristina continued, "your aunt went out with the baby strapped to her back, returned, and began shouting, crying." Her voice grew rough, jagged, and I could feel my eyeballs pulsing, the tears collecting behind them. "I had just come home from school and I was so happy because a boy I liked had given me a candy. But then," she said.

I already knew the ending to this story. This was *my* story, after all. My legend.

"I knew something very bad had happened."

Jane was hysterical, unable to communicate what was wrong, Cristina said. She followed her back to the apartment, where they found Doña Rojas with Margarita. They handed Cristina the baby.

The baby. Me.

"I held the baby—you—for the next five or six hours. You were so quiet, as if you knew your life had changed. Because I was busy with you, I didn't see them take your mother out on a stretcher or try to revive her, but my mamá talked about it her whole life. First the plane crash, then the mother. Such a tragedy."

"I'm so sorry," I said, even though it was my tragedy too.

In cartography, mapmakers have always had to wrestle with the different ways humans think and interpret information, how one person's up is another person's down, all depending on perspective. The loss of Juan Carlos—the plane bombing—was a tragedy to his family but also the country, and the death of Margaret was a loss for the Moores but also for the apartment building on calle 5 Norte. And of course they were my tragedies too, but there was more to the story. Without the loss of these two people, Jane and Elizabeth would never have become my mothers, we would never have become a family, a triad of women. I wasn't sure if it was true, but they had always told me that they knew they would—somehow—become mothers, that they had been waiting for me. Endings and beginnings were tied up in intricate knots, impossible to untangle.

Cristina and I sat in silence, both of us with tears streaming down our faces. She reached across the table and gripped my hand until her knuckles turned white.

1989
Cali, Colombia

If you were aware that talking to the dead was crazy, Margaret Moore told herself in those following weeks, then you must not be crazy. And, anyway, she couldn't stop herself. Whenever Jane left the apartment, she would curl up in the armchair and imagine that she was sitting on his lap, her back pressed against his chest like they had been all those months ago during the blackout. She had been frightened of the dark then, but now the electricity cuts didn't even register. Everything was darkness. Even though sun streamed through the window, Maggie felt weighed down and she lit the candle Doña Rojas had brought her the day after the terrible news. The old woman didn't cry with her and didn't tell her everything would be all right. She lit the vela.

"Tienes a tu hija," Doña Rojas had said. Your daughter.

Our daughter, Maggie had thought at the time.

"You will never be alone." The landlady had set the candle on the windowsill, the smoke billowing out of the apartment like a cleansing.

Later Maggie spoke aloud to the silent candle, the empty room. "I promise that Dolores will never be alone, either."

Although the baby had diluted his belongings somewhat, everything in the apartment reminded her of him. The postcard from Rome hung above the bed, the photo gallery she had made for him, the basket beside the window with his paperwork, and his worn leather slippers lined up near the door as if he were about to step into them again. But the coffee funnel had been set aside to make room for the bottles, his emptied dresser drawer had become a makeshift bassinet, and the sheets now smelled of newborn, not his cologne.

She tucked her feet underneath her as the baby fussed and then quieted. Through the apartment's walls she could hear a song playing on the radio, a popular tune that she heard a lot, one that Juan Carlos had tried to teach her.

"It's about singing," he had translated. "Singing and being together. Like us: we'll always be together." He had sung along at the time, and she had been surprised by his deep baritone as she caught words like *peace* and *whole world* and *forever*. The baby in her stomach had flipped and flopped at his voice and he brought his face close to her taut skin. "The song will make a good lullaby."

"You'll spoil our child, won't you?" she had teased. "You'll let her play all the time, never make her do chores for her poor mother."

"We'll have a baby muy contemplada," he had said.

The melody drifted and Maggie closed her eyes. Juan Carlos's voice sang to their daughter, and it sounded so real, so alive. But it was probably just the music coming through the window or the baby's sleepy coos.

The candle's flame flickered. She could imagine his laughter. At least she told herself it was imagined, because otherwise she really was going crazy.

Maggie leaned her cheek against the worn upholstery of the armchair and she swore she could feel his heartbeat.

Maggie wasn't feeling well and the baby seemed restless. Neither had slept, even after Doña Rojas appeared at the apartment's door with a bundle of herbs. "A sage smudge," whispered Jane as they watched the old woman snake the scented smoke into the corners of the room and around the unmade bed.

"Para quitar el aire malo."

Maggie had simply nodded, a headache building in her temples that was not helped by the astringent smell. That night the baby had slept—so perhaps the brujería had worked—but the mother had not. Even in the silence of the apartment, she could still hear the baby's breathing, a sound filled with gurgles and sighs that disrupted her as she was about to finally fall asleep. Juan Carlos had always slept like a vampire, on his back, arms folded, still. She hadn't known how restless, how noisy, an infant could be in her sleep.

"Let me take her out, give her some fresh air," Jane offered when she came back from a short break at her hotel. She had arrived with a few supplies—more diapers, a can of formula—that she had bought with the help of Cristina and had found her sister talking to herself, alone in the apartment, curled in the armchair again—always in that spot by the window—as if she were waiting for a bus that never came. It was surely sleep deprivation that gave her that faraway look in her eyes and those mumbled words. "You need some rest."

The new mother was too exhausted to object. Her head pounded like the sound of nails in the tree house Dad had built her when she was seven. Dolores's fussy breathing as her diaper was changed sounded like rush-hour traffic on Interstate 35. She felt a pain as if she had a stitch in her side like the ones she used to get when playing tag across the playground. She closed her eyes, wondering why she was flashing to moments of her childhood, times that she hadn't thought about for so long they didn't even feel like her memories. Her memories were filled with nothing but Juan Carlos. His smile that day in the piazza, his laughter as he ordered more tahini at the restaurant de los árabes, the way he reached for her in his sleep and clung to her.

"You can take my map," she found the strength to say. But as she opened Juan Carlos's map, the softened paper ripped along the folds, the whole thing coming apart in her hands. Bits fluttered to the floor, the circled locations, the pencil-lined routes. Her breath felt forced and broken. It was as if Juan Carlos had died all over again.

"This—" She gasped for air. "This was his."

Shredded roadways and rivers littered the apartment floor. The baby began to cry.

"I have nothing of his." Margaret had no choice but to sob.

Jane knelt beside her sister, rocking Dolores in one arm as she calmed Margaret. "You have her. She is his. The two of you made this beautiful thing."

The three of them—sisters and infant—stayed crumpled together for a long time, each silent, each with her own thoughts.

But as babies do, Dolores eventually began to fuss, her tiny pink mouth working itself into a desperate and hungry O. The aunt bounced her while warming a bottle of formula on the pan that was at the ready on the hot plate. She switched on the kettle; she needed a cup of coffee.

Maggie watched as Jane quieted the infant with a bottle. Both of them sighed at the relief, but not Maggie. The baby's cries still echoed in her head and made her blood vessels pulse. Her sister was right: she needed Jane to take the baby out. "I'll draw you a map," she said. "Do you have any paper?"

Jane handed her a pad of stationery from the hotel and a pencil with its logo etched on the side. Maggie fitted the pieces of Juan Carlos's ripped map together and quickly drew a rough outline of the neighborhood on the stationery, marking the spots she thought Janie would like.

"How long are you expecting me to be gone?" Jane asked, sipping her hot coffee as she watched her sister write in her familiar block printing.

"You don't have to go to all these places today, but you should see them—they're the places I visited with Juan Carlos or the ones he told me to see. The baby should see them too." She glanced at her daughter in her sister's arms and felt like she needed to promise them something. "We can go together when I feel better."

"I love that idea, Mags."

"Yes," Maggie said, more to herself than Jane. "We'll bring Dolores to the zoo together. So don't go there today." She added the apartment's location to the drawing and showed it to her sister, who set down her mug, spilling on the map.

"I won't go without you," promised Jane, kissing her niece's downy-soft head.

"Remember the hospital? That's over here." Margaret Moore tapped the hospital with the pencil lead. "If you end up there, you've gone the wrong way."

Jane strapped the baby to her back. "I'll follow your instructions exactly."

CHAPTER 23

Geography, my professor Dr. Foster would say, comes from the Greek word *graphe*. "To describe," he would say. "To describe the land. That's geography." As undergraduates, we would shift in our uncomfortable auditorium seats, knowing he was working up to a long lecture. "Maps let us visualize the world when—and *only* when—they describe it accurately."

I had just come back to my room after breakfast, where I had managed a few bites of rice and scrambled eggs. My mind was spinning with everything Cristina had told me, with images of the apartment on calle 5 Norte, Jane coming to the rescue, the terrible result. I hadn't slept much, just tossed and turned. Last night, Oscar invited me out for a drink and Franklin asked how I was feeling and sent me a picture of Django sleeping on Grandpa Bao's bed, but I didn't answer either of them. Trina and whoever else were coming to take me to San Antonio today before they left on their trip to the coffee region.

"One last stop on your map," Trina had insisted when she called me last night.

The hand-drawn map of Cali, Colombia, with its locations carefully labeled, would have met Dr. Foster's approval. It accurately depicted this city and, more important, my history in it. This map told a story in the way that the best maps do. This was the story, however partial, of my beginnings. La Ermita church with its plaque, the romance of a modern art museum, the nostalgia of calle 5 Norte. And now I knew why the hospital was on the map. It was all there.

"I'll pick you up around ten," she said, and then told me a funny story about Andrés.

I didn't really listen, but I agreed to go with my new friends to the next spot on the map because I didn't know what else to do. I couldn't imagine repeating out loud everything I had learned from Cristina; I didn't even know how to—*what* to—think about it all. The map, at least, provided some kind of direction.

A knock startled me. For a moment I had no idea where I was or what day it was.

"Dorrie!" called a voice.

I hadn't had a morning nap since grad school. The knocking started again.

"Dolores?"

I opened the door to find Trina standing in the corridor. "You didn't come down or answer my text. You okay?"

"Fine, yes." I yawned. "Just a little tired."

"We're going to Sunday lunch and then to San Antonio." Trina grinned. "Meet me downstairs in ten minutes?"

"Oh, I don't know, Trina. I'm not feeling up to it."

"Get dressed. We'll go to my favorite spot that serves really good food near the church. It's an adorable traditional neighborhood, you'll love it. And don't worry. Just me and Seb, and Andrés. They'll meet us there." She sat on my rumpled bed. "No Oscar."

"Oscar?"

"Well, I assumed you two . . ." she began. My face burned. She laughed. "No regrets, right? I never regret an experience."

"Oh, me neither," I said, although I was filled with regrets. But luckily not about Oscar.

"You have to take it all in—the good, the bad, the good in bed." She raised one eyebrow. "I assume he was good in bed?"

"Trina!" I threw a damp towel at her. "Me and Oscar? Never happened."

"Ah. Well. Either way, he wouldn't have come because Oscar prefers restaurants that serve foreign food, not these local places. He loves sushi."

At the mention of sushi, I moaned and beelined to the bathroom. When I came back, I plopped on the bed before I could make a fool of myself and fall.

"Wait, Dorrie, you're not—"

"What?"

She stood up and laid a hand on my forehead. Her perfume was overwhelming.

"You're not pregnant, are you?" she asked. "I was pukey like that my first trimester."

The faucet dripped. I remembered telling Franklin the story of Saint Isidore's drops of water on stone, great progress through small steps. "Exactly," he had said as we raked leaves in the yard of the Victorian. "You need to take it slow, in small steps."

Small steps. Get on with it.

Trina had insisted on taking me to a pharmacy.

"This is ridiculous," I had protested.

"You never know," was all Trina had said.

Now I was waiting.

"Do you want me to come up?" she asked when she brought me back to the hotel.

"No," I said. "Tell Seb and Andrés I'm sorry to miss lunch. I think I'd rather be alone."

Alone, not lonely.

I set the timer on my phone and sat on the bathroom floor, the black-and-white pattern reminding me again of the T-O map Isidore of Seville included in *Etymologies.* The symbol was meant to represent Christianity: a cross. Jerusalem is at the center of the cross, the center of the world, middle of the O. I ran my finger along one of the crosses on the tiles. Separated by the T or cross are the three continents—Europe, Asia, Africa—the truth as he understood it at the time. What was my truth?

My phone pinged. I reached for the test, but it wasn't the timer.

Becks: Can you call me?

"What's the matter?" I asked. Becks was saying words that didn't make any sense. Bleeding. Too much. Risks. Emergency room. The doctors were moving up the C-section, trying to wait until she hit thirty-seven weeks, but keeping her at the hospital just in case. As I listened, my phone chimed again, but I closed my fist around the stick without looking.

"Three more days," she said, teary. "If my body can just hold on to this baby for three more days."

"I'm changing my flight. I'll be there."

"No, Dorrie, I'll be fine. Charlie's here, my mother is flying in tomorrow."

"Becks—"

"Don't cut your trip short for me." I could hear her words, but her voice said something else. Becks and I had been friends since we were playing in sandboxes and dressing up in our mothers' high heels. She was the only person alive who knew me when I was young, a child—other than, I realized, Cristina Rojas Vargas.

"I'm coming," I said firmly, the way Trina insisted I let her help with the hotel, my luggage, the map. "I'll be in California as soon as the airlines will get me there."

Trina loaded my Travelpro into the back of the little blue car the next day after arguing with the gray señora to refund a portion of my unused nights. I had managed to get a flight through Houston and then on to San Francisco. It was so early, the sun hadn't yet peeked over the mountains surrounding Cali's valley, and the glow of streetlights reminded me of my first impression of this place, all dark and shadowy and full of mystery—and a little possibility.

"What a difficult time for your friend," Trina said. "She doesn't know me, but tell her I'm thinking of her."

The roads were nearly empty, just a few trucks and motorcycles buzzing here and there beneath the trees that hung over the wide road that ran through endless fields of sugarcane. The cane, really just blades of grass at this point, waved as if seeing me off, as if saying goodbye to me, a native daughter. I listened for the voices but all I heard was the rumble of the little blue car as Trina sped away from Cali. As we approached the Alfonso Bonilla Aragón International Airport, the sky turned pink and I told her how grateful I was for everything she had done.

"You'll have to come back," she said. "You haven't seen all the spots on your treasure map."

It was true, and yet I had found a treasure already. Trina and her friends had showed me my birth city, Oscar and the colibrí had shown me a bit of magic, the river cats had let me glimpse myself and my mothers here, and Cristina Rojas Vargas had given me a piece of my past.

Trina pulled up to the curb and hefted my Travelpro out of the trunk. She hugged me tightly. "And." She paused. "What about the test?"

PART THREE

SAN FRANCISCO, CALIFORNIA

San Francisco, California, is situated at the end of the San Francisco Peninsula in Northern California. Covering 46.9 square miles (121 square kilometers), it is surrounded by three bodies of water: the San Francisco Bay to the east, the Golden Gate Strait to the north, and the Pacific Ocean to the west. This hilly city has an average elevation of 52 feet (16 meters), with the highest point, Mount Davidson, at 928 feet (283 meters).

CHAPTER 24

In 1521, explorer Ferdinand Magellan set out to map the ocean and measure its depth. In his ship, he let down a line until it unspooled to its full length: 750 meters. And still it hadn't touched bottom. The sailors brought the line up again and, with that, Magellan declared the ocean to be immeasurable. So deep no man, he thought, could plumb its depths. It wasn't until many centuries later when sonar was used to chart the ocean floor that the first cartographers mapped the valleys, mountains, and plains below the water. Then, in the 1980s, a satellite spinning above the earth's atmosphere got a better look. The geodetic satellite measured the surface of the ocean, the dips and crests of the waves, which, the scientists knew, closely matched the topography of the ocean's floor. With these new calculations, oceanographers tweaked and adjusted maps. Four hundred years after Magellan explored the world, a satellite named after him took the most accurate measurements to date of the surface of Venus, a feat he couldn't have even imagined.

So many iterations, step by step fluctuations occur. Little by little, more and new information, new ways of thinking, and new discoveries change the way humans see the world around them.

═══

Sitting in a waiting room chair in the university hospital in Northern California, my worldview changed and fluctuated. Becks's mom—whom I still thought of as Mrs. Eastman—clicked knitting needles beside me. I could almost believe I had never been in Colombia, never visited the sites on my mother's map, as if the whole thing had been a dream, except that I had accidentally spoken Spanish to the taxi driver and the remnants of the sunburn lingered across my chest. I arrived in San Francisco less than an hour before the ob-gyn took my best friend in for an emergency C-section. I had come straight from the airport, my green Travelpro beside me; I wouldn't let it out of my sight this time.

"Nervous energy," Mrs. Eastman said, catching me staring at the growing length of a pink and blue striped blanket. "It shouldn't take this long, you know," she said. "My niece had a C-section and the whole thing was over in about forty-five minutes."

The lights glared. The knitting needles clacked.

"Something's wrong."

"I'm sure everything is fine, Mrs. Eastman."

(*She could be right. Things can go wrong so quickly,* said Elizabeth. *What do you know of childbirth?* snipped Aunt Judith. *About as much as you do,* retorted Jane, the nulliparous women argued over something none of them had experienced, *but I was there for Mags.* Gigi, the mother and grandmother, soothed, *Please, this is no time for arguments.* I listened carefully to see if any other voices spoke, but if Margaret Moore was with my chorus, she stayed silent.)

"They'll let us know," I said. "Soon, I'm sure."

The needles continued their rhythm. I found an outlet and plugged in my phone, which had died during the flight. Sitting on the white linoleum floor of the waiting room, I watched as the screen came to life, pinged with unread texts. Trina, Oscar, Franklin. It hadn't been a dream. I switched it off again.

"Becks said you were traveling," Mrs. Eastman said, knitting furiously. "She said you went to your birth country. How exciting."

I didn't want to talk about the trip right now, but Becks's mother's needles clicked faster. I thought of how Franklin had told me the trick was not to take in too much at once. Mrs. Eastman needed a distraction, so I asked, "Didn't you and Mr. Eastman recently get back from Europe?"

"Norway and Sweden. John wanted to do some genealogy. Sort of like you—a homecoming."

I nodded. I didn't want to be rude to this woman who had fed me after-school snacks and driven me to ballet lessons and hosted a joint graduation party, but their trip was nothing like mine. Genealogy was nothing like finding out what happened to the parents who had created you. Without a hobby on which to train my nervous energy, I absently pulled the hand-drawn map out of my bag, folding and unfolding the paper. I put it away and then took it out again.

"I wanted to visit the fjords. They were beautiful." Her voice trailed as a blue-scrubs-wearing woman in a tight ponytail and surgical mask entered.

"Who's waiting for Rebecca Eastman?"

A ball of pink yarn rolled toward me.

"John isn't arriving until tomorrow," Mrs. Eastman fretted when she returned and went to call her husband. I waited alone, then I waited with her. She had been right. There was something wrong. The doctor told us they would know more soon.

The clock on the wall of the family room ticked unnecessarily loudly. Like the *pa-thum* of a baby's heartbeat. I had gone along to one of Becks's prenatal appointments when I visited her and Charlie, very early on, just before Jane got sick, just before I lost my job, just before I broke up with Jason.

Pa-thum, pa-thum, pa-thum, went the fetal monitor.

"That's my baby's heartbeat," she had said, grinning so broadly I was afraid her face would split. I gripped her hand.

Pa-thum, pa-thum, pa-thum. Faster than I could have thought possible.

(*We didn't have those when my kids were born*, said Gigi. *I can't even imagine*, said Aunt Dot, whose one pregnancy was stillborn.)

Pa-thum, tick, pa-thum, tick.

My head lolled and I realized I'd fallen asleep, the sound of the ticking mixing with my memories of the fetal heartbeat.

"Her name is Daphne," Mrs. Eastman was saying, shaking my shoulder.

"Who?" I asked.

Becks's mother stared at me. Her eyes were wet, her mascara clumped in the corners. "I better call John," she said and wiped her nose with a crumpled tissue.

Daphne. "The baby," I said aloud, answering my own question.

A new person, a new life had entered the world. A new fluctuation.

"You made it," Becks whispered. I gave her a gentle hug, trying not to disturb the plastic tubing that snaked around her.

"I made it," I said, swallowing the catch in my throat. I wanted to say, *I'm so glad you're alive.* But of course I didn't, couldn't. And I couldn't say, *I'm so glad the baby is alive.* But I was. I was so relieved because I knew people could die, could easily leave you. Instead I said, "I wouldn't miss it."

(*What a relief she survived,* said Jane, and Elizabeth murmured her agreement.)

"And everyone is okay," I said. I knew better than most, better than I ever had, that everyone wasn't always okay, that childbirth was treacherous, could be dangerous, unpredictable.

"We're okay." Becks nodded. "The baby's in the NICU. As a precaution. With Charlie."

I wondered if a NICU and state-of-the-art medical care could have saved Margaret Moore, could have kept me from being an orphan twice—three times—over.

"But we're going to be okay," Becks added with false cheer. As if she was trying to convince herself. This was how she had been the summer of her second miscarriage, when my mothers rented a cottage along the Mississippi and invited her to join them. "You can come, too, Dorrie," Jane had added.

We spent a long weekend sitting on the screened porch, listening to the water flow beyond a grove of cottonwoods. Becks would insist she was fine, and Elizabeth would bring her cups of tea, and Jane would turn on the radio, letting soft strains of cello and flute float out the back door and wrap us in soothing notes. Neither of them had ever lost a baby, much less been pregnant, but they knew how to care for people. I didn't know what to say to my best friend, who had a desire and a pain I was sure I would never—could never—know.

The back lawn of the cottage had a garden that sloped toward the river. There was a little gravel space with a well-used fire ring, and Becks dragged a couple of plastic Adirondack chairs to the patio. The purple-and-yellow flowers—black-eyed Susans?—were in bloom, and a lazy bumble bee bounced from blossom to blossom.

Becks sat and watched the water moving south, heading toward its new life. My mothers and I would take turns sitting beside her as she healed, slowly.

"I don't know what to say," I said on the third day.

She sipped her coffee and looked across the river. A heron rose from the bank, hidden until it exposed itself. We watched its prehistoric wings flap as it flew upriver.

"You don't have to say anything," Becks said after the heron had disappeared. "Just knowing you're here is enough."

Hovering at the foot of the bed, Mrs. Eastman gripped her daughter's ankle through the thin blanket. Tears pricked my eyes and I felt faint again.

"We knew everything would work out, Becky." And then Mrs. Eastman began to weep, with relief or with fear. "Oh, my baby," she said.

First I passed the regular nursery, the one where nonparents can watch the nurses fuss with the newborns through a window down the hall from the new-mother suites. A set of grandparents waved at a blue-capped baby to the right. Closest to me was a baby in a pink cap, eyes screwed shut, arms escaping from her swaddle. Those were the healthy babies. The ones with full lung capacity and pink cheeks.

(*Dorrie was tiny like that. Tiny with a head full of black hair.* I could hear the weepiness and nostalgia in Jane's voice. *She cried, always.* Jane chuckled softly at the memory and somewhere behind the sound of her voice, I thought I heard another, quieter and unfamiliar murmur. But I was sure I had imagined it.)

To find Becks's baby, I needed to go past the regular nursery and follow the signs to the Neonatal Intensive Care Unit. As I came around the corner, I saw Charlie in too-large scrubs and a blue hairnet over his unruly hair, a blue mask hooked under his chin. Above his beard, his eyes were bloodshot, the skin beneath sallow.

He put an arm around me in an approximation of a hug. "This way, Dorrie."

We passed through two loud, aggressive fire doors. Another hallway. The door to the NICU. And a window.

"Want to see her?"

From outside, I touched the glass as he pointed to the isolette, inside of which was a tiny bundle with breathing tubes, matching her mother. The diaper was crooked, little legs flailing and then calming.

Charlie handed their house keys over to his mother-in-law. She and I would stay in their apartment tonight and come back in the morning. We didn't talk in the Uber to the Sunset. Late that night, after Mrs. Eastman had gone to bed with the help of an Ambien, I found a half pack of cigarettes in the back of Becks's kitchen drawer while looking for fish food. I took out the pack and held a cigarette to my nose. It smelled like a Cali street corner and I pictured the chaos of my birth city and then I remembered something else. Yes, it was the time—not that long ago—when Becks and I bought a pack in a fit of teenage nostalgia in Nebraska during our cross-country trip from Minnesota to the Bay Area. Charlie had flown out to start his job, while Becks and I drove there, navigating the route and the U-Haul trailer. We listened to music from our high school years (too much Britney Spears and Semisonic and Destiny's Child), singing along as the deserts of the west streaked by. We ate Doritos and drank Gatorade, stopping to pee at interstate rest stops, where we bought

magnets and a trucker hat and other tchotchkes, lighting one cigarette after another.

(*I might have expected this from Dorrie, but not Becks,* Grandma
June had scolded.)

When we arrived, we emerged from the car reeking, both of us
giggling like children who had gotten away with something. Charlie
scooped his wife in his arms, not even complaining about the stench
of smoke.

But now, tonight, instead of making me laugh at the memory,
the tobacco smell made me nauseous and I threw the rumpled pack
in the trash. They were the past and Becks—and I—were heading
into a new future.

because Mom keeps calling to tell everyone the gossip. Rebecca had a hysterectomy, so please send useless flowers."

I gasped and my hand flew to my mouth. "You—"

"It's the hormones," said Charlie, a whisper. "And the lack of sleep. She won't sleep."

"*Can't* sleep," Becks snapped.

A hysterectomy? My eyes burned.

Mrs. Eastman patted her daughter's leg. "What else do you need, Becky?"

I thought of Margaret Moore, going through this in a foreign country without her mother or her partner. Her sister must have been a poor substitute.

Becks looked at her mother, then me, then Charlie. "I'm sorry," she said, and her mood swung again and she began to cry.

"I can come back later," I said.

"No, I'm sorry." She smoothed the blanket over her lap. "I'd like to hear about your trip, Dorrie. Don't go."

So Charlie and Mrs. Eastman returned to the NICU, and I sat in the blue vinyl chair beside the bed.

"I'm so tired," she said, and I told her to sleep.

Becks closed her eyes. My phone pinged and I scrambled to silence it. But she didn't move. It was Trina. Her name across the screen was jarring. In the still of Becks's hospital room, it was hard to believe I had ever been to Cali and made friends with her and her husband and all the others.

Trina: Is everything ok?

I looked at the pastel flower arrangements and bed pads and sanitizing wipes. Everything was not okay, but it would be. Right?

Dorrie: My friend had an emergency hysterectomy.

Trina sent back a surprised face and a crying face.

Dorrie: She's sad.

I looked at the words I had typed and they seemed so inadequate.

Trina: I can't even imagine. We don't want more children, but I can't imagine not being able to if I wanted.

Humans like options, I thought. We like to be able to make choices and give ourselves the illusion of control. But that's all it really was—an illusion. We weren't in control. If we were, Becks wouldn't have had her ability to have more children taken away, I wouldn't have lost my mothers—so many mothers—and I wouldn't have a chorus chattering in my ear.

Becks jerked and then murmured in her sleep, and I tucked my phone in my pocket and stroked her fingers until she quieted. Her pre-birth manicure was starting to grow out, showing the moons of her nails. The rosy polish made her hands look even paler, especially next to my tan ones.

I wondered if Maggie Moore and Juan Carlos had held hands—hers pale, his dark—as they walked the river path along the río Cali. I remembered Franklin's long slender fingers taking my blood pressure, raking leaves, stroking my face. I thought of glimpsing Daphne through the glass of the NICU, her tiny fists pink and frail. All these thoughts crisscrossed one another, intersecting each other. Like a plus sign.

A plus sign like the one that had appeared in the little window on the test stick. Two lines like the T-O map. Or maybe like the cross atop the Iglesia La Ermita. Or an X.

Becks stirred and an alarm beeped. Her feet made the crisp sheets rustle and I laid a hand over her leg to calm her as she let out a soft cry. Then she opened her eyes. "Dorrie."

"There she is." I nestled a couple pillows behind her back.

"My should-be sister," Becks murmured, tears leaking down her cheeks. "Thanks for being here. I'm sorry. It's just that every time I wake up, I remember all over again."

The nurse came in and checked various machines, offered to bring the baby in later for her feeding. Becks looked so pale and exhausted lying against the sheets and I could feel that lump reappearing. But of course *she* wasn't going to die. Unlike Margaret Moore in 1989, Becks had excellent care in one of the best hospitals in the country. And unlike Jane, she wasn't riddled with cancer; she had had a baby—the most natural, wonderful thing in the world.

I swiped at my eyes and we talked about her pain for a moment, just the physical aspects of it. The incision, the soreness, the engorgement. All things I knew nothing about.

(*I remember all that like yesterday*, said Gigi. *They say you forget childbirth, but you never do*, agreed Grandma June.)

Someone came in with a tray and Becks picked at the food. "Jell-O?" she offered, and we laughed. "Sorry, the Percocet is for me." She sipped juice and I watched her, the two of us together in this room the way we had been in so many places, always together. And then she said, "Remember when I was trying to decide if I wanted to have two or three kids?"

Her words hit me like a bludgeon; I forced myself to keep a neutral face.

"Looks like I won't have to decide."

"I loved being an only child." I knew these were worthless words but I said them anyway. "Only children are the best."

She asked for water and I pointed the bendy straw toward her, just as I had for Jane. Tears streamed down her face, silent weeping, and yet this was the best I could do, the most I could offer.

She was awake, nursing the baby, and chatting on her phone. I had just returned from having some lunch in the hospital cafeteria with Mrs. Eastman, who ignored her turkey sandwich and repeated her husband's flight information several times. Becks's color looked better, and she was actually smiling. She mouthed to me to wait and I listened as she gave someone (a substitute teacher?) instructions on final collage projects.

"You must be feeling a little better," I said when she got off the call.

"It's the dopamine," she said, nodding at the baby. "The lactation nurse says I'm getting a shot of the stuff every time she latches. Or they just tell you that so you stick with it. The power of suggestion?"

"Whatever works. Is it hard?"

Becks flinched as she transferred Daphne to the other breast, but even so, she looked as if she'd been breastfeeding babies her whole life. My heart lurched. "It's tricky, but the nurse says Daphne's a pro. She's officially graduated from the NICU. Aren't you a professional eater?" she asked the baby, running an index finger along Daphne's cheek. "Tell me about your trip. Or anything. Tell me, keep me occupied."

So I showed her some pictures of Cali, a couple with Oscar to make her laugh, the apartment building, and one of Cristina Rojas Vargas. Daphne fell asleep on her mother's chest, and as I talked, Becks's eyes leaked again, almost like she was crying without meaning to. "But you've heard most of this."

"Tell me more. Ignore me."

I inhaled. Sighed.

"Well." I looked around the maternity suite at the bassinet, the wipes, the gauze. Three vases of flowers lined the windowsill. Daphne gurgled in her sleep and Becks smiled down at her.

Everything looked peaceful, hopeful despite the horrors of reality. Becks looked content with her hard-won infant.

And so I told her.

I told her what I hadn't told Trina. I told Becks what I hadn't told Franklin. He had texted several times, asking about my trip, about me.

Dorrie: Returning on Tues.

What else could I possibly say?

"You're going to be a mom!" Her tears were gone. "Dorrie, come here and hug me."

We hugged, careful of the baby, but then I whispered.

I whispered a truth, something I had been thinking but also not thinking.

I whispered a thought, just a thought.

And I ruined everything.

I said out loud the thing that I'd been thinking ever since those two lines appeared, the thought I didn't quite want to think but couldn't stop. I knew I shouldn't say it aloud to her; she was the last person who wanted to think about the choices women make. But I had to say it.

Maybe that's how my chorus functions. They say the things they need to say simply because to speak is to feel alive. To communicate— even without hope of reciprocity—is to assert your place in the world. Does doling out advice and opinions keep my family alive? Not just for me but for them? Are the things we say important not because someone else will hear them but because we've said them?

But words have consequences. And Becks wasn't ready to hear mine.

PART FOUR

MINNEAPOLIS–SAINT PAUL, MINNESOTA

The largest city in Minnesota, Minneapolis, lies on the west bank of the Mississippi River and its confluence with the Minnesota River, adjacent to the state capital, Saint Paul, which is situated east of the Mississippi. Together, these two urban cores, along with the suburbs of the surrounding seven counties, are known as the Twin Cities and create the sixteenth-largest metropolitan area in the country by population.

CHAPTER 26

Above the troposphere, the view is all marshmallow and cotton candy, the world turned upside down. Clouds become the geography, illusions of solid ground. Pilots tend to stay in this in-between space—called the tropo*pause*, where the jet streams form, blowing from west to east, making my flight home just a little faster. I slept fitfully, woke every twenty minutes to monitor our progress either out the window or on the map display in the seatback in front of me. Instead of the blinking cursor that's typically used on GPS, an out-of-scale airplane graphic followed an arc across the United States, shifting and angling to reflect the movements of our route. When we landed in Minneapolis, a tall man with neat gray hair offered to retrieve my Travelpro from the overhead bin.

It was dark when the airport taxi dropped me off at the Victorian. The streetlight in front of the house had gone out, and I had to use my phone's flashlight to see the lock on the front door. I switched on the foyer light and saw the stack of mail that Franklin had left on the side table. With the cats still at his house until tomorrow, the Victorian felt strangely empty, an odd hush hung in the air, alongside an odor of forgetting.

(*Coming home is the best feeling ever,* someone said. *Something seems strange,* Elizabeth said. *Home,* someone seemed to echo.)

Home. I *was* home, but I already felt a wistfulness for Cali, and I had that nagging ache at the back of my mind, remembering Becks's pained face. I pushed all thoughts aside and dropped my carry-on and suitcase with a thud. I just wanted to crawl into bed and sleep as long as possible.

For a moment, my eyes still closed, I believed I was still at the Hotel América. It was before. Before Becks's C-section, before the drugstore test, before the night of dancing and drinking. It was before my suitcase arrived, when I was without luggage or baggage—lost but also free and unencumbered. Then the buzz of a lawn mower and the tick of the clock on the highboy came into focus, and I knew that I was home—in my mothers' house. I sat up and the room spun and everything came back to me like a tidal wave.

I'm pregnant. My best friend hates me.

Becks had cried after I whispered in her ear, told her this secret within a secret. "You can't!" she said. "How can you even think about it? When there are some of us—some of us who would give anything—what would your moms say?"

Of course, I knew what my moms would say because they were saying it; even as I stood in front of my friend, my chorus had voiced their opinions. The voices of the childless women were the loudest. Becks railed and woke Daphne, whose cries brought first an aide and then Charlie and Mrs. Eastman.

"Dorrie has to leave," Becks had said stonily above the baby's cries. She didn't look at me, wouldn't hug me back when I leaned down to kiss her cheek. *I'm sorry*, I tried to say but failed.

Mrs. Eastman looked startled; Charlie looked tired. *It's the hormones*, he mouthed at me. *It's fine*, I mouthed back.

"Go, Dorrie," Becks had said again sternly, in her teacher's voice. Like the chorus, there was no arguing with her.

I had no choice.

When my mothers' bedroom stopped spinning, I propelled myself out of bed, dragged myself through the motions of morning: bathroom, a robe, Elizabeth's slippers. Today I would bring the cats home, unpack, go to the grocery store.

The odor hit me like a wall of discontent. On the first floor of my mothers' Victorian, the air was thick and choking. Something was off, something smelled strange, as Elizabeth had said. An acrid, bitter scent. As I came around the corner into the living room, the smell intensified, activating my gag reflex. I remembered Becks saying in her first few months of pregnancy, "I can't stand Charlie's deodorant. His smell makes me want to vomit." I breathed through my mouth and investigated.

Early Minneapolis city planners built an organized grid of neighborhoods and transit without regard for topographical disruptions: lakes, waterways, marshes. The roadways bumped into these landmarks and continued on the other side. The streets ran east-west, the avenues north-south, and I could never decide if I admired their adherence for order or thought they were fools for not adapting to the surroundings. My mothers' Victorian was just past one of those disruptions, a lake, and was sited on a north-south avenue facing west, exposing the back of the house—upstairs office, downstairs kitchen and dining room—to invigorating morning sun.

As I entered the living room, I took in the Victorian's 1893 woodwork and coffered ceilings. Its blond-brick fireplace. The built-in stained-glass window above the oak in the dining room cast green and yellow mirages. The light flickered and shone on the disaster.

(*What happened here?!*)

It was disarray, and not the kind that I had created before I left for Colombia. The plaster ceiling between the dining room and kitchen was shredded and brown, whole sections had fallen to the floor, everything soggy and the color of Jane's Darjeeling tea. The streaming sun was baking the damp, black mold speckling the edges of a cookbook, the corners of a photo of Bojangles taped to the fridge.

I gaped. Dizzy again. I flung open the window above the sink, fanning the air, hoping to dilute the stink that hung thick in the kitchen. The wooden fruit bowl that had sat on the counter my whole childhood, the folded pile of potato-sack dish towels embroidered with flowers and leaves by a great-grandmother, the Post-it notes on the corkboard in my mothers' handwriting. My mothers' house. My mothers' things. Everything was saturated. Fine gritty dust coated the coffee maker. Not one thing, whether valuable or worthless, whether sentimental or forgotten, had escaped damage. The yawning holes above me exposed foamy mush and dark wood beams. I was back on calle 5 Norte, seeing the empty storefront, the dilapidated courtyard of my family's apartment, realizing all over again that I could never truly go back, that the past, no matter what my chorus might believe, was gone, could never be revisited, not really. My stomach churned and my eyes burned.

(*Wasn't someone checking on the house? I thought that nice boy was taking care of the house.*)

After vomiting in the sink, I found my phone and called Franklin. This—everything—was his fault.

CHAPTER 27

While Europe was in the Dark Ages, Arabic and Chinese societies were making huge advances in science and math, giving them the ability to chart great distances, to travel across unknown oceans, to discover new lands. But they didn't. Professor Foster said that's because they didn't need to go anywhere. The Arabic people already had their spices and goods that Europe eventually sought. And the Chinese didn't care about converting anyone. They stayed put.

Like my mothers had. They lived in Minneapolis their whole lives, just like the entire Moore family—all but Margaret. And like me too. But now the legacy of my home was destroyed and I needed to blame someone.

When Franklin opened the door, Bojangles, like a traitor, rubbed against his legs while I reached down to stroke the cat's tail. It was impossible to believe that only a few weeks had passed since I ate rice pudding in the Liu kitchen.

"You're back!" Franklin said. His hair was more unruly than when I left, and his face was tanner. He was wearing gym shorts and a T-shirt. When he leaned toward me for a hug, the smell of him was so strong my eyes stung. But I pushed past him, past the hug, into Grandpa Bao's house.

"Are they ready?" I asked sternly.

"How was your trip?"

"Meow." Now Bojangles rubbed against my legs. I scooped him up and he purred as I held his warm body to my face. The feel of his soft fur triggered something, a memory, a moment. Mama and Mommy. A quiet Sunday morning with newspapers and cats and some music in the background.

"How's your friend? Did she have her baby?"

At the mention of Becks, I was catapulted to the present again. I swallowed whatever it was down.

"I know you were so worried—"

"I have to go." I cut him off.

"Okay, all right." He held up his hands in surrender. "I'll get their things."

He set the cat carriers on the floor with a thud. "The latches on these carriers don't seem to be—"

"It's fine," I snapped. Nothing was fine, but latches on carriers were the least of my worries right now. I thought of the Victorian, the mess I had to face. I just wanted to get out of this house, get away from Franklin.

"Django doesn't seem to want to leave," he said with a grin. In the living room, Django was curled up on Grandpa Bao's lap as if the two of them hadn't moved since I left, the whole house, the scene, frozen in time.

"Grandpa, I think Dorrie needs her cat back."

"Sorry," I apologized to both the cat and the old man, "but I need to get going."

"Can't you stay for lunch?" asked Grandpa Bao, and I felt a pang of regret, of disappointment, that familiar wondering: What if things were different?

But things were *not* different. The scene in the destroyed kitchen of the Victorian played on repeat in my mind. I apologized again and said goodbye to the grandfather and picked up Django, who seemed both disappointed to leave the warm lap but also pleased to see me.

"I can help—" Franklin began as I opened the carrier and put Django inside.

"Did you check on the house while I was gone?" I interrupted. I wanted to get to the part where I blame, find the one at fault. *There's no such thing as an accident,* Aunt Judith used to say.

Franklin gave me a funny look. "I told you I went over there a few times. Closed the kitchen window. Brought in the mail."

"Really?" My tone was harsh.

"Everything okay there?"

"No."

He laughed, maybe thinking I was joking, teasing like we had been doing to each other as friends. And then he stopped laughing. "Seriously? What's wrong?"

"It's destroyed. Everything is ruined." My cheeks felt hot and my eyes burned. The tears began. "I told you that you didn't need to do me any favors." I grabbed Bojangles and shoved him—gently, I promise—into his carrier. "I told you I could easily hire a service to house-sit."

"I'm so sorry. Everything looked fine when I was there last." Franklin reached out a hand, the fingers long and slender. I wondered for a split second if that was an inherited trait. "Sit down, Dorrie, tell me what happened."

"I just want to get back home." I shrugged away the hand he laid on my arm. Django meowed. "I need to go home."

"Dorrie, just calm down. Can you please explain? Did something happen to your house?"

"Don't worry. It's *my* house," I snapped. "My *mothers'* house. And no concern of yours." I took a deep, ragged breath. "You've done enough."

(*Why is she taking it out on this nice man?* asked Aunt Judith, who had always been so benevolent. *Well, you* saw *the house,* countered Elizabeth. *You're always so quick to judge,* began Judith, the two sisters falling back into their childhood bickering.)

Franklin protested, adding his voice to the noise, prattling on about the carriers and how much food was left and, wait, he could get the catnip mice he bought for them, but I headed to the door. I didn't want platitudes, I didn't want stories, and I didn't want to listen. I was so tired of listening. I had to get out of Franklin's— no—Grandpa Bao's house. Grandpa Bao's memories were pushing down on me, wanting something from me. Even with new floors and the fresh coat of white paint, I could feel the Liu family expecting something from me.

I allowed Franklin to haul the kitty litter and bag of food to the trunk, but I insisted on taking the cats myself. I settled them in the back seat, Bojangles behind the driver's seat, Django beside him. They yowled in protest.

"Slow down, Dorrie," Franklin tried again. "Can we just talk?"

I was in the driver's seat, the keys in the ignition. The car dinged, complaining about its open door. One of the cats—Django, I was pretty sure—also complained.

"Is this about that night . . . ?"

"It's not about that," I lied and slammed the door, jerking into reverse, wishing I could also back up, turn back, undo the past.

As I drove away, I wasn't entirely sure why I was crying. I wasn't sure why I didn't want to talk to Franklin or why I didn't tell him. If I had stopped to consider, I would have seen that the disaster of the house had nothing to do with him. But my tears blinded me, obscured the details of the city streets, the trees along the boulevard, the one- and two-story houses on Franklin's street. Everything felt irretrievably broken and changed. I felt like I was staring at the abandoned store-front on calle 5 Norte again. The sun on the dirty windshield splintered into an array of arrows, each pointing in a different, confusing direction.

It was *his* fault (wasn't it?) that the Victorian was in ruins. It had to be Franklin's fault because if it wasn't, then that just meant the universe made no sense, that things happened without reason, that any one of us can, at any time, be subjected to its whims. So it must be Franklin's fault. He probably got a glass of water from the kitchen sink when he closed the window, dislodged something in the pipes. Or maybe he went upstairs to take a leak, forgot to rattle the handle of the toilet (why didn't I tell him about the toilet?), and the disruption to the order of things caused the damage.

At the next intersection, I realized this wasn't the way I had come. I looked left, then right. The maples and ash trees along this Saint Paul street shaded the single-story houses, each containing their own lives, the humans inside bumping along their pathways. It looked like Franklin's street but wasn't. Which way back to the freeway? At the next stop sign, I pulled my phone out of my purse; I needed direction. GPS provides just the right kind—impersonal, analytical, and precise.

When I tried switching on my phone, I howled like the cats. "No!"

Django joined my cries. I reached for the glove box, but then remembered that the charging cable I usually kept in the car was still in my carry-on, which was on the floor in the foyer of my mothers' house.

(*She can be her own worst enemy sometimes.*)

Unlike the numbered or alphabetized city planning of Minneapolis, Saint Paul, the older of the Twin Cities, is less regimented, the streets more organic. Some twist and turn. The house numbers are continuous, without regard for the changes in blocks, and the streets' names are poetic or descriptive, like Bald Eagle Boulevard and Chickadee Lane. At a blue house on the corner, I turned right, only to find myself passing the same unfamiliar houses.

I tried a left turn this time and found myself at a T that looked familiar.

(*She's already come this way*, said Grandma June unhelpfully. *She needs to find Ayd Mill Road*, said Aunt Judith, who hadn't driven these roads in years. *If she takes a right* . . . began someone, each voice taking her turn as a back seat driver.)

I tried one more left and then a right. I was sure I'd passed the same brick Cape Cod several times now. One more turn. Ahead, beyond a gap between the houses, I glimpsed a freeway overpass. I was close. So close.

Django yowled.

"We're almost there," I promised.

Just because you can see where you want to go doesn't mean you can get there. I twisted and turned, searching for a way out as Django and Bojangles made their displeasure known. I considered returning to Franklin's house and asking for directions, but I didn't think I could find my way back, even if I wanted to.

Bojangles mewed behind me plaintively, accusingly, rattling the latch of his cage as if he, too, were judging me and my choices. I had told Franklin about the mess of the house, but I didn't tell him about *my* mess. *Our* mess. What would he say? What could he say? I allowed myself a fleeting moment to wonder how he'd feel. And then I squashed down the thought. I didn't even know how I felt.

That wasn't true.

I knew how I felt and that was nothing. Nothing and everything.

I saw myself seated in a pew at La Ermita, and then Margaret Moore in the same spot thirty-five years earlier. Both of us beginning a new life. Had she been as shocked as I was? Did she want to wish it away? Had she been hoping for me?

But Maggie, young as she was, had Juan Carlos, at least at first. She'd loved him, that's what Cristina had said. He adored her. And even though Maggie had probably never told thirteen-year-old Cristina that, I knew that you could recognize love, even from a distance.

And suddenly, there was the freeway. As I began the spiral of the cloverleaf entrance ramp, I heard a rattle from the back seat, another complaint. I didn't pay attention because I was so relieved to finally have found the interstate; I knew where I was.

Another clanking rattle.

Then, just as I prepared to merge, the clank was drowned out by a yowl. And suddenly, a huge orange tabby leaped between the seats toward me.

(*That cat!* exclaimed someone.)

"Django!" I cried, which startled him, and he used my right

shoulder as a launching pad, digging his back claws deep into my flesh. In a swirl of fur, he was on the floor and trying to slink under the passenger seat.

(*I hope he's okay*, worried Elizabeth.)

By this point, I had inadvertently slowed instead of accelerating into the lane, and a semi driver honked and passed me with a roar, which meant that I didn't hear the other carrier rattle. No warning. I saw Bojangles before I heard him. While Django had opted for the cocooning safety of under the seat, Bojangles decided that higher was better and was scrambling up the seat toward the top of my headrest. Instantly, my vision was completely obscured by his orange and fluffy tail. I reached up with both hands in an attempt to remove him.

And so, for a moment, I was completely unmoored. Hurtling through space and maybe time. I shoved at the cat's bulk, trying to push him off. As he flailed, I glimpsed the path—clear, but for how long, I wondered.

The last time I felt this out of control was when Jane was minutes away from death. I didn't know it was happening at the time, but I knew something was changing. She had extracted that promise from me and her breath came out ragged one moment, smooth and deep the next. Her face had gone pale, almost gray, and her eyes seemed to be looking not at me but beyond me, almost as if she were seeing other people. I wondered for only an instant if she had seen my chorus, who were silent in that moment. But it didn't matter what she saw or didn't see. What mattered to me was that I had known she was preparing to leave, that in some way, she had perhaps already left, had been leaving for a long time.

Maybe we're all just preparing to leave. Maybe that's all life is—a long preparation for the end. I had squeezed her hand but she simply stared ahead, and I felt a crushing strangle on my heart and lungs. There were no directions for how to be left alone. When Elizabeth passed, I had still had Mama. But now I was alone, in much the same way I had started my life. Juan Carlos was gone before I was born, Margaret Moore shortly after. One by one, people had left me.

CHAPTER 28

I was in pain. It was the bright light and the claws digging into the flesh of my upper thighs. Bojangles was half on my lap, and Django was partly on the passenger side mat and partly under the seat, his long, frightened tail and rear end exposed. The fat cat sat on a mat.

It's the sound I register first, even though I'm sure the impact happened simultaneously. Scraping, smashing, like a dropped frying pan or an unsteady desk. Smack. A jolt. An F-150 pickup was both beside and in front of me while also behind me. As red and dangerous as that bikini. The gleaming scarlet paint sparkled and my mind flashed to the color wheel: red and blue make purple. I thought I saw the shimmer of a hummingbird's wing. I closed my eyes or maybe my eyes closed me, protecting me from any more visions of what was happening. A crack, a crash, an earsplitting bang so intense it felt like it was coming from within me. Jostled from side to side, front to back. Even in this strange moment between the seconds, I noticed the silky back of Bojangles as he sprang to the back seat and, miraculously, aimed for Django's carrier.

Home, he might have been thinking. *Home.* We were all just trying to get home.

===

Later.

I'm not home.

Instead, I was in a hospital bed getting my blood pressure taken, filling out paperwork, and waiting for a provider to see me. I tried to tell the EMTs I was fine, just needed help getting home. But they shone lights in my eyes, just as Franklin had done all those weeks ago, and palpated my chest and insisted on a ride in the ambulance. The cats, those little fuckers, had both made a beeline for Django's carrier after the crash, the two hulking orange bodies crammed together in the safety of their cage. It was a simple thing to reach back and hook the latch again—the one Franklin had tried to warn me about, but I hadn't listened.

But I was so tired of listening. Advice, commentary, following rules and directions and maps. Besides, how could you tell whose advice to heed?

"How are you feeling?" the doctor asked. I had been sitting up, scrolling through my phone, trying to make decisions. The woman in the next bed had been sleeping since I arrived. I envied her oblivion.

"Sore. Like I got hit by a truck." I laughed. A joke.

The doctor murmured. Just like Olga had when I called her.

"How are you, Dorrie?" she said, as if we were the kind of friends who called, chatted. I had never asked her for anything before, other than to pass the crackers, another glass of wine, please, what did you think of the ending? But I didn't know who else to call. My best friend was . . . gone. My mothers were only in my head. Franklin? There was no way I could call Franklin now, not even if I wanted to.

"Where are you?" she asked when another semi roared past.

I had borrowed a charger from the fireman, the first responder to arrive. He took one look at the yowling cats in the back of the car and said, "You got someone who can pick them up?"

"I feel like I got hit by a truck," I had told Olga. "Because I did." She didn't laugh so I told her about the Ford and the two cats in one carrier.

"I'm allergic, you know," Olga said. I had forgotten. "But we can still help. My sister can take them." Relief turned into a sob. Olga and Rose Kumeh were both single professionals, avoiding matrimony, because, she had told our book group once, in their family, marriage meant giving up your career and having babies. But as spinsters, these two women could help me. Practically a stranger. "I'll be right there."

So while the EMTs and the police officers swarmed and the tow truck arrived and the cats meowed in righteous fear, I waited for Olga. I looked for Dante West, EMS, among the first responders. I knew EMT Franklin Liu was at home, wondering why I had left in such a huff. When Olga arrived, she took pictures, talked to the police, and winked at one of the firefighters, who had a smooth brown face, a broad smile, and a flawless fade, and had loaded my cats into the back of her Escalade for her.

"Everything's going to be okay," Olga said before she drove away, her voice so sure and comforting and present.

"Take a deep breath." The doctor landed his stethoscope on my chest with a cold thud. When he introduced himself, I didn't catch his name—something long and Slavic, I think. In a white coat over a dark green sweater vest, he had grown a goatee as if that would make him look older. I breathed. He moved the chest piece around: up, down, front, back. "Again."

(*They should warm those things up first.*)

I breathed again. He lifted my gown from the back, examined my flank, pressed with cold hands. I winced. He stepped back and his fingers clattered on the keyboard.

"Other than the bruising and lacerations, I'd say you got pretty lucky." His accent was aggressively Minnesotan—flat vowels, swallowed consonants. "I do want to watch that left side. Probably just a couple banged-up ribs, but we want to be sure the lungs aren't affected."

I shifted, breathed deeply again to check my lungs. The only thing out of place was that lump. Although it had shifted, the accident hadn't dislodged it.

Clacking, typing, mousing. "Your vitals look good."

I nodded, momentarily proud of my good-looking vitals.

Life was all about timing. If Juan Carlos hadn't been on that flight to Bogotá, he might not have died. And if he hadn't died, he might have been with Margaret Moore and their baby and prevented her death. And if they had been my parents, I would have grown up in Colombia, and I would have known my aunt Jane and her wife, Elizabeth, only from brief visits, and I never would have been their daughter. If the timing had worked out differently, half my chorus might not have been there—the Pelletiers wouldn't have been my family, I might never have known Great-Aunt Maureen. And perhaps I would have heard among my voices an abuela, the mother or even grandmother of Juan Carlos de la Peña. Maybe I would have even heard his voice. Depending on timing, you could gain so much or, just as easily, lose so much.

"We're going to do an ultrasound on your side there, Ms. Moore, just to make sure everything's okay. I'll order it now. And while we're at it, I think we should take a look at the baby too."

Even before humans used maps, even as simple as a T-O map, we navigated by the sky. The stars and the moon allowed the Phoenicians in 2000 BC to cross both land and sea. Long before conquerors and pillagers came to North America with their sextants and sea charts, the Ojibwe and Dakota were using pictures in the sky to find their way. Polaris, Orion, Andromeda. The bear, the hunter, the crab. Humans imagined a menagerie of creatures above our heads. Later, the imagery was drawn on parchment, on bark, on paper to be preserved, but the idea was the same.

Finding the North Star could orient a person—as long as the weather was clear.

(*Oh my*, breathed a voice.)

The wand slid in, the gel cold.

(*It's true*, said another voice.)

The doctor (a new one, this time a woman with short no-nonsense brown hair, a teal shirtdress under the white coat) smiled, pressed harder. The image on the screen became a Rorschach test, then a painting, then a map. Then a blur.

(*She is* . . . the women of the chorus murmured, a low hum below the medical opinions of the providers.)

The ultrasound looked good; the doctor said everything looked normal. Although to me, the swirling gray mass looked anything but normal. Where was the key? The compass rose? How could anyone find their way in the darkness of my uterus? It didn't seem possible. The whole thing felt theoretical. Two-dimensional.

Of course, all of cartography was built on theories for centuries. Until there was photography and satellite and radar, there were just men making guesses, formulating theories. And even though there wasn't proof for many years, everyone still believed, followed the instructions.

Seven weeks, the doctor told me.

Seven weeks pregnant. Embarazada.

I told the doctor this was unplanned, a surprise. She was all business, no reaction. She handed me information on healthy diets and on "other options" as the literature called it—two different road maps—and she seemed unbothered by whichever path I might choose. *Prenatal Nutrition*, *Living for Two*, and the most ambivalent: *Choices in Your First Trimester*.

"Just in case," she said as I shoved them in my purse.

(*What are those for?* asked Gigi, who had always been a little slow.)

"Any questions?" the doctor asked.

I looked away, bit my lip. All I had were questions.

My instructions were to take it easy, to use Tylenol but no opioids or NSAIDs on account of the pregnancy. No heavy lifting until the bruising heals. But which bruising? I wanted to ask the doctor if all organs heal, too, with enough rest and no exertion.

CHAPTER 29

The sun coming through the Victorian's western-facing windows caught dust motes and cat hairs, all suspended like stardust. The drive to Franklin's house, the truck, the hospital felt like a lifetime ago even though it had only been three days. Django leaped at a sliver of light as if it were a gnat, but Bojangles didn't notice and jumped onto the bed beside me. I rubbed his ears.

"You're my favorite, aren't you, Bo?" Olga's sister, Rose, had cooed yesterday when she returned the cats, giving special attention to Bojangles. Olga had arrived in a separate car, and after the two felines had been let loose in their own house, the three of us sat on the porch, away from the noxious smells of the kitchen and the allergens of the cats, and I tried to make conversation, tried to be easy and friendly in the way Trina and her friends had been.

"Thank you so much for taking them, Rose."

"They're the cutest," she said. She was tall like her sister, with the same upturned nose. "I could have kept them longer. I think I'm in love."

(*Those women are so nice*, said Aunt Judith. *They remind me of the Ahmed sisters—remember them, Jane?* asked Elizabeth. *Where are they from?* wondered Gigi—the same question I hated being asked. *They're so dark!* I flinched, glad, as I often was, that no one other than me could hear my chorus.)

"Why don't you have your own cats?" I asked Rose.

"I'm gone too much, and my sister would be a useless cat aunt with her allergies."

"What do you do?"

"She's a pharmaceutical rep," Olga said proudly. "She used to love to pretend to be a traveling salesman when we were little. Fala had an old suitcase we played with, packing and unpacking. I was always the customer."

The sisters had smiled at each other, and I felt my jaw tighten, missing my should-be sister, who should be here, talking with me. The voices were only for listening, not talking. The Kumeh sisters didn't stay long after that, and I thanked Olga for everything—she assured me she would help if my car insurance balked. Then I thanked Rose, thinking later about how I was indebted to another stranger.

But we're all strangers first, aren't we? I thought of my instant friendship with Trina and Seb and even María Sofía. I thought of Franklin. Sometimes we return to being strangers. While he tried to warn me about the carrier latches, I had been a wall, unwilling to listen, certain that the damage to my mothers' house was his fault. Even now, even as my nose tickled with the unpleasant scent of something terribly wrong, I knew it wasn't his fault, that old pipes can burst, old friends can become strangers as easily as lovers come from friends.

When Franklin arrived at the house a week later, I was sitting on the porch steps, waiting. Two little girls walked a dog, maybe a terrier, and struggled to choose a path. Each of the three wanted to go in a different direction, one little girl pointing, the other turning around, the dog straining on the leash. At the sound of a car pulling up along the curb, I looked away and would never find out which way they chose.

"Dorrie!" he gasped coming up the walk. The bruise on my cheek had turned a garish purple and the cat scratch on my forehead was as obvious as Harry Potter's scar. After ignoring first his texts and then his calls for nearly a week, I had finally answered this morning. With the benevolence I had seen in Olga and Rose, I told him what I'd found when I got home. I told him about the disarray and destruction.

"I had no idea, I promise," he had said, explaining how he had checked on the house, hadn't touched anything. And then I told him about the car crash and he had said, "I'm coming over."

At first I wanted to say no, knowing I could handle this alone. After all, I wasn't lonely—I had the voices suggesting bleach solutions and recommending local handymen who were probably long gone. But then I thought of the paperwork at the hospital. The tech had asked me to verify my information. I clicked the pen, hovering over the clipboard. *Current address.* I crossed out the one I had shared with Jason, added in the Victorian. For my emergency contact, I scratched out first *Jane Moore* and then *Relationship: Mother,* and the lump in my chest exploded into my sinuses, clogging and disturbing their intricate network. I looked at the crossed-out words and wondered who I would add. Would Rebecca Easton be able to help from halfway across the country—or would she *want* to? I considered entering Olga's name—after all, I had just called her in an emergency—but she already had a sister, a big family. Obviously, Trina and Seb were too far away, part of a different lifetime. My chorus muttered as I filled in Becks's name. There was no one else. And so this morning, I had accepted Franklin's offer.

Now he reached out and gently touched the scrape on my cheek, peered at the bruise.

"You should see the other guy," I said. Baba used that line when he got hit in the face with a softball. I was ten at the time, and I thought it was the funniest joke ever, mostly because I got it, knew what the line was meant to imply. Sometimes just knowing something is enough.

But Franklin didn't laugh; his frown was deep, and my heart squeezed tightly for a moment until he switched into healthcare mode. He squinted, asked me medical questions, repeating the same things the doctors and EMTs had said. The only information I didn't give him was the thing he most needed to know.

He took my hand and turned it over as if palm reading.

"What are you looking for?" I asked.

"I'm just glad you're okay." He dropped my hand. "You're okay, aren't you?"

Instead of answering, I showed him the kitchen, watched his nose wrinkle at the stench. Rank, dusty. The damp had cooked in the summer heat. I had been avoiding the mess, eating delivery and going to the coffee shop in the mornings as if I were still in Cali, where everything was within walking distance. We stood silently in the stench for a moment. My eyes burned.

Across the mess of the kitchen, Django approached Franklin, who squatted and held out a hand. The cat sniffed his outstretched finger and then meowed plaintively.

"I think he misses your grandfather," I said.

We both watched the cat for a moment. And then Franklin said, "I had no idea this could happen."

I nodded, as if to say that I didn't know it either or that it was clear that he hadn't known. Either way, it felt a little like a truce.

"I know about leaking pipes, but usually that's a winter problem. Frozen lines and everything."

"It can happen anytime, according to the internet. I should've seen it coming. I guess I should have had that mysterious brown spot inspected earlier. Jane always worried about it."

"No, you couldn't have known, Dorrie. It's not your fault."

I led Franklin back out to the porch; I couldn't bear to look at the mess in the kitchen.

"It's not the worst I've ever seen," he assessed in his medical voice. "Grandpa Bao's basement had water damage. And you can get rid of all that plaster and lath while we're at it."

While we're at it. He sounded like the doctor. Check out my uterus *while we're at it.*

"Maybe it's a good time to do a full remodel? Your insurance will probably cover it."

I wasn't even sure how to access the home insurance. I might not even officially own the Victorian, which was probably still caught up in probate. Franklin talked on of plumbers and construction and offers of help. He recommended the contractor who had remodeled his own kitchen. His words were gentle waves washing over me and I chose to float on them. In the background, the chorus discussed the house, my body, the choices I could be or should be making. My head hurt and I closed my eyes. The peonies were blooming and their scent reminded me of Elizabeth for a fleeting moment.

"It's a mess, but fixable."

(*Has she told him about the test?* asked Aunt Judith, like someone who had gone to the bathroom and missed key plot points of a movie. *She needs to do it now,* said Elizabeth. *She'll do it when she's ready,* said Jane. And on and on they talked.)

Then he paused and I opened my eyes. "Dorrie, I—"

A wasp nearby hummed.

"I'm sorry." Then he added, "I don't know what else to say."

"Me neither." The first truthful thing I'd told him since return-ing from Colombia.

But it wasn't enough, I knew.

Dr. Foster used to lecture that we needed to think geographically. "All the most innovative human inventions and discoveries have been a result of man thinking geographically," he would say. "Use your brains, consider the world around you, not only as it is but as it *could* be."

I considered the topography of my mothers' unmade bed, the slope in the hardwood floors, worn by years of footsteps. I forced myself to look at the kitchen, the contours of the walls, the stalac-tites of ripped insulation, and tried to picture something different, new. As soon as Franklin gave me the number for Jim the contractor, a sixtysomething man with a bushy gray mustache and no hair on his head, I hired him and his team. He had had a break in his sched-ule due to a back-ordered something and could begin the next day. He had come by and discussed what needed to happen: demolition, plumbing, framing.

Over the past few days, I was asked to make decisions on cab-inet colors and countertop materials, and I gave vague responses. Paint chips and squares of tiles littered the dining table, which I passed—and ignored—every time I walked through the living room. The insurance company—both auto and home—called and sent long emails. My primary care doctor left a message with a referral to an ob-gyn. Franklin left a few voicemails, but I didn't respond. If I couldn't tell him the truth, I didn't know what else to say.

(*If you don't have something nice to say, don't say anything at all,* the chorus sometimes quipped.)

I let messages from Trina go unanswered too. Colombia felt very distant, like a dream, and I wasn't supposed to talk about my dreams. I wasn't sure if I had gained what Jane had wanted me to. Yes, I had found out something about my history—something important—but I wasn't sure I liked what I knew now, the tragedy of my legacy. Maybe we're better off in ignorance; understanding only a small portion of the story can be comforting, the version our parents play for us. Maybe we never really wanted the truth.

If it hadn't been for texts from Olga asking how I was doing and Rose requesting pictures of the cats, my phone would have been useless.

I didn't talk to Becks. According to Charlie's social media feed, she was barely sleeping, the baby needing feedings every hour and a half around the clock. The photos he posted of them—Becks bleary eyed and smiling, baby Daphne crying or sleeping beatifically—made my heart feel like it could snap in half if I couldn't talk to her. But I didn't know what I would say. I still didn't know what path I would choose.

Over the next few weeks, I tried to think geographically as I listened to the rending of plaster and boards, the clatter of tile and clink of fixtures. The work will go quickly, Jim the contractor said.

I tried to picture the world as it could be.

1989
Cali, Colombia

A Sunday morning melancholy hung in the air. The trumpets and their staccato cumbias had gone to bed, the dancers with sore feet had slipped off their Cuban heels, and the brawls that spilled out of the discotecas had ended in handshakes. That morning even the líderes of the cartels were looking forward to their family lunches and an afternoon siesta later. And on calle 5 Norte, a woman with a baby strapped to her back stepped onto the sidewalk.

Jane pulled out the map her sister had drawn for her. She turned the paper until she was oriented. The X marked the apartment and there was the Hotel América, the hospital where the baby was born, the river. Already familiar with the route to her hotel, she decided to go the other direction and headed down the hill.

While her niece slept, Jane wondered what she would tell her parents when she got home—hopefully with Mags and the baby in tow. They knew nothing about this infant or the tragic story of their youngest daughter. They didn't know that Margaret (at nineteen!) had a baby, that the father had died, that mother and daughter were alone in Colombia. Her parents thought Jane—always doing her own thing, they said—had simply taken it into her head to travel to a war-ravaged country, that she had suddenly decided it would help the thesis on gender roles in traditional marriage she was writing, and that the sisters missed each other. Jane hadn't lied, but she hadn't corrected them either. Maggie had sworn her to secrecy when she asked her to come. And what a secret it was.

She *did* know what she would tell Elizabeth. She would tell her how in love and how tragic her sister was, how beautiful the baby was, how unlucky and lucky she was. Just the smell of the baby's milky breath made Jane's heart thud from someplace deep within her. Elizabeth was finishing her first semester of grad school and had told Jane she wasn't ready to talk about children yet—even though Jane had thought of little else since turning thirty. But Jane would focus on their love, she decided. Talk of babies could wait.

What couldn't wait was convincing Maggie to come home. If she didn't, what would happen to her and this baby? With no father, no job, there was nothing to keep her here in this country. Maggie couldn't—or wouldn't—explain why she wanted to stay in this place where, as far as Jane could tell, she had no future and, really, no past. The vacant look in her sister's eyes scared Jane, and each day she tried to convince her to come home. "But *this* is home," Maggie had pleaded. "This *is* her home."

Maggie had said this even as she handed Jane the baby. As the days passed, Maggie seemed less and less connected to her daughter, asked more and more of Jane. So, just as she had when Maggie was a baby, Jane changed diapers, mixed bottles of formula, and sang lullabies.

"Here, hold her," she told Maggie, but it was as if her sister were slipping away.

Taking a left onto a tree-lined boulevard, Jane used the map, followed her sister's instructions exactly, just as she said she would. Now she was walking parallel to the river, the squawking of foreign-sounding birds loud but not loud enough to wake a sleeping newborn. She wasn't sure where she was, but she made a point of noting the landmarks so she could get back. Unlike her sister, she didn't like leaving anything to chance. She spun the map and traced her path along the river. Judging by the not-so-straight lines, she was just a couple blocks from the spot labeled *La Ermita*.

Maggie had told Jane about the baby's father, and when she did, her eyes became misty and her face relaxed as if she were experiencing something from beyond and her voice would trail off. Jane tried not to get frustrated—she did know what it was like to love someone like you were the first person on the planet to ever experience this kind of love—but Maggie didn't even know the man's last name. How could a woman be so in love and know so little, wondered Jane. But then she examined Maggie's face and she knew it wasn't up to her to judge. Some things are better left unexplained.

The baby stretched one delicate arm, escaping the binding of the carrier. Jane paused and carefully tucked the little hand safely back inside. Then she looked up to see that she was across the street from what appeared to be a church. It had spires and a strange cross and an odd, Gothic look to it, out of place here among the palm trees.

"Señora," called a man pushing a cart.

Her instinct was to flinch, back away, protect the baby from this stranger, but then she saw mounds of fruits displayed under his brightly colored umbrella and felt foolish for being afraid of a peddler. She shook her head, wishing she could communicate. She should have brought Elizabeth, who had taken four years of high school Spanish, with her on this strange trip.

Another vendor rolled his cart onto the plaza across from the church and then another and another, and soon crowds began pouring out of the church doors, women in hats and smart suits, men in shined shoes, little children in tights and miniature blazers. Jane suddenly felt very out of place in her peasant dress and Earth Shoes. A priest in a robe stood by and Jane saw a habit-clad woman scurry around to the back of the church, which made her think of the stories Elizabeth had told her about the nuns in her parochial all-girls high school. Imagine being surrounded by all those women—it sounded both beautifully idyllic and incredibly trying.

The church's bell pealed and the baby cooed in her sleep, and Jane wished she were hers.

CHAPTER 30

As the crew gutted the kitchen, I tried to stay out of their way. I was practicing the art of staying out of everyone's way. No more mothers, no more Becks, no more Jason. Franklin? I wasn't sure. He had offered to help with the house, but I couldn't imagine going back to the easy camaraderie we had while raking leaves and cooking rice before . . . before everything.

And so I focused on Bojangles, Django, and the Victorian. And as progress was made in the kitchen, I began to picture the future. I saw that my old bedroom could be a nursery, the upstairs bathroom had its original cast-iron tub ready for rubber duckies, and the backyard could easily be the site of either tea parties or ball games. Right? I kept asking myself.

(*This will always feel like Jane and Elizabeth's house*, said Aunt Dot unhelpfully. *If Dorrie isn't going to bring back the symposia*, complained Great-Aunt Maureen, *what's the point of such a big living room?*)

I pushed aside their comments, and while the reconstruction took shape, I sorted through my mothers' belongings. In the linen closet upstairs, I started with a set of twin sheets that used to go on my childhood bed, long ago donated to an immigrant family from Somalia. Elizabeth's dresser drawers were filled with Woolrich sweaters and L.L.Bean corduroys that still smelled like tea tree deodorant. Downstairs, the coat closet in the foyer held Elizabeth's cross-country skis, a collection of gardening shoes, and a fur coat from Great-Aunt Maureen. Something was caught in the back of the closet, tangled in an old brown winter coat and a plaid scarf. Suspended on a wire hanger was the wooden mobile that used to hang over my crib, made by Uncle Harris, who had passed away from COVID before vaccines but was not part of my chorus. I held it up, the wood stars (a little crooked) and moon dancing on invisible fishing line. My chorus of women chatted and exclaimed as each item was revealed. Everywhere were memories, and not just for me.

In the living room, I tackled the built-in bookshelves that flanked the fireplace. Three decks of cards bound with brittle rubber bands, several board games, and a string of Christmas lights were wedged beside a yeast cookbook and Sylvia Plath's best-of collection. And behind all of it, hidden in the back of the shelf, was an album. The voices murmured, some saying they remembered this photo album, others anxiously waiting to see what was inside. I knelt on the floor, shifting the other books aside, and opened the plasticky pages with a crackle. After following the hand-drawn map through Cali, I knew a treasure when I saw one.

Inside the front cover of the album, in Grandma June's swirling script, was Margaret Moore's name. My first mother, my original mother. Ask any adoptee, anyone with an absent parent, and they will tell you. There will always be something missing. A piece of you, no matter how small. My mothers had tried to fill in the gaps with the stories I had heard as a child (and those doled out from my chorus), and I knew that was why Elizabeth had learned how to make empanadas and Jane wanted me to go to Colombia. And, yes, seeing Cali, the apartment, meeting Cristina—all those things filled more blank spaces. But the truth was that something was still missing, and perhaps always would be. Even if you're sure it's a very small piece, everyone knows that a 5,000-piece puzzle will never be complete with 4,999 pieces.

In the first photo—black and white—I recognized my grandparents' rambler in the winter, the sidewalk lined in snowbanks. The Moore family pose on the front step: Grandma June, Grandpa Vic, and Jane as a young woman. The only missing member must have been behind the shutter. On the next page was a black-and-white photo of Jane, her head bent over a book, her features relaxed like she doesn't know she's being photographed. The light falls on one side of her face, almost obscuring it in overexposure. A tree is out of focus behind her, making Mama's presence in the photo even more vivid.

(*I was so young!*)

I pulled back the plastic and peeled up a corner of the picture. "Dec 1988" was written on the back. I knew that handwriting. It was the same square print as the map, which was in my still-unpacked Travelpro. The photographer and the mapmaker were one.

Page by page, I leafed through the album, sitting cross-legged on the living room floor, past a series of half a dozen photos of plants and rocks, each taken extremely close up, the veins and imperfections and symmetry visible, the absence of color giving the viewer a sense of what the photographer saw.

There were several landscapes that, without color, looked almost moonlike. Then I found myself looking at a younger version of the Victorian itself in full, if faded, color. I let out a burst of laughter— there was something so charming about seeing my home when it was dark forest green with white trim, before the hydrangea in front had been planted. Without the shrubs, the front walk looked like a center part on a balding man.

"Meow," chirped Bojangles, and stretched and pawed the plastic. I gently pushed the cat off and shifted the album to my lap. As I did, something fell from its pages. A faded envelope with a logo for Foto-Rápido stamped on the front, wrinkled and torn along one edge. Several snapshots and a few strips of sepia negatives slipped to the floor. I could feel my chorus holding its collective breath as I examined each one.

The first: an old woman, so wrinkled it looked like her face could fold up into itself. She wore a black or very dark scarf wrapped tightly around her head like a nun or witch. But she had an interesting smile on her face, not exactly as enigmatic as, say, the Mona Lisa's but still—it felt like she knew something, maybe something about the woman behind the camera. It was a sibling of the photo of Doña Rojas in Cristina's apartment. I would send a copy of it to her, as a way to thank her for . . . everything.

The second photo was a blurry image of a person—a man. There was something familiar about the angle of his head. Even though the face was obscured by movement, I could tell the subject had broad shoulders, the same dark hair as mine.

(*Juan Carlos*, gasped a voice.)

I wasn't sure who in my chorus said it, but she was right. It had to be Juan Carlos. My father. Juan Carlos de la Peña, through new information and stories and now this photo, newly alive but also newly lost. I squinted and held the photograph close to my face as if I could dive into that moment. I stood up and switched on the lamp beside Elizabeth's chair. No matter what I did, the face didn't come into focus. But behind the out-of-focus face, I could see what looked like Italian architecture. I felt a great realization.

Bojangles leaped into the chair and rubbed his face against my hand, and his purr filled the quiet of the living room. My ears strained; what else could I hear? If I listened hard enough, I thought, maybe I could hear a deep, low voice, Spanish words, maybe a song. I wondered if my father had whispered to me while I was in my mother's belly. And, if he were part of my chorus, would I recognize his voice? It had never seemed odd that the voices I heard included no men, but maybe they had been there the whole time and I just had never listened for them.

I wiped my eyes and took a deep, shuddery breath before flipping to the last photo in the envelope. This one was not blurry. Crisp and so clear it felt like I could reach out and touch its subject: my mother. Margaret Dolores Moore, hugely pregnant, leaning on the railing of a stairway in the courtyard of an apartment building in Cali. Her belly protruded in front of her like a moon orbiting a planet, and I instinctively brought a hand to my own belly, which was just beginning to outgrow the elastic-waist pants I had found in Jane's dresser. In the photo, the mango tree behind Maggie Moore was lush and heavy with fruit. In her eyes, creased in a grin, I recognized the same self-conscious glint I always saw in my own photos. I sank into Mama's floral sofa and held the two photos in my hands. The blurry Juan Carlos in my left hand, the in-focus Maggie Moore in my right. Together.

"My parents," I said aloud to the empty room. Bojangles meowed and my voice cracked as the tears came. "I look like them."

The image on the screen was in black and white. The exam room paper underneath me crinkled and the too-cold air-conditioning whirred as a shape came in and out of focus. I tried to look at it with an artistic eye like Margaret Moore might have. But it was just a blob that twitched and moved. And it was blurry. As blurry as the photo of Juan Carlos. Or maybe that was my eyes stinging.

(*Goodness, this is exciting,* said Gigi. *A great-grandchild!* exclaimed Grandma June. *Don't get attached,* warned Elizabeth, *she gets to decide what to do. The right to choose is one thing,* said Aunt Judith, *but look at that profile.* The voices spoke over one another and contradicted each other, the image having finally solidified the reality of what was happening with me.)

I thought of the ultrasound taped to Trina's refrigerator in Cali. Back then, it hadn't seemed any more important or interesting than the crayon drawings of houses and robots. Since I left, she had texted me multiple times, always upbeat and cheery, always telling me to book another trip, always asking about Becks. I had finally answered last week and told her the baby had been named Daphne. It was a true thing I could tell Trina without telling her how I destroyed my relationship with my best friend.

"About ten and a half weeks," the sonogram tech told me.

Eleven weeks ago I had a mother. Two years ago I had two. A lifetime ago I had another mother, a father. And now what did I have?

I saw him across the clinic's busy lobby before he saw me. Some days, rattling around in the Victorian, I could almost imagine Franklin didn't exist, that he and I had never been together, had never had that night or those months long ago, but here he was, pushing an old man in a wheelchair; his gait was unmistakable, that lolling list to the left, the errant hairs at the top of his head that escaped his comb. I had once watched him walk across the quad from an upstairs library cubicle, and he had that same stride—purposeful and polite. He had detoured around a couple who stopped mid-sidewalk, then he cut across the grass, his footsteps leaving prints in the early spring turf. We hadn't seen each other since that night over cafeteria pizza a couple months earlier and he seemed so familiar that I lost my place in the paper I was writing, a mistype that deleted an entire page.

In 1742, a map of Lake Superior included the outlines of two islands: Isle Royale and Isle Phelipeaux. The two islands, perhaps mirror images of each other, were described in detail in the 1783 Treaty of Paris, which officially ended the Revolutionary War. But someone, somewhere, had made an error—whether a copyist's mistake, the faulty communications from an explorer, or a mapmaker's duplicate—because the Isle Phelipeaux isn't real. Its partner, Isle Royale, is there off the Minnesota shore of the biggest of the Great Lakes; you can go visit the pine forest and wolf habitat. But there is no landmass beside it, no evidence of Phelipeaux. It never existed.

But here he was, an island in the sea of strangers. I tucked the black-and-white printout into my purse. We were on a collision course and it was only a matter of moments before he glanced up.

"Dorrie!" he cried. "Look, Grandpa, it's Dorrie."

Grandpa Bao grinned. "I'd stand up and hug you," he said, "but I'm afraid I'm stuck in this thing."

"He fell and twisted his ankle," Franklin explained. "We just got X-rays and we're glad it wasn't his hip, right, Grandpa?"

Mr. Liu reached out his hand, brown and wizened, and I shook it. He didn't let go. "You're lovely," he said, and then kissed my palm.

(*How cute*, exclaimed Aunt Dot. *I hate when old people are called cute*, complained Gigi. *But you have to admit that he's sweet.*)

"How are you, Miss Dorrie?"

Franklin nodded and repeated, "How *are* you?"

(*Tell him!* said my chorus. *Secrets always come out.*)

"I'm good." I smiled at Grandpa Bao. "The cats miss you."

Grandpa Bao squeezed my hand. Franklin tilted his head and seemed to study me. "You look a little . . ." He paused and appraised me, a look that was both intimate and clinical. "A little crooked."

"I'm—" I began. I could feel my chorus (the potential grandmothers in particular) holding their collective breath, waiting for me to say the truth. "It's the construction, so much noise. Thanks for referring me to Jim, he's—"

And then a woman was at Franklin's side, laying a hand on his arm. "It's going to be twenty minutes," she said. She was shorter than me, petite with long black hair curled in beachy waves. She wore glasses with little flowers at the temples.

"I'm Dorrie," I said—which was a truth.

"Sorry!" exclaimed Franklin. "This is Dorrie, Sasha."

(The chorus gasped.)

How complicated everything was, I thought, suddenly deeply weary, exhaustion sinking over me.

"Hi," Sasha said absently and then continued. "They won't have his prescription for twenty minutes, so I can wait while you take him home."

Home. I was reminded how powerful the word was.

"No, you go back to work," Franklin said. "We'll wait." And then Sasha handed him a piece of paper, a ring on her finger flashing in the harsh fluorescent clinic lights.

Sasha, an ultimatum, my mother's ring. His words echoed in my head as clear as my chorus's voices. I clutched my bag closer, thinking of the printed ultrasound. He had made a decision, which meant I could too.

"Nice to meet you, Sasha," I said. She turned to me, her face blank, and it was clear she'd never heard of me. I had told Jason about Franklin—we had shared all our past romances—although, I realized now, I had never used his name. "My college boyfriend," I used to say, as if that was his only title. "Freshman-year Franklin," Becks had always called him. "I'm an old friend of Franklin's."

"Are you a paramedic too?" Sasha asked.

"Cartographer."

"Is that a job still? Sounds so old-fashioned. Like what's-his-name. Mercator?"

"Yes, well, we work a little differently now, but it's sort of the same thing. People always need to know where they're going," I said flippantly, as if cartography were that simple, as if we mapmakers could solve that sort of existential dilemma.

"Nice to meet you, Lori."

No one corrected her.

"I really should get back to work, Frank," Sasha said.

Frank. I didn't like the way she shortened his name, the way he seemed smaller when she said it. Grandpa Bao didn't seem to like it either, because he reached up for my hand again. I gripped his fingers and placed my other hand on his shoulder, reveling in the way he took up space, the way his bones felt solid and present. I'd become too accustomed to accepting whispers of people.

"It's so nice to see you," I said, reluctantly letting go of Grandpa Bao's hand. My lump pushed against my breastbone as Franklin steered the wheelchair across the lobby to the elevators.

CHAPTER 31

In the air-conditionless kitchen, box fans did little more than move around the hot, sticky air of late July, and Jim the contractor and his workers sweated, adding a new, sour scent to the bouquet from the water damage. I tried to chat with them in my newly honed Spanish, but I found their colloquialisms different and their accents difficult to understand no matter how much we smiled and nodded at each other, and so after that, I got out of their way as much as I could—often escaping to the love seat on the porch, where the laughter of neighborhood children mixed with the Mexican Spanish and the voices of my chorus.

(*I did not care for that woman*, they said after the run-in with Sasha. *She's not right for that boy.*)

I appreciated their opinions, but I was ready to move on, to forget all about Franklin Liu. To get on with it.

But getting on with things was more difficult since the nausea I had experienced in Cali had been replaced by bone-deep exhaustion. My whole body begged for sleep as if I had never known a full night's rest in my life. It reminded me of the way Jane had slept near the end, often and deeply. I felt a change in my body that, for once, echoed the changes in my life. I had begun to take daily naps in the afternoons, after the workmen left for the day, and every day, in the lazy breeze of a ceiling fan, I had dreams of Colombia.

In one, I'm at the apartment on calle 5 Norte and instead of an invisible, early pregnancy, my belly is huge, protrudes awkwardly out in front of me. I'm in the courtyard, sweating under the mango tree, when I spot a face in an upstairs window. First it's a worried Cristina and then it's Margaret Moore, as peaceful as she looked in her high school photo, staring down at me. In another, I'm walking along the río Cali, the call of birds echoing in a blue darkness. I realize I can't move my feet; they're heavy as if chained to the earth. "Dolores," says a voice, and Oscar is there in the dark, his hands on my stomach, my face, my shoulder. I try to cry out but my voice comes soft as a whisper. Suddenly, I realize that in my hand is a bell, like the one on the reception desk at the Hotel América. I begin to ring it. Ring, ring. "Here's your baggage," the gray woman says. My Travelpro appears. "And this too," she says. Another, a duplicate. Then a larger one, then a vintage Louis Vuitton makeup case, then an old-fashioned steamer trunk, then more roller bags and duffels and satchels. "Your baggage is all here," the unfriendly concierge says. "I'll call for the porter."

Ring, ring.

I slowly awoke as the ringing in my dream morphed into the ringing of a doorbell.

"Jason."

I hadn't planned to ever see Jason again. We had exchanged our belongings, switched our social media profiles, untangled our lives. He had been so certain of our breakup that he had been efficient in every area: the gas bill, the Costco membership, the shared cell phone plan. He had extricated himself from me firmly and, I had thought, permanently. When I had needed someone with me as I cared for Jane, he had vanished.

So his appearance at my front door felt as surreal as my dream. Real-life Jason seemed to blend with a ghost of Oscar, and the two of them were standing together in the Victorian's foyer, each so different and yet with me in common. I blinked. And only Jason was standing there.

(*What is he doing here?*)

"What are you doing here?"

"Your mail," he said, pushing past me into the house as if he owned the place. "It looked important."

(The voices debated. *He's a nice man. He was never good enough for Dorrie. Better someone than no one.*)

Jason handed me the stack and he was right, the one on the top did look important. A document from the state somehow got routed to my old address. The death certificate. I had seen enough of these envelopes to know what it was: proof of my aloneness in black and white. I didn't open it. Instead, I thanked him, but he was already heading into the living room, getting a glimpse of the kitchen and disaster beyond.

It was like being caught with your skirt tucked in your pantyhose or spinach in your teeth. I knew that the destruction wasn't my fault, but seen through his eyes, it felt like it must have been—a complete contrast to the Flynns. His immaculate duplex, the neat suits and chinos he wore, his mother's fastidiousness. I had never been quite right for Jason; he had always wanted to change me. For a while, I thought that was the best thing about him.

"What happened here?" He was already appraising, using his Realtor's voice. "Nice workmanship," he said, and slapped the counter.

I had been there when Jim's two strong, young workers inched the new countertop in place. I didn't have any preference for materials or the desire to make decisions, but he had insisted I needed composite stone, the same thing Franklin had put in Grandpa Bao's kitchen.

"Sure," I had said, and pretended to care about stone samples, pointing to one that I thought I could live with—a dusty tan with flecks of something shiny and new. Once the workmen had finished, Jim the contractor wiped it clean with a cloth, and it looked like it belonged, like it had always been here in the Victorian's kitchen, and at the same time, it also had a bit of sparkle.

"It doesn't matter," I snapped at Jason. "Not your concern."

"Who'd you use?"

"This doesn't have anything to do with you anymore."

"You know, Dorr, I could still help you sell."

Ever practical, Jason had first begun to talk about property values a few months after Elizabeth's funeral. Along with Becks, he had been a rock for me and Jane during those first confusing months of not quite believing Mommy was gone. He picked out movies to watch and touched up scuffs and peeling paint from half-empty cans in the basement. His mother sent brownies and pints of ice cream as Jane lost weight from what we thought was grief but later found out had more to do with the return of her cancer. During that time, I would curl around his warm body at night, comforted by his solid presence, the certainty of our life. But then, as the months went on, he began to talk about a retirement community, where his parents lived, how low-maintenance it was, how Jane would love it.

(*Community!* Great-Aunt Maureen had scoffed. All of my relatives lived in their own homes until the end.)

He said that his father, Tom, was on the recycling committee at Lasting Memories, and Gail was in charge of field trips. I had rolled my eyes at Jane and she snickered. I could just imagine Gail Flynn bossing around her new neighbors and organizing the best outings.

"Jane doesn't want to sell," I told him as she had nodded her agreement.

Now Jason, looking around at the unfinished work, tried another tack: "You could sell this place 'as is' and walk away with good money."

"Jason," I said, "is there anything else you need?"

He shook his head and, with one movement, knocked a stack of papers from the countertop. Magazines that hadn't yet been canceled, several issues of the neighborhood newsletter, and the pamphlets from the ob-gyn slid to the floor.

Jason stooped, picked them up, and began to hand them to me. It felt like time slowed down, like he was acres away, moving through thick air. *Prenatal Diet* and *Choices* inched through space.

I tried to grab the papers, but he registered their contents before I could move.

"What is this?" His face was white.

When we first moved in together, I had had a late period. Six days, which was unheard of for me. At first, the delay didn't worry me; after all, I had been lugging boxes and moving furniture into Jason's new duplex. He had bought the building and would rent out the other half while we lived in the updated side, all stainless-steel appliances and gray walls. Then, by five days overdue, I knew it was time for a pregnancy test. I hadn't told him but he had seen the box, and he jumped to conclusions, eager like a puppy.

"I can explain—" I began now.

"You're pregnant?"

"I'm—"

"—is it mine?"

I tried not to roll my eyes. His optimism was exhausting.

"Jason—" I tried. Speaking in hyphens, in dashes, as if my very words could turn to lines, roads, boundaries. "—it's not what you think."

"Dorrie," he said. I pulled at the pamphlets but he held them fast. "Dormouse." He only called me that when we were together, alone, intimate. "You're having a baby?"

That day four years ago, I hadn't been pregnant. To my great relief and his disappointment.

"It's—"

But he wrapped his arms around me, squeezed me, lifted me off the floor that still needed tiling.

"I knew you would change your mind!"

When we were together, I would remind him that I never wanted children, but he would shush me, rub my back, and say, "I know your birth mother died, but I'd make sure you were okay, I'd get you the best medical care. And, anyway, *your* mother died in a third-world country." I bristled at the memory of his use of that outdated term.

"My mother knows the number one obstetrician in Minnesota," he said now, reminding me again of the story of his sister who had had a difficult birth but it all turned out okay. "I would never let anything bad happen to you."

The world swirled and I could feel an attack of vertigo coming on. "Please, Jason, you don't understand."

I suppose I should have guessed how he'd react. Even after I had assured him the result was negative that day in his duplex, he still hoped for another twenty-four hours until I started bleeding. Now, as we talked and I tried to explain things, told him I wasn't with the father, that it was a surprise, I realized I should have known that he'd take my accidental pregnancy personally, that he'd expect me to come back to him. It would look to him like I *had* changed.

"I don't mind that this one isn't mine," he said. That's how badly he wanted a family.

(*That's sweet*, said a voice. *It's creepy*, said another.)

"We can be a family, Dorrie. We'll have more babies. This was meant to be."

"No." I shook my head. "I'm sorry." I didn't love him anymore—perhaps I'd never loved him—but I was sorry I couldn't fulfill his desire. I had stepped back, but now I moved toward him, feeling his pain and forgiving him for not being the man I wanted to be with. I reached for the pamphlets, taking them one at a time and stacking them on the countertop. "It's not—it's not meant to be with us, Jay. This is about me. Just me."

We both looked down at our hands, and in his was the last pamphlet: *Choices*. And that's when an anger that perhaps he'd been holding on to since our first conversations, our first disagreements about children and families, exploded. It was so unexpected, Jason Flynn with his sweater vests and neat part and pleasant aftershave. He railed at me now, hurled words at me. He took the pamphlets and ripped them apart. He shredded them, letting their confetti sprinkle across the subfloor until a breeze from the fan lifted them and they swirled like snow. I thought for a moment of Joaquim: *Snow, can you imagine?*

"I can't even believe you'd consider this," Jason said before ripping the *Choices* pamphlet. "I should have known. My mother warned me it would be like this. But I kept defending you. You and your fucking hippie baby-killing dyke moms."

(*What?!* Outraged shock rippled through the chorus.)

His words were daggers, poison darts heading straight to my heart. My vision went black, I stumbled. I wanted to yell, *I'm not a fainter!* But I had to grab the countertop to keep my balance and when I could see again, I took in the sparkle and it seemed to give me strength.

"Get out!" I yelled with all the force of my body, my history. "This is *my* life!" I declared.

CHAPTER 32

Late July is always hot in Minnesota, and this year the humidity reached tropical levels. Due to its latitude and its inland location, far from the moderating effects of the oceans, the Upper Midwest is known for its wide temperature swings from life-threatening cold to sweltering heat. Minnesota is parallel with Washington state, France's Normandy region, and Germany's Rhineland, but has none of the vineyards or rocky cliffs of those places. Instead, the forty-fifth latitude ensured that my mothers' Victorian was too cold in the winter and too hot in the summer.

Now that I was at the beginning of my second trimester, I was increasingly overtaken by an exhaustion at a level I had never before experienced. Those were the times I missed my mothers the most—when my limbs felt leaden and my head fuzzy—and my solitude in the Victorian palpable. The voices offered bland suggestions, but I ached for Becks and the sympathy and advice she would have given me if I hadn't destroyed everything.

Before he drove away, Jason had told me I'd be sorry, that I'd never get an offer like this again, that he'd never be back.

But what was another absent person? People go, I reminded myself. Things disappear. Life, at its very core, was fragile and temporary. My role as daughter was cut short by Elizabeth's massive heart attack and Jane's cancer. My trip to Colombia was abbreviated by Becks's emergency, and our friendship had been severed by my tactlessness. And I never even got a chance to know my father or biological mother.

In the sweltering kitchen, the sour scent of the workmen still hanging in the air, Bojangles leaped onto the sparkling composite stone. The subfloors had been tiled, but the Sheetrock needed painting and the light fixtures needed installing. Otherwise, it was almost complete. The cat meowed and I scratched him under the chin. Jim the contractor had selected the dishwasher and the stainless steel sink and the induction stove. But maybe it was time for me to make a decision. Maybe I could move forward, I told myself. Take it one step at a time. The least I could do was choose a color for the walls.

I wandered up and down the aisles of the home improvement store, feeling out of place. Elizabeth had been the tinkerer, seeking grout or flathead screws, and even though she and Jane had tried to free me from gender expectations by buying me both trains and dolls, I had never been enamored with trucks like Andrés was, and Becks and I obsessed over the secret lives of our dolls. I knew nothing of fittings and flanges.

I pushed the unwieldy cart and tried to think geographically. In the tenth century, explorers from the Ottoman Empire left China and crossed the Mediterranean, passed through what would eventually be named the Strait of Gibraltar, and meandered the shoreline of the Atlantic Ocean, mapping the coast of Greenland. Unlike the warring Christians, they hadn't come to convert or conquer and they didn't claim; they had come to explore.

The paint department appeared to be one of the few places where women congregated, and I scanned the rows of chips alongside them, holding the colors up to the artificial light, trying to see

into the future. Squares of Sea Foam and Linen White made my throat catch. I impulsively grabbed the light green; I would complete the study while I was at it.

While I'm at it. I put a hand on my low belly. The weeks had gone by and I knew that by not making a decision, I had essentially decided. *Colombians make the best babies,* Trina had said.

Despite my penchant for strategy and deliberation, I found myself trying to imagine one future I had never planned, never thought I wanted, over another just as unknown. One path would be stasis and stability, the other meant movement.

(*Was Dorrie always this passive?* Elizabeth wondered.)

Was I? I knew I should apologize to Becks, to tell her she had been right to be angry at me, to beg for forgiveness for burdening her with my indecision, especially at that time. I wanted her back in my life, but I was somehow also becoming more and more accustomed—again—to solitude. Trina and Oscar and all the rest seemed like a dream I had had once. Franklin was . . . I didn't know but I wasn't ready to talk to him any more than I was ready to talk to Becks. I didn't know if she would ever forgive me. Instead, I listened to my chorus, enjoyed their comforting, inane commentary.

I turned to the riot of colors displayed on the racks. A woman with a toddler in a cart reached around me and grabbed a blue. Blue with a hint of purple, reminding me of the feather of the colibrí that landed—however briefly—on my wrist. It was the color of the sky in Cali just after the sun dips behind the mountains. I thought of the new cupboards in pale maple and grabbed the chip too. Perhaps this would be my new kitchen, remade in shades of Colombia.

"Dorrie?"

I turned and there he was. Of course. Inescapable. There were dozens of family-owned hardware stores across the city. Multiple and competing big-box home improvement stores were scattered around the suburbs, each open long hours, plenty of time to shop without running into anyone. And yet, here we were.

"Franklin." My first thought was vain. How did I look? I was wearing one of Jane's loose-fitting blouses and baggy jeans. Would he know or would he think I had put on weight, perhaps from the grief? "Hello."

I fiddled with the blue paint chip—True Blue—turning it in my fingers like a card dealer in Vegas, not that I'd ever been to Nevada. Franklin pushed a cart filled with planks (Is that what they're called?) of wood (Two-by-fours?). "Got a project?"

"Trestle tables. It's for Grandpa Bao's funeral." His face was ashy.

I tried not to gasp in shock, tried to make my voice steady. "I'm so sorry." Tears pricked my eyes, saliva built in the back of my mouth, and I squinted. "When?"

"The funeral is tomorrow. He died last week."

(*That nice man, what a shame.*)

"You didn't tell me," I said, and then felt foolish to think I would be the one he would call. He had Sasha, after all, someone to lean on, to depend on.

He didn't respond, so I reached out across the aisle, put my hand on his forearm. He grabbed it and pulled me into an embrace. And then Franklin was shaking, his body trying to keep the tears from coming, resisting what must happen.

"I had so hoped to see him again," I mumbled into Franklin's chest. "The cats miss him, especially Django."

He chuckled through his sobs and clung to me more fiercely.

"Would it be okay if I came to the funeral?"

"Please," he said, his voice strangled. "It wasn't sudden and it wasn't a surprise, but it still hurts." I rubbed his back, the spot where his shoulder blades jutted, and he told me about the shock of discovering that Grandpa Bao had passed in his sleep, the surreal duty of telling his father. The phone calls and the conversations.

"I understand," I said, and he gripped me tighter.

Back at the Victorian, brand-new brushes and rollers were scattered across the subfloor. When I got home from the store, I peeled off the blouse on which Franklin had shed tears and changed into a pair of Elizabeth's baggy army-green shorts and a college-branded T-shirt threadbare with age. I taped off the edges of the new cabinetry and thought about the loss of Grandpa Bao and the raw grief in Franklin's eyes, and how we're never prepared. Franklin had asked me if I had ever seen someone die. He knew how profound—and inevitable—death was, and yet nothing prepares you for your specific loss.

As I pried off the lid of the can of True Blue, all the losses came back to me—Jane at home in that hospice bed, Elizabeth before I could get to the hospital, Maggie in an apartment in Colombia, Juan Carlos falling from the sky. So much loss. I worked in silence, methodically tearing at the blue tape, lining up the edges as precisely as possible and admiring Jim and his workmen's handicraft. I was getting on with it. *Again.* I dipped my brush into the paint.

(*Is she sure about that color?*)

My phone buzzed in my pocket, and I set down the paint brush. It was a college number. All the phone numbers at the college started with the same prefix, which I would dial when I called Mama in her office or Mommy in the library. They would answer and immediately ask what was wrong, as if an only child can't call her mothers to ask about where the extra roll of toilet paper is or whether she can sleep over at the Eastmans' again. My eyes stung as I looked at the three numerals.

"Dorrie Moore? Or is it Pelletier?"

It wasn't my mothers, of course. The only way I heard their voices now was in my chorus.

"Yes?" I said cautiously. "Moore. Dolores Moore," I confirmed.

"Dorrie, this is Hank."

I waited. I knew of no one named Hank. This must be a fund-raising call, probably an undergraduate earning twelve dollars an hour asking alumni for money—not that I was alumni.

"Hank Lundgren. Dean. Sciences." He paused. "How are you holding up, Dorrie?"

I looked down at the bump under my T-shirt. "I'm fine, Dr. Lundgren."

"I'm calling," he said, clearing his throat with a phlegmy cough, "about a position in the Geography Department."

As he talked about curriculum and enrollment and interviews, I stared into the can of True Blue, thinking of Cali's sky and the Hotel América's sparkling swimming pool. While he explained that the position would be adjunct this year but was set to be tenure-track the next, I heard my mothers' voices, the voices of my grandmothers and my aunts chattering and considering. But I was thinking about which room I would paint next, whether I would paint my child-hood bedroom yellow or lavender.

"We would be so pleased if you would consider interviewing," Dr. Lundgren said.

I dipped the brush and painted broad strokes, leaving behind vibrant color, making the kitchen new again. Mine.

CHAPTER 33

My chorus had been right all those weeks (or was it months?) ago: sitting on the porch floor in my wool skirt *had* snagged the weave. In addition, I couldn't button it, so I found a pair of black ponte pants in Jane's closet and covered the elastic waist with my black V-neck, which now showed off more cleavage than I'd ever had. An approximation of the funeral outfit I never thought I'd need again.

(*Has she even had that dry-cleaned yet?* complained the voices.)

Bao Liu's funeral was beautiful and joyous and sad and heartbreaking. I sat in the back of the church but spotted Franklin and his family members, their faces solemn. I looked for Sasha—I would smile politely at her, I told myself—but didn't see her anywhere. Three floral arrangements contrasted with one another at the pulpit—one of organic daisies and long grasses, one with neat and formal lilies, one a riot of brightly colored gerberas. Staid recorded music played quietly through unseen speakers as people shuffled in.

The program I had been handed featured a younger version of Grandpa Bao on the cover in shades of black and white. I studied the photo, noting the parts of him that reminded me of Franklin. The way the eyes crinkled at the corners, the particular slope of the forehead.

(*Good genes*, said someone. *Handsome.*)

The hair on my arms stood up as I realized that Grandpa Bao's genes now had something to do with me. Throats cleared, noses sniffed, an organist hit a wrong note. The hard pews, the up and down, the hymnal—it all reminded me of funerals past. Grandma June's Lutheran service with Communion, Aunt Judith's memorial in the rec center where she had volunteered, Aunt Dot's dignified affair at the storied and venerated cemetery chapel. Elizabeth's and Jane's send-offs at the college where they had devoted their professional lives. These services and memorials and funerals never quite captured the essence of my relatives, but they acknowledged their lives, their impacts.

Even though I had only met Franklin's grandfather a few times, my eyes grew misty as one of the Liu siblings choked up during the eulogy. *Thank you*, I wished I could say to Jane, *for not making me do this.* Every time someone we know dies, we are reminded of our own mortality. I supposed that was why Jason had wanted children so badly, why most humans do. Leaving behind progeny is the ultimate act of ensuring something of yourself is left in the world. Tangible DNA, maps for the next generation and the next and the one after that.

As I opened the hymnal and pretended to recite the words of "A Mighty Fortress" or whatever it was, I realized that my chorus was part of what had kept me from that primal desire. I had never seen death as the end. A change, yes, but not the end, not an absence. I pictured myself, five or six years old in a cherry-red headband, chatting with Grandma June. How could I possibly have imagined creating my own offspring when I was already surrounded by my relatives, burdened with the needs and wants of past generations? I didn't blame them, not really, but I did see, suddenly, as I stood to recite the Lord's Prayer alongside the Liu family, that if I could let them go, maybe I could make room for whatever was to come next, even if it wasn't in my original plan.

A map is simply one interpretation of a set of data. The GPS on your phone, the competitors' apps, the road atlas. These are different ways of seeing the same information—none more right or more wrong, simply different. What had always intrigued me about maps was that the cartographer's version of the world was what became reality for the map user. The mapmaker got to define our space and places, add clarity to what was otherwise confusing and chaotic. A map made order out of chaos. You didn't have to obey its grids or markings, but you knew it would be foolish not to, not if you hoped to get where you wanted to go.

And I had always felt that my relatives, my Greek chorus, were serving that same purpose: making order out of chaos, showing me the way, defining reality. The voices didn't insist, didn't demand. Like a map, they were there, available, and it had seemed ridiculous to even ponder not consulting them, not letting them guide me.

But what if their voices were just one interpretation of the world? What if they did not represent, simply by virtue of existing, the definitive path of my life? I thought about the hand-drawn map of the sights of Cali, and I thought about what I actually saw there. I had expected the map to represent the reality of my birthplace. But it was only one interpretation, a rendering by my parents, yes, but still only one way of looking at the city. I had found friends and mangos and vistas and experiences even without the map. Even my life, one I had started out charting, had strayed many times from what I thought I had mapped for myself. Caregiving and deaths, the end of relationships and jobs, a trip to South America, a friend lost and found again. These things hadn't been part of my life map, but they had been rich and meaningful and each one had led to something new and fresh and spectacular in their newness. And, I realized, each of these things had happened without the guidance of my chorus; these events and choices had been a result of my life lived.

We filed out of the sanctuary, following the Liu family: the head mourners. I remembered being part of that processional, watched by the damp eyes of other mourners, feeling somehow proud to be acknowledged as the saddest one. When it was my grandmother, my uncle, my great-aunt, my mother, I earned the right to not glance up, to keep my eyes focused on the carpeted aisle or linoleum floor. Franklin did not look at me when he passed my pew.

In the vestibule outside the sanctuary, the Liu family greeted friends and acquaintances, shook hands, nodded. I recognized Franklin's mother, whose brown hair was now mostly gray. His father, shorter than I remembered him, stood uncomfortably in a black suit, and beside him were Franklin's half-siblings. Two brothers with shy wives; a sister, unmarried.

As my family members had each passed, one by one, my place in the funeral receiving line moved up until I was at the front of the parade, until I was the only one left. The last of the Moores. The endling.

I felt a fluttering, remembering that word. Endling. That's what Franklin had called me, and that's what I assumed I would be always. The fluttering continued at the thought of his words. And then I realized the fluttering wasn't emotional or in my head. The fluttering was very real and it was coming from my abdomen. I wasn't an endling. Not anymore.

I went through the line, pressing my flesh against the flesh of these strangers until I came to Franklin. He stood a little apart from his family, alone. I saw no sign of Sasha.

"Dorrie," he said.

Franklin. This tall and lanky EMT whose feet were too big for his frame. My college boyfriend, holder of memories that even I had forgotten. I reached up and hugged him, mumbled something sympathetic in the direction of his ear. My boyfriend who had become an ex, a choice I had made but had never really understood. His suit jacket was smooth, the fabric slightly slippery under my hand. My friend, this helpful, thoughtful man, who could take care of his grandfather and rake leaves and rub Bojangles under his chin. This man who was going to be a part of my future, even though that had never been on the map.

The reception was held at the yellow house, where I could see what Franklin had used the lumber from the home improvement store for. A long makeshift table was set up in the driveway, its two-by-four legs just visible under several damask tablecloths.

Women—as at every gathering—brought Crock-Pots and platters out from the house, arranging them in a predetermined array that they wouldn't let me help with.

(*Such a nice spread,* said Grandma June. *Such variety,* agreed Gigi, still unhappy about the meager college catering at Jane's reception.)

"Please, eat," the women insisted.

I stood to the side as people arrived, nibbling a dumpling, thinking about my mothers' parties, their symposia and holiday gatherings. The Victorian, now so quiet, had once been a sort of Alexandria. In the first century, people from three continents converged on that city, the largest of the ancient world, which was an intellectual center for nearly a millennium. Like the Alexandrians, my mothers welcomed their coworkers and friends, sometimes even their enemies. They held discussions and heated arguments, wine tastings and cooking marathons. My mothers might not have been adventurous, never leaving the comfort of their house, but they had invited the outside world in. I remembered the pile of coats on their bed, the smells of cheap perfume and stale incense, the shiny clatter of the breaking of the occasional glass. I would sit on the third-from-the-bottom stair and peer through the slats, where I could watch and listen but not be seen. I was always a good listener.

As the driveway filled with people in their black suits and navy dresses, I faded into the background, feeling out of place and in the way and wishing I had a stair on which to perch. There was still no sign of Sasha or her beachy waves and I told myself to stop looking for her, to assume she would appear at some point, a manicured hand on Franklin's arm. A path that wound along shrubbery and snaked around the house to the backyard caught my eye. I followed the flagstones and squeezed past a potting bench tucked next to the house with half-empty bags of soil underneath. A pegboard held tools, each labeled: trowel, shears, snippers.

For Alexandria, time marched forward, tastes shifted, wars were fought, and eventually the mecca moved elsewhere, the ancient city fading from popularity. My mothers' house, too, had become more of a passing place, a port, an interim location. If I wanted, I thought, I could use it as such, I could think more like Maggie than Jane, I could venture farther from home. After all, you can always return—can't you?

I ran my hand along Grandpa Bao's tools, artifacts of his existence. A flashback of him on his knees in the garden that day when I was nineteen and in love. I continued to follow the stepstones into the garden and between small trees and beds of flowers. I could hear Elizabeth listing off names: rudbeckia, aster, sedum, allium. Gigi was adding her opinions on their hardiness and the appropriateness of their placement in this garden. Jane suggested which plants would work well at the Victorian, which corners needed more or less sun, amended soil, rabbit fences. But I didn't keep track of their commentary and, anyway, my vision was clouding as my eyes filled with tears.

I couldn't imagine leaving the Victorian. But I also couldn't imagine a stagnant life, a life lived exactly as Jane and Elizabeth had lived theirs, with their voices in my head guiding and guarding me.

At the rear of the backyard, along a fence that divided this city lot from the next, I found a bench. Its wooden slats were smooth and carefully hewn, the handiwork of either Bao or the grandson. I lowered myself down and leaned back, inhaling the scent of lavender and pine. A low hum of voices drifted from the house and driveway, too far away to be heard clearly. But I was used to mumbled voices.

My own chorus had quieted. Maybe they were listening too, or maybe they had gotten bored, moved on to whatever else they did when I couldn't hear them. A cardinal whistled and flew past, and I remembered the birds Oscar and I had seen in Cali. A charm of hummingbirds. The wings had been such bright colors—blues and purples and turquoise—that it almost felt like a dream, and I wished I had kept the feather. I wanted evidence of my life.

I laid a hand on my abdomen. I *had* evidence. The calm of the Liu garden's yellows and purples seemed familiar, something I couldn't quite remember. I pulled out my phone and snapped a photo of the purple blossoms and the black-eyed Susans, the tall stalks of grasses and the frill of ferns. I studied the image and realized what it reminded me of. My fingers hovered over the screen. And then I sent the photo to Becks.

Dorrie: I'm here.

I didn't expect—or deserve—a response. I had been greedy, I realized, to burden Becks with my unasked-for fertility, at that moment, to position myself in the middle of her trauma. Sometimes we needed to hear other people's thoughts and feelings, and sometimes we need others to listen. I hadn't been listening to my friend that day. That was the problem with being an only child, *the* only child. It's easy to do childish, selfish things.

I looked out at Grandpa Bao's cedars. And then my phone rang. "Becks?"

"I'm so sorry," she blurted.

"You're sorry? I'm sorry!" We spoke over each other, each apologizing. "I'm so sorry about what happened at the hospital."

"I should have been there for you," she said. I began to protest and tell her that I had been selfish, that I never should have broken my news that way. "No, Dorrie. I'm the one who should have been your friend. You needed me and I shut you out. It's just . . ." she began and I could hear a clog in her throat. She went on. "I've always envied you, Dorrie, you and your cool moms, who understood about girls and teens and the way we wanted to live our own lives. I had Ellen and John—nice but so boring. You had this exotic background, that perfect black hair, that mysterious past. It always seemed like everything came so easily to you—I mean, you went to graduate school, have an amazing, interesting career."

"You thought I had it easy? I'm unemployed, Becks. I'm single! You know I was always envious of your family, so perfect like a TV show. Mom, dad, two kids. I wished you could be *my* sister instead of Kyle's sister."

"He would have preferred that too," Becks interrupted, her voice snagging.

"And your mom was always there, always reliable. Unlike my

mothers, who you never knew about. Would they be home? Would it be a family dinner or would there be a roomful of strangers drinking something odd like port. Who drank port in the nineties? And your dad . . . John might have been a bit boring, but you had a dad. You still have a dad, a mom."

"I know and I'm sorry now. I said things . . . well, my hormones, as Charlie keeps saying, are very out of whack. That's not an excuse, but it's true. And I know now that you've had a hard time too. But after I moved away, it just seemed like you began to live your own life, apart from me. I'm lonely here, Dorrie. And while I was stuck on bed rest you were gallivanting across South America with hot guys." Her words were falling now, caught between a hysterical laugh somewhere between crying and giggling. She never used words like *gallivanting*, and I knew I was forgiven. "But you never wanted children, so for you to magically get pregnant—it was a lot."

"I know," I said softly. "My timing was terrible."

Becks chuckled that great, beautiful guffaw she did sometimes. "Okay, I agree, it was terrible timing!" Then she asked where the picture I had sent her was taken. "It looks just like that place your moms rented."

Behind me a cardinal chattered and the song buoyed the full feeling in my heart. I explained to Becks about Grandpa Bao, the funeral. I could hear the babble of a baby in the background. I pictured my best friend bouncing in place, soothing her infant.

"Is that the sound of your beautiful baby?"

She sniffed. "Oh, Dorrie. Daphne is amazing, but it's heartbreaking to know she'll never have a brother or sister."

"Well, it might not be exactly the same thing," I said, "but, Becks?"

A beat of silence. Was it a void or was she there for me?

"I'm keeping it." Without a map, without instructions, I was plunging into the unknown.

(*She'll be fine*, said Gigi.)

I would be. I wanted to silence their commentary. I didn't need my chorus to tell me I'd be fine. I had Becks, I had Olga, I had . . . new friends. And I could make more; Trina and Seb and Hannah and even María Sofía had taught me that. I was smart, I was capable. Even with the pamphlets shredded and unreadable, I had already begun to increase my intake of fresh vegetables and water, and had found, to my dismay, that coffee had a new, musty, chalky taste, so I was drinking tea in the mornings now. Rooibos and Darjeeling in stoneware mugs. I was turning into my mothers.

"Maybe our babies can be should-be sisters."

(*Is she really going to be able to handle becoming a mother?* asked Aunt Dot, who had never had children of her own.)

"Oh, Dorrie."

Another beat of silence. Neither of us could speak, I knew. We were sharing a moment of silence, together. Words didn't always need to be spoken for people to understand one another.

"It's the hardest most wonderful job." Becks was crying.

"I'm gonna need a lot of help, then."

CHAPTER 34

I stayed hidden in the corner of Grandpa Liu's garden long after Becks and I ended our call. Our reconciliation. Dappled sunlight coming through the branches of the maple above blinded me and I squinted. In the darkness behind my lids I caught glimpses of the río Cali, a swaddled baby, a mango tree. I blinked again—tears?—and saw the faces of my relatives blurry and superimposed one over another. Jane, Maggie, Gigi, even Baba and Grandpa Vic.

"Here you are."

I turned to see Franklin following the path toward my bench. A flurry of chattering surrounded me.

(*Tell him now. You don't need to tell him anything. You can do this alone. You don't have to do it alone.*)

The words and advice and opinions of my Greek chorus swirled like a charm of hummingbirds.

"I was looking for you."

"I'm sorry," I said, standing up. All the visions and voices slid away. "It's just such a lovely spot."

"Sit," he said, lowering himself. "I could use a moment of quiet."

Wishing I hadn't stood, I looked at the slats of the bench and tried to determine where I should sit, what was the appropriate distance from him. If I was going to talk to him, I needed to be close; if he was going to be upset, I needed to be distant. If I wasn't going to tell him, I could be near; if I was never going to speak to him again, I needed to be far. It was an impossible equation to solve. I closed my eyes and plopped; I ended up a hand's width apart.

He sighed and stretched out his long legs, putting one arm along the back of the bench, just brushing my shoulder. The silence was unnerving.

"It was nice to meet Sasha," I said at last. "Where is she? I didn't see her at the service."

He shifted, crossed and then uncrossed his legs.

"Remember I told you she gave me an ultimatum?" I nodded, remembering how sick I felt then and how I hadn't known why. "I ended up giving her my mother's ring."

I could picture the sparkle on Sasha's finger. I laid a protective hand across my belly, reminding myself I would not be alone. Not even lonely.

"I see."

"No, Dorrie," he said. "I gave her the ring but not because I wanted to marry her, or even be with her anymore. I gave her the ring because my mother wanted me to and sometimes you do things your mother asks you to do."

I was holding my breath, thinking of Jane, my promise to her. I had done what she asked—I had gone to Colombia—but it wasn't the answer to everything; it didn't fill a void or tell me where I came from. The magic Jane thought I would find in that apartment wasn't in a certain location. I had already known that. Like Dorothy, who needs to leave home to come home, I needed to step outside myself and see Dolores Moore from another angle to know that I have always been home. Going to Cali, seeing the places where my parents had met and loved and died, showed me another side of myself. It showed me one version of my origins, but it wasn't my entire past, and it wasn't going to be part of my future. Yes, I would visit again. Next time I might try harder to find out more about the de la Peña family, maybe visit the crash site, but going to Colombia had erased the feeling I had had my whole life that I was missing something, that I was incomplete, that I was half one thing and half another. But maybe, I realized, a person could be a whole half American and a whole half Colombian. I was whole and belonged exactly where I was.

"But Sasha could see that I wasn't promising anything with that ring. It was just a thing, an object. Once she saw it on her hand, she realized it too."

"Realized . . . ?"

"We aren't in love, we haven't been in love for a long time. I know that now, it just took me a while." His hand brushed my back so gently it might have been a butterfly's wings. "When you told me about hearing the voices of your family, I began to listen, to pay attention. I've always wanted to jump in and help and save people. When I stopped to listen—not to voices in my head, I'm not as goofy as you," he joked, "—I knew I needed to listen to myself."

My own voices were silent now. We listened together.

"Before he died, Grandpa Bao made peace with the idea of his own death. It was the night before, actually. He wasn't feeling well, so he had gone to bed early. I went in to check on him, and when I leaned down to pull up the blanket, he opened his eyes. He told me that he was happy, that he had had a good life because he had always listened to his heart. He had never let anyone tell him what to do, even when he wanted advice, even when he wasn't sure." Franklin inhaled. "I want to be like that, Dorrie. I want to listen."

I nodded. Franklin was so close—four, maybe five inches away. What scale would that be, I wondered. I could feel the warmth radiating off his thigh, his hand, his arm. Shouts and laughter rose from the front yard. I'd forgotten the way funerals often turned joyful as family and friends remember the best of their loved ones, the idiosyncrasies, the ridiculous, the old stories. Everyone the deceased has left behind gathers and mourns—and remembers—together.

I'm eight years old. Mama is on my right; Mommy is on my left. We're in our funeral best—plus headwear as requested by Great-Aunt Maureen. The Moore matriarch had passed away after a short battle with lung cancer (died, actually, with a cigarette in her mouth). I had always been a little afraid of the loud opinions of Grandpa Vic's sister, but I was thrilled to be wearing one of her old pillbox hats, complete with a netting veil. Mama wore one of her aunt's hats from her 1970s cowboy phase: a shiny red cowgirl hat with a white velvet band. Mommy, not much of a hat wearer, had agreed to one of Maureen's vintage Hermès scarves as a headband.

Grandpa Vic took his place at the podium in a dark gray suit topped with a plaid hunting cap and began telling stories about his sister. At first, Mama sniffled and Mommy handed her a rumpled tissue, but as my grandfather kept talking, she began to smile, tentatively at first, then more broadly. I was having trouble following the stories he was telling about Great-Aunt Maureen; I was curiously watching Mama and the rest of the mourners as they began to chuckle. Soon the entire congregation gathered at the cemetery's chapel was laughing. I had already been to three funerals by then, but I had never heard this kind of laughter at a memorial. That loss—and remembering those who have passed—could be amusing was a strange idea. I looked up at my mothers, who were wiping their eyes with their sleeves, and saw simultaneous smiles and tears.

I snickered at their faces even though I wasn't sure what had been so funny. I could even hear Gigi giggling in my chorus joined by Aunt Dot. We were sad, I knew, but we were also joyful with the memory of the old woman.

Humans, I realized, could hold two emotions at once.

Franklin shifted and his hand brushed mine with more certainty. I was thrilled; I was terrified. Two emotions at once. I both wanted to tell him and didn't want him to know. Two thoughts simultaneously. I wanted to listen to my chorus; I wanted them to leave me alone. Two opposing desires.

I looked down and brushed the back of his hand with my thumb. He didn't flinch and didn't move. This was it, I knew. I needed to tell him. It was time, and I would have to accept whatever happened next. I inhaled.

"Your bruises have healed," he said, and touched my cheek with a long slender finger.

You've always been searching, Dorrie, Jane had said. I had always thought maps would show me the way, but life had no map. I thought about the hand-drawn sketch with its history and coffee stain and creased folds. I thought about how I had been certain it would show me all the answers. Maybe it was never about the map? What if accidents, mistakes, could actually show the way?

A tear collected in my right eye, and I realized how frightened I was, how much this moment would change my life. Maybe he wasn't in love with Sasha, but did that mean . . . ? I didn't know and I didn't want to know. And if I didn't say anything, I wouldn't have to know.

"Just a faint scar," I said, pointing at the crooked line across my forehead where Bojangles's claws had slid.

"Good," he said, and took my hand, laced his fingers through mine, and then looked at me as if to ask if this was all right. I gripped, squeezed.

I opened my mouth. *Tell him,* I could imagine my chorus saying. *Be brave,* they should have been saying. I clenched my fists and glanced at my abdomen, grateful for the elastic waistband. *Take a leap. Live.*

A shout of a laugh from inside the house, the call of a mourning dove, the buzz of a mosquito.

He squeezed back, an act so intimate—the touch of a human. Not simply words, advice, musings, but actual physical contact, proof of existence as felt by nerve endings and synapses. This was real. We both nodded, gripping hands.

"Again, I'm sorry about—" he began. "I wanted to know if you ever—"

"IjustwantedtotellyouImpregnant," I blurted.

"What?"

"I'm pregnant," I said, slower. Now that I had said it once, I could do it again. "I'm having a baby."

Franklin stared at me. He didn't say anything, and he didn't nod. Commentary rattled around my head, but I pushed the noise away.

"In January, I guess."

His hand went limp, but he didn't let go.

"A baby," I said. I grabbed both his hands in both of mine and hung on as if they were going to escape or fly away. He looked down at our entwined fingers and then at my face. His head moved up and down, but I wasn't sure he understood. I realized I needed to clarify.

"*We're* having a baby."

1989
Cali, Colombia

Margaret Moore held a hand to her forehead, pressing to try to beat away the headache. No tears. No crying without the baby. She closed and then opened her eyes. The room went blurry. She closed her eyes again. She was tired, so tired. She knew she should sleep while Jane had the baby. But how could she sleep with this pain in her head. It radiated down her body, seemed to seize her arms and legs.

She collapsed on the mattress and dozed or maybe just existed. *We'll get a real bed*, Juan Carlos had promised. *We'll find a bigger apartment*, he had said, but she had been afraid that she would lose him if they had too much space. And she had.

"¿Señora?" called the dueña, who cautiously pushed open her tenant's door. Doña Rojas was worried about the young mother. She never could have foreseen the tragedy, but from the moment the couple had told her they were expecting a baby, she had felt protective of the two of them. They seemed so alone in the world, even if they insisted they liked it that way. The young man traveled a lot, left his young bride too often, especially after the baby was on its way. Cristina—a teenager who thought she was wise because she spoke English—told her not to interfere with them, but it was clear to Doña Rojas that la americana needed her. She had tried to cleanse their apartment and had practiced the most powerful incantations she knew, ones she had learned from her grandmother, but it hadn't helped. She had hoped that the sister who had arrived from the United States would solve the poor woman's plight, but she didn't seem to know much more about babies. *Ciegos guiando a ciegos.* The blind leading the blind.

"Señora, te traigo almuercito."

Maggie wasn't sure how long Jane had been gone, but she could smell something tangy and smoky as Doña Rojas stepped inside. Soup? Vegetables?

"¿Señora?"

It was the old woman, her head covered as always with a black scarf. Fine wrinkles rimmed her eyes, which peered at Maggie. Where, she wondered for a fleeting moment, was her camera? She hadn't thought of the Nikon since she had heard the news about Juan Carlos. Photos were no substitute for the real thing.

Maggie struggled to sit up. "Buenos días, Doña Rojas." The sound of her voice surprised her. It was strange, weak, fragile.

"I saw your sister leave with the baby, so I brought you food," the old woman said.

Margaret pressed her temples again. When had the dueña learned English, she wondered. "Gracias," she said. Or maybe she said, "Thank you." Was she speaking Spanish or was Doña Rojas speaking English? She wasn't sure and didn't have enough energy to wonder.

Doña Rojas bustled around the tiny apartment, lifting a lid off the pot she had brought and pouring something into one of Juan Carlos's three mugs. The phosphoric smell of matches drifted across the room, and Maggie glimpsed the vela lit beside the bed. How long would it burn? she wondered. Would it burn long enough to make a wish?

"You don't look good, mija." The old woman mumbled a few words that sounded like prayers or maybe spells. "Eat. You need food to feed a baby."

"My sister has Dolores. Jane is a better mother than I could ever be. Tell her that, please."

Doña Rojas shushed her and sat on the edge of the mattress, her knees creaking. She smelled like herbs and soil and something sweet.

"I'm all right," Maggie insisted. "If you leave the soup, I'll manage."

"No one should be alone, especially a new mother with a baby."

She felt she should explain that she had asked Jane, but Maggie nodded in agreement. "Juan Carlos is gone." Gone. "Mi amor." Her voice rough like sandpaper. "I'm alone."

"We aren't alone as long as we have family," soothed the old woman.

It felt like the words were being spoken from far away or from inside a deep well. Maggie's vision was as cloudy as her hearing, everything underwater, blurry, unreal. She couldn't move, she felt strapped to the bed. She couldn't swallow the broth Doña Rojas brought to her lips.

A pain shot through her skull but then slowly dissipated. She knew, the way she had known she loved Juan Carlos the moment she saw him, the way she had known she was home the moment she stepped out of the airport, the way she had known she was pregnant, that this was the end.

"If only . . ." she began. A rough, small hand took hers and pressed. "If only I didn't have to leave my baby. If only . . ." she said again. The hand in hers squeezed. She thought of her sister and her baby, somewhere in Cali, in the city that was home. As long as they were together, it would be okay. "If only someone would watch over her, advise her, help her find her way. Even if it can't be me."

Somewhere in the mist of her consciousness, Maggie thought she heard a knock on the door of Juan Carlos's apartment. Or maybe it was her childhood bedroom with the pink curtains and dotted swiss bedspread. She tried to look around for her mother. Was that her aunt? She was disoriented, unsure which way was up, down, east, or west. She heard voices, maybe her sister in two pigtails? The talking turned serious, low. Maybe it was Juan Carlos. He was back. Was he back? Had he come home? Had her wish come true? She was too weak to look for him, but maybe he had found her.

Or maybe it was the landlady's young daughter, the two of them talking about hospitals and ambulances.

"Where's Dolores?" Margaret murmured. "Don't let Dolores be alone." She wasn't sure Juan Carlos would have approved of the name she chose. She hadn't told her sister what it meant after Cristina had translated the name.

Doña Rojas shushed her as if she were the child, not the mother. There were hands on her, warm and gentle. "Your daughter will never be alone, she will always be surrounded by family," she assured her.

A gift. Or a curse.

"Guided by them for as long as she needs them."

"Dolores . . . ?" Margaret Moore repeated: "Dolores."

CHAPTER 35

I scratched Django under the chin and then shoved him off the composite stone so I could reach the coffee maker. I licked a finger to gain enough traction to remove a filter from the stack and then filled it with grounds—Colombian arabica. As the coffee maker gurgled, a tender, earthy smell filled the kitchen. I leaned against the sparkly countertop and admired the new-to-me vintage yellow enamel table and the way Great-Aunt Maureen's Navajo rug, which I had moved out of hiding in the study, filled the space of the kitchen and warmed my bare feet. The True Blue walls shone like a tropical sky. Steam from the coffee maker fogged the window behind me, and I made a fist and cleared it away with the back of my hand.

Snow and leafless trees had transformed outside as much as my home improvements had transformed inside over the past months. Even in the pale blue light of not-quite morning, I could make out the garage—still falling down but freshly painted deep burgundy to match the house—banked with snow from the narrow path made by shoveling. The birdbath from Grandpa Bao's garden was nearly buried, pretty as a picture. I told myself I would remember to photograph the yard to send it to Becks, who didn't have to face January in Minnesota anymore, although she and Charlie and seven-month-old Daphne had celebrated Christmas here. I would send it to Trina, too, so she and her friends could see what real winter was like. *So much snow,* I could just imagine Joaquim saying.

It was remarkable, I thought: the only voices I heard lately were those I imagined.

The coffee maker gurgled and I filled two mugs.

In contrast to the fresh coat of paint outside and the neat and tidy re-modeled kitchen, the rest of the Victorian was a disaster. But it was *my* disaster. I carried the mugs through to the living room, passing by the dining table, which was still a repository for mail and detri-tus. A slipper (that's where that went!), the novel I had started but couldn't quite get into, the official letter from the college welcoming me as adjunct instructor of geography, part-time assignment (*Sorry we didn't have a full-time appointment at this time*). There was also a package I hadn't opened yet.

I set down the coffee cups and tore open the padded envelope. Blue and orange stripes, polka-dot print. It was a corduroy dress with a coordinated onesie, so tiny they fit in my open palms. I felt a tear prick my eye. "From all of us at Book Group," said the note in Olga's handwriting. "And Rose too." I laid the two items on the back of Mama's floral sofa.

Bojangles leaped up, leaving a dusting of long white hairs on the baby clothes, size 0–3 months.

I didn't think I could ever be—or want to be—a parent. I had had mothers and motherlike figures opining my entire life. I had had too many mothers, not enough mothers. I thought I had enough data, enough information, to make the choice.

But ultimately, we can't know for sure without ground truthing.

"Just because we think we know where something is or what something is," Dr. Foster used to say, "doesn't mean that's where or what it *really* is." Some student, usually a philosophy major, would raise his hand and contest the idea of knowledge. Or a statistics student might try to defend mathematical certainty. Dr. Foster would patiently shake his head, maybe sigh, and command, "There must be ground truth."

Surveys and radars and satellites can provide enough data to map an area in minute detail, and GPS can locate coordinates within six to ten meters—remarkable accuracy for machine learning—but in order to find geographic reality, as it's called, cartographers still need to confirm the measurements on the ground. No matter how much data is collected, they must find the truth for themselves.

"I desperately need coffee," said Franklin from what had become his side of the bed. My mothers' bedroom was nearly unrecognizable. Sure, the bones were still there: view of the backyard, the highboy, the Colombian wool blanket on the bed. But their belongings had been replaced with the stuff of a messy life: my clothes, most of which I was sure I would never fit into again; Franklin's running shoes and down coat and pajamas and changes of socks, more than either of us admitted he kept here at the Victorian; and then there were the swaddles and diapers and pacifiers and burp cloths. A handmade crib that she never slept in.

"Here you—" As I took another step toward the bed, I tripped on something (the other slipper!) and half the coffee in the cup in my right hand sloshed to the floor. "Save what you can," I said, handing the other cup to Franklin and mopping the spill with a lone sock. "What a mess."

(*Life gets messy sometimes*, said a voice, so quietly, I wasn't sure I had heard it.)

"Did you hear that?" I asked Franklin, who looked like he was about to make love with the coffee. I hadn't heard the chorus in so many months, I had almost forgotten what they sounded like. This voice didn't sound familiar.

"Hear what?"

(*Our apartment was a mess like this*, the voice said, louder now. *And we loved it.*)

The bundle beside Franklin twitched and wiggled, and the voice faded.

He looked down at our daughter. "Margarita is going to need a feeding soon," he said.

I dropped the damp sock and climbed into bed beside them both.

ACKNOWLEDGMENTS

It takes a village to publish a book.

Thank you to Thao Le, my extraordinary agent, for being an unwavering cheerleader (and sometime therapist) and for believing in me and my work. Thanks, of course, to Carrie Feron, Ali Chesnick, and everyone at Gallery Books. Carrie understood the story I was trying to tell and helped me make it what she saw it could be.

Special thanks to my dad and his wife, who have helped me understand and embrace my Colombian half. And gracias for indulging me in a tour of Cali, Colombia, including visits to all the (real) places on Dorrie's map.

Lots of love to my mom, who faithfully read aloud to me when I was a child and has always supported my passion for reading and writing. I'm grateful for her stories about her brief time in Colombia as an American abroad.

I'm so grateful for my virtual writing group, which emerged from the Latina writers' collective Las Musas. For the past three years, the talented and lovely Reina Luz Alegre and Ismée Williams have generously provided support and feedback. These authors were instrumental in shaping the novel's narrative (particularly the love story). Thanks also to Eric Smith for his time and generous accolades.

I am indebted to more writers than I can possibly name from

Minneapolis's vibrant and active literary community, but a special shout-out to Karlyn Coleman, Sara Dovre Wudali, and Carolyn Williams-Noren for their camaraderie, talent, and cooking skills. Thanks to everyone in our little kidlit group for the fabulous retreats and gatherings, and to our de facto leader, Trisha Speed Shaskan. Thanks also to Karen Latchana Kenney for her beautiful cabin retreat, where I finished the first revision of this novel.

Thanks to the Minnesota State Arts Board, which has provided generous grant funding over the years for this and other books. Thank you to Jerod Santek and his writing center, Write On, Door County, for the space and peace in which to write.

I'm not a cartographer, but I was a librarian, and I'm indebted to the people whose research and passion I mined. I relied heavily on Thomas Reinertsen Berg's *Theater of the World: The Maps That Made History*, as well as *How to Lie with Maps* by Mark Monmonier. I also visited the (sadly now closed) Map & Atlas Museum of La Jolla, where I got to view many historical maps, including an original T-O map. Any cartographic errors are mine alone.

Finally, huge gratitude and love to my husband and daughter, who have been there with me through it all: publishing ups and downs, plot holes and procrastination, successes and setbacks. You two, Dave and Sylvia, are my world.